LEFT
at the
ALTAR

MARGARET
BROWNLEY

sourcebooks
casablanca

Published by Sourcebooks Casablanca, an imprint of Sourcebooks,
Inc.
P.O. Box 4410, Naperville, Illinois 60567-4410
(630) 961-3900
Fax: (630) 961-2168
www.sourcebooks.com

Printed and bound in Canada.
MBP 10 9 8 7 6 5 4 3 2 1

For George, till we meet again

"Time does not change us. It just unfolds us."
—Max Frisch

One

"FIFTY-FOUR MINUTES."

Her father's booming voice made Meg Lockwood want to scream. But airing her lungs in church wasn't an option, and thanks to the whalebone corset beneath her wedding gown, neither was breathing.

"Mama, make him stop."

Her mother straightened the garland of daisies in Meg's hair for perhaps the hundredth time so far that day before turning to her husband. "Henry, must you?"

Papa kept his gaze glued to his gold pocket watch rather than answer, his wagging finger ready to drop the instant the minute hand moved. Not by any means a formal man, he'd battled with Mama over his wedding attire until, like a defeated general, he'd thrown up his arms in surrender. Unfortunately, the knee-length coat Mama had chosen emphasized Papa's ungainly shape, which bore a striking resemblance to a pickle barrel.

The finger came down. "He is now fifty-five minutes late."

Meg's hands curled around the satin fabric of her skirt. Where *was* her bridegroom? She hated to keep the wedding guests waiting, but she didn't know what to do. Time meant nothing to her erstwhile fiancé, but he'd promised not to be late for their wedding. She'd trusted him to keep his word.

Just you wait, Tommy Farrell!

When he finally did show up, she wouldn't be responsible for her actions.

Tommy wasn't the only reason for her ill temper. As if her too-tight corset wasn't bad enough, the ruffled lace at her neck made her skin itch, and the butterfly bustle hung like a brick at the small of her back. Worse, the torture chambers disguised as dainty white slippers were killing her feet.

The church organ in the nearby sanctuary moaned louder, as if even the organist's patience was spent. The somber chords now rattled the walls of the tiny anteroom, threatening the framed picture and forcing the glass beads on the kerosene lamp to jiggle in protest.

She met her mother's worried gaze in the beveled-glass mirror. At forty-five, Elizabeth Lockwood still moved with the ease and grace of a woman half her age. The green velvet gown showed off her still-tiny waist and slim hips.

A wistful look smoothed the lines of worry on her mother's face. "You look beautiful."

Meg forced a smile. "So do you, Mama."

Meg had inherited her mother's honey-blond hair,

turquoise eyes, and dainty features, but her restless countenance was clearly thanks to her father's side.

"Fifty-*six* minutes late," her father exclaimed, and Meg's already taut nerves threatened to snap.

Clenching her hands tightly, she spun around to face him. "You never change!"

"Change? Change!" Papa looked indignant as a self-righteous preacher. "Why would I? Someone has to maintain a healthy respect for time."

The door swung open. *Thank goodness.* Meg whirled about again, ready to give her errant fiancé a piece of her mind, but it was only her older sister. The worried frown on Josie's face told Meg everything she needed to know, but still she had to ask.

"Anything?"

Josie shook her head. At twenty-three, she was two years older than Meg, and at five foot ten, stood a good six inches taller. Today she wore a dusky-rose gown that complemented her dark hair and gave her complexion a pretty pink glow. She took after Papa's side in looks, but of the three Lockwood girls, she was most like Mama in calm disposition.

"Ralph looked all over town." Ralph Johnson was Josie's husband, and he owned the saddle shop at the end of Two-Time's main street. "You don't suppose something might have happened to Tommy, do you? An accident?"

"It better have," Meg muttered.

Gasping, Mama looked up from straightening Meg's gown. "Of all the things to say!"

"Sorry, Mama." Hands balled at her sides, Meg gritted her teeth. Her mother was right, of course; such uncharitable thoughts didn't belong in church.

Neither did thoughts of murder.

"Fifty-eight minutes," her father announced.

"I'm sure he'll be here soon, Papa." Josie always tried to see the bright side of things, but even she couldn't hide the doubt in her voice.

Papa's gaze remained on his watch. "Soon's already come and gone. Now he'll have to answer to me for keeping my daughter waiting!"

Her father didn't fool Meg one whit—he'd been against the marriage from the start. If she didn't know better, she would suspect him of causing her fiancé's absence just to prove he was right.

"Fifty-nine minutes!"

"Henry, please," her mother cajoled. "You're upsetting her."

"She *should* be upset. The boy's irresponsible and will never amount to a hill of beans. He's like a blister; he never shows up till the work's all done. Doesn't even know whether to wind his watch or bark at the moon. I should never have agreed to this marriage."

"You didn't agree to anything, Henry."

"And for good reason! Furthermore—"

A knock sounded, but before anyone could answer it, the door cracked open and Reverend Wellmaker popped his head into the room. "Is everything all right?" he asked, eyes round behind his spectacles. "We're almost twenty minutes late."

"*Fifty-nine* minutes late!" her father roared.

The difference in times raised no eyebrows, since no standard time existed in Two-Time. It was common practice for communities to set watches by the local jeweler, but unfortunately, their town had two—Meg's father and Tommy's pa. Both stubbornly insisted they alone had the right time.

The feud dividing the town for more than fifteen years was expected to end the minute the two families were joined by marriage. Both fathers had agreed—albeit reluctantly—to standardize time once the deed was done.

"Shh, Henry, not here." Her mother gave the minister an apologetic smile. "Soon."

Josie left with the pastor, and Papa continued his sonorous count until interrupted by another knock on the door.

"Meg, it's me, Tommy."

"It's about time!" She hiked her skirt above her ankles and started across the room.

Her mother grabbed her by the arm. "It's bad luck for the groom to see you in your wedding gown," she whispered.

"It's worse luck for the groom to be an hour late for his own wedding." Meg pulled free from her mother's grasp and ripped open the door. "Where have you been? You agreed to get married on Lockwood time and—" Suddenly aware that something was terribly wrong, she bit back the rest of her sentence.

Tommy looked as sober as an owl in a barn. Even more worrisome was his attire—old canvas trousers held up by blue suspenders. He appeared haggard, as if he hadn't slept, and his unruly red hair stood on end like a rooster's comb.

"We have to talk." He grabbed her by the hand and pulled her out of the room and down the hall.

She held back. "Thomas James Farrell, stop right now. You hear me? I said *stop*!"

But he didn't stop, not until they reached the cemetery behind the church. It took a moment for Meg's eyes to adjust to the bright autumn sun.

Tall, granite grave markers stood at attention like pieces on a chessboard waiting for someone to make the first move.

She snatched her hand from his. "What do you think you're doing? What's going on?"

Tommy grimaced. "Meg, I'm sorry, but I can't do this. I can't marry you."

She stared at him, dumbfounded. *This can't be happening.* "What are you saying?"

"I'm sayin' I can't be the husband you want. I can't spend the rest of my life workin' on watches in my father's shop. All those hairsprings and gears and stems and—"

"*This* is how you give me the news?" She gave him an angry shove. "Tommy Farrell, I've known you nearly all my life, and you've caused me plenty of grief along the way, but this takes the cake!"

"I'm sorry." He slapped his hand to his forehead. "I'm goin' about this all wrong. It's not that I don't want to marry you. I just can't."

"And you waited for our wedding day to tell me this?"

"I feel bad, I do."

"*You* feel bad? How do you suppose our guests feel after being kept waiting all this time? And what about the town? Our fathers promised to end their feud—"

"I know, I know." He grimaced. "Right now, I'm only thinkin' of you."

"By humiliating me in front of the entire world?" She stared at him as if seeing him for the first time. For years, she'd made excuses for his lackadaisical ways and had even defended him to his own father. She'd forgiven him for forgetting her birthday—not once but twice! But this…this was by far the worst thing he'd ever done.

"I'd make you miserable," he continued, his Texas twang even more pronounced than usual. "I'm not ready to settle down. I want to see the world. To travel to Europe and Asia and…and the Pacific Islands. I read somewhere that they're real nice."

"You've said some mighty dumb things in your life, but this has got to be the dumbest."

"I knew you wouldn't understand."

"No, I don't understand," she cried. "I don't understand how you could wait till today to throw me over for a bunch of islands!" She backed away from him, fists at her side. "I should have listened to Pa."

"Meg, don't look at me like that. It really is for the best. Maybe in a year, or two or three, I'll be ready to marry and settle down. Maybe then we can—"

"Don't you dare say it, Tommy Farrell. Don't you even think it! I'd sooner die a spinster than marry the likes of you."

"You don't mean that…"

"I mean every word. I don't ever want to see you again. Not ever!"

"Meg, please."

"Just…just go!"

He stared at her as if making certain she wouldn't change her mind. Then he swung around and rushed along the narrow dirt path leading out of the cemetery as if he couldn't escape fast enough.

Watching him flee, Meg felt numb. Today was supposed to be the happiest day of her life, but instead, it had turned into a nightmare. How would she break the news to her family? To the guests? To the folks counting on this marriage to bring peace to the town? She pulled the garland from her hair, threw it on the ground, and stomped on it.

A movement caught her eye, and a tall figure stepped from behind an equally tall grave marker. Her gaze froze on the man's long, lean form. A look of sympathy—or maybe even pity—had settled on his square-jawed face, crushing any hope that the humiliating scene had somehow escaped his notice. Her cheeks flared with heat. Could this day possibly get any worse?

He pulled off his derby and nodded at her as if apologizing for his presence.

"Sorry, ma'am. Forgive me. I couldn't help but overhear." If his dark trousers, coat, and vest hadn't already marked him as an easterner, the way he pronounced his words surely did.

In no mood to forgive a man—any man, even one as tall and good-looking as this one—she grabbed a handful of satin, turned, and rushed to the church's open door, snagging her wedding gown on the doorframe. She glanced over her shoulder to find him still watching her. In her haste to escape, she yanked at her skirt, and it ripped. The tearing sound might as well have been her heart.

Inside, the thundering organ music rang like a death knell. Hands over her ears, she kicked off her murderous slippers and ran down the hall in stocking feet.

Two

GRANT GARRISON LEFT HIS BOARDINGHOUSE AND rode his mount down Peaceful Lane. Two-story brick residences lined the street, the boardinghouse where he lodged among them. Either the street name was a misnomer or someone had once had a strange sense of humor, because the street was anything but peaceful.

Even now, angry voices filled the morning air, the loudest coming from Mr. Crawford, who took regular issue with his next-door neighbor's bagpipes. But he wasn't the only one airing his lungs.

Mr. Sloan was yelling at the Johnson boy for stealing his pecans; Mrs. Conrad could be heard expressing her disapproval at the goat eating her flowers. Next door to her, Mr. Quincy was arguing with the paperboy, who had thrown the morning newspaper on the roof for the second time that week.

Grant tipped his hat to the two women gossiping over a fence and steered his horse around the wagon belonging to the dogcatcher. A terrible commotion drew Grant's attention to an alleyway, and the dog-catcher emerged running, chased by a big yellow hound.

A half block away, the widow Rockwell walked out of her tiny house carrying a lamp. Compared to the other buildings on the street, the two tiny residences she owned looked like dollhouses. She waved at Grant, and he tipped his hat in greeting.

"Need any help?" he called. He'd already helped her move twice that week.

"No, not today."

The widow's two houses were located directly across from each other. Almost identical in size and style, they were called Sunday houses and had originally been built so that immigrant farmers could stay in town during weekends to run errands and attend church.

The problem was, the widow could never make up her mind which one to live in. No sooner would she haul her belongings to one side of the street than she decided to live on the other. So back and forth she traipsed from house to house, moving, always moving.

It had rained the night before, and puddles of mud dotted the dirt-packed road, causing the widow to pick her way across the street with care.

Except for a few lingering clouds, the sky was clear, and the air smelled fresh with just a hint of fall.

It was a normal day on Peaceful Lane—except for one thing. In the middle of the roadway, a woman was fighting with a pushcart.

Grant reined in his horse and narrowed his eyes against the bright morning sun. Did he know her? He didn't think so. Still, something about her small, trim frame struck a familiar chord.

The lady pushed the cart one way and jerked it

the other. A trunk or chest of some kind was perched precariously on top of the hand wagon, and it teetered back and forth like a child's seesaw.

Apparently seeing the futility of her efforts, she leaned over to examine one of the wheels stuck in the mud. This afforded him an intriguing glimpse of a white lace petticoat beneath an otherwise somber blue dress. She surprised him by giving the pushcart a good kick with a well-aimed boot.

Hands folded on the pommel of his saddle, he leaned forward. "So what do you think, Chester? Should we offer to help before the lady does injury to her foot?"

For answer, his horse lowered his head and whickered.

"I quite agree."

Urging his horse forward in a short gallop, Grant called, "May I be of service, ma'am?" He tugged on the reins. "Whoa, boy."

She whirled around, eyes wide as she met his gaze. Two red spots stained her cheeks, but whether from exertion or embarrassment at being caught in a less-than-ladylike predicament, he couldn't tell.

"Thank you kindly," she said with a soft southern lilt.

"My pleasure."

Her face looked vaguely familiar, but he still couldn't place her, which struck him as odd. Her big turquoise eyes should not be easily forgotten. Hatless, she wore her honey-blond hair piled on top of her head, but a couple of soft ends had fallen loose. The carefree curls didn't seem to belong to the stern, young face.

He dismounted and tethered his horse to a wooden

fence. He guessed the woman lived nearby, but that still didn't tell him where they might have met.

He tipped his hat. "Name's Grant Garrison."

She studied him with a sharp-eyed gaze. "You!"

Since she looked fit to be tied, he stepped back. At that point, the flashing blue-green eyes jarred his memory.

"You're the"—he almost said *jilted*—"bride." He hardly recognized her out of her wedding gown. According to local tongue-waggers, her name was Meg Lockwood. Best not to let on how last week's disastrous nonwedding was still the talk of the town.

She glared at him, eyes filled with accusations. "That day at the church…you had no right to eavesdrop on a private conversation."

He extended his arms, palms out. "Please accept my apologies. I can assure you the intrusion was purely unintentional. I was visiting my sister's grave."

Uncertainty crept into her expression, but her combative stance remained. "You…you could have announced yourself."

He also could have stayed hidden, which might have been the better choice. "I considered doing just that. I'm afraid that had I done so, I might have flattened your bridegroom's nose."

This failed to bring the smile he hoped for, but at least she looked less likely to do him harm. She glanced up and down the street as if trying to decide whether to accept his help.

"I would be most obliged if you didn't mention… what you heard."

Her request confused him. Everyone in town knew the wedding had been called off.

"About the Pacific Islands," she added.

Never would he profess to understand the way a woman's mind worked, but her concern was indeed a puzzle. Would she *rather* her fiancé had left her for another woman, as some people in town suspected?

"I promise." He pretended to turn a lock on his mouth. "Not a word."

She let his promise hang between them for a moment before asking, "What brings you to Two-Time, Mr. Garrison?"

He hesitated. "I'm a lawyer. Since the East Coast is overrun with them, I decided to try my luck here. I just opened an office off Main." He replaced his hat and tossed a nod at the cart. "Where are you taking that?"

"To my sister's house." Her gaze shifted to the end of the street. "She lives in the corner house with the green shutters."

"Well, then." He grabbed hold of the handle and yanked the cart back and forth before giving it a firm push. The wheels gave a reluctant turn and finally pulled free of the gooey sludge with a *slurp*. But just as it cleared the mudhole, the cart tipped to one side and the chest shot to the ground, splashing mud everywhere.

Miss Lockwood jumped back, but not soon enough to prevent mud from splattering on her skirt. "Oh no!"

Muttering an apology, Grant quickly turned the chest upright, leaving an intriguing assortment of corsets, petticoats, and camisoles scattered on the ground. He never expected to see such a fancy display in a rough-and-tumble town like Two-Time.

While she examined the chest for damage, he quickly swooped up the satin and lace dainties and shook off as much mud as possible. Did women actually need this many corsets?

"I have to say, ma'am," he began in an effort to make light of the situation, "there are enough underpinnings here to fill an entire Montgomery Ward catalogue." He couldn't help but look at her curiously before dumping the garments back into the chest.

Checks blazing, she slammed the lid shut and double-checked the lock.

He offered her his clean handkerchief, which she turned down with a shake of her head. Silence as brittle as glass stretched between them, and Grant couldn't help but feel sorry for her. They seemed doomed to meet under trying, if not altogether embarrassing circumstances.

Since the lady seemed more concerned about the wooden chest than the corsets...uh...contents, he studied it more closely. It was obviously old but had been well cared for. Intricate engravings of birds, flowers, and a ship graced the top and sides, along with several carefully carved initials.

"No damage done," she said, her voice thick with relief. The red on her cheeks had faded to a most becoming pink. "My family would kill me if something happened to it."

"A family heirloom?" he asked.

She nodded. "All the way from Ireland. It's called a hope chest."

Grant knew about such things, of course, from his sisters. But never before had he been privy to a hope chest's contents. It was hard to know what disconcerted him more—manhandling Miss Lockwood's intimate garments, or the possibility that something of a similar nature filled his sisters' hope chests. Whatever happened to filling a hope chest with household goods?

Tucking the handkerchief into his trouser pocket, he struggled to lift the chest off the ground. He set it atop the cart and wiggled it back and forth to make sure it was balanced just right. "I'm afraid the contents may be ruined."

"Th-they'll wash," Miss Lockwood stammered, refusing to meet his gaze.

He brushed off his hands and grabbed hold of the cart's handles. This time, the wheels turned with ease, and he pushed it slowly down the road. She fell in step by his side, and a pleasant whiff of lavender soap wafted toward him. With heightened awareness, he noticed her every move, heard her every intake of breath.

"You said you were visiting your sister's grave," she said in a hesitant voice, as if she wasn't certain whether to broach the subject.

He nodded, and the familiar heaviness of grief rose in his chest. "Mary died in childbirth a month ago. Her husband owns a cattle ranch outside of town."

They had reached the gate leading to the two-story brick house with the green shutters. The rail fence enclosed a small but well-cared-for garden. A hen pecked at the ground next to a row of sprouting squash plants.

Miss Lockwood afforded him a look of sympathy. "I'm sorry for your loss," she said.

"And I'm sorry for yours." In danger of drowning

in the blue-green depths of her eyes, he averted his gaze. "Where would you like me to put it?"

"Put it?"

He shot her a sideways glance. "The corset…uh"—he grimaced—"hope chest."

She lowered her lashes. "The porch would be just fine," she murmured.

Since the cart wouldn't fit through the gate, he had no choice but to haul the chest by hand. Fortunately, only two steps led up to the wraparound porch. Even so, he was out of breath by the time he set the heavy chest next to a wicker rocking chair.

She'd followed him up the porch steps. "I'm much obliged." Her prettily curving lips made the sadness in the depth of her eyes all the more touching.

"My pleasure." He studied her. "I hope you don't mind my saying this, but…if I had someone like you waiting at the altar, I would never walk away. Not in a million years." The expression on her face softened, and he was tempted to say more but decided against it. Better stop while he was ahead.

With a tip of his hat, he jogged down the steps and headed back to his horse. The memory of all that silk and lace remained, as did the shadow of her pretty smile.

❦

Meg stood on her sister's porch, surprised to find herself shaking. *If I had someone like you…*

Never had anyone said anything like that to her, not even Tommy. Just thinking of Mr. Garrison's soft-spoken words sent a shiver racing though her, one that ended in a sigh.

Pushing such thoughts away, she knocked and the door sprang open almost instantly.

Josie greeted her with a questioning look. "Who's that man I saw you with?"

"Just...someone passing by. He stopped to help me." Meg seldom kept anything from her older sister, but she didn't want to discuss Mr. Garrison. Not in her confused state.

Josie looked her up and down. "Oh dear. You're covered in mud. What happened?"

Meg glanced down at her skirt. "I had a little accident."

"I told you to wait for Ralph," Josie scolded. "That hope chest is far too heavy for a woman to manage alone."

Meg hadn't wanted to ask her brother-in-law for help. Not with the way he'd been coughing lately.

"It's a good thing I have you to help me, then." Meg cleaned the sludge off the soles of her high-button shoes on the iron boot scraper, then shook as much of the mud off her skirt as possible. Satisfied that her sister's pristine carpets would not be soiled, she circled the hope chest. "Grab hold of the other side."

Carved by her great-grandfather, the wooden piece had been handed down to family members for generations. Each bride carved her initials into the old wood before passing it on to the next woman in line. Mama had passed it down to Josie who, after her own wedding, had handed it over to Meg during a ritual that had made all three Lockwood sisters roll on the floor with laughter.

Today, however, no such happy ritual was in play as she and Josie struggled to carry the massive chest inside the house and into the small but tidy parlor. They set it on the brick hearth so as not to get mud on the carpet.

"Whew! I forgot how heavy it was," Josie said.

Meg brushed a hand over her forehead. Good riddance. The hope chest that once held her girlish dreams was now a dismal reminder of a day she'd sooner forget.

"I don't know why Amanda refuses to take it. It's only fair. You and I both had our turn."

Josie frowned, as she was inclined to do whenever their younger sister's name came up. "Amanda's too independent to get married. She's only interested in stirring up trouble."

By trouble, Josie referred to Amanda's many causes. One—her campaign to close saloons during Sunday worship—had almost created a riot. Their youngest sister was the black sheep of the family and was always on the warpath about one thing or another.

"Poor Mama," Meg said. "All she ever wanted was to see the three of us married and bouncing rosy-cheeked babies on our laps." She gasped and quickly covered her mouth. "Oh, Josie, I'm so sorry."

"It's all right." Josie patted her on the arm. "I haven't given up hope that one day I'll have a child of my own. Some things just take time."

Meg flung her arms around her sister's shoulders and squeezed tight. "I wish I had your patience."

Josie hugged her back. "I love you just the way you are."

Meg pulled away and smiled. Spending time with Josie always made her feel better. "Thank you for taking the hope chest off my hands. If I have to look at it one more day, I'll scream." She and Josie had spent hours working on her trousseau—and for what?

"I'm afraid the clothes inside are a mess. The chest tipped over, and everything is covered in mud." Just thinking about that handsome new lawyer's hands all over them made her cheeks blaze.

Josie opened the hope chest to check the contents. She lifted the carefully sewn garments one by one and examined them.

While her sister inventoried the damage, Meg glanced out the parlor window and froze. There rode Mr. Garrison on his fine black horse. Her breath caught, and she quickly stepped behind the draperies so as not to be seen gaping. Did she only imagine him staring at the house? *If I had someone like you…*

Josie's insistent voice brought her out of her reverie. "I'm sorry?"

"I said I'll wash and press the garments, and they'll be as good as new." Josie studied her a moment, and her expression softened. "Are you okay?"

Meg moistened her dry lips. "I'm fine."

Josie lowered the hope chest's lid and stood. "It's been nearly a month. You can't keep hiding. Papa misses you at the shop. You know what a terrible bookkeeper he is, and with Christmas just around the corner…"

Guilt surged through Meg like molten steel. How selfish of her. Staying hidden like a common criminal had done nothing but place an extra burden on Papa's shoulders. It was her job to keep the shop records, order supplies, and serve the customers, thus freeing her father to spend his time repairing watches and clocks. And yet...

"I don't know that I'll ever be able to show my face in public again."

"Meg, that's ridiculous. No one blames you."

Taking the blame wasn't what bothered Meg; it was the feeling that she had let everyone down. Papa had promised to make peace with Mr. Farrell as a wedding present. Now that the wedding had been called off, the feud between the two men had resumed. If anything, their animosity toward each other had grown worse, each blaming the other for the disastrous affair.

"Go and clean up while I fix us something to eat."

Meg nodded and started down the hall, but not before taking another quick glance out the window. The deserted road looked as forlorn and lonely as she felt.

∽

Moments later, Meg joined her sister in the sun-filled kitchen, her skirt still damp where she'd washed off the mud.

Josie's kitchen table had become the sisters' sounding board. Everything that happened—good, bad, or otherwise; every crisis, every problem—was hashed out, analyzed, resolved, or left to die upon that maple table.

Meg pulled out a chair, plopped down, and rested her elbows on the smooth-polished surface. "I don't understand why Papa and Mr. Farrell continue to fight." For as long as she could remember, bad blood had existed between the two men. Mama blamed it on professional differences, but Meg was almost certain their warfare had more personal roots.

Josie filled the kettle and placed it on the cookstove. "Sometimes I wonder if even they remember what started it. It happened so many years ago." She wiped her hands on her spotless white apron and pulled a bread knife out of a drawer.

Through the open window over the sink came the sound of bells pealing out the noon hour for the residents living and working north of Main. The rest of the town, including her father, had stopped for the noontime meal a good forty minutes earlier.

"Josie…how did you know you were in love with Ralph?"

Josie gave her an odd look. "What a strange question."

"I'm serious. How did you know?"

Josie thought a moment, cheeks tinged a pretty pink. "It was the way he made me feel. The way my heart leaped whenever he came into sight."

Meg chewed on a fingernail. She had known Tommy nearly all her life. Next to her two sisters, he was the best friend she'd ever had.

In school, he'd dipped her braids in ink and helped her with geography and science. In turn, she'd teased him about his red hair, drilled him on his numbers, and made him read aloud until he became proficient.

Knowing how their fathers disapproved of their friendship only strengthened the bond between them and forced them to meet in secret. It had been Romeo and Juliet all over again. Still, during all those years she'd spent in Tommy's company, never once had her heart leaped at the sight of him.

Josie dumped a loaf of bread out of a baking tin and proceeded to slice it. "I know you're still hurting, Meg, but I never did think you and Tommy belonged together."

A month ago, Meg would have argued with her sister, but now she only nodded. "I guess there're worse things than being jilted for the Pacific Islands."

Josie laughed. "I hope we never find out what those things are."

Meg laughed too, and for the first time in weeks, her spirits lifted.

Three

THE BELLS ON THE DOOR OF GRANT GARRISON'S OFFICE danced merrily. Grant slid the last of his legal books onto the newly arrived bookshelves and stood to greet his visitor.

The welcoming smile died on his face the moment he turned. He knew the man at once—the gangly fellow with the pasty skin was Miss Lockwood's wayward bridegroom. He'd recognize those flyaway ears and that carrot-colored hair anywhere. Although today, the former groom's hair was neatly combed and parted down the middle.

"Mr. Garrison, is it? I'm Thomas Farrell." He offered his hand.

Swallowing his dislike, Grant shook the man's hand before walking around his desk. He sat, and the new leather chair squeaked beneath his weight.

"What can I do for you, Mr. Farrell?" Grant asked, his manner as cool and abrupt as his voice. A man so heartless as to leave a woman at the altar didn't deserve the time of day, let alone civility.

If Farrell noticed anything odd about Grant's

demeanor, he didn't show it. Instead, he lowered himself onto the ladder-back chair in front of the desk. He mopped his forehead with a handkerchief and crossed and uncrossed his legs. He looked like a man about to be hanged.

Grant waited. One minute passed, then two. The *clip-clop* of horses' hooves and the rumble of a wagon floated through the open window. The clock on top of the bookshelf clucked like a hen on a nest. It was exactly two—or two forty, depending on which time zone one favored. According to railroad time it was probably closer to three, but few people paid attention to train schedules unless they were leaving town.

"Mr. Farrell?" Grant prodded at length, if only to save what remained of the hat clutched in the young man's hands.

The man gulped, and his Adam's apple bobbed up and down like a rubber ball. "I'm bein' sued," he said.

Grant's eyebrows shot up. For the love of Pete, what other dastardly deed was Mr. Farrell guilty of? "Do you owe someone money?" he asked.

"No, no, nothin' like that."

"Did you cause injury?"

The question seemed to perplex the man, or at least render him momentarily silent.

"No…not really."

"Then why are you being sued?"

Setting his misshapen felt hat on the desk, Farrell reached into his trouser pocket and drew out what looked like an official document. He carefully unfolded the sheet of paper and smoothed out the wrinkles before sliding it across the desk.

It *was* a legal document. Grant scanned it quickly until he came to Meg Lockwood's name. A vision of a pretty, round face seemed to float up from the page. He remembered everything about her: her pretty pink cheeks, small dainty frame, and large, expressive eyes. He also remembered how she had struggled to smile the day they met on the street, even though her heart had been so recently broken by this very man.

Grant sucked in his breath and forced his gaze down the rest of the document. "It says here you're being sued for breach of promise." Miss Lockwood was asking for damages amounting to ten grand. That was a lot of money, even by Boston standards.

Farrell rubbed his chin. "Can she do that?"

"'Fraid so. It says you broke a promise to marry her and left her at the altar." The memory of Miss Lockwood standing alone in the cemetery in her wedding gown tugged at Grant's insides, and his hands clenched. It took every bit of professionalism he possessed not to toss Farrell out on his ear.

Farrell grimaced. "I don't deny any of that, but there were extinguishin' circumstances."

Garrison tossed the document on the desk. "I believe you mean *extenuating* circumstances."

"Yeah, that too." Farrell leaned forward. "I need a lawyer, and no other lawyer in town will touch my case."

Elbows on the desk, Grant tented his fingers. "What makes you think I will?"

"You're new in town. You can take sides, and no one will think the worse of you."

Grant opened his mouth to say something, but Farrell quickly stopped him.

"Before you go sayin' no, let me explain what happened."

Rubbing his neck, Grant considered Farrell's request. Personally, he disliked the law that allowed a woman to sue a man for promises that were so often only implied, or even imagined. The Boston courts were filled with such cases. Recently, one unfortunate man had been forced to pay twenty thousand dollars to a woman he hadn't set eyes on in eighteen years. His one mistake had been peering into her baby carriage and declaring her a beauty. Based on that one innocent gesture, he was accused of backing out of a promise of marriage when she came of age, and he was financially ruined.

Of course, in Miss Lockwood's case, no question existed about the nature of the promise. As much as he found such lawsuits distasteful, Grant didn't blame the lady for taking revenge.

He tapped his fingers together. "I don't handle these kinds of cases."

A lawyer could hang a reputation on a single sensational case. In that regard, a heart-balm tort was made to order—alienation of affection, seduction, breach of promise; they were all sensational. But fame didn't pay the bills and was often more of a hindrance than an asset. A lawyer's real bread and butter came from land disputes and routine legal chores, and that's what Grant had intended to concentrate on when he'd moved here.

"Please, there's no one else. At least listen to my side."

"I don't have much time." He had all the time in the world.

Farrell's gaze traveled over Grant's desk, empty

save for the blotter and inkwell. "It'll only take a few minutes."

Grant blew out his breath. "Very well."

Farrell sat back. "I guess you could say it started at last year's winter dance." His skinny red mustache twitched. "Everyone kept askin' when Meg and I would set the date. Meg said she wouldn't marry me unless her pa and mine stopped bickerin' and agreed to a single time zone."

Farrell pulled out his handkerchief and dabbed his forehead. "Then my pa surprised us all by sayin' he would agree to such a thing if Mr. Lockwood did the same." His twang grew more distinct as he continued. "Everyone badgered Meg's pa until he finally agreed to end the feud and"—he snapped his fingers—"just like that, Meg and I were betrothed."

Grant narrowed his eyes. He didn't want to sympathize with the man, but he could see how small-town peer pressure might have put Mr. Farrell in a difficult position.

"How could you have gone along with this if you didn't love her?" A promise to marry was considered a legally binding contract. A man would be foolish to pledge such a thing unless he was serious.

"Oh, I love her all right. I've loved her ever since I was five and she was three, and I saw her runnin' down the street stark naked."

Grant blinked and cleared his throat. Erasing the memory of her intimate garments from his memory took considerable effort. "Did…did Miss Lockwood feel the same about you?"

"I-I think so."

"You think so?" Grant frowned. "Did…Miss Lockwood have no other suitors?" he asked.

"Oh, plenty," Farrell said with a nod. "But old man Lockwood chased them all off. He tried to get rid of me too, but I refused to go away." Farrell rubbed his chin. "Meg was the best friend I ever had, and I miss her somethin' awful, but we're as different as night and day. She's perfectly content to stay in Two-Time, and I want to see the world. Her idea of a good time is to curl up with a book." He wrinkled his nose. "I want to sail an ocean, and she wants to read about it."

Farrell looked so distraught and sounded so sincere that Grant felt sorry for him despite all his efforts to the contrary. At least Farrell had been man enough to own up to his feelings before ruining Miss Lockwood's life. His instincts were sound, even if his methods left much to be desired.

"Please, I need a lawyer. You're the only one in town who didn't turn me down before hearin' my side."

Grant hesitated. His office had been open for a month, and to date, Farrell was the only one soliciting his services. He'd had no idea it would be so difficult for a big-city lawyer to earn a small town's trust.

He mentally ran through his options. If he could talk the two feuding families into accepting a compromise, perhaps people would view him more favorably. Eighty percent of the breach-of-promise cases in Boston were settled out of court. Still, he didn't want to take sides against the lady.

"By way of disclosure, you should know that I happen to be acquainted with Miss Lockwood and my sympathies lie with her."

Farrell nodded. "She has my sympathies too, but not ten thousand dollars' worth."

Grant folded his hands on the desk. "Hell has no fury like a woman scorned."

Farrell leaned forward. "It's not Meg's fury that worries me. It's her pa's. He's using this as an excuse to ruin my pa and run him out of business. Please say you'll help me."

❧

No sooner had Meg sat down to supper with her family than she sensed something afoot. Mama, seated at one end of the polished dining room table, must have sensed something too, because her gaze kept darting in Papa's direction. Seemingly oblivious to his family's questioning glances, Papa stood at the head of the table, carving the roast beef and whistling.

The whistling was what worried Meg. Papa was seldom in such good spirits before he ate. She met her younger sister's gaze. As if to confirm Meg's suspicion, Amanda rolled her eyes.

Unlike Meg or Josie, who had taken after either Mama or Papa in appearance, Amanda had inherited a little from each parent. She had Mama's turquoise eyes and Papa's brown hair, but her personality was strictly her own.

Though only nineteen, she had already made a name for herself designing hats. Having inherited her father's flair for the dramatic and her mother's eye for design, she was determined to open her own hat shop, an enterprise her parents bitterly opposed. Making hats as a pastime was one thing, but doing so professionally was quite another.

Papa finished cutting the roast beef and set the carving knife aside, but waited until halfway through the meal before addressing their unspoken questions. He dabbed his mustache with his napkin and cleared his throat.

"I have an announcement to make."

Meg's heart stilled. Papa's announcements were always met with skepticism and more than a little dismay. That's because they usually involved some harebrained scheme to outsell his competitor and bitter enemy, Mr. Farrell.

"What is it, dear?" her mother asked, her pinched face belying the calmness of her voice.

Papa glanced at the wall. Twenty-two clocks in all shapes and sizes graced the dining room. The shiny faces stared back like an eager audience waiting for the next act in a stage play. Pendulums swung back and forth like a trainman's lantern. The constant rhythm of *ticktocks* marked each passing second with the precision of a military cadence.

"I have filed a breach-of-promise suit against Tommy on Meg's behalf."

As usual, his timing was impeccable. No sooner were the words out of his mouth than a cacophony of chimes, bells, cuckoos, and gongs announced the hour of seven. He had planned his announcement precisely so that the clocks would effectively drown out any protests his family might feel obliged to offer.

Stiffening in shock, Meg took a quick swallow of water and forced herself to breathe. Her mother looked no less alarmed. Amanda just stared and for once looked tongue-tied.

Meg didn't even wait for the last of the chimes to fade away. "Papa, you didn't!"

"Henry, how could you?" her mother gasped.

"How could I?" His mustache twitched in righteous indignation, and the fork in his hand stilled. "A grave injustice was done to my family, and you expect me to do nothing? It's time to abandon the handkerchief and pursue the matter legally."

Meg's throat threatened to close, and she could barely get the words out. "I don't want my name dragged through the court." It was embarrassing enough to be left at the altar without having to relive her horrible wedding day all over again.

"No one's dragging you anywhere. All you'll have to do is sit and look appropriately heartbroken." Papa calmly helped himself to the sliced meat and handed the platter to Amanda. "Barnes has agreed to represent us. I asked Miller, but he plays faro with Farrell and said it would be a conflict of interest." Papa cut a small piece of his meat with his knife and stabbed it with his fork.

"Breach of promise. Conflict of interest." Papa waved his fork. "Don't you just love all those legal terms?"

"Yes," Amanda said. "And deciphering them is what keeps lawyers in fancy suits and thoroughbred horses."

Ignoring his youngest daughter's comment, Papa's gaze traveled the length of the table. "Why do you all look so surprised? It's the proper thing to do. Barnes assured me it's done all the time."

Meg felt sick. "But I don't want to sue Tommy. I just want to put this whole thing behind me and forget it ever happened."

"And forget we shall," Papa said with a magnanimous

nod. "Just as soon as he hands over a check for ten thousand dollars."

"Ten—" Meg jumped to her feet. "That's…that's outrageous!" Tommy didn't have that kind of money, and even if he did, she would never accept it.

"Henry, I beg you to reconsider," Mama said.

Even Amanda, who seldom took sides in family arguments, nodded vigorously, the platter of meat bobbing up and down in her hands.

"What is the matter with you all?" Papa looked genuinely perplexed. "The Lockwoods have never backed down from a fight, and we're not about to start now."

"This is between Tommy and me, no one else!" Meg cried.

"Nonsense. I'm your father, and it's my responsibility to see that you're taken care of. Now that you're damaged goods—"

"*Henry!*"

"You know what I mean, Elizabeth. A woman left at the altar is often regarded with less-than-customary respect. Every man will look at her with a more critical eye and naturally assume she's lacking in some way. Who would take a chance on marrying her now?"

Meg stared at her father in shock. Did he really think she was damaged goods? "I don't need a man," she cried, "and I certainly don't want Tommy's money!" Jumping to her feet, she slammed her chair against the table and stormed from the room in tears.

❧

The following morning Meg decided to walk to town rather than wait for Papa to rig the horse and buggy and ride with him. She was still upset over the lawsuit and had hardly slept a wink. Maybe a walk would be the thing to help clear her head.

It was still early and few shops would be open, but already the widow Rockwell was hauling a box of belongings across the street.

Normally, Meg would stop to help her move, but not today. Nor did she pay any heed to Mr. Crawford raising Cain with Mr. McGinnis, his bagpipe-playing neighbor. She hardly even noticed when the Johnson boy almost ran her down while escaping the clutches of Mr. Sloan.

Nor did the big yellow hound running down the street with his tail between his legs earn more than a cursory glance. This time it wasn't the dogcatcher giving chase. Today the hound's tormentor was Cowboy, Mrs. Rockwell's black-and-white cat.

Something had to be done about that annoying tom, but not today. Today Meg had other things on her mind.

As if her father's latest plan wasn't bad enough, the editorial in the morning paper denounced breach-of-promise suits as a whole and referred to her *by name* as a manipulating gold digger!

Ooooooooh, her father made her so mad, and this ridiculous lawsuit was the least of it. Papa was the most stubborn, mule-headed man to ever inhabit the face of the earth. He never spoke when he could shout or walked when he could run.

Reaching the edge of town, Meg stomped onto the boardwalk. The heels of her boots hammered the wooden boards like two angry woodpeckers. Halfway down the block, someone called her name.

She spun her head in the direction of the male voice. Seeing her former fiancé waving to her, she quickened her steps. She was in no mood to see anyone, and she certainly had nothing to say to Tommy Farrell.

Yanking the hem of her skirt up to her ankles, she stepped onto the muddy street and sidestepped a pile of horse manure, hoping to reach the sanctity of her father's shop before Tommy caught up to her.

No such luck. With unprecedented speed, he grabbed her by the arm and spun her around.

They were standing in the middle of Main Street. A horse and wagon swerved around them, causing the driver to rend the air with curses.

Meg pulled her arm away. "I have nothing to say to you, Tommy Farrell. Go to your precious islands and leave me alone!" She whirled about in a circle of skirts and stormed across the street to the other side.

"I can't go now," he called after her. "I can't leave town until this lawsuit is settled."

"That's all you care about. Leaving—"

"You don't understand."

"Oh, I think I understand just—"

"Meg, listen—"

"No, *you* listen—"

She stopped to tell him that there would be no lawsuit, but Tommy wouldn't let her get a word in edgewise. He joined her on the boardwalk, his mouth flapping up and down like a broken cellar door. Never had she seen him so riled.

"Your pa's a stubborn old fool and…"

On and on he went like an indignant jaybird. In the process he called her father every name under the sun, managing to insult not only him, but also a good number of God's creatures.

Knuckles planted firmly at her waist, Meg glared at Tommy. "How dare you talk about my father like that!" Much as she hated to admit it, everything he said was, to some extent, true. But that didn't give him any right to say it.

"Come on, Meg. You know I'm right. Now thanks to his money-grubbin' ways, I'm under orders not to leave town."

"My father is not money-grubbing. Nor is he a scoundrel or—"

"So what do you call suin' me? For ten thousand bucks, no less!"

"Honor," she said. "Which is something you know nothing about." If he did, he would never have waited until their wedding day to break off with her.

"Honor?" Tommy reared back. "Great Scott, you call that honor? It feels more like betrayal to me."

"You should know!" She turned and stormed away.

"If you go through with this lawsuit, then you're just as bad as your old man," he called after her.

Seething through gritted teeth, Meg let herself into her father's shop. Pocketing the key, she slammed the door shut with her foot. After the way Tommy had talked about her father, it would serve him right if she did go through with it. Yes, indeed it would.

Four

GRANT SAT THAT MONDAY MORNING IN THE DINING room of Mrs. Abbott's boardinghouse. A former bordello, the house now had sturdy, prim furniture and muted colors that made it look as respectable as a preacher's wife. The same was true for its owner, whose demure countenance belied her less-than-virtuous past.

For inside Mrs. Abbott's full-rounded body beat the heart of a woman who had once answered to the name of Good Time Sal. All that remained of the red-haired beauty of yesteryear was the painting on the parlor wall. Her once-glorious red hair was now snowy white, her lively blue eyes were faded, and her ivory-pink skin had long lost its luster. Thankfully, the gown in the portrait, with its eye-popping neckline, had been discarded along with the woman's youth.

Grant helped himself to a second cup of coffee and lingered over the morning headlines, the front page all that was left of the newspaper. His landlady had confiscated the rest of the *Two-Time Gazette* and sat opposite him at the table, clucking at the town's latest gossip. The other four tenants had already gone for the day, leaving just the two of them alone.

The breach-of-promise suit had made the front page, and the editor had made no effort to mince words. Grant frowned. Was Miss Lockwood really a gold digger? Or was she just lashing out from hurt? If it was the latter, she might be willing to settle out of court for less money. But if she really was a gold digger...

"Oh my!" Mrs. Abbott exclaimed. "You won't believe the letter someone wrote to Miss Lonely Hearts."

Grant never read that particular column and had no interest in it, but that didn't keep his landlady from reading it aloud to him each morning. Today's letter had been written by a wife with a philandering husband.

"I bet Mrs. Trollope wrote that letter," Mrs. Abbott said. "It sounds like her. Or maybe it was Mrs. Garner. Her husband is as trustworthy as a wolf in a henhouse." She wasn't alone in playing the Miss Lonely Hearts guessing game. The column's daily letters were the subject of much speculation in town and a topic of conversation everywhere Grant went.

So far, he was at a loss to explain what his sister had found so appealing about Texas in general and Two-Time in particular. Her letters had been filled with glowing reports of wildflowers, rolling hills, vast skies, and friendly folks. That was a far cry from reality. He now knew the state was populated with fat cattle, lean men, and short tempers. Friendly? Hardly. Fistfights broke out with little or no provocation. Gunfire was as common as houseflies. The only things saving this town from extinction were bad aims and fast horses.

The day he arrived in Texas had been the worst day of his life. Instead of finding his sister waiting for him at the Two-Time train depot, he had been greeted by his brother-in-law, Joe.

One look at Joe's face told him something was terribly wrong, and his words bore that out. His sister had gone into premature labor, and neither she nor her child had survived. It had been a stunning blow.

Grant would have left town then and there, had Joe not talked him into staying. "Mary was convinced you'd love it here."

Mary, his twin. The one person in the world who had known him better than anyone else. As children, it had seemed that she could even read his mind. For that reason, he had reluctantly agreed to stay. He'd give it his best shot if for no other reason than to honor his sister's memory.

So far, he'd found nothing to love about the town or the people. How could his sister have been so wrong about Two-Time? So wrong about him?

The tall, stately clock in the corner of the parlor sighed just before the hammer hit the bell. Deep, rich dongs filled the room, commanding attention with the same force as a judge's gavel. Out of habit, Grant pulled the watch from his vest pocket. A fifteen-minute difference in time meant that either the tall clock was slow or his watch was fast. Shrugging, he pocketed his watch and reached for his coffee cup. Might as well sit here as in his empty office.

It sure did look like staying in Two-Time was a mistake. He should have turned around immediately upon learning of his sister's death and gone back to

Boston. Now he was obligated to stay, at least till the rent ran out on the office.

So far he had only one client, and he wasn't even sure about that. He'd told Farrell he would think about taking on his case and get back to him. There were risks involved in handling such a high-profile, controversial lawsuit, and it might do more harm to his business than good. He was viewed as an outsider and was likely to remain so if he took sides. On the other hand...

Startled out of his reverie by a sudden loud pounding at the front door, Grant spilled his coffee. He set his cup down and reached for his napkin. "Shall I see who it is?"

Mrs. Abbott rose and brushed a strand of white hair behind her ear. "I'll get it." She frowned. "It's probably Mrs. Walters wanting to borrow more flour."

She hastened from the dining room to the parlor, tottering from side to side like a child just learning to walk.

The banging persisted with an urgency that brought Grant to his feet.

Mrs. Abbott swung the front door open. Before a word escaped her mouth, a barrel of a man pushed his way inside, forcing her back against the wall.

"Your clock is running slow," he said as brusquely as one might sound an alarm. He crossed to the tall clock in the corner of the parlor with quick steps. It seemed like the only time a man walked or talked fast in this town was when he was interfering in somebody else's business.

After opening the clock's glass case, the man pulled

a screwdriver from his pocket. Bending slightly at the waist, he turned the screw on the pendulum disk.

"You must check the clock each time you hear me ring the bell," he scolded as he worked. "It's the only way to ensure accurate time. If I hadn't heard the gongs as I walked by your house, you'd have ended up on Farrell time."

Mrs. Abbott's eyes rounded in horror. "Oh dear!"

Watching from the dining room doorway, Grant frowned. The two of them made Farrell time sound like the end of the world.

The visitor stepped back and pulled out his watch. After checking the time, he made one more adjustment before closing the cabinet. Seemingly satisfied, he doffed his hat and left with nary a good-bye.

Mrs. Abbott shut the door after him and walked back to the dining room.

"Who was that man?" Grant asked, taking his seat.

"Why, that was Mr. Lockwood—"

"Lockwood!" Meg's Lockwood's father? He should have known.

"When the bell in front of Lockwood Watch and Clockworks rings, I'm supposed to check the time on my clock." She wrung her hands. "Sometimes I get busy and forget."

Grant shook his head. "What business is it of his if your clock runs fast or slow?"

Bells rang throughout the day at all different times. The bells from the large clock in front of Lockwood's shop had a deeper tone than the bell from Farrell's, which allowed Two-Time residents to tell them apart. The gongs were so loud and insistent that not even a blind man could ignore the passage of time. Mercifully, the bells stopped at night or no one would get any sleep. It was hard enough sleeping through the gunfire.

"Oh, Mr. Lockwood is just being thoughtful," Mrs. Abbott assured him. "He doesn't want me to be late. My boarders depend on me serving meals on time."

"I still think he had his nerve barging in like that."

"It's a good thing he did. Look what happened to Mrs. Fitzgerald. She missed her husband's funeral, and all because she refused to keep her clock properly wound. When she finally arrived nearly two hours late, they had to open the grave and repeat the whole service over again just for her benefit."

Grant rubbed the back of his neck. He'd never heard of anything so ridiculous. No such problems existed in Boston, which adhered to the standard time established by the Harvard College Observatory. Prior to regulated time, train crashes in the area had been a frequent occurrence. More than a hundred accidents were the direct result of engineers leaving or arriving at depots too early or too late, and not knowing the location of other trains.

Mrs. Abbott still looked distressed as she returned from the kitchen to refill Grant's cup. "I'll try to remember to check that the clock runs on time. I don't want you to be late for the office," she said.

"Thank you." Not that anyone in town would notice if he was late or altogether truant. Lockwood's unwelcomed interruption had served one purpose though. Grant's sympathy for Tommy Farrell had increased tenfold. No wonder the poor fellow got in over his head. The possibility of a father-in-law like that was enough to make any man have second thoughts about marriage. Taking on the Farrell case no longer seemed like such a bad idea.

Five

THE MEETING AT MR. BARNES'S LAW OFFICE TO DISCUSS the breach-of-promise lawsuit was scheduled for 1:00 and 1:40 p.m. consecutively to accommodate both parties.

Meg insisted upon arriving early. She had something to say, and she needed to say it before Tommy and his attorney made their appearance.

Mr. Barnes greeted Meg and her parents at the door and then ran around the office clearing books and papers off chairs to make room for them to sit. A man of extremes, he had a rotund body perched upon pencil-thin legs. His full beard hardly seemed to belong with the shiny, bald head it sat upon.

He pushed a pile of papers aside and perched on the corner of his desk, arms folded. "Well now, little lady, your father said you have some questions."

Seated between her parents, Meg pulled off her white gloves and laid them across her lap. Normally the lawyer's condescending tone would infuriate her, but today she had other things on her mind.

"Only one," she said. "What do we have to do to drop the lawsuit?"

This brought an immediate reaction from her father. "Meg, we've been through this a hundred times. We can't let Tommy get away with what he did to this family." His voice rose until it rattled the windows. "To you!"

"Henry, you promised not to shout," Mama said.

"I'm not shouting!" her father shouted.

Meg clenched her hands tight. "I'm the one he walked out on, not you. And you didn't want me to marry him in the first place."

"That's neither here nor there. The man hurt you and deserves to pay."

"I don't want his money. I want nothing from him!" Her voice rose to an unladylike level, but it was the only way she knew to penetrate her father's thick skull.

"Now, now." Mr. Barnes waved his hands up and down like a housewife shaking out the wash. "Let's all remain calm. It wouldn't do to let the other party know we're not in full accord." He cleared his throat and pushed his spectacles up his nose. "So, Meg, what exactly are you saying?"

"I'm saying that I want no part of this lawsuit. What happened between Tommy and me is over, and I want to forget about it."

Her father reared back. "What crazy talk is this? Next you'll be telling me you forgive him."

Meg glared at her father. "Maybe I do."

Her father shot to his feet like a popped cork, and everyone started talking at once. Soon they were all on their feet, even Mama.

"Now, Henry, you promised…" Mama tugged on Papa's sleeve.

Meg seethed. "And I am *not* damaged goods!"

Mr. Barnes's eyebrows shot up. "Good heavens! Are you saying you broke the code of maidenly modesty?"

That got her father's attention, and he looked as puzzled as she did. "Maidenly what?"

"I was simply asking if your daughter and Mr. Farrell had engaged in—"

"Certainly not!" Meg exclaimed. The very idea. She and Tommy had shared, at most, a couple of chaste kisses. "I just want to forget about the wedding—"

Mr. Barnes cleared his throat and straightened his bow tie. "Don't forget that the wedding took a healthy chunk out of your father's finances." He reached for a piece of paper. "The wedding dress alone cost—"

The door to the office sprang open, and Barnes stopped reading. All four heads swiveled toward the newcomers. Papa pulled his watch out of his vest pocket, a not-so-subtle reminder of the differences between the two families.

Tommy's father entered the office first. Robert Farrell gave Mr. Barnes a curt nod, but didn't as much as glance at Meg or her parents.

A thin man with a saucer-size bald spot on his crown, he was the physical opposite of her father. Papa was tall and round as a rain barrel, while Mr. Farrell was a good five inches shorter and thin as a measuring stick. It was as if by some mutual agreement the two men had decided to look as different in appearance as their personalities and philosophies dictated.

Behind him, Tommy slinked into the office as cautious as a minnow swimming through shark-infested waters. Meg couldn't help but feel sorry for him. But it was the tall man walking in last who commanded her attention. She recognized him at once and suddenly couldn't breathe.

Oh dear God. This can't be happening.

Barnes cleared off three more chairs and quickly introduced his clients to Tommy's lawyer. "I'd like you to meet Mr. and Mrs. Lockwood and their daughter, Meg."

Grant Garrison pulled off his derby and tucked it beneath his arm. His tailored dark trousers and frock coat made him look even taller and leaner than Meg remembered. Thick brown hair fell from a side part and tapered neatly to his collar.

He shook hands with her father and took her mother's offered hand in his before releasing it. He then turned his handsome face to Meg and locked her in the depths of his golden-brown eyes. He picked up the gloves she didn't know she'd dropped on the floor. As he handed them to her, his fingers brushing hers, a corner of his mouth quirked upward.

"We meet again."

❦

Grant had attended many meetings with opposing counsel, but he'd never witnessed anything quite like this. If the raised voices weren't bad enough, Mr. Lockwood's habit of pounding the desk with his fist as he spoke was downright annoying.

The only thing Grant could compare the meeting to was a Boston labor riot from which he'd been lucky to escape with only a slight wound to the shoulder. The way things were going, he doubted his luck would hold a second time.

With each booming eruption of Henry Lockwood's voice, the windows rattled and the beaded lampshade on Barnes's desk shook like it was about to explode.

The defendant's father responded in kind, his voice thinner but no less virulent.

The lack of alarm, surprise, or even disapproval on the women's parts suggested that such outrageous behavior was not unusual and, indeed, quite normal for the family patriarchs.

Things were different in Texas, that was for sure, but never had Grant imagined having to deal with such unbecoming behavior. His ears were already ringing. Mr. Lockwood had a voice like the biblical bulls of Bashan.

Since Mr. Barnes had called the meeting, it was his job to restore order. When he failed to do so, Grant stood and positioned himself between the battling twosome. Enough was enough.

"Gentlemen!"

The two men glowered at each other but thankfully fell silent. Their heaving chests and daggerlike glares suggested the reprieve was only temporary, and a second round was imminent.

"If you would kindly take your seats, we will get started," Grant said in a voice usually reserved for a biased jury.

Lockwood looked about to argue, but his wife tugged on his coattail, and he lowered his generous bulk onto the chair next to hers.

Only after order had been restored did Mr. Barnes read the charges lodged by his client. He then folded his hands on his desk and cleared his throat.

"Mr. Garrison, would you care to comment?"

"Thank you," Grant said. He was still standing and decided to remain so for security purposes. Holding on to the lapel of his frock coat gave him a feeling of control. "While I have nothing but sympathy for Miss Lockwood…"

Pausing, he leveled his gaze at her and almost lost himself in her bold regard, her turquoise eyes as unfathomable as the deepest ocean. She sat perfectly composed, feet together, hands on her lap, chin up. She certainly didn't look like she needed his sympathy. Nor anything else, for that matter.

He averted his gaze and continued. "The fact is that my client was pressured into asking for Miss Lockwood's hand in marriage and—"

Lockwood popped up from his seat—a regular jack-in-the-box. "That's absurd!"

"Papa, please," his daughter pleaded. "Listen to what the man has to say."

"We'll have a chance to present our side in due time," Mr. Barnes assured him.

Lockwood's mouth puckered, and he looked about to argue. Finally, at his wife's urging, he lowered his bulk onto the chair again with a silent scowl, arms folded across his ample chest.

Grant continued. "My client is willing to pay a reasonable sum to cover expenses but not the exorbitant fee listed in the complaint. Furthermore—"

Once again Lockwood sprang to his feet. "Considering the mental anguish Tommy put my daughter through, ten thousand dollars is more than reasonable."

Mr. Farrell leaped up, and the two men faced each other like combatant soldiers. "Now see here, Lockwood—"

"No, *you* see here!"

"Gentlemen." This time Mr. Barnes took charge by pounding his desk with a brass paperweight. "If you would be so kind as to take your seats, you'll both have a chance to speak at the appropriate times."

Grant waited for the men to comply before continuing. "The defendant wishes to make it clear that he never meant to hurt Miss Lockwood. But the truth is that he was forced—"

"Forced, my foot," Mr. Lockwood shouted. "He sneaked behind my back and damaged my daughter!"

Meg's hand flew to her throat, and her protest escaped in a strangled whisper.

"Henry!" her mother said sharply.

"It's true, and you know it."

Cheeks blazing, Meg rose from her chair and glared at her father. "How…how could you?" she sputtered.

Feeling sorry for her, Grant quickly restored order. "Would you care to make a statement, Miss Lockwood?"

Shooting him a look of disdain, she appeared about to say something, but after a quick glance at her father, she abruptly changed her mind. Whirling about in a flutter of skirts, she stormed out of the office, slamming the door so hard that the lamp on the desk shook.

Miss Lockwood's departure relieved Grant of any hope that the dispute could be brought to a quick and civil conclusion.

Six

"DO HURRY, MEG, OR WE'LL MISS THE TRAIN,"
Amanda shouted as they hurried around a horse and
carriage and dashed down the narrow, dirt-packed
streets of San Antonio toward the train depot.

"I *am* hurrying!" Meg retorted. It was overcast and
cold that late afternoon in November, and the threat
of rain hung precariously in the air. The streetcar
driver had told them that the town clocks were set to
train time, but neither she nor her sister could imagine
anything so perfectly synchronized.

They raced past rows of single-story adobe buildings. Clay waterspouts jutted out from beneath flat
roofs, and the fenced yards were filled with goats,
chickens, and brown-faced children.

Twenty thousand people called the city home, but
the crowded streets around Market Plaza suggested
many times that number.

Balancing an armload of gaily wrapped packages,
Meg followed Amanda past stalls of hand-tooled leather
goods, bright shiny jewelry, and colorful shawls called
rebozos. Booths were strung between mule-driven

wagons and the Spanish mission. Mexican vendors vying for Christmas shoppers outshouted each other, and trail-driving cowboys traded stories with charros, their Mexican counterparts.

An artist seated behind an easel was painting the portrait of a young Mexican woman dressed in a bright-blue peasant dress. A man sat cross-legged on a blanket selling clay pots, and three men played guitars while another sang. The music could hardly be heard above the cries of the vendors.

Hurrying to keep up with her sister, Meg couldn't help but cast an envious gaze at the twirling dancers. Colorful skirts made them look like flowers caught in a whirlwind. Normally at this time of year she would be putting last-minute touches on her gown for the winter ball. However, no one had asked her to go this year, and the thought of sitting out the dance at home filled her with dismay. But that wasn't the only reason for her depressed mood.

Why, oh why had she allowed Amanda to talk her into traveling to San Antone? On a shopping spree, no less? Her feet hurt, her head ached, and if she had to look at another ostrich feather or peacock plume for her sister's hats, she would scream. It was just her luck to belong to a family that did everything in excess.

"If you hadn't spent so much time pondering velvet ribbons, we'd be on the train by now," she huffed, her breath coming out in white plumes.

"Oh, stop complaining, Meg. Here I thought I was doing you a kindness by inviting you to spend the day shopping instead of moping around."

"I was not moping around!"

Fine, maybe a little. She felt guilty for giving Amanda a bad time. It wasn't her sister's fault that she felt out of sorts. At home, she couldn't go anywhere without people stopping to stare. Two-Time was no longer divided only by time—the pending breach-of-promise lawsuit was now the talk of the town. Everyone had an opinion, and more than one fistfight had broken out because of it. Half the town sided with Tommy; the other half, with her.

"Oh, look," Amanda called. "The clocks were right. The train hasn't left yet."

"Thank God," Meg muttered. Her feet couldn't hold out much longer.

The uniformed conductor motioned them to hurry with a wave of his hand. White teeth flashed against his ebony skin as they neared. "All aboard," he called as if to encourage them to run faster.

No sooner had they stepped onto the train than the door closed behind them with a *whoosh*, followed by a high-pitched whistle.

Stretching her neck to peer over her packages, Meg followed Amanda down the narrow aisle in search of empty seats. The train was packed with weary-looking shoppers, harried young mothers, and distracted businessmen.

"Over here," Amanda called.

Just as Meg slipped past a man standing in the aisle, the train started with a lurch, forcing him to bump into her.

The packages flew out of her arms and into the lap of a male passenger.

Regaining her balance, Meg murmured a quick apology and reached for one of the packages that had spilled. She lifted her gaze and was greeted by an all-too-familiar face.

"Mr. Garrison!" she gasped, pulling her hand back as if from fire. What was Tommy's lawyer doing here?

Grant handed her the package, and the surprise on his face faded into amusement. "Miss Lockwood. Fancy meeting you."

Amanda grabbed the package out of Meg's hand. "Do you two know each other?" she asked, struggling to reach the overhead baggage rack.

Mr. Garrison nodded. "We've met a couple of times."

Cheeks blazing, Meg picked the remaining packages off the floor and struggled to place them on the iron-rod shelf above her head.

"Let me help you with those." Mr. Garrison stood, his commanding height making it necessary for him to remove his hat. His arm brushed against hers as he reached up to place the paper-wrapped boxes on the baggage rack.

He moved with an air of authority that gave no heed to the swaying motion of the train. In short order, all their parcels were stacked neatly overhead.

Pulse skittering, Meg sat. She pulled off one glove and then the other, laying both across her lap. She then untied her cape and let it hang loosely over her shoulders.

Mr. Garrison took his place directly opposite her and donned his hat.

Since Amanda was looking at her rather strangely, Meg felt compelled to make introductions.

"Mr. Garrison is Tommy's lawyer," she said and added, "This is my sister Amanda."

He acknowledged Amanda with a polite nod and doffed his hat. "A pleasure."

Amanda lowered herself onto the seat next to Meg. "Isn't this a conflict of interest or something? You two being seen together?"

Mr. Garrison waved off her concern with slight shake of his head. "Not unless we discuss the case, which I have no intention of doing." His congenial expression did nothing to conceal the warning in his voice.

"Nor I," Meg assured him, inclining her head. It was bad enough that this man had been privy to her most intimate garments. She certainly didn't want to think about the embarrassing scene that had followed. Did he think she was damaged goods too?

"Ah, for once we're in accord." His intriguing smile made Meg's heart do a funny flip-flop. Or maybe it was simply the motion of the train.

A young lad with jet-black hair shuffled along the aisle hawking newspapers. "Read all about it," he called above the *clickety-clack* of the wheels on the railroad tracks and the drone of voices. "Stage attacked…"

Mr. Garrison reached into his pocket. "I'll take one," he called with a raised hand. The boy handed him the paper in exchange for a coin. "Keep the change."

The boy's grin practically reached his ears. "Thank you, sir."

"Would you ladies care for a newspaper?" Mr. Garrison addressed them both but gazed directly at Meg.

Meg afforded him a polite smile. "We'll pass, thank you."

The boy continued on his way, and Mr. Garrison

opened the *San Antonio Daily Times* with a snap and began reading.

The top of the newspaper came up to the tip of his nose. This allowed Meg to study him at length. He really was a fine-looking man. Everything from his highly polished shoes to his black felt bowler was impeccable. His square face lacked the leathery look of local ranchers, making him appear younger than his years, which she guessed to be somewhere in his late twenties or perhaps early thirties. But what he lacked in sunbaked lines he made up for in commanding presence.

He was no doubt a force to be reckoned with in the courtroom. That's what worried her. Next to him, Mr. Barnes looked like a rank beginner.

What a pity Mr. Garrison had chosen to pursue such a profession! Lawyers got rich off other people's misfortunes, and she had no patience for the lot of them.

Next to her, Amanda fingered the velvet ribbon purchased that day and gave a contented sigh. "I can hardly wait to get started on the new hat I'm making for Mrs. Wellmaker. The color will go perfectly with her eyes. Don't you agree?"

"I'm sure it will," Meg said, as if she cared what the pastor's wife wore.

The church was the only neutral territory in town because the pastor refused to show favoritism by using either Farrell or Lockwood time. He chose instead to ring the church bells at random on what he called *the Lord's time*. That meant Sunday worship could be anywhere between seven and noon, depending on when the good reverend felt compelled to preach.

Anyone who didn't wish to be caught racing to church in less-than-stylish attire had to plan ahead.

"And this one is perfect for Mrs. Evanston," Amanda was saying. "It's a lovely shade."

It was a bright red that would look more appropriate on Madame Bubbles, owner of Two-Time's house of ill repute, than a politician's wife. Amanda insisted that hats made a statement, giving women a presence in a society that basically treated them as invisible. Her philosophy was simply the higher, the wider, the bolder, the better. She had nothing but contempt for the modest, ladylike hats favored by Mama, Josie, and Meg.

"Shouldn't the mayor's wife wear something more sedate?" Meg asked, trying not to sound critical.

"Hats aren't meant to be sedate. They're supposed to make a statement about a person and make her presence known. Sort of like those old hoop skirts we were forced to wear as children. Feel it. Isn't it soft?"

Meg rubbed a finger along the satiny length. "Yes, it is soft." How anyone could carry on so about ribbons she would never know. "Papa will have a fit if he finds out that you're making hats for her." The mayor favored Farrell time, and that infuriated their father.

Amanda made a face. "I don't care. I love Papa dearly, but sometimes he can be so stubborn."

With a slight tilt of her head, Meg reminded her sister that they weren't alone. Such private discussions should never be aired in public. Not only did it show disrespect for their father, but who knew how Mr. Garrison might use Amanda's words to his own advantage during the trial?

The lawyer seemed completely engrossed in his

newspaper, but that could be an act. While Meg was watching him, an idea about how to stop the lawsuit popped into her head. What if she could convince Mr. Garrison that he didn't have a chance in Hades of winning the case? Maybe then he'd advise his client to settle out of court, bringing a swift end to the ordeal. If the two lawyers worked together, perhaps they could persuade her father to accept a more modest settlement. One that wouldn't send Tommy to the poorhouse. At this point, she was desperate enough to try anything.

"I do agree with Papa in one regard," she said, her voice a tad louder than necessary to make sure it could be heard over the rumble of wheels on track.

Amanda's head pivoted in her direction. "That's a first, you agreeing with Papa."

The careless shrug of her shoulders belied Meg's anxiety. She didn't want Tommy's money. She didn't want anything from him.

"In this case, he's right. The wedding cost him a great deal of money. Not to mention the inconvenience Tommy caused the family and wedding guests. All hundred and fifty of them, if I'm not mistaken."

Amanda's mouth fell open, but fortunately she was too stunned to voice her surprise at Meg's change of heart.

Not so Mr. Garrison. The newspaper inched downward, and he greeted her gaze with raised eyebrows that quickly knitted into a frown.

"I thought we agreed not to discuss the case, Miss Lockwood."

Aha! It was just as Meg had thought. He *was* eavesdropping. With a careless toss of her head, she brushed an imaginary piece of lint from her skirt. "I wasn't talking to you, Mr. Garrison. I was talking to my sister."

He inclined his head. "My mistake."

"Yes, isn't it?" she said with meaning.

He studied her for a moment before lifting his newspaper to eye level and blocking himself from her view.

Convinced her little plan was working, she continued, "The bridal dress alone cost more than two hundred dollars. So—"

"Two hundred and fifty-nine dollars to be exact," Mr. Garrison said without lowering his newspaper.

Meg stared across the narrow aisle. "Did you say something, Mr. Garrison?"

The paper collapsed onto his lap, exposing an expression that was the model of innocence. "Oh, I apologize, Miss Lockwood. I was talking to your sister."

Amanda's gaze swung back and forth between the two of them, a puzzled frown on her face.

Arms spread apart, Mr. Garrison lifted the newspaper until only the top of his hat could be seen above the headline. Meg had heard that looks could kill, but right now she would settle for hers burning a hole right through the center of all that paper and print.

"In addition to the dress and other expenses," she continued, spacing each word precisely, "there's the matter of mental anguish…"

✎

Behind his newspaper, Grant Garrison almost laughed out loud. Mental anguish? The woman had to be kidding. Nothing was wrong with Miss Meg Lockwood's mental faculties, that was for sure. She knew exactly what she was doing. She had his ear and meant to make the most of it.

Keeping his gaze hidden, he listened as she rattled on. "I haven't been able to sleep for a month," she said.

Ha! An outward lie if he'd ever heard one. He lowered his paper until she came into full view. No woman could look so downright attractive without adequate sleep. Today, her eyes fairly sparkled, and not so much as a shadow or line marred her pretty, round face. Not only did the turquoise dress beneath her cape match the color of her eyes, but it also showed off her tiny waist and slender hips.

Her hair was swept into a tidy bun this time, allowing only the most stubborn tendrils to escape. A perky hat sat upon her head, the feather as rigid as her ramrod back.

Purposely ignoring his gaze, she continued to cite every possible expense imaginable, words spilling out like water from a pump. Invitations, stamps, ink, paper, cake, decorations, trousseau, and shoes—on and on she went.

At mention of her trousseau, his mind traveled back to the day her hope chest overturned, revealing its intriguing contents. Tommy Farrell would never know what he'd missed. All that lace and satin and...

"And then of course there's Mama's dress and yours and—"

His head fairly spun. Did a wedding really require so much folderol? And what was wrong with wearing a previously worn pair of shoes? Or even a dress for that matter? No one looked at anyone other than the bride. So why did her sisters need all that new frippery?

These were questions he would present to the court, but he suspected they'd have little impact. Her father was a force to be reckoned with and his daughter no less so. Her big eyes alone could sway even the likes of Judge Isaac Parker, the hanging judge of Fort Smith, Arkansas.

And that's what worried him.

Seven

MEG STOOD BEHIND THE COUNTER OF THE LOCKWOOD Watch and Clockworks shop examining the pocket watch the widow Mrs. Burberry had brought in for repairs.

The eleven-jewel timepiece was a finely crafted Waltham made by the American Watch Company. Housed in a silver hunter case, it was similar to the one Abraham Lincoln had carried. No doubt it had been purchased sometime during the War Between the States. Watches with metal lids had been originally designed for hunters, the clamshell casings protecting a watch's delicate face from dirt and physical shocks. They became especially popular with soldiers during the war.

With neatly written figures, Meg carefully recorded the make and serial number into the store's watch book. Her mother had insisted that working in her father's shop would take Meg's mind off the disastrous wedding and pending lawsuit.

Her mother was wrong.

Even now, Meg felt Mrs. Burberry's faded gray eyes watching her every move like a detective shadowing a suspect. Nearly six weeks had passed since that fateful wedding day, but there still appeared to be no end to the stares. Some sympathetic. Most critical.

The strange looks she got were the least of it. Everyone seemed to have an opinion about what had gone wrong, and some were not afraid to express it. Worse, many placed the blame squarely on Meg's shoulders. According to the town's meddling matrons, it was a woman's job to not only land a man, but also to keep him.

"Your husband's?" Meg asked. Alvin Burberry had died last spring.

Mrs. Burberry nodded. "Yes, I want to mail it to our son."

"It's a very well-made watch," Meg said. "I'm sure Papa will have no trouble repairing it. Probably just needs a good cleaning."

"My Alvin wouldn't buy a watch that wasn't well made." The dowager sniffed. "He said a watch should be chosen with the same care as a wife and should run with the same efficiency as a well-run household."

Meg afforded the widow a wan smile. "I would imagine a watch has an easier time of it than a house-wife and is probably more appreciated."

She meant it as a joke, of course, but you would never know it by the look of disapproval on the widow's face.

"Being a housewife is a noble profession, as the good Lord intended." The older woman snapped her thin lips shut in a way that signaled her opinion was not to be questioned. "Men want us to cook the bacon, not bring it home. Nor do men care for independent women with minds of their own." Though she fell short of accusing Meg outright of such folly, her expression said it all.

Meg bit back the retort that flew to her lips. Even though she dreamed of getting married and raising a family, she saw no reason why she couldn't still work in Papa's shop on occasion if that's what she chose to do. Why should marriage limit her options?

The widow was a product of her upbringing, the same as Meg's father. But times were changing. Women were now allowed to attend college, and Meg had heard that women in big cities such as Boston and New York thought nothing of working outside the home. But she kept such thoughts to herself. Offending a customer was strictly forbidden.

Instead, she handed a receipt across the counter with a forced smile. Like it or not, the customer was always right—at least till she walked out the door, which thankfully Mrs. Burberry soon did.

Ohh! People like that made her so mad.

Worse than the verbal advice or criticisms were the articles cut from *Godey's Lady's Book* magazines and left surreptitiously on the counter for her to find. The bold-printed headlines promised everything a woman needed to know about landing a husband.

Never act smarter or more knowledgeable than the object of your affection. So went the typical piece of advice. Reading novels was discouraged, as was voicing one's opinion on religion and politics. Women were counseled instead to stick to such mind-numbing topics as fashion and the weather.

That was all well and good when talking to *some*

men. But one as educated and refined as, say, Mr. Garrison would surely expect more from a lady friend than such drivel. Not that it mattered what the eastern lawyer expected or preferred.

Even if it did, Meg supposed she could never compete with the fancy women he must have known in Boston. She stared down at her plain gingham frock and sighed. If only he didn't keep popping into her thoughts.

If I had someone like you waiting at the altar...

Annoyed at herself for entertaining such thoughts, Meg slammed the watch book shut.

Looking up from his workbench, her father pulled the small magnifying glass away from his eye. "Mrs. Burberry didn't mean any harm. She was only trying to help."

"I don't need her help or anyone else's." After all the bad publicity, Meg's marriage prospects looked far from promising. She might as well just resign herself to spinsterhood and be done with it. "What do I need a husband for anyway?"

Her father's eyebrows lifted. "Now you sound like your sister."

"Maybe Amanda has the right idea."

"In time you'll change your mind." Regret edged his voice as he said it, as if he dreaded to think of such a thing. He was funny that way. He talked about his daughters marrying but disapproved of any suitor who happened to come along. He hadn't even approved of poor Ralph. It wasn't until Mama put her foot down that he finally gave Ralph permission to court Josie, albeit with utmost reluctance.

"Amanda will change her mind about marriage one day. All it will take is for a certain man to come along. The same will be true for you."

Maybe her father was right about her, but Meg doubted a man existed who could change Amanda's mind.

She joined her father at his workbench and slid onto a stool next to his. How she loved watching him work! For such a large and expansive man, he had a surprisingly gentle touch. He could repair the most delicate of mechanisms, even the ones in women's pendant watches.

If only he was as good at repairing relationships. "What happened between you and Mr. Farrell?" She'd asked her father this before but never got an answer. At least not one that made sense. "What happened to make you hate each other?"

"Nothing happened," he said in a voice that signaled the matter was not open for discussion. Normally, she would take the hint and change the subject, but not today.

"Mama said you two were once the best of friends and inseparable all though school."

His hand stilled. "You know your mother. She only sees what she wants to see. I still can't believe she actually approved of your marriage to that scalawag's son." He shook his head. "She has no idea what Farrell is really like."

"Oh?" The bad blood between the families had prevented Meg from getting to know Mr. Farrell personally. All she knew was that Tommy held his father in high esteem and was as puzzled by the feud between the two families as she was. "Tell me, what is Mr. Farrell really like?"

"You don't need to know."

He turned his attention back to the watch he had been working on, relieving her of any hope she would find out more.

He lifted the watch to his ear. His mouth curved upward, and the corners of his eyes crinkled. He pulled the timepiece away and held it toward her. "Listen."

"I know what a watch sounds like, Papa."

His eyebrows shot up. "That's like saying you know what every songbird sounds like based on hearing but a few."

Knowing she would never win such an argument, she took the watch from him and held it to her ear.

"Hear that?" he asked excitedly. "Six ticks to the second."

The *ticktocks* sounded like all the others he had made her listen to through the years.

"That's the sign of a good watch." His eyes shining, he followed her gaze to the wall of clocks. "After the Declaration of Independence was signed, the bells rang out in Philadelphia announcing America's freedom. But do you know what amazed John Adams the most? The fact that thirteen clocks had been synchronized to chime at the same precise moment. He didn't think such a thing was possible."

He waved his arm to indicate the myriads of timekeepers that filled the walls from baseboard to tin ceiling. "What would Mr. Adams think about all this, do you suppose? Hmm?"

"He would think you overdid a good thing, Papa."

Her father laughed. "Would he also think I'm just an addlepated old man like you do?"

"I never said that, Papa. I never even thought it."
Old was not how anyone could describe her father.
Stubborn. Obsessed. Opinionated. But never old.

"Did you know that when I was a young man, I
wanted no part of the family business?"

"That's hard to believe, Papa," Meg said. "What
made you change your mind?"

"The war." The sparkle in his eyes had now been
replaced by a more somber expression. His "war
look," as Meg called it. "Do you know what soldiers
requested most in their letters back home? Pocket
watches. The war was rough on watches. Windup
keys were lost. Rain and mud gummed up the works.
Suddenly your father was in high demand as a watch
repairman." He laughed. "There are many ways to
fight the war, and I did it with this." He held up a pair
of needle-nose pliers. "Time is the ruler of all things."
He winked. "He who controls time has the power. He
also helps to win wars."

She studied her father's profile. "Is that why
you and Mr. Farrell are always fighting about time?
Because of power?"

Her father's expression darkened, and she immediately regretted bringing up Mr. Farrell a second time.

"Power has nothing to do with it. He knows nothing about the art of clock making. He uses olive oil to
lubricate the works. Can you imagine?" Papa would
never think of using anything in his shop other than
the more expensive sperm oil.

"I set my clocks by the sun, which is the way the
good Lord intended. Farrell sets his by some convo-
luted planet configuration known only to himself."

"What about the trains?" Meg asked. There had been talk about coordinating zones across the country to railroad time like on the East Coast, but so far only a few towns had seriously considered it.

Her father pursed his lips in disapproval. "That's all we need. To eat, sleep, and work at the whim of an iron horse." He handed her the watch. "Wrap this up. Thomson is stopping by later to pick it up."

Mr. Thomson owned the shoe-repair shop on the other side of town. Meg stared down at the heavy, ornate watch in her hand. "Papa, is there a way we can settle out of court?"

The question hung between them for a moment before he opened his mouth to answer.

Then, all at once, the hands of every clock reached the quarter-hour mark. A short but impressive symphony of gongs and chimes drowned out her father's reply, but did nothing to erase the stubborn expression on his face. It was a look with which Meg was all too familiar.

If he were a clock, he would tick to the tune of *no, no, no*—six beats to the second.

Eight

GRANT STOOD IN THE FRONT OF THE POST OFFICE staring at his watch.

It was after ten. Why was the post office still closed? In Boston, stores and businesses posted business hours, a tradition he'd taken for granted until coming here. No such helpful signs existed in Two-Time. Shopkeepers opened their shops seemingly at will and closed them likewise. Still, he had expected more from the United States Post Office Department.

"Excuse me, sir," he called to a cowpoke who was leaning against a post while he rolled a cigarette. "Could you tell me when the post office opens?"

The man peered at him from beneath a floppy felt hat. His cratered face was as brown as old leather, and the knees of his bowlegs spread wider than his shoulders.

"What week is this?"

"Week? I believe it's the last week of November," Grant said.

"The second or fourth week means the post office is on Farrell time. The rest belongs to Lockwood. The U.S. Post Office don't like to show favoritism."

Grant grunted as he calculated in his head. Farrell time meant that the post office wouldn't open for another forty minutes or so. "That's right nice of them. I guess we should be grateful for having only two time zones in town."

"You got that right. Heard tell that a town in Kansas has seven." The cowhand gave the cigarette paper a dab of his tongue. "By the way, name's Jackson. Ain't seen you 'round these parts."

"That's because I only recently moved here. Name's Garrison. Grant Garrison."

Jackson stuck the cigarette in his mouth and struck a match. "Hey, I know you," he said, the unlit cigarette jiggling up and down as he spoke. "The jilted bride case, right?"

"Actually, I prefer to call it the Lockwood versus Farrell case."

After lighting his cigarette, Jackson dropped the match and ground it out with the heel of a spurred boot. "That's one feud you don't wanna mess with." He shrugged. "A'course, it's not as bad as some of the others."

"Others?" Grant asked. "You mean there're other disputes around?"

Jackson scoffed. "Are you kiddin' me? We've got more grudges here in Texas than they ever thought of having in Kentucky, and that's saying somethin'. There are the Early-Hasley strife and the Sutton-Taylor feud." He went on to list a dozen or so more. "Then there was the Patton-Manner feud, but that ended a year ago when they shot each other good and dead."

Grant blew out his breath in disgust. What had his sweet, gentle sister ever seen in a town like this? "Unbelievable."

Jackson regarded him with slitted eyes. "Don't you have feuds where you come from?"

"In Boston?" Grant shook his head. "Not like they have here. We just sue each other."

"A good shootin' is faster and less costly."

"Can't argue with you there. What's the reason for all this hostility?"

"Reason? Feuds don't need no reason. Or at least none that matter." Jackson puffed on his cigarette before adding, "Most started during the war. I think the Patton-Manner quarrel began over a goat. Or maybe a sheep. Some are second-gen'ration grudges, and the original offense is long forgotten."

"What about the Lockwood-Farrell feud? What started that?"

"Heck if I know. Don't think even they know. But I'll tell you somethin'. If that fight don't end soon, there's gonna be trouble to pay in this town. Big trouble. And I sure don't want to be 'round when it happens."

❧

Meg had just walked into the house when her sister Amanda beckoned from the top of the stairs. "Psst."

After a hard day at the shop, Meg longed to drink a cup of hot tea and sink her tired feet into a pair of soft slippers. Normally she would think nothing of hiking her skirt clear up to her knees and taking the stairs two at a time—a habit her mother deemed unladylike. Today, she would have earned Mama's approval, because she was far too tired to do more than climb one stair at a time.

"What is it?" she asked, after reaching the landing.

For answer, Amanda hustled Meg into her bedroom and closed the door. Amanda's room had almost as many handbills on the wall as the sheriff's office. But instead of having wanted posters of every known criminal from Mexico to Indian Territory, the walls were plastered with leaflets and handbills from charitable, political, and advocate organizations. The Irish Relief Fund, Children's Home Society, and Prohibition were the most prevalent.

Amanda thrust a pamphlet into Meg's hands.

"Oh no, don't tell me. Not another cause…"

"Read it," Amanda said.

Meg studied the pamphlet. The bold print read: *Miss Brackett's Training School for Volunteer Workers of the Suffrage Campaign.*

"Oh no, you didn't."

Amanda nodded. "I signed up yesterday. This represents our future. Yours and mine. You should be thanking me."

"Papa will have a conniption."

"Only if he finds out." Amanda snatched the pamphlet out of Meg's hand. "It's only a five-day course and will be held at the hotel. You should sign up too."

"And how do you suggest I explain my absence for five whole days?" December was the shop's busiest month.

"You could always pretend to be ill."

Meg shook her head. "Mama would insist I go straight to bed. Besides, I can't think of anything new right now until I get through this lawsuit."

"Have it your way, but you'll be sorry. Lucy

Stone plans to stop by. Can you imagine anyone still traveling and giving speeches at her age?" Amanda had the highest regard for the vocal women's rights advocate, now in her seventies and still going strong. "Did you know that she's married but still uses her maiden name?"

"Is that what you wish to do when you marry?"

"Bite your tongue. I never intend to marry." Amanda emphasized her stance with a determined nod. "I have too many other things to do, and I certainly don't want to waste my life like Mama."

"Shame on you, Mandy. How could you say such a thing? We would all be wise to follow in her footsteps. She's the best possible wife and mother. You know she is."

"And do you know how she spends her days? Scrubbing floors, washing clothes, cooking meals, and beating rugs." Amanda sighed. "There has to be more to life than cleaning house and putting up with Papa's demands."

"Papa doesn't mean to be so demanding. He only wants what's best for us."

"I shudder to think. He's still stuck in the old ways. He has no idea that women can do different things now. Lucy Stone has a college degree. Can you imagine what Mama could have done with that? She could have had a career."

A career? Her mother? Meg shook her head. It was impossible to imagine. "Mama would never work outside the home except for charity."

"That doesn't mean *we* can't."

"I have a job."

"You're working for Papa, and that's the same as Mama."

"I like working at the shop." Or at least she had before she became the talk of the town. "I keep the shop's books in order and get to work with numbers."

Amanda shook the pamphlet in Meg's face. "I'm just saying that there're other opportunities."

Meg sighed. Her sister meant well, but Amanda's ways weren't hers. The truth be told, the only thing Meg had ever wanted was to marry and raise a family.

"What a fine couple we are. You don't want to marry, and no one wants to marry me."

"Don't say that, Meg." Amanda's expression softened. "Don't even think it. If you ask me, Tommy leaving you at the altar was the best thing that ever happened to you."

If it wasn't for the pending lawsuit, Meg might have agreed. "Poor Mama. All she ever wanted was to see the three of us happily wed."

"Thank God for Josie," Amanda said. "If she ever gets around to presenting Mama with a grandchild, that will take the pressure off the two of us."

"Do you really think so?"

Amanda made a face. "I can hope, can't I?"

Nine

THAT THURSDAY AFTERNOON, MEG LEFT THE CLOCK
shop early and scurried along the boardwalk as quick
as a mouse.

Others stepped aside with curious stares, and she
could well imagine what they were thinking: *Where's
that crazy jilted bride off to in such a hurry?* Well, let them
look. See if she cared!

Two-Time had grown in leaps and bounds since
the first arrival of the train, and today, Meg would
have to pass all twenty-two saloons on the way to
Jackleg Row—a derogatory name given to the street
housing the town's lawyers.

The number of doctors and lawyers in a place said
a lot about a town's reputation, and Two-Time had
plenty of both. No fewer than four attorneys occupied
offices on Jackleg Row, though most were kept busy
by land or railroad disputes. A disturbing number of
clashes were still battled out at twenty paces, keeping all three doctors in fine Kentucky whiskey and
Cuban cigars. That didn't count the numerous snake-
oil peddlers who traveled through town hawking

"miracle elixirs" that supposedly cured everything from ingrown toenails to gray hair.

Meg had just breezed by the post office when a bearded man stepped in front of her, blocking her way. He stuck his leering face in hers.

"Well, looky who's here," he slurred.

She waved away the sickening smell of alcohol. "Kindly step aside, sir!"

He jeered. "Unfriendly, ain't you? You're not still pinin' for the Farrell boy? Whatcha see in that fella, anyway?" He clamped his gnarly fingers around her arm, and his eyes glittered. "I'll show you what a real man is like."

"Let me go!" She kicked him on the shin. When that failed to convince him, she bashed him over the head with her parasol.

"Ow!" Releasing her, his hands flew up to grab his injured head. "Why, you little—"

Meg didn't wait to hear the rest. Instead, she picked up her skirt and ran. Papa had been right. In the eyes of some, she was damaged goods, and that made her the target of unwanted advances.

The man's curses followed her into the general store. She slammed the door shut behind her and swallowed the bile in her throat. Standing on tiptoes, she peered over the pyramid of tinned goods to see out the window. Satisfied that she hadn't been followed, she willed her heart to stop pounding.

"What happened to you?"

Startled by a voice behind her, Meg gasped and spun around. Oh no! Of all the people she could have bumped into, why did it have to be Sallie-May

Hutton, the town's worst gossip? Willing her stomach to stop churning, Meg shook her head.

"Nothing happened. Why do you ask?"

Sallie-May stared at the broken parasol in Meg's hand but didn't pursue the question.

"I read all about the lawsuit in the paper," she said. The tight corset beneath her figure-hugging blue dress made her sound breathless.

Sallie-May made no secret that her goal was to land a husband, preferably one who was rich. Given the booming cattle business and the number of local ranch owners who benefited from it, her goal wasn't all that preposterous, even with her annoying personality.

Meg tried not to let her irritation show. "If you don't mind, I'd rather not talk about it."

"Testy, aren't we?" Sallie-May patted her carefully coiffed black hair and changed the subject. "Do you think that lawyer will ask me to the winter ball?"

Meg stared at her. "You want to go to the ball with Mr. Barnes?"

"No, silly. I'm talking about Tommy Farrell's lawyer." She clasped her hands together and sighed. "Honest to goodness, he's the most handsome man I ever did see. He's so tall and…" She rolled her eyes to the ceiling with a sigh. "My, my, my, what broad shoulders!"

"I hadn't noticed," Meg lied. She'd have to be blind not to notice Mr. Garrison's good looks and considerable charm, but she wasn't about to admit as much. Knowing Sallie-May, she'd jump to all the wrong conclusions and spread them all over town like flower seeds by sundown.

Sallie-May stared at her with a look of disbelief. "Really?"

"Yes, really." Meg tossed her broken parasol into the oak barrel used for trash and left the shop. A wave of apprehension rushed through her as she peered up and down the street. Her assailant was nowhere in sight. With a sigh of relief, she continued on her way.

❦

Moments later, Meg reached Jackleg Row. The fine black steed tied to the hitching post in the middle of the block was Mr. Garrison's, which meant that Tommy's lawyer was in his office. She hadn't seen him since the day they'd been on the train together.

The memory made her pulse skitter. As much as she hated to agree with Sallie-May, she was right about one thing—Mr. Garrison really was a most handsome man, especially when he wasn't frowning. Although even then he held a certain appeal.

If I had someone like you waiting at the altar...

The voice, the memory—coming as it did out of nowhere—quickened Meg's pulse. Heat rose up her neck, and she forced herself to breathe.

Refusing to look in Mr. Garrison's office window, she held her head high and her shoulders back. She kept her gaze focused ahead as she passed, and the whole time her heart was racing to beat the band.

Three doors away, she barreled into Mr. Barnes's office like someone seeking shelter from a storm.

The lawyer lifted his bald head with a startled gaze and pushed his spectacles up his bulbous nose. "Miss Lockwood."

Closing the door behind her, Meg stepped up to his weathered desk. She drew in a deep breath and fought to recall what she was doing there.

"How can I help you?" he prompted.

"I wish to drop the charges," she managed at last. "But as you know, my father would never agree."

"And rightfully so." Mr. Barnes stuck his pen in the penholder. "Mr. Farrell put you and your family through a dreadful ordeal." The lawyer shook his head, the jowls beneath his beard wobbling like jelly. "Simply dreadful. It's only right that he make retribution."

"But even you must admit that ten grand is excessive." Not in good conscience could she accept such a large settlement.

"By Texas standards perhaps, but by eastern standards it's little more than average." He narrowed his eyes. "Surely you're not suggesting we settle for less?"

"There's more at stake here than money."

He blinked. "More, you say?"

"What are our chances of getting Mr. Farrell to drop this ridiculous feud with my father and accept Lockwood time?"

Mr. Barnes folded his hands across his stomach and gave a mirthless laugh. "Never going to happen, and you know it."

"Both men agreed to make Two-Time a one-time town as a wedding gift."

"Yes, but the agreement involved a formula based on East Coast time, not Lockwood or Farrell time. Now that the wedding has been called off, neither is willing to pursue that course of action."

Meg chewed on her lip. Now that marriage was out

of the question, Papa would never agree to anything other than Lockwood time. She'd hoped that Farrell would be more reasonable, if for no other reason than to keep his son from financial ruin.

The lawyer cocked his head. "If you're worried about the outcome of the trial, you needn't be. The cards are stacked in our favor." He lifted his eyebrows. "Surely your father isn't worried about losing the case?"

Such a thought would never cross Papa's mind. "He doesn't know I'm here, and I'd be most grateful if we keep it that way."

"Ah." Mr. Barnes stood and walked around the desk. Reaching out, he patted her on the arm in that condescending way that made her feel like she'd stepped into a gopher hole. "Don't you worry your pretty little head about a thing. Go on home and leave everything to me."

❧

Grant looked up from his desk just as Miss Lockwood passed his window for the second time that day. Earlier, he'd peered out the door after her and watched as she sailed into her lawyer's office. This time, she charged down the street like the cavalry, hips swinging side to side. She looked madder than a wet hen, and he couldn't help but laugh.

For such a small package, she sure could get riled up. He had to look twice to make sure steam wasn't coming out of her ears.

Whatever her lawyer had said to her sure wasn't sitting well. Grant tapped his fingers together. What was it that had her and Barnes at odds? Another one of her schemes? Like the one she'd pulled on the train? Even now, he could envision her as she'd looked that day. Her wide-eyed, rosy-cheeked innocence hadn't fooled him a bit. She'd known all too well what she was doing.

He hated feeling sorry for the man who was set to oppose him in court, but the lawyer Barnes had his hands full. No question about it.

Ten

Meg spent a busy morning helping customers pick out the perfect clock or just the right watch to give as Christmas gifts, and, of course, no watch was complete without a sturdy chain.

Owning a watch often caused more anxiety than it cured. Watches weren't cheap, and owners feared losing them or having them stolen by pickpockets. This fear had resulted in all manner of security devices. Men preferred the single or double Albert chains attached to a fob or medallion that made it easier to pull the watch from the pocket. Women wore watches either on brooches or around their necks on slide chains.

Poor Mrs. Cooper attached her watch to both a chain *and* a brooch. Even with that, she was so fearful of something happening to the watch that she'd ended up with a nervous disorder that caused her to lose her eyebrows.

After the morning rush, Meg replaced the watches and chains in the display cabinet beneath the counter, locking the sliding door.

"I'm just going to get some fresh air," she called to her father.

Papa looked up from his workbench but said nothing.

Outside, the sky was gray, and the cold air nipped at her cheeks like a playful puppy.

The sound of music drew her attention down the street. A parade was heading her way. It was one of many spontaneous parades that streamed down Main every few weeks or so. Most were political, but this one looked as though it was purely for fun.

A group of mariachi players, dressed like peasants in white cotton pants and shirts, led the way, followed by all manner of horses, buggies, and people on foot. Two violinists and a guitarist strolled alongside a painted wagon carrying a harpist.

Meg marched next to the street musicians, absorbing the sweet, salty sound of the music. She felt like a flower opening up beneath the warming rays of the sun. It wasn't her nature to be somber or morose, but since the disastrous wedding, she'd been both. She was ready to throw off the shroud of gloom and have some fun.

"*Ay-ya-yay-ya!*" she shouted in time to the music, and the wagon rolled to a stop.

A Mexican man wearing a large straw hat and a red sash around his waist stepped from the wagon and held out his hand. "Senorita?"

Meg drew in her breath. The senor—a stranger—was asking her to dance. In the middle of the street, no less.

Her first thought was to say no—a lady would never accept such an invitation! But before she could demur, she discovered her feet already moving to the music.

Taking this as consent, the man bowed from the waist. He then drew her into the street in front of the musicians. Facing her, he dropped his arms to his sides and, heart pounding, Meg followed suit. It had been so long since she'd kicked up her heels that she wasn't sure she remembered how.

A guitarist struck a chord and the horns blared. Soon she and her partner were moving their feet in time to the up-tempo music.

Aware that a crowd was gathering to watch, Meg felt self-conscious at first. *Oh, sweet heaven. What must they think of this jilted bride now?* Fortunately, the music soon took over, and her usual carefree self returned.

Keeping her upper body rigid as the dance required, she followed her partner's lead, pounding her heels into the ground with swift, precise movements.

Lacking the traditional wide skirt, Meg moved her arms to imitate the colorful swirl of fabric, twisting her body from left to right. The dirt road prevented the sound of stomping feet, but spectators made up for that lack with the clap of hands.

It felt good to let herself go and not think about her disastrous wedding and all that had happened since. Now she knew how a butterfly felt emerging from a dark cocoon. As her feet moved to the rhythm, her spirits soared. Laughing, she lifted her face to the gray, swollen sky and cried, "Olé!"

⁓

Music greeted Grant as he walked out of the barbershop, rubbing his clean-shaven chin. A crowd had gathered around a couple dancing in the middle of the street. He almost didn't recognize the carefree, light-hearted, and nimble-footed woman as Meg Lockwood.

But now that he did, he stepped off the boardwalk

for a closer look and couldn't take his eyes off her. Never had he seen her look so joyful.

She stomped her feet and twirled as effortlessly as a child's whirligig. Eyes sparkling, she tossed a coquettish smile at the spectators and beamed up at her partner, cheeks rosy red. She dipped right, left, and spun around, imitating the whirl of a colorful skirt with the graceful flow of her arms and hips.

The tempo of the music increased, and Miss Lockwood's feet became but a blur beneath her.

Her skirt flapped against her slim ankles, revealing glimpses of a lace petticoat beneath the hem. A disturbing but not unpleasant memory popped into his head—the memory of her hope chest and the intriguing underpinnings contained within.

Forcing the thought away, Grant sucked in his breath. His manly interest battled with professional integrity. The woman was intriguing—no question. Still, that was no excuse to forget, even for a second, that she was the plaintiff in a lawsuit filed against his client.

Because of that, he forced his thoughts back toward legal matters. So this was how the *heartbroken* lady spent her time, was it?

Miss Lockwood, if you are as dejected and inconsolable as your father claims, would you please tell the court why you were seen dancing in the street?

No sooner did the thought occur to him than another followed in its stead. How would it feel to be her dance partner? To hold her in his arms? To twirl her around and make her laugh and…

Startled by the wayward turn of his mind, Grant steered his thoughts back to the case, as hard as that was.

What else did the lady do to soothe her so-called dejected spirit? It was a question any lawyer worth his salt would ask. Nevertheless, that led to disturbing speculation involving the lady's sweet lips.

Grant shoved his hands in his coat pockets and blew out his breath. What was it about her that affected him on so many levels? Yes, she was a looker, but it had to go deeper than that. There had been no shortage of pretty women in Boston, yet none had turned his head as effectively as Miss Lockwood.

Perhaps it was the memory of her standing forlorn in the cemetery the day Farrell had left her at the altar. Maybe it was the recollection of her pushing her hope chest, along with her broken dreams.

Whatever it was, he'd better get over it, or he wouldn't be in any condition to handle his client's case in court.

Eleven

THE SKY WAS METAL GRAY, AND CLOUDS HUNG LOW with the threat of rain when Meg opened her father's shop that Saturday morning. Already a line of customers waited, anxious to take advantage of the ten percent discount advertised in the morning's newspaper.

During the next couple of hours, eight-day clocks, fine men's timepieces, and ladies' pendant watches inset with foreign gems flew out the door like bats from a cave.

It was midafternoon before the rush was over. The moment the last of the sale items left the shop, Meg leaned against the counter and ran the back of her hand over her heated brow.

"Whew!"

Papa rubbed his hands together. "It's going to be a fine Christmas." A broad smile crossed his face. "Yes, indeed." He plucked his hat and coat off a wall hook and reached for the bulging sack of money. "I'm off to the bank. I'll unpack the new shipment when I get back. Need anything?"

"No, Papa. I'm fine."

"Don't forget to ring the bell on the hour."

She glanced at the wall of clocks. It was quarter to three. "I won't, Papa."

Whistling to himself, her father left the shop amid a jingle of bells.

It was only then that Meg noticed the Malone boy on the other side of the counter, perusing the watches displayed in the glass case. How he was able to see anything through the thick curtain of straw hair in front of his eyes was a puzzle.

His name was Tucker, Tucker Malone. His pa owned a farm outside of town, and Tucker was one of twelve children. The family had gone through hard times in recent years. The railroad had caused local farms to fall out of favor, and fruits, vegetables, eggs, and even hog meat transported from out of town were considered more desirable than local fare.

At eleven years old, Tucker was small for his age. It pained Meg to see the boy running around barefooted even during the winter months. His clothes were at least two sizes too small. Buttons were missing from his shirt, and the holes in his ankle-high trousers were patched as close together as shingles on a roof.

"What can I do for you, Tucker?"

The boy stared at her though a slot of parted hair. For answer, he dug into his pocket and fished out a shiny quarter, which he slid across the counter with a grimy hand.

"I want to buy my pa a watch for Christmas."

Meg's gaze dropped to the quarter. About all it would buy was a watch stem, but Meg didn't have the heart to say as much. "Let's see what I have."

Stooping, she slid the door of the display cabinet open and reached for the cheapest watch in the store. The fat, open-face watch had a winding stem at twelve o'clock. The bulky timepiece was of the kind derisively known throughout the business as a turnip and had been traded in for a newer model.

Looking up, she noticed the boy staring at another watch—a fine watch in a hunter case that needed no key because it had a wind-up stem at the three o'clock position. She hesitated for a moment before selecting the higher-priced watch and drawing it out of the cabinet.

It was a sturdy silver watch made by the American Watch Company. The case was engraved with an eagle.

"What do you think of this one?" she asked, setting it on the counter between them. Normally she would go into her practiced sales pitch and mention the high-grade jewels, fine workmanship, and twenty-year guarantee, but she doubted the boy was interested in such details.

Shaking the hair away from his face, he gaped at the watch with rounded eyes.

"You can touch it," she said.

He glanced up as if to see if she really meant it before moving his hand across the counter. The moment his fingers made contact with the polished case, he jerked his hand back as if he'd been burned.

Meg picked up the watch and opened it to show him the white enamel face. "It keeps excellent time," she said. "And only has to be wound once a week. Here, you can hold it." She handed the watch across the counter. Taking it from her, he held it in both hands like an injured bird.

"Do I have enough money for this?" Tucker asked. The eyes meeting hers pleaded for a positive response.

She hesitated but a moment before relieving his worry with a smile. Her father would have a fit, but how could she say no?

"Absolutely. Do you think your pa would like it?"

"Yes, ma'am!" he shouted. As if remembering his manners, he lowered his voice but not his enthusiasm. "I think he would like it a lot!"

"Then it's a deal." Meg held out her hand, and he placed the watch in her palm. She then helped him pick out a sturdy silver chain. After placing both watch and chain in a small, square box, she slid it into a paper sack.

She handed the small parcel over the counter. "Merry Christmas."

The boy held on to his father's gift with both hands as if never intending to let it go. "Merry Christmas."

The sudden spring to his step as he left the shop brought a smile to her face—a smile that turned to alarm as soon as the door closed after him. Papa wouldn't necessarily mind her giving away a cheap watch, but he would take issue with an expensive one.

Reaching into the glass case, she quickly arranged the watches until the empty space looked less obvious. She stepped back. It would have to do. With a little luck, Papa wouldn't notice the watch missing until after she'd paid for it out of her salary.

❧

At precisely two minutes to three, Meg stepped outside the shop to ring the bell announcing the hour.

An argument raged a half block away, but she paid the angry voices no heed.

Instead, she turned her attention to the stagecoach parked directly in front of Papa's shop. The driver, known simply as Bullwhip, leaned next to the coach smoking a stogie as he did six days of every week, though never at the same time twice. No one could figure out his schedule, or if he even had one. As far as anyone knew, he left when he was good and ready and arrived whenever circumstances allowed. Anyone wishing to hitch a ride had better be ready to leave on a whim, or miss out.

Bullwhip wore a long linen duster, a low-crowned felt hat, and high leather boots—a uniform that never varied, no matter what the season. A burly man with a full red beard, he let nothing keep him from arriving at his destination. Not rain nor hail—or even concern for life or limb. Not even being robbed eleven and a half times at gunpoint.

Her father had little patience with the man, and not just because he refused to abide by Lockwood time. Papa considered the stories of death-defying escapes nothing but tall tales. "How can a person be robbed eleven and a *half* times?" he'd asked. "You're either robbed or you're not. There's no halfway."

Today, Bullwhip greeted Meg with a nod of his grizzly head. "Miz Lockwood."

"Bullwhip." She unwound the rope from a hook attached to the side of the building, careful not to let the clapper hit the bell mouth before it was time.

There was a trick to ringing a bell with clear, sharp rings and no stuttering. Other than Papa, Meg was the only one in the family who had mastered the technique. Holding a watch in one hand, she pulled the rope until the bell tilted forward. Not until the clapper hung straight down and the minute hand on her watch pointed straight up did she let the bell fall. The bell pealed in perfectly spaced dongs on precisely the hour.

Cigar held between his teeth, Bullwhip checked his watch, as did all passersby, though why he bothered was anyone's guess. Adjustments were made as needed before other watch owners continued on their way, but Bullwhip made no changes to his.

When all that remained of the last gong was a fading echo, Bullwhip put his watch to his ear, then shook it—a habit that drove her father crazy. Shaking a watch made as much sense to Papa as blowing on the muzzle of a gun after firing.

Meg turned to go inside, but the heated voices at the end of the street were now so loud that she could no longer ignore them. What had begun as a small knot of people gathered in front of the stables had become a good-sized crowd.

She hesitated, but curiosity got the better of her. Fishing the key out of her pocket, she locked the shop and headed toward the angry crowd.

Nearing the stables, she recognized one of the voices as belonging to Mr. Steele, the blacksmith. "I'm a-telling you, something's gotta be done about the crime 'round here. Why, just yesterday, someone walked off with one of my tools. And if local thieves ain't bad enough, the train brings in every scalawag 'twixt here and Missourah."

"The train ain't done much for my cattle either," yelled a local rancher. "All that shakin' ground has made them stop eatin'. They're so skinny, they're beginnin' to look like bed slats."

Meg walked around the circle of grumbling citizens, but she couldn't see much over the high-crowned hats favored by most of the men.

"Yeah, well, we can't do nothin' about the outsiders, but we can do plenty about the local thieves. What the boy needs is a good whuppin' and maybe some time in the hoosegow. That'll teach him."

Everyone started talking at once.

Meg stepped onto a crate in front of the hardware store and stretched as high as her short frame allowed. She blinked. Was that...?

Tucker!

The butcher—a large, beefy man with a pockmarked face and crooked nose—held Tucker by the ear with one hand and the boy's gift for his pa in the other. His name was Bruce Burrow, but everyone called him T-Bone.

The boy's eyes were as round as wagon wheels as he stared at T-Bone's bloodied apron.

Oh no. "Wait! Stop!" Meg shouted, but her cry could barely be heard over the loud voices of the others. She hopped off the crate and quickly cleared the steps leading off the boardwalk. Shouldering her way through the mob, she yelled, "Let me through."

After barreling her way to the front of the throng, she faced T-Bone, eyes blazing. "Take your hands off that boy at once!"

T-Bone furrowed his brow. "And who's gonna make me?"

Before she could respond, a male voice answered for her. "I am."

Meg recognized the cultured eastern accent even before Mr. Garrison emerged from the crowd and joined her in the small clearing. His long, lean form was attired in dark trousers and frock coat, and he stood out among the crowd of shopkeepers, farmers, and cowpunchers. All eyes turned to him in hostile silence.

T-Bone spit out a stream of tobacco; it fell to the ground with a *plop*. "Well, well, well. If it's not the fancy lawyer from the East." His eyebrows met and curtsied. "And what business is it of yours what I do?"

Garrison regarded the man with a look of disdain. "I happen to be this lad's lawyer."

"Is that so?" T-Bone looked skeptical, but he released the boy's ear.

Tucker rubbed the side of his head. "He's got my watch."

"I'll take it," Garrison said, holding out his hand.

The butcher gave him a quick visual check before handing over the timepiece. It didn't take a soothsayer to know that Mr. Garrison had the advantage in height, age, and probably even strength.

"Don't know how the boy affords a lawyer," T-Bone growled. "Cain't even afford one meself."

Mr. Garrison placed a hand on Tucker's shoulder. "In that case, I suggest you make it your business to avoid litigation."

T-Bone scratched his temple. "What's that supposed to mean?"

"It means to stop looking for trouble," Meg said.

Garrison met her gaze. For once, he'd dropped

his guarded look, and she saw approval in his eyes. Touching the brim of his hat with the tip of his finger, he led the boy away.

The butcher watched until the lawyer disappeared in the crowd. "The boy's a thief."

"He's not a thief," Meg said and told them how Tucker had picked the watch out for his pa. "He bought that watch with his own money."

T-Bone made a derogatory noise. "If that's true, I promise you that money didn't come from no legal means."

"Watch with the promises," someone yelled from the back of the crowd. "You don't want the jilted bride suing you."

This brought an outburst of laughter. Cheeks flaming, Meg bulldozed her way past the jeering men with as much dignity as she could muster.

❧

A moment later, Grant entered the Lockwood Watch and Clockworks shop to a riot of jingling bells. Hand on the boy's bony shoulder, he guided him inside.

The walls fairly vibrated with the sound of ticking clocks, some loud, some soft. Shiny brass pendulums swung back and forth. Minute hands moved a notch en masse like drilling soldiers. Never had Grant seen so many clocks in one place.

Yet he had the eerie feeling that even with all the improvements made to clocks and watches in recent years, no one really knew what time it was—or even how much time was left. His sister certainly hadn't.

Lockwood looked up from behind the counter,

eyes flat as wallpaper. He glanced at the boy before setting his tool down and closing the case of the mantel clock in front of him.

Grant led the boy up to the counter. Lockwood made no effort to temper his dislike. Even the wall of ticking clocks couldn't hide the tension that stretched as thick as pea soup between the two men.

"You better have a good reason for being here, Garrison," Lockwood said.

Grant nodded. "I'm here on behalf of this young man. He's been accused of stealing this watch." He set the paper bag on the counter and pulled out the square box. "He claims he purchased it from this shop fair and square." He opened the box and held it so Lockwood could see inside.

Lockwood gave the watch a cursory glance. "You'd have to be rich to afford a watch like that."

Grant raised an eyebrow. He didn't want to believe the boy was a liar, but it certainly appeared that way. He turned to Tucker. "What do you say to that?"

"I was rich till I bought the watch." The boy looked close to tears. "Cost me a whole twenty-five cents, it did."

Lockwood grunted. "Twenty—" He cleared his throat. "The boy's lying. No one but a fool would sell a watch like that for mere peanuts."

Jingling bells announced someone entering the shop, and all eyes turned to the front of the store. Miss Lockwood was framed in the doorway with the light at her back, and suddenly, Grant felt the need to catch his breath.

She wasn't dancing this time, nor was she standing

up for a boy too young to stand up for himself. Still, she sure did look pretty as a picture, her tiny waist and trim hips hugged in all the right places by a blue floral dress.

Tucker pointed his finger at her. "She sold it to me!"

Miss Lockwood turned her gaze to Tucker, and a shadow of a smile touched her lips.

Wishing the smile was for him, Grant doffed his hat, but all he got for his efforts was a wary glance.

She shut the door and joined them at the counter. "What seems to be the problem?" she asked, sounding oddly breathless, as if she'd been running. Two red spots stained her cheeks.

Her father grunted and tossed a nod at the watch on the counter. "This boy claims you sold him that there watch."

"His name is Tucker." Meg lifted her chin. "And what he said is true. I did sell him the watch."

Lockwood's glance sharpened. "For twenty-five cents?" he sputtered.

"He bought it for his pa for Christmas," she said, her voice thick with meaning. "I'm afraid it took *all* of his hard-earned money."

Father and daughter glared at each other, and neither looked about to back down.

"I guess that settles it then," Grant said, anxious to whisk the boy away before the real battle began.

"Nothing is settled." Lockwood slapped his hand palm down on the counter. "That's an expensive watch, and—"

"I'll cover it," Meg said beneath her breath.

Father and daughter continued to glower at each

other with the same stubborn look. Much to Grant's relief, Lockwood threw up his hands, spun around, and vanished into the back of the shop.

Miss Lockwood slipped the watch back into the box and handed it to Grant. Their fingers touched as he took the box from her. Quickly pulling her hand away, she moistened her lips and lifted her lashes.

"Sorry for the confusion," she said, "but the watch is his to keep."

"Glad to hear it," Grant said. "Much obliged."

She lowered her gaze to the boy, and her expression softened. "You go straight home now, you hear?" she said. "And wish your father a Merry Christmas for me…from the whole Lockwood family."

Tucker nodded. "Yes, ma'am."

"I'll see that he gets home," Grant said, reaching into his pocket for a golden eagle. Tucker shouldn't be roaming around with an expensive watch. Better to see him safely home, but first things first. The boy could definitely benefit from a decent meal and a new pair of trousers.

Grant slid the twenty-dollar coin onto the counter and steered Tucker toward the door.

He glanced back at Miss Lockwood as he left, and this time her pretty smile was most definitely for him.

Twelve

PAPA WAS UNUSUALLY QUIET THAT NIGHT AT SUPPER. Mama gave him a questioning look but said nothing. His silence made the ticking clocks sound like hail on a tin roof.

Meg exchanged a glance with her sister.

"Does Papa know?" Amanda mouthed.

At first Meg didn't know what Amanda meant, but then she remembered the suffrage school. She gave a silent shake of her head. No, Papa didn't know. At least she didn't think so.

A look of relief crossed Amanda's face, followed by a knitted frown that seemed to say, *Then what? What is on Papa's mind?*

Meg lifted her shoulders in a slight shrug. Surely he wasn't still upset about the watch. Not after Mr. Garrison had paid at least double what it was worth.

She looked down at her plate and was startled when the vision of a crooked smile and velvet-brown eyes came to mind.

"Is everything all right, Meg?"

Meg lifted her gaze. "What, Mama?"

"Is there something wrong with your meal?"

Meg shook her head. "No. Everything's fine."

Her mother studied her for a moment before glancing at the wall of clocks. In five minutes a cacophony of chimes would announce the hour.

"How long do you intend to keep us in suspense, Henry?"

Papa looked up from his plate. "What are you saying, my dear?"

Mama finished buttering her roll. "It's obvious that you have something on your mind."

Setting his fork down, Papa dabbed his mouth with his napkin and cleared this throat. "What I have to say can wait until after we have finished eating."

Mama set the buttered roll on her bread plate. "I'd rather you say it now."

"Very well, my dear, if you insist." Papa cleared his throat and glanced at the clocks. Reprieve was still four minutes away. "Barnes wants to meet with you in his office. Wants to go over your testimony."

Mama sat back in her chair. "*M-my* testimony?"

"Since neither the plaintiff nor defendant is allowed to testify in a breach-of-promise suit, it's up to the rest of the family to take the stand."

Meg's heart skipped a beat. "But why, Papa? You know how Mama hates talking in front of an audience."

"What are you talking about? Audience? A courtroom is not a theater. All she has to do is address her comments to the judge."

"But what on earth would I say?" Mama asked.

Papa laid his napkin by the side of his plate. "The truth. You just have to tell the court how devastated our daughter is. How it's affecting the entire family."

Her mother glanced at Meg as if to determine the truth of his statement.

Amanda crossed her eyes and mouthed, "*Devastated?*"

Meg pushed her plate away. "This is ridiculous. I won't have it, Papa. It's bad enough that you're putting me through this, but now Mama."

Her father dismissed her concern with a wave of his fork. "We're family. That means we're in this together."

Meg's temper flared. "If that's true, then why didn't you consult us before filing the lawsuit?"

"As head of this household, I'm required to make certain decisions I think are best for the family." He arched an eyebrow. "Surely, you're not questioning my judgment. Hmm?"

That was exactly what she was doing. She blew out her breath in an effort to calm herself. "I've always tried to be a good daughter and do what you've asked of me. But this time you ask too much."

The silence that followed was as brittle as broken glass. Even the ticking clocks couldn't fill the void.

"Would you please pass the salt," Amanda said at last.

Meg reached for the salt dish and handed it to her sister. Amanda met her gaze and tossed a slight nod at their father, calling attention to his bright-red face.

Alarmed, Meg softened her voice. "I'm sorry, Papa. I don't mean to question your judgment, but I'm very much against this lawsuit."

"I didn't think you'd fight me on this, Meg."

"And I didn't think you would go against my wishes."

She had already done battle with him twice today,

but it couldn't be helped. She felt like she was fighting for her life.

He struck the table with the palm of his hand, rattling the dishes and causing Mama to jump. "You'll do what I say, young lady, and—"

"Henry, please," Mama said gently.

"This is a matter of honor." Papa toned down his voice, but the stubbornness remained on his face. "Tommy Farrell caused great injury and embarrassment to my family."

Meg glared at him, and this time she made no effort to hide her anger. "This has nothing to do with me or even Tommy, and you know it. It's all about your ridiculous feud with Mr. Farrell."

"Meg…" Mama said. "You don't know what you're saying."

"It's true, Mama. You know it's true." Meg pushed her chair away from the table and jumped to her feet. "And I won't have Mama testifying! I want nothing to do with your blasted lawsuit!"

Her father rose so quickly that his chair fell back. He opened his mouth to speak but instead tugged on his tie, his neck thick with blue ropelike veins.

Meg slammed her chair against the table at the same time the minute hand of every clock struck the hour. The bells, cuckoos, and gongs sounded like a bunch of scolding jurors all mocking her. She clapped her hands over her ears.

"Meg, please," her mother pleaded, her voice barely heard above the chiming clocks. "Let's talk about it."

"There's nothing to talk about!"

Her father opened his mouth to say something, but

his voice faltered and he gasped for air. Before Meg's startled eyes, he folded like a rag doll and collapsed to the floor.

Horrified, she was the first to reach his side. "Papa!"

Thirteen

MEG WAITED IN THE HALL OUTSIDE THEIR PARENTS'
bedroom door with Josie and Amanda. It seemed as if
they'd been waiting for hours for either Mama or Dr.
Stybeck to exit.

Amanda had fetched Josie, and Meg was filling her
in on what little they knew about Papa's condition.
While the two stood whispering, Amanda paced the
narrow hall like a dog with a bone to bury.

"How's Mama?" Josie asked with a worried frown.

"You know Mama," Meg said, her voice wobbling.
"She's as calm as the moon."

Josie's forehead creased. "I don't understand.
Father's never had trouble with his heart before.
What would cause him to have trouble now?"

"It's all my fault." Meg dabbed at the corner of her
eyes with her handkerchief. "We had an argument."

"Over the lawsuit," Amanda added, though it was
unnecessary. Josie knew that Meg was against it and
had been from the start.

Meg tried to breathe, but it felt like a brick
had lodged in her chest. "If…if he dies, I'll never

forgive myself," she said and immediately burst into fresh tears.

Josie wrapped an arm around Meg's shoulder. "Papa's strong, Meg. You know that. That old ticker of his is never going to run down. He's like an old clock."

Comparing Papa to an old clock usually brought smiles if not laughter, but not today. Even the most expensive clocks ran down eventually.

The bedroom door opened, and all three women swung around to face it. Dr. Stybeck stepped into the hall, black case in hand. Round and compact as a ladies' watch, he had a full head of white hair and a goatee to match.

Meg waited for him to close the door. "How is he?"

"He's asleep right now. The mustard plaster helped, and his pulse is now normal. I left your mother something to relieve his pain and laudanum to relax him."

"What would cause a problem with his heart?" Josie asked.

"Mental strain and excitement are the chief causes of heart disease," the doctor said. "He'll be fine with some bed rest. Just keep him calm. If he gets upset, he could have another episode, and we might not be so lucky next time."

"Does that mean we have to do everything Papa says?" Amanda asked.

"Amanda!" Josie said, looking shocked.

Amanda's eyes glistened with tears she seemed determined not to shed. "Knowing Papa, he did this on purpose just so he can have his way!"

Meg put her arm around her sister's waist. "It'll be all right," she whispered. "Don't cry."

"I'm not crying," Amanda exclaimed, brushing away evidence to the contrary.

Josie turned to the doctor. "My sister is just upset. We all are."

"Your father has a strong constitution. With some rest and good care, he'll be up and about before you know it," Dr. Stybeck said. "Just keep him calm."

Meg nodded. "Thank you, Doctor."

He donned his derby. "I'll check back in the morning."

"I'll see you out." Josie followed the doctor to the stairs. She paused with her hand on the newel post and glanced at the closed bedroom door, her face etched with worry. "I'll stay the night."

Meg shook her head. "There's nothing you can do. Go home to Ralph." He had been laid up again with a lung infection, and nothing could erase the worry from Josie's face these days.

Josie hesitated before finally nodding. "You both better get some sleep. I'll be back first thing in the morning."

After Josie and the doctor left, Amanda said, "I'll sit with Papa so Mama can rest."

Meg nodded. "We'll take turns."

Amanda swiped at a tear. "How are we supposed to keep Papa calm? That's like trying to hold back the wind. If he finds out I've enrolled in that school—" She caught her breath. "I'll withdraw my application."

"Don't do that," Meg said, twisting her hand-kerchief into a ball. "It's only for five days, and it means a lot to you."

Amanda chewed on a fingernail. "I don't want to upset him."

"I'm afraid I'm the one most guilty of that, but I'll make it right. You'll see."

Amanda blinked away the last of her tears, but her eyes remained red. "Oh, Meg. I'm so sorry. I was thinking of myself, and here you—"

"I know." Meg pushed a strand of hair away from her sister's forehead and gave her a loving hug. Amanda could be distracted at times, maybe even self-centered, but when push came to shove, she always rose to the occasion.

Amanda searched her sister's face. "What are you going to do?"

"The only thing I can do." Meg's confident voice belied her true feelings. Her life was spinning out of control, and there didn't seem to be a blasted thing she could do about it. No matter how much she dreaded the trial, she couldn't take a chance on further upsetting her father or his heart. Not now.

"I'll go through with the lawsuit. Just like Papa wants."

❦

"Mama?"

Surprised to see her mother and not Amanda seated by Papa's side, Meg pushed the bedroom door open all the way. The first blush of dawn crept along the windowsill, but the shadows of night still clung to the corners of the room. A slight breeze from the open window tugged at the lace curtains, and the cool air felt refreshing.

"Come in, Meg."

Closing the door softly behind her, Meg moved to her mother's side and dropped to her knees. "Have you been here all night? I thought Amanda—"

"Shh." Her mother's gaze fell on Papa, who hadn't stirred. Even in the dim light, his face looked deathly pale. "Amanda sat with me for a while. Then I sent her to bed."

"Oh, Mama," Meg whispered. "You shouldn't have done that. You need sleep. Go to my room and rest. I'll stay here."

"Thank you, precious, but when your father awakens, he'll want me by his side."

Meg placed her folded hands on her mother's lap. "Forgive me, Mama. I never meant… If he doesn't recover"—she shuddered at the thought—"I'll never forgive myself."

Mama cupped Meg's hands in her own. "You mustn't blame yourself, child."

"But I'm the one who upset him."

Her mother's gentle sigh sounded like a summer breeze. "Your father feels things deeply, and that includes an obligation to protect his family. He's convinced that Tommy leaving you at the altar caused you great harm and distress."

"But that's not true, Mama. I mean…" Meg hesitated. She felt distressed all right, but only because of the pending lawsuit. Why wasn't she more upset with Tommy after what he had done? If anything, she felt… what? Numb? It was as if that awful scene at the church had happened to someone else.

Shocked by the realization, she was momentarily struck speechless. When she agreed to marry Tommy, she had honestly thought she loved him. But if that was true, shouldn't she feel utterly miserable? Heartbroken even—or something? Anything?

"What were you about to say, Meg?"

Meg studied her mother. *What would you think of me, Mama, if you knew what was in my heart? If you knew I wasn't as devastated as everyone thinks I am. Would you think me cold and unfeeling? Perhaps think less of me?*

"I—I'm so confused. I don't know how I feel or which way to turn. I keep waiting for something to happen, but I don't know what."

Her mother's expression softened. The gray morning light picked up the gold in her hair, the warm lights in her eyes. "It hasn't been that long. You'll sort it all out soon enough."

"But when, Mama? How long will it take?" She was at sixes and sevens, and she hated feeling that way.

A hint of a smile touched her mother's lips. "Patience, my dear. Some things can't be rushed. Each heart has its own clock. Grief has its own time, its own season."

Grief? It had never occurred to Meg that she was grieving. Now that she thought about it, it made perfect sense. Being left at the altar had been a loss on so many levels. Even her friends avoided her, as if they didn't know what to say. Or maybe they just didn't want her bad luck rubbing off on them.

Her mother's words gave Meg a measure of comfort—or at least an excuse for feeling so unlike herself. Still, it didn't feel like grief. Not like the horrible sadness that had fallen over her like a shroud when Grandmama Lockwood passed away. Or even when her beloved pony died the winter she turned twelve. But maybe grief came in different shapes and sizes.

Like love.

Fourteen

THREE DAYS LATER, MEG STOPPED TO READ THE SMALL, understated sign on the door of Grant Garrison's office.

His name was printed in tasteful gold letters followed by the words *Attorney-at-Law*. It was a far cry from the blatant signs favored by the other lawyers in town. It hardly seemed to belong to a man whose larger-than-life presence seemed to suck the air out of every room he entered.

She braced herself with a deep breath before reaching for the handle. The door flew open at her touch, and she jumped back.

"Oh!"

Mr. Garrison looked surprised to see her standing there. "I apologize. I didn't mean to startle you." He was wearing his hat and held a brown portfolio at his side.

"It's fine. I"—she glanced at the leather case in his hand—"caught you at a bad time."

"Not at all. I just have an errand to run, but it can wait." His brow creased. "Does Barnes know you're here?"

"No. Nobody does."

He hesitated. "If you have a question about the case, you should talk to your lawyer."

She moistened her lips. "I'm not here about the case." At least not exactly.

He studied her a moment before glancing up and down the street. "Come in."

"Are you sure?" Just being around him made her pulse throb, and she suddenly felt like a stammering schoolgirl. "I-I don't want to keep you."

"You're not."

She stepped across the threshold, her gaze traveling from wall to wall. Unlike Barnes's office, this one was sparsely furnished. Only a blotter, inkstand, and oil lamp broke the wide expanse of the polished oak desk. A tall, well-stocked bookshelf stood like a sentinel on guard duty, with rows and rows of law books arranged in precise military order. Only the town's lending library had more volumes.

The other walls were bare except for a framed diploma from Harvard Law School. The office said much about the lawyer but little about the man.

"Have a seat." He motioned to a brown leather chair that looked as if it had never been occupied. He pulled off his hat and set it on the desk next to his portfolio, his movements unhurried and precise.

Meg sat and folded her gloved hands in her lap. Her mouth dry, she lifted her chin and tried to ignore the butterflies in her stomach.

What hold did he have over her? Why did he affect her so? He was so unlike the local cattlemen and farmers. He didn't talk like them, and he sure

didn't walk like them, his long strides more purpose-
ful and precise. But neither was he like the big-city
dandies who drifted through town on occasion.
It didn't seem possible, but even with his immaculate
dress and cultured voice, he was the most masculine
man she'd ever encountered.

Instead of taking his own chair, he slid a hip on
the corner of his desk and folded his arms across
his chest—a simple movement that emphasized his
virile appeal.

"You said you weren't here about the case. So
why *are* you here, Miss Lockwood?"

"I came to return your money." Relieved at
having something to do, she pulled off a glove.
Fishing the twenty-dollar gold piece from her drawstring purse, she placed it on his polished desk. The
money provided an excuse for coming today, but it
wasn't the only reason.

He glanced at the Liberty coin before turning his
gaze back to her. He really did have nice eyes, though
today they were more gold than brown. His slightly
mussed hair gave him a boyish look that hardly
seemed to go with his broad chest and wide shoulders.

"Your father agrees to this?"

She debated how to answer him without making
her father look bad. "Let's just say he's not in a position to agree or disagree."

Garrison angled his head, brow furrowed. "In other
words, he doesn't know."

A surge of guilt rushed through her. She hated
going behind her father's back, even when she knew
it was the right thing to do.

"Papa has a…health problem. He had an episode. His heart—"

A shadow of concern fleeted across Garrison's face. "I'm sorry to hear that. Is he all right?"

"Right now he is, but the doctor said we have to keep him calm." She chose her next words with care. "As you might imagine, that won't be an easy task."

He commiserated with a nod of his head. "You could ask your lawyer to petition the judge for a postponement. To give your father time to recuperate…"

She'd suggested that to her father, but he'd absolutely insisted on the trial proceeding on schedule. Truth be told, she was as anxious as Papa to have it all over and done with. The last thing she wanted was to face the new year with a trial hanging over her head.

"That won't be necessary. My father is recovering nicely and expects to return to the shop next week."

"Glad to hear that."

He sounded sincere, and her opinion of him went up another notch, which worried her. She was having a hard enough time trying not to *like* the man.

"I'm afraid he won't be completely out of the woods." She gazed at Mr. Garrison through a thick fringe of eyelashes. Time to get down to business. "If you could perhaps…be gentle with him, I would be ever so grateful."

He tilted his head, eyebrows arched. "By gentle, do you mean on the witness stand?"

She lifted her gaze and looked him square in the face. "Yes, that's exactly what I mean."

He rubbed his chin. "Under the circumstances, I'm afraid what you're asking might not be possible." His gaze locked with hers. "My duty is to provide my client with diligent representation. I've never found a *gentle* approach to be that effective."

Recalling how gentle he had been with Tucker, she asked, "Never, Mr. Garrison?"

"Perhaps when dealing with children and horses. But not in a court of law."

She noticed he left women off his list. "I know the plaintiff and defense are not allowed to testify in such cases, but I wonder if the judge would be willing to make an exception in my case."

"Are you saying you wish to take the stand?"

"It could be bad for Papa's heart to testify, and Mama…has a hard time speaking in public."

"Putting you on the stand in a case such as this would be highly unusual."

"But not impossible?" she asked hopefully. When he didn't correct her, she added, "You can be as rough as you wish with me."

He smiled, and it was as if the room suddenly filled with sunshine. "Now there's an intriguing thought."

She blushed and her pulse quickened. "What I meant is—"

"I know what you meant, Miss Lockwood." His smile had died but not the memory. That remained firmly engraved in her mind. "It's been my experience that judges seldom make exceptions. Especially in breach-of-promise suits."

"That makes no sense." Who knew the facts better than the parties involved? "A marriage proposal involves only two people and is generally not made public."

"Agreed," he said. "But the courts consider such testimony prejudicial."

"Perhaps in light of my father's recent health problems, the judge would reconsider."

"To be fair, that would mean that my client would also have to testify. Is that what you want?"

Tommy's testimony was the least of her concerns. "What I want is to protect my father's health."

He studied her. "If you're worried about your father's condition, perhaps you should reconsider. About dropping the suit, I mean."

"I'm afraid that might place an even bigger burden on my father's health," Meg said.

"I wouldn't know. I'm better at law than matters of the heart."

She regarded him, curiosity whetted. Did his statement have a deeper significance, or had she only imagined it? "And yet you take on a heart-balm lawsuit."

A muscle tightened at his jaw. "I hope to see the day such legalized extortions are outlawed. They're nothing but a racket devised to bring men to financial ruin and disparage women."

Disconcerted by his sudden cold contempt, Meg met his icy stare straight on. "Disparage women, Mr. Garrison? How so?"

"By assuming that women are weak and defenseless and unable to support themselves."

She folded her hands together in her lap. She couldn't argue with anything he said, but neither could she verbally agree without sounding critical or disloyal to her father.

Still, it was a statement she couldn't altogether ignore.

"I'm afraid you'll have to change the way society thinks and who employers choose to hire before you get your wish," she said.

Just getting her father to let her work in his shop had been a battle. He was convinced that allowing his daughters to hold down jobs reflected poorly on him and his ability to care for and support his family.

"Perhaps," Garrison said wryly. "Right now, I just wish to change the mind of the court."

"I would say that your work is cut out for you then. The court tends to favor us weak and *defenseless* women."

"Of course"—his expression lightened, as did his tone of voice—"that's only if you can convince the judge that you are indeed...defenseless." There was that smile again. It was just a quick flash, but it made her heart flutter. "And that's a mighty big if."

"If the judge is like most men, he won't need much convincing," Meg said.

A faint twinkle appeared in the depth of his eyes. "In that case, it seems that you have me at an unfair advantage."

"I certainly hope so," she said, as if such a thing were possible. "Just so you know, I intend to ask my lawyer to speak to the judge about letting me testify in place of my parents. I trust you won't object."

"About questioning you on the stand?" A look of anticipation crossed his face. "He'll hear no objection from me. In fact, I'll be happy to tell the judge that myself, if it would help."

Why, the sneaky dog! He *wanted* her to take the stand. "I'd be much obliged," she said with a sense of unease.

He looked a tad too arrogant for her peace of mind, like a man who not only enjoyed a good fight but welcomed it.

"I won't keep you." She stood. Better leave before he guessed how close she was to losing her composure.

Standing, he picked up the gold coin and held it out to her. She glanced at his hand but made no move to accept the money.

"Take it," he said. "You owe me nothing."

"I'd prefer to keep it that way." It was bad enough having to ask him to go easy on her father. She walked to the door but, before leaving, glanced over her shoulder. "Thank you for your time."

"The defense should be thanking *you*, Miss Lockwood," he said.

Fifteen

PAPA SHOWED UP AT THE SHOP THAT MONDAY MORNING, anxious to get to work.

Meg had promised her mother that she would keep an eye on him, but there was no slowing him down. He even insisted he felt well enough to perform the hourly bell ringing.

Still, she couldn't help but fuss.

Finally, he threw up his hands. "You're treating me like an invalid."

"The doctor said you have to take it easy and—"

"Bull!" He thumped on his chest. "You know what will stop this old ticker? Boredom, that's what. Now go. I need you to drop this ad off at the *Gazette*." He handed her a hand-drawn sketch. "Have Buttocks run it in Friday's paper."

"Buckham, Papa. Buckham," Meg said with a sigh.

Trying to get her father to stop calling the man names was a waste of effort. The editor steadfastly refused to abide by Lockwood time. Unfortunately, the town had only one newspaper, so her father's threats to boycott fell on deaf ears.

Meg tucked the advertisement into her drawstring purse. "All right, you win. No more fussing."

A cold wind greeted her outside, cutting through her woolen skirt like icy knives. Half a block away, she spotted the swaybacked horse and rickety old wagon belonging to Mr. Mutton, the dogcatcher. Stray dogs had become a problem in recent months, and things had come to a head when the mayor's two-year-old grandson was bitten. Fortunately, the dog showed no sign of the dreaded rabies, but the town went up in arms and a dogcatcher was hired.

The town council voted to pay him by the dog rather than a flat salary. A big mistake, because it left no canine safe from the man's greedy clutches.

Now armed with a snare pole, he crept along the side of a building like a thief in the night.

A glimpse of the man's furry target made Meg stop in her tracks. "Hey!"

Lifting her skirt above her ankles, she ran across the street with such haste that the driver of the hotel's horse-drawn omnibus was forced to jerk on his reins and come to a quick stop.

"Watch it!"

Paying no heed to the driver, Meg frantically waved her arms and called, "Mr. Mutton! Wait."

By the time she'd reached the alley, Mutton had already snared the dog. The poor thing trembled and whined, tail between its legs and its neck caught by a loop of horsehair.

"That's Blackie," Meg said upon reaching the dogcatcher. "He belongs to Mr. Steele. Can't you see the tag?" Mutton would have to be blind not to see it.

"Git outta the way, miz. I got work to do."

"Yes, but this isn't it."

He pulled on his pole. Blackie reared back on his hind legs, but this only made Mutton pull harder.

Meg grabbed the pole and glared at him. "That dog is licensed."

"That dog is a nuisance!" Mutton snarled back.

"Then complain to the owner."

"I ain't complainin' to no one." His nose was mere inches from Meg's. "Now git outta my way."

He yanked on the pole, but Meg held on with both hands. They were fairly evenly matched in height, but Mutton didn't have to battle with a wind-blown skirt.

A tug of war ensued, with Meg yanking the snare pole one way and the dogcatcher another.

"Let go!" he barked.

"You let go," she yipped.

Meg didn't realize that Deputy Sheriff Jeff Boulder had arrived until he spoke. "I suggest you both let go."

Instantly obeying Boulder's command, she released the pole. Mutton flew backward, hitting his head against the wall with a sickening thud.

Hand on her mouth, Meg stared in horror as the man slithered to the ground.

❧

Sheriff Clayton greeted Grant with a nod of his head and feet firmly planted on his desk. His light, sandy hair brushed against skin as leathery and worn as the soles of his boots.

"What can I do fer you, Garrison?"

"Got a message that your prisoner wants to see me."

The sheriff leveled a thumb toward the open door leading to the jail cells in back.

"Much obliged."

There were three cells in all, but only one was occupied. That was a surprise. Considering the noisy street brawls that kept him awake half the night, Grant had expected the jail to be packed.

The prisoner sat on a cot rubbing his foot. A fat, hairy toe poked through a hole in his gray woolen sock.

Grant introduced himself. "You said you wanted to see me."

The prisoner dropped his foot and stood. "Kinda young, ain't you?"

At nearly thirty, Grant didn't feel all that young. "Old enough to know the law."

The prisoner frowned. "'Round here that could be a hindrance. Case you're wonderin', name's Kidd. Jacob Kidd."

"I know who you are." Kidd was a notorious stage robber who had managed to avoid the law for a good many years. For a man with such a bad reputation, he sure was small in stature. If he stretched, he might reach all of five feet tall. He had a drooping mustache and wore his shoulder-length hair pulled back like a donkey's tail and tied with a piece of rawhide.

"You asked to see me."

"Shore enough did." Kidd looked him up and down, and Grant felt like a horse on the auction block. "Heard that you were handlin' the jilted bride case."

The image of a pretty, round face flashed through Grant's mind, and he was momentarily jolted by the clear vision.

"Well, is you or ain't you?"

"I'm sorry. Yes, I am. But I prefer to call it the Farrell versus Lockwood case."

Business had indeed picked up since his name had appeared in the newspaper, mostly from people unable to get any other representation. Like the two Chinese men who had smelled a need and decided to start a laundry in town. Victims of the anti-Chinese movement, they faced community objection to their plan, which is why they hired Grant.

"The judge found me guilty." Kidd made a face. "Dadgummit. If my blasted horse hadn't thrown a shoe, I would never have been caught."

Grant shrugged. "So what can I do for you?"

"Well, here's the thing. I've been sentenced to hang next Friday at noon, Lockwood time." He paused.

"Go on."

"I wanna be hung on Farrell time."

Grant frowned. He'd heard a lot of requests from condemned men, but this was the first he'd heard of one wanting to change the time of execution.

"May I ask why?"

"Farrell time lets me live a whole forty minutes longer. A man can accomplish a lot in forty minutes. In my younger days, I coulda robbed both a bank and a stage in that amount of time—and don't forget it took only an eighteen-minute battle with Mexico for a third of what is now the good ole USA to change ownership." Kidd fell silent for a moment. "Heck, forty minutes is even enough time to fall in love."

Grant glanced around the dismal area with its empty cells and rough adobe walls. Didn't seem like the place offered much chance for falling in love—or anything else for that matter.

"Have you talked to your lawyer about this?"

Kidd made a face. "Why would I do that? The fool man couldn't even keep me from bein' sentenced to hang."

Grant hesitated. His top priority was the Lockwood trial, but requesting a time change shouldn't take too long. Less than an hour was in question, after all. "I'll talk to the judge, but I can't promise anything."

Kidd nodded. "You get me more time, and I'll tell you where I stashed the loot from the last holdup."

"I'm sure that would make the sheriff very happy."

"The sheriff?" Kidd chuckled. "Well, what do you know? My last week on earth, and I finally find me an honest man."

"Maybe you were just running with the wrong crowd."

Kidd shrugged. "Maybe so."

A sudden commotion rose from the adjacent office, followed by loud voices, but it was the high-pitched one that caught Grant's attention. The woman's voice sounded vaguely familiar.

"Looks like I'm about to git me some company," Kidd said.

"Sounds like it."

"A petticoat by the sounds of it. I might have more need for that extra forty minutes than I thought. I'm in love already."

"Sounds like you're asking for more trouble than you already have."

Kidd shrugged. "Get me those forty minutes, and I'll take my chances."

❧

Grant stepped into the open doorway separating the cells from the sheriff's office and tried to make sense of the scream-fest in front of him.

A man and woman were going at it tooth and nail, but Grant couldn't make hide nor hair of what they were carrying on about. The citizens of Two-Time were a passionate lot, that's for sure. He'd witnessed more verbal disputes, fistfights, and shoot-outs during his short time in town than a dog had fleas.

Looking more befuddled by the moment, the sheriff was trying to calm the fighting couple, but his efforts went unnoticed. Clayton seemed more suited to restoring order at a church meeting than in a town as wild as Two-Time.

The undersheriff finally had enough. "Quiet!" he snapped, leaving no room for argument.

Taking advantage of the blessed silence that followed, Grant stepped through the doorway. Though her back was turned, he recognized the woman at once as Miss Lockwood. No wonder her voice had sounded familiar. Holding herself ramrod straight, hands planted firmly on her hips, she looked and sounded fit to be tied.

"May I be of service?" Grant asked.

He addressed the sheriff, but Miss Lockwood replied. "Not unless you're offering to conduct a funeral service."

"I'm afraid that's outside my job description."

She spun around, and her eyes widened. "Mr. Garrison."

Grant doffed his hat. "Miss Lockwood. Didn't expect

to see you here." The target of her fury was a thin man holding a handkerchief to the back of his head.

She lifted her chin in an act of self-righteousness, a far cry from the cool, reasonable woman who had graced his office on her father's behalf a couple of days earlier.

The sheriff lifted a key ring off a hook on the wall. "Suppose you tell me what this is all about."

"She—"

"He—"

"One at a time!" the undersheriff snarled. He pointed at the skinny man. "Since you're the injured party, I'll let you go first, Mutton."

The man named Mutton drew himself to his full height. "I was mindin' me own business and this…this pit bull of a woman attacked me."

Pit bull? Grant kept his gaze firmly on Miss Lockwood's indignant face but remained silent.

The sheriff's head swiveled toward her. "Is that true?"

Miss Lockwood glared at the man. "I did not attack him."

Her denial bought an immediate response from Mutton, and the argument escalated again from there. Try as he might, Grant couldn't understand the crux of the problem. The number of references to donkey's anatomy flying back and forth did nothing to unravel the mystery.

It wasn't until after the sheriff locked both parties in jail for disturbing the peace that he filled Grant in on the details. It seemed that Miss Lockwood was protecting the blacksmith's dog.

"Are you representing Miss Lockwood or Mr. Mutton?" the sheriff asked.

"Neither," Grant said. Representing Miss Lockwood would be a conflict of interest. Even paying her bail might be considered suspect, and he couldn't take the chance. As for the dogcatcher, if indeed he was snaring tagged dogs as the lady proclaimed, jail was too good for him.

Clayton tossed the keys to the cells on his desk. "I was a-hopin' you'd handle Lockwood. He don't take kindly to me lockin' up his daughters."

Grant wasn't sure he'd heard right. "You mean this isn't the first time?"

The sheriff's eyebrows lifted like a hot-air balloon. "Heck no. Though usually it's her sister Amanda that I have to jail. Just last month, I had to lock her up for causin' a riot at the Golden Spur Saloon. And then there was the time…"

Listening with growing disbelief, Grant rubbed the back of his neck. He'd met the sister only once, and that day on the train she had acted perfectly sensible and sane. Looks could sure be deceiving. Was there no one in this town who knew how to behave in a civilized manner?

"The only one of the three sisters who hasn't given me trouble is the oldest one, Josie."

Grant had yet to meet her. "Barnes represents the family. I'll let him know that Miss Lockwood requires his assistance."

The sheriff nodded. "Much obliged."

Grant glanced through the open door separating the office from the cells in back. He couldn't see the lady, but it sure did look like Kidd was counting on those extra forty minutes.

Sixteen

GRANT READ THE SIGN ON MISS LOCKWOOD'S LAWYER'S door. Barnes had gone to San Antone, and the note gave no indication of when he would return.

That left Grant with only one option, and not a pleasant one at that. He hated having to break the news to Lockwood himself, but he didn't want to leave the man's daughter in jail. It was no place for a lady, not even one as unconventional as her.

Grant swung back into the saddle with a grimace and moments later reached the Lockwood Watch and Clockworks shop. He dismounted and wrapped the reins around the hitching post.

"If I don't come back in ten minutes, Chester, you better fetch the sheriff," he said half-jokingly.

The wind was cold and the sky thick with dark clouds. The locals claimed Texas had no climate, but it did have weather—though supposedly it seldom snowed in Two-Time. The most Grant had been told to expect was an ice storm or two before winter's end, but it sure did smell like snow now.

He blew on his cupped hands and rubbed them

together before reaching for the brass doorknob. A clamor of bells announced his arrival.

Lockwood was adjusting one of the tall clocks. At the sound of the bells, he turned toward the door with screwdriver in hand. "Mr. Garrison." His voice as cold as the expression on his face, Lockwood closed the clock's glass door and walked behind the counter. "If you're here about the trial, you'd best speak to my lawyer."

Grant pulled off his hat. "That's not why I'm here," he said. "I came to tell you that your daughter has been arrested."

Had Grant expected Lockwood to show surprise or even dismay, he would have been sorely disappointed.

Instead, Lockwood only shrugged. "What has Amanda done this time?"

"Nothing that I know of. She's not the one in jail."

This time Lockwood did look surprised. "You're not saying that Meg…"

"I'm afraid so."

Lockwood rubbed his chin. "Hmm. What do you know? What's *she* doing there?"

"I believe she assaulted someone."

"Really?" Lockwood's eyebrows practically disappeared into his hairline. "Who'd she assault? Tommy Farrell, I hope."

"Sorry to disappoint you, but I believe it was the dogcatcher."

Lockwood pondered this for a moment. "Wonder what beef she has with him. Far as I know, he's on Lockwood time."

Grant ran a finger along his upper lip. Did everything in this town have to be about time? "Not anymore," he said wryly. "He's now on *jail* time."

Lockwood blew out his breath. "How much is that mercenary sheriff gonna charge me this time?"

"I believe the customary bail is five dollars."

"Harrumph." Lockwood pulled five singles out of the cashbox and locked it. He reached for his hat, plucked his keys off a hook, and stormed around the counter, stopping only to turn the sign in the window to *Closed*.

Recalling that Lockwood had had a recent health scare, Grant followed him outside and waited for him to lock the door. The man certainly looked robust enough. Was it possible that Miss Lockwood had exaggerated her father's condition?

"Do you have daughters, Mr. Garrison?" Lockwood asked.

"No, sir. I'm not married."

Lockwood pocketed his keys. "Well, if you're smart you'll keep it that way and raise chickens instead." With that, he turned and headed for the jailhouse.

❧

Meg hurried to keep up with her father's long strides. For a man who had recently suffered a health scare, he was in rare form. "Papa, do slow down. Your heart…"

"There's nothing wrong with my heart," he insisted, but he slowed his pace. "It's bad enough that Amanda gets herself arrested with clocklike precision, but I thought you had more sense."

"I'm sorry, Papa, but—"

"But, but." He threw up his hands. "There's always a *but*." He stopped abruptly in the middle of the boardwalk and faced her. "In my day and time, a woman knew her place, and it certainly wasn't jail!"

"It wasn't my fault—"

"Then whose fault was it? You girls carry on like you've been raised by wolves."

"That's not true, Papa—"

"Isn't it? If Amanda spent half as much time learning domestic skills as she does chasing trouble, she might get somewhere. As for you, young lady…"

Her father was so busy ranting that he failed to notice the group of protestors marching down the middle of the street. There were close to twenty in all, each carrying a sign urging people to join the American Woman Suffrage Association. Leading the parade was a hefty woman dressed in black. The only bits of color on her person were a white band on her ample chest that read *Votes for Women* and a large, red plume on a hat that stood three stories and an attic tall—Amanda's work, no doubt.

Amanda followed at the rear of the small procession, waving an American flag and holding up traffic. Meg groaned. No doubt the group was purposely trying to get arrested to earn sympathy for their cause.

Papa had handled bailing one daughter out of jail with no apparent injury to his health, but Meg doubted his heart could handle two on the same day.

"And furthermore," Papa was saying, oblivious to his youngest daughter's latest endeavor, "your misconduct could be used against you in court and—"

"Oh, look, Papa." Meg grabbed him by the arm and all but hauled him into the nearest shop.

Her father pulled away from her clutches and glanced around like a man who had suddenly found himself on the moon. "What are we doing here? I have work to do, and so do you."

"Don't be so serious, Papa," she said, giving his arm a playful tug. "I wish to pick out a Christmas present for you."

"For me?" His lip curled. "Here?"

Meg looked around and her heart sank. Oh no! Of all possible places, she had inadvertently dragged her father into Walker's Gun Shop.

Rifles and shotguns hung from the walls between shelves of ammunition, and handguns were displayed in a glass case. Walking into Madam Bubbles's parlor couldn't have been more ill advised. Having served in that terrible war, Meg's father had sworn off guns forever. No wonder he looked so utterly affronted.

"What can I do for you, Lockwood?" the gunsmith, Mr. Walker, called from behind the counter. A blunt-jawed man with a thick nose and receding gray hair, he smelled of linseed oil and stale tobacco.

Her father waved his watch and tossed a nod at the clock on the wall behind the shop's owner. "You can set your clock to the right time. It's four minutes slow." He pocketed his watch and turned to Meg. "Come along. We've got work to do." He turned to leave just as the marchers began to pass by the front of the store.

"For me," Meg cried out. "I want a gun for me."

Her father stiffened momentarily before whirling

about, a look of astonishment on his face. "You want a gun? What in the name of Sam Hill for?"

She tried to think of an answer and then remembered the fear that had run through her when she'd been accosted by that awful man. Who knew what might have happened if she hadn't been able to bash him over the head with her parasol!

"To protect myself."

Her father's eyebrows arched. "Protect yourself? From what?"

"From…from…" She cleared her voice. "Men who think I'm damaged goods and that they can have their way with me."

"Oh, for the love of Pete." Her father threw up his hands and called over to Walker, who was listening to their conversation with wide-eyed interest. "Help my daughter select a gun. And make it quick. I haven't got all day."

"Will do." Walker scurried over to a corner cabinet where an array of small pistols was displayed. He pulled out a single-barrel derringer and held it up for her to examine.

"This here's a fine gun for your purposes," he said.

"Are you sure it will work?" she asked. "It seems awfully small."

He drew back, waving his hands like a man trying to hold back a stampede. "I'm not making any promises here, mind you."

"Oh dear goodness." She sighed. "I'm not going to sue you."

Every man in town walked on eggshells around her now, even Reverend Wellmaker. During a recent sermon, he'd looked directly at her and, after promising life everlasting, qualified his statement. "Of course, there are no guarantees…"

Walker explained the merits of the weapon and how to carry it safely. He then showed her how to load it.

By the time Meg and her father left the shop fifteen minutes later, the marchers were nowhere in sight. Either they had returned to the hotel or were now in jail, heaven help them.

Her sister owed her big time. In her purse was a derringer she was now obliged to carry.

❧

The following morning, Meg finished dressing and reached for her purse, the heavy weight an unpleasant reminder that she now owned a gun.

Grimacing, she pulled out the weapon and glanced around the room for a place to hide it. Did Walker accept returns? Not all shop owners did.

Without warning, her bedroom door flew open and Amanda burst inside waving a newspaper.

Upon seeing the gun in Meg's hand, she froze, a look of horror on her face. "Oh!" She closed the door behind her. "Where did you get that?" she asked, her voice hushed. "You know how Papa feels about guns."

Meg stuffed the gun in her purse and struggled to close the clasp. "He knows I have it."

"What?"

"And it's all your fault." Meg explained about dragging Papa into the gun shop. "I saved your hide. Again."

Instead of thanking her, Amanda grimaced. "You better have another trick up your sleeve. I'm gonna need all the help I can get."

Meg rolled her eyes. "Now what have you done?"

For answer Amanda held up the *Two-Time Gazette*. The bold headline read JILTED BRIDE'S SISTER MARCHES DOWN MAIN.

Meg's jaw dropped. "Oh no!"

"Meg, I'm sorry. I never dreamed they would use *your* name. Not with a real celebrity in town. They didn't even mention Lucy Stone." Amanda looked as indignant as a newly shorn sheep. "Imagine ignoring a fine woman like that!"

Meg stared at her sister in disbelief. She was the one who needed pity, not Lucy Stone. "That *fine* woman could have gotten you arrested." What a field day the editor would have had with that!

"It would have been for a good cause," Amanda said and frowned. "What am I going to do? If Papa sees the paper..." She shuddered.

Meg sighed. She could never stay irritated or angry at her sister for long. "We'll hide it from him."

"Do you think that will work?"

"No, but we can try." No sooner were the words out of her mouth than the sound of a slamming door shook the very walls, followed by Papa's booming voice.

"Amanda! Come here. Now!"

❧

Two bodies came shooting through the batwing doors of the Last Chance Saloon and onto the boardwalk, missing Grant by mere inches. Grunting like bears, the two men rolled off the wooden sidewalk with pummeling fists and landed next to a brown horse tied to the hitching post in front.

"Hey!" Grant yelled. "Quit it. Both of you."

The two men raised their heads from the ground to stare at him, fists pulled back ready to do bodily harm to each other.

Grant regarded them with disgust. "That's no way to settle your differences." He pulled two white cards printed with his name from his coat pocket. Leaning over, he handed one to each man. "We can settle this dispute in my office."

"Well now…" one man said, pocketing the card. "That's mighty nice of you to offer your services."

"Glad to help," Grant said. "That's what I'm here for."

Lip curling, the second man wiped the blood from his jaw with his shirtsleeve. "Don't know where you hail from, mister, but out here the quickest way to settle differences is this." With that, he let his fist fly, the knuckles making contact with his foe's face with a sickening crunch.

"Take that, you son of a…"

"Why, you—"

Shaking his head, Grant shoved his hands in his pockets and continued on his way to the Silver Spur Saloon and Dance Hall. He pushed his way through the swinging doors, pausing for a moment to let his eyes adjust to the dim light.

As far as the town's saloons went, the Silver Spur was the most respectable. That was partly because of the posted sign forbidding floozies, suffragettes, Methodists, and other troublemakers from entering its hallowed doors. Someone, probably the proprietor, had written Amanda Lockwood's name at the bottom of the sign.

The bartender was a giant of a man standing well over six foot six. His friends called him Stretch. His enemies called him Stretch too, preceded by an expletive.

Grant's gaze zeroed in on a corner table where the newly arrived circuit judge currently sat. Rumor had it that this was the judge's favorite watering hole, and that had proven to be true. His name was Judge Thomas Lynch. He was known for being firm but fair. Today he sat alone and looked like he wanted to keep it that way.

Grant walked over to the table. "Your Honor." He introduced himself and pulled out a chair. "Do you mind?"

"What? What did you say?"

Grant had been warned that the judge was hard of hearing. He repeated his request, this time a little louder.

The judge lifted his glass to his lips and tossed back the contents in a single gulp. He set it down and wiped his mouth with the back of his hand. "Does it matter to you whether I mind or don't mind?"

Accepting that as an invitation to join him, Grant sat.

"If this is about the jilted bride case…"

"Not entirely."

"Ay? What did you say?"

"I said not entirely," Grant said loud enough to draw the bartender's attention to their table.

"Well, get on with it then," the judge said with an impatient wave of his hand. "What's on your mind?"

"A last wish from a condemned man." Grant emphasized each word. If he spoke any louder, everyone in the saloon would be privy to the conversation.

Judge Lynch made a face. "What does Kidd want now?"

"To change the time of his sentence."

The judge signaled to the bartender for a refill. "So the man's finally showin' repentance."

"Sentence," Grant repeated, this time louder. "He wants to change the time of his *sentence*."

"Why? What better time to meet one's maker than high noon?"

"Noon's not the issue." Grant leaned forward so he could speak directly into the judge's ear. "He wants to meet his maker on Farrell time instead of Lockwood's."

"Well, I got news for him. Once he hangs, he'll be judged on his deeds. Which time he keeps won't get him any special favors at the golden gate."

Grant shrugged. "I don't think he's looking for heavenly favors. Only one earthly one. We're talking forty minutes."

"You're right about that. The man knows no limits. I'll grant his request this time, but he better not ask for anything more." The judge paused for a moment. "Is that all?"

"Not exactly." Grant hesitated. "Mr. Lockwood is having health problems. His daughter would rather that he not testify."

"Is he able to sit up and take nourishment?"

"I believe so. He's already back to work."

"Then he testifies. Anything else?"

Grant hesitated again. Usually he looked forward to

trial, but he was beginning to have grave reservations about this case. As if Lockwood and his intriguing daughter didn't offer challenge enough, he now had a tin-ear judge to contend with. Would he have to shout his opening and closing statements?

He cleared his throat. "Barnes wants to put the defendant and plaintiff on the stand, and I have no objection." After repeating this sentence three times, Grant drew a notebook and pencil out of his portfolio and wrote it down.

The judge stared at Grant's bold handwriting for several moments. "You do realize that letting the parties testify might tempt me to take sides."

"I have no problem with that," Grant said and added too quietly for the judge to hear, "As long as you take my side."

"All right, but no tears. I won't have anyone weeping in my courtroom. Nothing tilts the scales of justice faster than tears, and we can't have that. Understood?"

Grant stood and pushed in his chair. "You have no fears in that regard." With a tip of his hat, he walked away.

"Tears!" the judge shouted after him. "I said *tears*!"

Seventeen

THE HANDWRITTEN SIGN HANGING ON THE DOOR OF the courthouse was designed so that everyone, except the pastor who favored God's time, would arrive in an orderly fashion. It read:

THE **JILTED BRIDE** TRIAL WILL BEGIN PROMPTLY
AT THE FOLLOWING POSTED TIMES.
LOCKWOOD TIME: 9:20 A.M.
FARRELL TIME: 10:00 A.M.

Upon reading the sign, Meg gritted her teeth and tightened her grip on her purse. The gold clasp wouldn't stay closed. She should have left the gun at home, but that wasn't the only thing that irritated her.

"I wish everyone would stop calling me the jilted bride."

Her mother smoothed a stray hair away from Meg's forehead with a gloved hand. "This will soon be over, Pet. You'll see."

"I know." Meg forced a smile. She didn't want

Mama worrying about her. Heaven knew Mama had enough on her plate worrying about Papa. Despite the doctor's warning, he refused to curtail either his deportment or his activities.

Rising on tiptoes, her mother craned her neck. "Have you seen your sisters?"

"No, Mama."

Amanda had sworn Meg to secrecy about both the suffragette school and Lucy Stone. She was already in trouble with Papa for marching down Main. Meg's only hope was that her sister didn't land in jail—again. Poor Mama. What did she ever do to deserve the trouble her family put her through?

"Wait here, and I'll go and look for them."

No sooner had her mother vanished into the crowd than Sallie-May appeared by Meg's side, her tight corset making her sound breathless, as usual.

"Oh, you poor dear. You must be petrified. I know I would be."

"It is a bit scary," Meg admitted. Who would have thought that a court case could attract so much attention?

"Just wanted you to know that me and the others are rooting for you." Sallie-May pointed to a knot of Meg's friends from school who waved back.

"Thank you," Meg said. Right now, she needed all the friends she could get.

Sallie-May shook out a white glove. "Lord knows, there're a few men I'd like to sue. Is he taking on new clients, do you know?"

"Who? Mr. Barnes?"

"No, silly. Mr. Garrison."

"I have no idea," Meg said. Just then, she spotted

the newspaper editor, Mr. Buckham, heading her way. He looked like a hound sniffing out fresh meat.

Meg held nothing but contempt for the man, and for good reason. The editor avoided facts like a boy avoided soap. Such was his imagination that every newsworthy event read like a piece of yellow journalism, even something as innocuous as a cat in a tree. Meg shuddered to think what lamentable press was in store for the trial.

"I better go," Meg said. "Talk to you later."

In an effort to escape, she quickly ducked into the courtroom and bumped headlong into Mr. Garrison.

She dropped her purse, and the gun shot across the floor, spun around like a bottle in a kissing game, and stopped. As luck would have it, the muzzle pointed directly at the toes of the lawyer's shoes.

"Oh!" Meg took a step back. "I'm s-sorry," she stammered. She'd thought she was ready for today, but the mere sight of Tommy's lawyer made her feel like a bumbling schoolgirl.

Mr. Garrison picked the weapon off the floor with his thumb and forefinger and examined it before handing it to her grip first. "I see that you came armed. Does that mean you aren't willing to let justice run its course?"

"Oh, I'm willing, Mr. Garrison. I just want to make sure that it does."

"I see," he said, his tone coolly disapproving.

He swooped her purse off the floor and handed it to her, his gaze never leaving her face.

"Much obliged." She dropped the weapon into her purse's satiny depths. "I also thank you for the other day."

"The other day?"

"I understand you informed my father of my"—she searched for an appropriate way to soften her shameful incarceration—"predicament."

"I thought he should know." Mr. Garrison held her gaze. "I trust your…*predicament* didn't cause you any inconvenience."

"It did not." She studied him. "Are you planning to use my jail time against me in court?" Her father was convinced that Tommy's lawyer would.

Mr. Garrison arched a brow. "Should I?"

"A gentleman would not."

"Perhaps, but a *lawyer* wouldn't hesitate if he thought it would help his client." He slanted his head. "You did say that I could be as rough with you as I like. On the stand, that is."

"Yes, but only because I believed you were indeed a gentleman."

"Don't feel bad, Miss Lockwood. I made a similar error in thinking ladies didn't end up in jail for assault. Or carry guns on their persons."

She lifted her chin, conveying more confidence than she felt. How could a small-town girl like her expect to hold her own against a sophisticated man like him? "Let that be a warning, Mr. Garrison."

He afforded her a brief flash of a crooked smile. "I'll keep that in mind." With a sweep of his arm, he stepped aside to let her pass. "Have a good day."

Not missing the irony, Meg gave her head a slight toss. "You too, Mr. Garrison. You too."

❧

The courtroom was packed and the air as heavy as wet wool. The building had previously been used as a schoolhouse, but only two things remained from its former function: the bell tower on top of the building and the blackboard on the wall behind the judge's bench.

A railing served as the bar separating the defense's side from the plaintiff's. The court recorder sat hunched over a small desk in front of the bench, his spectacles clinging to the tip of his nose.

To the right of the blackboard stood a flagpole displaying the American flag with its thirty-eight stars. On the opposite side hung the Lone Star flag of Texas.

Meg took her place at the plaintiff table between her father and Mr. Barnes. Though she'd taken pains with her appearance, her bright-red skirt seemed wrong for the seriousness of the occasion. She had never been in a courtroom and hadn't known what to expect. She just wanted the trial to be over quickly with a minimum of pain or embarrassment.

Her father nudged her arm. "Look at that." He pointed to the display of hourglasses on the judge's bench. "I ask you, what kind of man still keeps time with an hourglass?"

"Maybe he just collects them, Papa."

"Hmm. Maybe I should give him a watch."

"Not a good idea. That would look like you're bribing the judge—"

"Bribing the judge?" her father exclaimed, his voice rolling like thunder from the front of the courtroom to the back. All eyes turned to him, including the bailiff's.

Barnes frowned, his forehead creased all the way to

his bare head. Before he could caution her father to keep his voice down, Meg had already tugged on his arm.

"Shh, Papa."

Tommy sat at the defense table across the aisle, but it was his lawyer who commanded everyone's attention. Mr. Garrison had dressed for court in a dark coat and striped trousers, and his unfeigned confidence and dash of arrogance left a strong impression. He looked far more polished and capable than Barnes, and Meg's heart sank. If the case was judged on appearances alone, Garrison would win hands down.

Tommy was dressed more casually, but apparently his lawyer had insisted he exchange his usual overalls for conservative trousers, a boiled shirt, and a bow tie. Even his normally unruly red hair had been combed back neatly and plastered down.

He didn't so much as glance at Meg, but Mr. Garrison certainly did and made no bones about it. Then he did the most unbelievable thing imaginable—he winked!

Heat rose up Meg's neck to her face. As shocked as she was—and as indignant—she couldn't help but be intrigued. She had judged a book by its cover, so to speak, and been proven wrong. The man gave the impression of being a very proper and conservative lawyer, but there was definitely more to him than met the eye.

He held her gaze, his face full of challenge. Refusing to look away, she glared back. *Oh, no you don't, Mr. Garrison. You're not going to intimidate me, either here or on the stand!*

As if having received her message, he gave a slight

nod and maybe a hint of a smile. They were like two opponents "shaking hands" before combat. He then turned to his client.

Feeling more nervous than she dared let on, Meg glanced over her shoulder. The courtroom was packed to the gills, but she had no trouble picking out her sister and mother.

Mama acknowledged her with a flutter of her hand, but neither she nor Josie seemed to have noticed Mr. Garrison's shocking disregard for propriety.

Her father leaned sideways, shoulder pressed against hers. "Are you all right, Megs?" he whispered, using his pet name for her.

"I'm fine."

Drawing back, he frowned as he studied her. "You don't look fine. Your face is all red. Maybe you're coming down with something."

She focused her gaze on the judge's empty chair. "I'm perfectly all right, Papa." She lowered her voice so Barnes couldn't hear. "I'm just afraid that Tommy's lawyer is more experienced at this sort of thing than ours."

"Experienced, my foot!"

"Papa, please. He'll hear you." She glanced at the defense table, but Mr. Garrison appeared to be in deep conversation with his client.

Papa lowered his voice. "He's nothing but a petti-fogger. His fancy lawyer talk might have worked in Boston, but it won't work here."

Meg blew a strand of hair away from her face. Pettifogger? Mr. Garrison? Hardly. "I just want this to be over."

Her father patted her hand. "Soon, dear daughter.

Soon. Once I get on the stand and tell the judge what happened, that will be the end of it. You'll see."

Her lips parted, and she swiveled her attention to Barnes. "Papa's testifying?"

The lawyer leaned toward her. "The judge agreed to allow you and the defendant to testify but refused to excuse your father."

"But his heart—"

"Pshaw!" Papa said, and for once didn't have to be reminded to keep his voice low. "There's nothing wrong with my ticker that winning our case won't cure." He reached for his watch.

Meg wished she had her father's confidence, but something told her that win or lose, things wouldn't be that easy. Barnes was a good solicitor, but she doubted he was a match for a big-city lawyer like Mr. Grant Garrison.

❧

The bailiff rose from his seat and pushed his glasses up his nose. "All rise."

Grant stood, his gaze fixated on the plaintiff table. Today Miss Lockwood wore a bright-red skirt and a white lace top tied at the neck with a perky red ribbon. The outfit showed off the intriguing valleys and peaks of her feminine form to full advantage. Did she wear the bold ensemble to send a message, or to bolster her own confidence?

Whatever the reason, it worked. Miss Lockwood currently looked determined and poised, with none of the vulnerability or hot temper she'd exhibited on previous occasions.

Still, he'd been more than a little surprised to find the lady carrying a gun. What other weapons did she have in her arsenal?

Grant wasn't sure why he'd winked. He certainly hadn't meant it in a lecherous way. It was more of an attempt to let her know that he was merely doing his job. Whatever happened in court should not be taken personally.

It wasn't like him to be so forward, but something about her brought out a protective streak he didn't know he had. Even when she'd faced assault charges and looked unbearably self-righteous, he'd ached to protect her.

He glanced at his own fumbling client, but only to remind himself whose side he was on.

Judge Lynch emerged from his chambers, his robe trailing behind like a cloud of black smoke. His refusal to excuse Lockwood from testifying was a surprise, especially given the circumstances of the man's health, but supposedly there was bad blood between the two. Would that have any bearing on the current case? Even a judge supposedly as fair as this one could show bias. He'd as much as admitted it.

Taking his seat, the judge reached into his robe pocket, produced an ear trumpet shaped like a ram's horn, and held it to the side of his head. With the other hand, he banged the gavel once, then turned over an hourglass.

Barnes wasted no time while presenting his case, though he had to keep repeating himself so the judge could hear. By the time the lawyer called his third witness, he was practically shouting and already showing signs of throat trouble.

Various vendors took the stand, all testifying to the validity of the wedding expenses that had been presented as evidence. Grant waived his right to cross-examine. Lockwood had spent a bundle on the wedding—no question. The only way to lessen the impact was to hasten the departure of those testifying to the facts. As Grant kept telling his anxious client, his time would come.

❧

The hours dragged on, and Meg's brain felt like day-old porridge. Even Judge Lynch had dozed off a time or two, his hog-calling snores disrupting the proceedings.

Not even the short break for lunch had helped. Meg tried to stay awake by watching the sand drip in the hourglasses on the judge's bench, but that had the opposite effect. In an act of desperation, she turned her attention to the bailiff and tried to guess how long it would be before the glasses fell off the tip of his nose.

What she *didn't* do was allow her gaze to wander over to the defense table. She was tempted, oh yes, but there was no way she would give Mr. Garrison the satisfaction of knowing how much his brazen attempt to unsettle her had actually worked.

Just when she thought Barnes was about to wrap up his case, he nodded toward the back of the room. "I would like to present into evidence exhibit number twenty-three." The double doors swung open, and all heads turned toward the back of the courtroom. A moment of anticipation was followed by the appearance of two men carrying the Lockwood hope chest.

Meg's jaw dropped, and her hand flew to her

mouth. Oh no! She glanced over her shoulder at Josie. Surely Josie had emptied the trunk of its embarrassing contents! Josie relieved her of that notion with a wide-eyed shake of the head. She mouthed something, but Meg couldn't make out what it was.

Meg frantically waved her hand, beckoning Barnes to the table. In response, he turned to say something to the judge.

Her father nudged her shoulder. "What is it, Meg?"

"You have to stop him, Papa," she said, keeping her voice low. "Please!"

"Stop him? But why?"

"I don't want my personal belongings flaunted," she whispered.

"Flaunted? What are you talking about? Flaunted?"

Meg forced herself to breathe. She shouldn't have listened to her sister. It had been Josie's idea to fill the chest with unmentionables in the first place! She'd insisted that an alluring nightgown or chemise was more conducive to a happy marriage than table linens.

"Do you have any idea what's in that hope chest, Papa?"

"Of course I know." Her father patted her on the arm. "Everyone knows. Items for a home. Linens and such. Towels. No need to be embarrassed." He chuckled softly. "When your mother and I were first married, she made me sleep on embroidered pillowcases from her hope chest. I awoke each morning with my face looking like floral wallpaper."

Meg's stomach churned. Her life was about to unravel, and her father was going on about pillowcases! This couldn't be happening.

After gaining permission from the judge to confer with his clients, Barnes hurried over to the table and leaned toward her. "What is it? What's the problem?"

"You mustn't open that hope chest," Meg said, voice low but firm.

Barnes straightened. "Why ever not? Receipts are all good and proper, but nothing impresses like seeing the real thing."

"Yes, yes," Papa agreed with a nod of his head. "Listen to Barnes. He knows what he's doing."

"No, no, you don't understand…"

The judge pounded his gavel. "Let's get on with it, shall we?"

Barnes stepped back. Hand on his chest, he cleared his throat. "I present as evidence Miss Lockwood's hope chest. My intent is to show the court the time and effort Miss Lockwood put into planning for the home she expected to share with her husband."

Meg closed her eyes and held her breath. If there was ever a time for the ground to give way beneath her feet, let it be now.

"Objection!" Mr. Garrison rose, and all eyes, including Meg's, turned to him.

"On what earthly grounds?" the judge demanded, his patience clearly spent.

Garrison caught her gaze in his. Lips parted, she covered her mouth with the tips of fingers.

"Mr. Barnes has already presented the court with enough wedding receipts to paper the entire town. It hardly seems necessary to waste Your Honor's time with the display of "—he ran a finger across his chin and shot a meaningful glance at Meg—"trivial household goods."

Judge Lynch inclined his head. "I quite agree." He banged his gavel. "Sustained."

Meg sat back with a *whoosh* of relief. She glanced at Mr. Garrison, cheeks burning. Though she was grateful for the way things turned out, it was foolish to think the lawyer had done it for her. He must have thought the contents were damaging to his case.

Garrison took his seat and then did something that made her heart lurch and threw her into utter confusion. He winked at her for yet a second time that day.

Eighteen

FOLLOWING A VERY TIRING AND TEDIOUS DAY IN COURT, Grant looked forward to a good meal and early night. He rode his horse down Peaceful Lane toward his boardinghouse. It was cold outdoors, but after sitting indoors all day, he welcomed the fresh air. It wasn't yet dark, but already the lamplighter was making his rounds.

Little had changed on the street since that morning. Mr. McGinnis and his bagpipes were at it again, and as usual, Mr. Crawford was yelling out a second-story window, trying to make his neighbor stop.

Cowboy the cat streaked across the street, but it was hard to know if he was chasing or being chased.

The two housewives were still yakking over the fence as they had been that morning, and that crazy widow was dragging an empty bookshelf across the street.

Grant sucked in his breath. The last time he'd offered to help, he ended up having to move three rooms of furniture. Still, she was having a heck of a time. And at her age.

He reined in his horse. "Need a hand?" he called against his better judgment.

A look of relief crossed her face. "Bless your heart," she said.

Swallowing his irritation, Grant dismounted and looped the reins around a fence post. He then grabbed the bookshelf out of her hands and hauled it the rest of the way across the street.

This time, he only had to move one room of furniture, because she had already managed the rest. The whole time he worked, she talked about her deceased husband. To hear her tell it, the saintly man deserved to be canonized.

Grant got everything moved but her cat, which was now stuck in the old oak tree.

The widow Rockwell wrung her hands. "Oh dear, I don't know what gets into Cowboy. I told him to stay out of that tree. Would you mind getting him down? I hate to bother the volunteer firemen again."

"I'll see what I can do."

Someone, probably the firemen, had left a ladder leaning against the tree, so climbing up wasn't a problem. Climbing back down with a snarling cat was. For his efforts, Grant ended up with a nasty scratch across the back of his hand.

The widow took the cat from him. "Oh, you naughty boy. Look what you did to the nice man."

Grant pulled out his handkerchief and wrapped it around his hand.

"Come inside, and I'll bandage you up."

"No need to bother. It's just a scratch."

Mrs. Rockwell set the cat down, and a look of confusion crossed her face. "Oh dear. I don't know.

It doesn't seem right. I think my Charley is telling me he wants me to live in the other—"

Grant backed away. He had no intention of moving her again. Not tonight anyway. "Let Charley sleep on it." It was a strange thing to suggest a dead man do, but she seemed to understand. "He might change his mind in the morning."

"Do you think so?"

"You never know." With that, Grant raced down the walkway and let himself out through the gate.

No sooner had he mounted his horse than he spotted Miss Lockwood a short distance away, pushing a cart with her hope chest. His gaze reached the heavens. Not again.

She was apparently returning the chest to her sister's house. Suddenly he had trouble breathing. A delayed reaction, no doubt, from moving all that furniture.

Should he offer to help? Good manners dictated that he must. Good sense cautioned him against it.

What if the hope chest tipped over again? The last time had put them both in an embarrassing position. Worse, it had…what? Messed up his brain. All that softness. All that lace. All that feminine allure…

While Grant debated the pros and cons of lending a hand, Miss Lockwood stopped to adjust the chest, which had tipped to one side.

She lifted her head, her wide-eyed gaze meeting his, and her lips parted. Blast it! Now he had no choice but to help—or chance looking like an ill-mannered cad in her eyes. Not that it mattered what she thought. Why would it? Still…

"Your hope chest puts on as many miles as Mrs.

Rockwell's sofa," he called, closing the distance between them. He then reined in his horse and dismounted.

His attempt to make light of the moment was met with a smile that did nothing for his peace of mind. The smile faded all too quickly, a frown taking its place.

She pointed to his handkerchief. "Your hand."

"Just a scratch."

"Cowboy?" she asked.

"How did you know?"

"Everyone who tries rescuing him gets branded. That's why he's called *cowboy*."

"Ah."

Miss Lockwood lifted her gaze to his. "I was hoping I'd bump into you."

"Oh? Why is that?"

She gave him a soft-eyed look. "I wanted to thank you." Her cheeks turned a pretty pink. "What you did in court…"

"I didn't do it for you." It was a lie, of course. He had done it entirely for her—not something he was proud of. Any thought of how it affected his client's case hadn't even been a consideration until later. Much later.

"Regardless, I'm much obliged."

He studied her. "You do know that the contents… would have supported your case."

"Perhaps," she said, and her eyes flashed with mischievous light. "But that's not the kind of support they were intended for."

Grant threw his head back with appreciative laughter. Who knew? The lady had a sense of humor.

"I'm just relieved that the judge sustained your motion," she said.

He grinned. "It's not often that a plaintiff's thankful for a defense attorney's win."

She smiled. "Are you as good at losing as you are at winning?"

He cocked his head. "Losing, Miss Lockwood? I'm afraid that's something with which I have no experience."

"I guess there's always a first time. I hope that if you ever do lose, you don't take it too hard."

He grinned. "Worried about me, are you?"

She lifted a finely shaped eyebrow. "Should I be?"

"I'd rather that you save your concern for that." He pointed to the hope chest that was still tipped to the side.

"Oh!"

"Let me do it," he said. He thrust the reins of his horse into her hands and bent over to shift the hope chest back and forth until it was properly balanced. He then took the pushcart by the handle. This time, the wheels turned with ease on the dry dirt road.

Miss Lockwood fell into step by his side, leading his horse by the reins. "What's your horse's name?"

"Chester."

She slid him a sideways glance. "Such a serious name for such a sweet horse."

"Don't let him hear you say that," Grant said. "He likes to think he's a warhorse."

"A warhorse, eh? So did you name him after a general or something?"

"Chester is short for Rochester, the name we gave the whale in my first big court case."

"You represented a whale?"

He grinned. "Actually, I represented the whaler who refused to pay the fish oil tax because he said whales were not fish."

"And you won?"

"Of course I did. With the help of a scientist, I was able to prove to the court that, contrary to popular belief, whales are actually mammals."

"I don't think you'll be representing many whales in Texas," she said.

Grant laughed. "Probably not."

Her face grew serious. "Speaking of trials…"

"I'd rather we didn't."

"I'd rather we didn't either, but…Mr. Barnes said that Papa still has to testify."

"Sorry, the judge was adamant. It seems your father's reputation precedes him." Grant afforded her a sideways glance. "As you know, a man is judged by his deeds."

"And a woman by her misdeeds," she quipped.

He arched an eyebrow. "Is that a confession, Miss Lockwood?"

"Just an observation, Mr. Garrison."

"Ah."

Upon reaching her sister's house, she said, "If you will kindly put the chest on the porch…"

He grasped the hope chest with both hands and heaved it up the porch steps. Since arriving in Two-Time, moving furniture had occupied as much of his time as the law.

He set the chest down and brushed his palms together. He then jogged down the porch steps and took the reins from her.

"Much obliged," she said.

"My pleasure." Catching himself staring, Grant mounted and touched the brim of his hat. "See you in court."

"Yes, you will, Mr. Garrison," she said. Her gaze clung to his as she ran her hand along Chester's neck. "Take care of your wound."

"So you *are* worried about me," he said.

"Just want to make sure you're still around when the judge rules in my favor. I wouldn't want to miss seeing your face."

"Oh, I'll be there, all right, Miss Lockwood. I just hope you're not too disappointed by what you see." Tugging on the reins, he rode away.

He kept his hat pulled down low and his gaze straight ahead. If Mrs. Rockwell was planning on moving again, he didn't want to know. And he most certainly didn't want to know whether Miss Lockwood was still watching from her sister's porch.

⌘

"How did you think it went?" Josie asked moments later as the three sisters gathered around her kitchen table.

Meg lifted her face out of her hands to find Josie and Amanda looking at her with furrowed brows. Good thing they didn't know what was really on her mind. She couldn't stop thinking about her latest encounter with Mr. Garrison.

How handsome he was; how dashing. He looked nothing like the serious-minded lawyer who'd appeared in court. And the smile! Oh my! Was there ever a more attractive dimple? Or a more intriguing chin cleft?

"Meg?"

She blinked. "What?"

Josie frowned. "I asked you how you think the day in court went."

"I suppose it was all right," Meg said. Mr. Barnes had done an adequate job, but it was hard to compete with Mr. Garrison's commanding presence.

Josie exchanged a worried glance with Amanda. "It didn't help that Mr. Barnes lost his voice, but it was only the first day."

Meg's heart sank. If Josie couldn't think of an encouraging thing to say about the start of the trial, then it was worse than she'd thought.

"I still don't know why you allowed Mr. Barnes to get his hands on the hope chest."

A pained expression crossed Josie's face. "I didn't, Meg. That was Ralph's doing, but don't blame him. He had no idea what was inside. When Mr. Barnes asked for it, Ralph thought you had approved."

Amanda frowned. "Mr. Barnes must have known what the hope chest contained. Why would he want to embarrass you like that?"

Josie shook her head. "It was locked when Ralph gave it to him. I was out at the time, and Ralph didn't know where I kept the key."

Meg rubbed her forehead. "Papa must have given him the spare key." No doubt Papa would be shocked to learn what was really in his daughter's hope chest. That would only add to his idea that she was damaged goods.

Thank God Mr. Garrison had objected. Still, as grateful as she was to Tommy's lawyer, Meg hated being beholden to him. Hated even more the way he kept intruding on her thoughts in ways that were… disturbing. He made her think about things that no lady should be thinking. Things like…

"Did you know that whales are mammals?" she blurted out.

"For goodness' sake, Meg," Josie said, looking startled. "What are you talking about? Whales…"

Meg dropped her gaze to her lap. "I just thought it was interesting," she murmured.

"Does Papa still have to testify?" Amanda asked, bringing their attention back to the trial.

"I'm afraid so," Josie said.

"I dread him taking the stand." Meg heaved a sigh. It was hard to know what worried her more: his heart or what he might say. Once Papa started talking, he often got carried away, and there was no telling what would come out of his mouth.

"If you ask me, that's Mr. Garrison's doing," Amanda said. "He wants Papa on the stand and doesn't care a fig about his health."

"That's not true," Meg argued. "Mr. Garrison is a very caring man." How could she forget his kindness to Tucker?

Both sisters stared at her.

"Why are you defending him?" Amanda asked.

"I'm not defending him." She wasn't, was she? "I-I was simply stating a fact. Not all lawyers are manipulative—or pettifoggers."

Amanda looked dubious. "We'll see if you still feel that way after *you* take the stand."

The very thought made Meg's blood run cold.

Even Barnes had been surprised by the judge's decision to allow Tommy and her to testify.

You can be as rough as you wish with me.

Now there's an intriguing thought.

Meg was so caught up in the memory that it took a moment to realize her older sister was talking to her. "I'm sorry, Josie. What did you say?"

"I asked what Papa said about having to bail you out of jail."

Meg shrugged. "He didn't say much of anything. Just that he should have been a chicken farmer."

Josie frowned. "A chicken farmer? Papa?"

Amanda laughed. "He doesn't even like chickens."

Josie stood and reached for the heated teakettle on the stove. "Meg, do you remember the time you brought home that rooster with the broken leg?"

"I remember," Meg said, grateful for the chance to talk about something other than the trial. She couldn't have been more than nine or ten at the time, and after fitting the fowl's leg in a splint, she'd nursed him back to health.

Josie poured hot water into a porcelain teapot. "I still laugh every time I think of how that rooster followed Papa around."

Amanda nodded. "He kept telling the rooster to go away." She giggled. "That silly bird thought *Go Away* was his name."

The memory brought others to the fore. Meg and her animal hospital were the butt of many family jokes. At one time Meg dreamed of becoming a veterinarian, but no college would allow a woman to study the veterinary arts. It was one of many dreams to fall by the wayside, including, now, her dream of marriage and children.

Their girlish laughter brought Josie's husband, Ralph, into the room. A quiet, unassuming man, he was ten years older than his wife. He had brown hair, blue eyes, and an easygoing smile. A mustache adorned his upper lip. No one could tell by looking at him that he had a breathing problem that caused him to tire easily and miss out on many family gatherings.

"It does me good to hear you all in such good spirits," he said. "Have you told them the news, my dear?"

"Not yet," Josie said.

Meg held her breath. Could this be the news she'd been waiting to hear? Were Josie and Ralph going to have the child they so desperately wanted? *Please, God, let it be so*.

"Don't keep us in suspense," Meg coaxed with a stealthy glance at her sister's middle.

"I have a job," Josie announced.

Meg blinked, not sure she'd heard right.

Amanda frowned. "What are you talking about? What kind of job?"

"I'm working for the newspaper," Josie said, barely able to contain the excitement in her voice.

Meg and Amanda stared at her, neither saying a word.

"I thought you'd be happy for me," Josie said, sounding hurt. "I expected more from the two of you. You know how much I like to write."

Meg did know. When they were growing up, Josie would regale them for hours with her stories of beautiful princesses sailing the seas and traveling to faraway places. "But I never thought you'd write for that awful newspaper."

The *Two-Time Gazette* was better known for its gossip than news. On the few occasions a newsworthy article appeared, it was so riddled with opinion that fact was hard to separate from fiction.

"No, no, you don't understand." Josie exchanged a fond look with her husband. "You're looking at the new Miss Lonely Hearts."

Meg blinked. "You're writing a column for the lovelorn?"

"I am." Josie laughed. "Don't look so shocked. The original writer was, believe it or not, a man, and he has retired."

Amanda shook her head. "You're married. What do you know about lonely hearts?"

Josie laughed before growing serious. "Most people who ask for advice already know what to do. They just want permission to do it."

"Papa will have a fit," Amanda said. "You know what he thinks about women working outside the home."

"And marching down the middle of Main Street," Meg added with a meaningful look at her younger sister.

"I'm a married woman," Josie said. "I don't need Papa's approval." A dimple appeared on her cheek. "I also don't intend to tell him."

Meg turned to her brother-in-law. "How do you feel about Josie's new job?"

Ralph gave his wife's shoulders a loving squeeze. "I encouraged her to take it. A talent like hers shouldn't be kept hidden. And who knows? Maybe this will lead to something else."

Meg chewed on her lower lip. Did this mean the two of them had given up hope of becoming parents?

"I was hoping you'd be happy for me," Josie said.

"I *am* happy for you," Meg said, reaching for her sister's hand.

"Me too." Amanda stretched her arm across the table to take Josie's other hand.

Later, Josie walked Amanda and Meg to the door and waited for them to don their wraps. A cold wind greeted them outside.

Josie hugged Amanda and then turned to Meg. "Don't worry. The trial will soon be over."

"I sure do hope so." Meg loved seeing her sisters happy, and Josie was practically floating on air. "Ralph is so supportive of you. You're lucky to have found him. Do you think there'll ever be anyone like that for me?"

Josie patted Meg gently on the cheek. "I think that's a question you should send to Miss Lonely Hearts."

Meg laughed and hurried down the porch to catch up to Amanda. "Maybe I will," she called over her shoulder. "Maybe I will."

Nineteen

FOLLOWING A BRIEF WARM SPELL, A BLUE NORTHER swept through town, stirring up dust and lifting shingles off rooftops. The temperature dropped so quickly that the owner of the coal company had to scramble to meet demand.

Head lowered against the wind, Meg held on to her hat with one hand and held a basket over her other arm while she waited for the mule-driven coal wagon to rattle past.

Judge Lynch had some legal business to attend to, so court was in recess. That meant that the trial would drag on for yet another week—a prospect she dreaded.

The bitter cold nipped her cheeks and cut through her woolen skirt. Upon arriving at the sheriff's office, she reached for the handle with a gloved hand. The door flew open to her touch and banged against the wall. A gust of wind lifted a whirlwind of papers off the sheriff's desk and ripped Wanted posters off the walls.

Meg's hat blew off as she tried closing the door, and Sheriff Clayton hurried around his desk to help her. It was like trying to push a locomotive uphill, but they finally managed to battle the door shut.

"Whew!" She retrieved her hat and arranged it on her head again, pinning it in place.

"What brings you out on a blustery day like today?" the sheriff asked.

"I came to see Mr. Kidd."

If the sheriff thought anything odd about her wanting to see the prisoner, he kept it to himself. He slanted his head toward the door leading to the jail cells and bent to pick up the Wanted posters from the floor.

Meg stepped through the open doorway and suddenly couldn't breathe. "Mr. Garrison!" What was Tommy's lawyer doing here?

Mr. Garrison turned and doffed his hat. "Miss Lockwood."

Despite the tempest outside, he looked as well put together as a fine Waltham watch. He was probably the only man in town who hadn't lost his hat to the wind.

"I'm s-sorry," she stammered. "Am I interrupting something?"

Kidd motioned her over to his cell. "Nah. My lawyer just stopped by to tell me the good news." Today was the day he was scheduled to hang, but you would never know it from his toothless grin.

"I didn't know you were Mr. Kidd's lawyer too," Meg said.

"My services are in much demand of late." Garrison's dimple deepened, and suddenly, she had a hard time breathing.

"I believe I owe it all to you," he continued, locking his gaze with hers. "I see you're here strictly as a visitor this time."

"I am." She gave him a slanted look. "I guess that means you won't be able to use this against me in court."

"Looks that way."

The shadow of his smile made her heart jolt. The moment shimmered between them like morning dew and might have lasted longer had Kidd not intervened.

"Ain't you gonna ask what my good news is?"

Pulling her gaze away from the lawyer's, she turned toward the cell. "Oh yes, of course. Do tell."

"My necktie party has been postponed on account of the wind." Kidd laughed as if he got some perverse pleasure from having the weather determine his fate. "Last week, I got me a reprieve on account of the sheriff bein' called out of town. Now this week, the wind…"

"That *is* good news." Feeling self-conscious beneath Mr. Garrison's steady gaze, Meg pulled a small package out of the basket. "I brought you something. I baked it special for you." She handed the wrapped tart though the bars, a small token of appreciation for his kindness during her short stay in jail. "You said you liked blueberries."

"That I do," Kidd said, grinning. He lifted the package to his nose and sniffed. "Hmm. I think I died and went to heaven."

"Time's up," the sheriff called from the doorway.

"But I just got here," she protested.

The sheriff shrugged and vanished.

"I'll walk you out, Miss Lockwood," Mr. Garrison said, "but only if you promise not to take advantage of my kindness."

"Why, Mr. Garrison. Whatever do you mean? Take advantage?"

"I wouldn't want you to try and influence me in any way. Into taking your side, I mean. Like you tried to do that day on the train."

She smiled at the memory. "If you insist upon putting such limits on me, I'll see myself out. But thank you anyway." With a wave to the prisoner, she started for the door. "Good day, Mr. Kidd."

"Same to you, Miz Lockwood."

❧

On Monday, Barnes rested his case, and a collective sigh worked its way across the courtroom. Having to shout for the judge's benefit had left him with only a low, gravelly rumble that no one could make heads or tails of.

The judge peered at Grant. "The defense may present his case."

Grant rose and buttoned his frock coat. His list of witnesses was considerably shorter, and he expected to wrap things up by tomorrow at the latest, if not by the end of the day.

"I call as my first witness, Mr. Henry Lockwood."

The crowded courtroom grew quiet. From the corner of his eye, Grant saw Miss Lockwood sit forward. She was dressed in a subdued blue frock today, but the combination of resolve and concern on her face as her father lumbered toward the witness stand touched Grant to the core.

Again, he was obliged to remind himself which side he was on.

Lockwood spoke in an uncommonly soft voice as he took the oath, stretching each vowel to ridiculous lengths.

"No tears," the judge reiterated. It was an unnecessary reminder, because the only one who looked close to tears was Grant's own client.

Grant faced the witness. "Mr. Farrell asked for your daughter's hand in marriage, is that correct?" Though he addressed the witness, he kept his voice directed to the judge's hearing horn.

"Yes, it is."

"And what was your reply?"

"My reply?"

"How did you respond to Mr. Farrell when he asked to marry your daughter?"

Lockwood cleared his throat and ran a finger along his upper lip. "I can't say that I recall."

Not for one moment did Grant believe this witness lacked in memory. "Would you say that you were delighted at the prospect of your daughter marrying Mr. Farrell?"

"Well, I…um…"

Miss Lockwood suddenly had a coughing fit. The woman's timing was impeccable. She took after her father in that regard. A certain skill was required for interrogating witnesses. Even a seemingly innocent question required much in the way of preparation. It also meant having to maintain control, and Miss Lockwood had effectively and momentarily shifted that control away from him.

The bailiff handed her a glass of water, and her attorney popped a hard candy into his mouth. Feet shifted. A buzz of voices rose from spectators. Seated in the gallery, the newspaper editor scribbled something on a yellow pad. Next to him, T-Bone had dozed off, his head wobbling back and forth like a marble circling a hole.

Grant waited until Miss Lockwood had recovered before turning his attention back to Lockwood.

"I'll repeat the question. How did you respond to Mr. Farrell's request for your daughter's hand?"

"Like I said, I can't recall."

Grant let Lockwood's answer hang for a moment for effect before continuing. "Permit me to refresh your memory. Isn't it true that you were against the marriage from the start?"

"Grrughshun!"

All heads, including the judge's, turned to Barnes, the source of the inhuman sound. "What did you say?" the judge asked. "Speak up."

Lockwood's lawyer coughed in an effort to clear his throat, but it did no good. His voice came out in a series of croaks. To move things along, Grant interpreted.

"Whether Mr. Lockwood did or did not agree to the marriage has no bearing on the case," he said on the plaintiff's behalf.

The judge blinked. "Does this mean you're objecting to your own question?"

"No, I'm simply stating Mr. Barnes's objection."

After several tries, Grant finally got the judge to understand who was objecting to what. He then offered his own rebuttal. "I believe Mr. Lockwood's opinion has a bearing on the case. A father's disapproval could put a terrible strain on a marriage. It would certainly give a man second thoughts about the wisdom of following his heart's desire."

"Is that your opinion or Mr. Barnes's?" the judge asked.

"It's all mine, Your Honor."

"Sustained."

"Eh, I believe you mean overruled," Grant said.

The judge narrowed his eyes in annoyance. "Whatever I mean, the witness must answer the question."

Grant turned back to Lockwood and repeated the question for the third time.

Lockwood pulled out his watch and flipped the case open with his thumb. Another delaying tactic. Like father, like daughter.

Grant frowned. "Are we keeping you from an appointment, Mr. Lockwood?"

Lockwood snapped the case shut and returned the watch to his vest pocket. "Not at all. I just noticed that the clock on the wall is fifteen minutes slow."

Judge Lynch frowned. "What's about to blow?"

"He said the clock was slow," Grant explained.

The judge glanced at his hourglasses and motioned Grant to continue.

Lockwood cleared his throat. "I didn't want that scalawag anywhere near my daughter." He quickly added in a more subdued voice, "But of course, it was my daughter's choice, and I had to respect her wishes."

"Like you respected her wishes not to go through with this lawsuit," Grant said beneath his breath.

"Speak up, I can't hear you," the judge said.

Grant stepped back. "I have no further questions." He waited for Lockwood to vacate the seat before calling his next witness.

"I call to the stand Miss Meg Lockwood."

❧

A hushed silence filled the courtroom as all spectators watched Miss Lockwood take the stand.

Never had Grant dreaded questioning a witness more. He had to be tough with her. His oath of office required it. His duty toward his client demanded it.

Meg laid her hand on the Bible and swore to tell the truth. Head held high, she spoke in a strong, clear voice. If he hadn't noticed the slight tremble of her lower lip, Grant would never have guessed the lady was nervous.

She took the witness stand, and he stood directly in front of her, blocking her view of her father. Holding herself rigid, she looked ready to fight him, and their gazes clashed.

Grant needed her to drop her guard, so he tried to look friendly, relaxed. "Could you please tell the court how long you and Mr. Farrell have known each other?" he asked in a conversational tone.

"I've known him almost all my life." She glanced at the defense table. "We grew up together."

"Can we also assume the two of you were good friends?"

"Yes."

"And in all that time, did you ever have occasion to doubt his word?"

"No. Never."

Grant paused. Witnesses often filled in silences with additional information, much to their detriment, but when Miss Lockwood failed to accommodate him, he continued, "So when he indicated he wanted to marry you, there was no reason for you to doubt his sincerity."

"No, none."

He dropped his casual tone and got down to business. "Miss Lockwood, is it true that you were against this lawsuit from the beginning?"

"Yes."

"Could you please speak up," the judge said.

"Yes."

"If Mr. Farrell reneged on his promise to marry you—"

"You know he did."

Something flared in her eyes, and Grant stepped back. "If the defendant broke his promise to wed, why were you against this lawsuit?"

"I—" She glanced at her father. "I just wanted to forget the whole thing."

"Forget the whole thing?" Grant let her statement hang for a moment. "Are you saying that you wanted to forget you ever wanted to marry Mr. Farrell?"

"Yes."

"Does that mean you forgive him for leaving you at the altar?"

She hesitated. "Yes."

"Is it also safe to assume that you were anxious to get on with your life?"

"Yes."

He moved closer, so close he caught a whiff of her

lavender perfume. It suddenly became necessary and indeed crucial to toughen his stance.

"Excuse me for saying this, Miss Lockwood. That hardly seems like the sentiments of a heart-broken bride."

She stared at him with bold regard, earning his begrudging admiration. "How would you know, Mr. Garrison?"

The judge's gavel hit the bench. "Will the witness please refrain from making unsolicited remarks?"

"Sorry, Your Honor," she said.

Grant leaned forward. "Hold on, I'm almost done," he whispered. Pulling back, he lifted his voice. "Did you love him?"

She blinked. "I—"

Barnes rose and made a god-awful sound—something between a foghorn and a wounded bear.

"I take it you are objecting," the judge said.

Barnes nodded and popped another hard candy into his mouth.

Grant addressed his comments to the judge. "If we don't know Miss Lockwood's true feelings, how can we determine if the charges against my client have merit?"

"Overruled." The judge turned to the witness. "Answer the question."

Meg bit her lower lip, and the look on her face felt like a knife to Grant's heart. He averted his gaze to gather his thoughts. Sometimes he hated his job.

"I'll repeat the question. Did you love Mr. Thomas Farrell?"

"Yes," she said. "I…loved him.".

Grant narrowed his eyes. She sounded sincere

enough, but why the hesitation? "Do you expect us to believe that, Miss Lockwood?"

This time the judge objected on behalf of the plaintiff. "Badgering the witness." He then added, "Sustained."

"I'll restate the question." Hands pressed together steeple-like, Grant tapped his chin. "You said you were heartbroken, Miss Lockwood. Could you tell the court exactly what that means?"

Her gaze dropped to her lap, and her lush lashes cast shadows on her cheeks. "I'm not sure I understand the question."

"Ah, then allow me to assist you. Were you too heartbroken to, say, go shopping?"

She lifted her gaze. "A woman can shop under almost any circumstance," she said, giving him a triumphant look.

"A simple yes or no will do, Miss Lockwood. Did you or did you not go shopping in San Antonio?"

"Yes, I went shopping." She turned to the judge. "To buy Christmas gifts for my family."

"What about dancing?" Grant asked quickly in an effort to minimize her last statement.

The question was meant to get her off-balance. Instead, it had the disconcerting effect of making him remember how she'd looked twirling in the street, head thrown back in laughter. Another, more disturbing thought followed. He'd wanted to be her partner that day. To be the one who made her eyes shine. The one holding her in his arms…

"Were you too heartbroken to dance?" he snapped in an effort to erase the memory.

Judging by her look of dismay, his carefully planned

strategy to disprove mental anguish was working. Still, it cost him plenty—a piece of his soul.

The spectators stilled, and the room grew so quiet a fly could be heard buzzing in the window.

Meg gave him a withering look, her eyes two turquoise pools of appeal. "That's not fair," she whispered. "You were spying on me."

"All's fair in love and law as long as it's legal," he whispered back. Louder he said, "I'll repeat the question. Isn't it true that despite being heartbroken, you were seen dancing in the street?"

Barnes jumped to his feet and made a gurgling sound.

"I take it you are objecting," the judge said with a roll of his eyes.

Barnes gave a vigorous nod and reached for a glass of water.

The judge continued. "Let me see if I have this straight. What Miss Lockwood does with her spare time has no bearing on the case. Is that your objection?"

"I think it does," Grant argued, not waiting for Barnes to agree or disagree with the judge's assumption. "You claimed Miss Lockwood suffered emotional devastation. Her public celebrations seemed to show otherwise."

"Overruled."

Grant turned back to his witness, and his breath caught in his chest. Tears swam in her eyes, and she looked every bit as devastated as her lawyer had described. Grant didn't want to feel sorry for her, but she was making it difficult for him not to.

"I said no tears," the judge declared with a bang of his gavel.

Grant handed her a clean handkerchief and gave her a moment to compose herself. "Would you like me to repeat the question?"

She shook her head. "No, that won't be necessary." She lifted her chin and flashed him a look of disdain. "I danced because I didn't want anyone to know how much I hurt."

It wasn't the answer he'd expected, and it sure in Hades wasn't the answer he wanted. Now he had no choice but to repair the damage. "Dancing, laughing, and flirting?" Oh yes, she had definitely been flirting with her dance partner. "Is that how you soothe your hurt, Miss Lockwood?"

Her mouth fell open, and he quickly switched tactics. He had made his point.

"Isn't it true that you told Mr. Farrell that you would rather die a spinster than marry him?"

"I—"

"Isn't it also true that you thought Mr. Farrell leaving you at the altar was the best thing that ever happened to you?"

"I never thought that."

He arched a dark brow. "Really, Miss Lockwood?"

Her face suddenly seemed to crumble, and her eyes filled with horror. She then jumped to her feet and cried, "Papa!"

Grant whirled about just in time to see Lockwood grab his chest and slip sideways. It was only fast action on Barnes's part that kept Meg's father from falling to the floor.

Twenty

CHAOS FOLLOWED MEG'S OUTCRY. THE JUDGE BANGED his gavel and called a recess. Spectators jumped to their feet and crowded around her father like cows around a feeding trough, forcing Meg to elbow her way to his side.

"Water, we need water." Her cry brought the bailiff running with a glass in hand. Water sloshed over the rim and splashed to the floor.

"Someone fetch the doctor," Garrison ordered, his voice loud enough to be heard over the murmurings of the crowd.

Tommy raised his hand. He looked shaken and pale as a winter moon. "I'll go," he said and raced to the back doors.

Slipping her hand under her father's neck, Meg lifted his head and raised the glass to his lips.

He pushed the glass away. "No doctor—" he murmured.

"Papa, please," Meg pleaded. After handing the glass to Josie, she pressed her hand against his forehead. He didn't feel hot or clammy. Not like last time. She moved her hand. He tried to say something, and she leaned closer.

"What, Papa? Tell me again."

Instead of answering, he winked and then quickly closed his eyes.

She drew back with a gasp. Papa was faking!

She looked up. Fortunately, no one seemed to have detected anything amiss. Not even Mr. Garrison, who was deep in conversation with the judge, his back turned. That man didn't miss much and would have probably noticed, had he been looking their way.

Fortunately, although Sallie-May and her friends were standing a short distance away, they were whispering among themselves and probably hadn't noticed either.

Neither had Mama. She was too busy unbuttoning Papa's collar and trying to make him comfortable.

"Henry," Mama said, shaking him gently, face etched with worry. "Talk to me."

Josie wrapped an arm around Mama. "The doctor will be here shortly."

Mama's lips trembled. "Do…do you think he'll be all right?"

Mr. Garrison finished his conversation and turned. Meg met his gaze. "That's up to Tommy's lawyer," she said.

❧

By the time the doctor arrived, her father had "recovered," though he still clutched at his chest and managed a hacking cough. No Shakespearean death scene was as dramatic as her father's performance. Even Mama was fooled.

Dr. Stybeck checked Papa's pulse and thumped on his chest. "I told you to remain calm," he scolded.

Her father lifted his head from the floor to glare at opposing counsel. "Calm? How can I remain calm while my daughter is being hammered to death?"

Barnes shook his head and croaked.

"What did you say?" Papa asked.

"I think he said you knew it wouldn't be easy," Meg replied.

"You didn't tell me it would be this hard." Papa struggled to sit up. As if recalling he was on death's doorstep, he clutched at his throat and made a gasping sound.

Alarmed, Mama patted his back. "Now, Henry. You're getting yourself all worked up again."

"And for good reason." *Cough, cough. Groan. Gasp.*

"Maybe you should take him home, Mama," Meg said. Papa's theatrics were bound to rouse suspicion sooner or later.

Her father wagged his head from side to side. "I'm staying," he said in a strained deathbed voice that would make any martyr proud.

Barnes and the doctor lifted him off the floor and helped him to a chair, where he sat limp as a rag doll.

The judge gave the bench several sound raps with his gavel. "In light of Mr. Lockwood's health, I suggest we bring this hearing to a close as soon as possible." He turned to Mr. Garrison. "Do you have any other witnesses?"

Mr. Garrison rose and Meg held her breath. "Just one, Your Honor. My client. Tommy Farrell."

"And do you have any more questions of this witness?"

Garrison locked her in his gaze. "No, Your Honor," he said.

Meg sagged in her chair. The worst was over.

Tommy took the stand but didn't really have much to say in his own defense. He did admit he'd felt pressured into marrying Meg by a town eager to put an end to the feud.

After Barnes cross-examined him, Tommy was excused.

Judge Lynch addressed both lawyers. "You may present your closing arguments. Court will then be in recess until after the first of the year." He glared at her father. "I'll announce my decision then."

Meg's heart sank. Papa was well meaning, but she had a terrible feeling that he'd earned them no favors with the judge.

Twenty-one

ON THE DAY AFTER CHRISTMAS, MEG SAT IN THE parlor reading the morning newspaper.

She had never paid any attention to the Miss Lonely Hearts column until Josie took it over. Now she read it religiously. It was the first thing she turned to each morning after breakfast. Today was no different.

The letters were entertaining. Some were downright hilarious, others more serious and even sad. Still, why anyone would write a stranger for advice was a puzzle. Today the first letter read:

> *Dear Miss Lonely Hearts,*
>
> *I am a twenty-year-old man with a respectable job and small savings. My problem is this: I've been in love with a certain girl for as long as I can remember, but she doesn't even know I'm alive. How can I get her to notice me?*

The letter was signed *The Invisible Man.*

She read Josie's answer with great interest.

Dear Invisible,

The fairer sex has a disadvantage in affairs of the heart, as each woman must wait for the male to make the first move lest she be thought forward or brazen. It's possible your maiden of choice is waiting for you to make your intentions known so that at long last she can reveal the true longings of her heart. So don't keep the lady waiting. Present yourself at once on her doorstep with a bouquet of flowers in your hand and words of love flowing from your lips.

Meg laughed at Josie's answer. Who knew that Josie had a previously hidden flair for drama? It seemed that even calm, composed Josie wasn't immune to Papa's influence.

Sighing, Meg tossed the newspaper aside. She certainly would notice a man standing on her doorstep, flowers or no flowers. Not that such a thing was likely to happen now that her name was mud. What man in his right mind would take a chance on a woman known to sue for promises not kept? Her father had made her every man's nightmare.

As she faced the harsh realities of a bleak, lonely future, Meg's spirits sank even lower.

The grandfather clock in the corner groaned, and the wall clocks sighed. Seconds later, the cacophony of alarms struck the hour of eight. Only today, bongs, gongs, cuckoos, and chimes weren't what bombarded her ears. It was mocking laughter.

Jilted bride, jilted bride, jilted bride…

She covered her ears, and when that failed to bring relief, she ran around the room, turning each clock in such a way as to disrupt its delicate balance. She knocked against the Christmas tree, and a glass ball fell to the floor and shattered.

Giving it no heed, she continued to dislodge pendulums, push birds into little wooden houses, and force minute hands to move until a strange and unaccustomed silence blanketed the wall.

This abrupt silence brought her father racing down the stairs, watch in hand, suspenders flapping at his sides. He stopped when he reached the parlor and stared at the tilted clocks.

Expecting him to scold her, Meg stood with arms crossed and waited. It wasn't like her to be so defiant or out of sorts, but Papa and this dumb lawsuit had pushed her to the limit.

Papa surprised her by not saying a word. Instead, he calmly walked from clock to clock. Like a doctor breathing life into his patients, he straightened wood casings, adjusted pendulums, and reset minute hands. Only after the last clock had been adjusted did he speak, his voice oddly quiet and controlled.

"When we soldiers came back to town after the war, there were no bells to greet us," he said. "They had all been melted for the war effort, even the church bells. Without bells, there was no way to announce the birth of a child or death of a loved one." He stopped to straighten one last clock.

"We had no way of calling people to worship, warning of a fire, or summoning a doctor. The citizens lived in total isolation, and I vowed to change all that.

And so I melted down every piece of metal I could find, even watches. That's how I made the bell that now hangs over the shop."

Meg had been only two when her father went to war and was nearly six when he returned. She remembered the first time the Lockwood bell rang and how she thought it was the most amazing sound in the world. She also recalled the tears in her mother's eyes. It was the first time Meg understood that tears could be shed for joy as well as sorrow, though nothing good that happened to her had ever made *her* cry.

Her father paused for a moment to adjust another clock. "Mine was the first bell in town after the war. We rang the bell for soldiers who returned and soldiers lost. The chime of clocks and ringing of bells that you find so objectionable brought people together then, and they bring people together now."

"And your ridiculous feud with Mr. Farrell is what tears them apart!"

Her father's hand froze on a regulator clock. "That's Farrell's fault. Not mine."

Shaking now, she fought for control. "Tommy told me his father wanted to go into business with you after the war, but you refused."

"Why do you keep harping on this, Meg?" He gazed at her over his shoulder. "Hmm?"

"Why do you keep refusing to answer my questions?"

"Questions, questions." Her father tugged on the chains of the grandfather clock. "What time is it when ten dogs run after one cat?"

Teeth gritted, she seethed. As a child she'd fallen for

her father's distracting tricks, but those days were long gone. "I don't know, Papa, and I don't care."

"Ten to one."

A footfall sounded, and Mama swept into the room. She took one look at Papa and then turned to Meg. "Is everything all right?"

"No, Mama. It's not all right." Meg turned and fled from the room. Things would never be all right, not ever again.

❧

Less than a week later, on New Year's Eve, Josie saw Meg to the door. "Must you leave so early?" she asked, her forehead lined with worry. The chimes of the gold clock on the mantel rang out. It was only thirty minutes to midnight.

"Can't you at least stay to ring in the new year?"

Meg pulled her cloak around her shoulders and tied the ribbon beneath her chin. "I'm sorry. I'm just not in the mood to celebrate tonight."

It had been hard enough to get through Christmas, but nothing compared to the depression that weighed her down now. Her sisters were so certain that '81 would be better than the last year, but Meg was less optimistic. It was hard to think much past the reading of the verdict next week. However the judge ruled, there would be no winners, only losers.

"I don't want to spoil your fun," she said.

Josie's expression softened. "You could never do that."

Meg forced a smile. She didn't want her sister to worry. "It's better this way."

"At least let Ralph walk you home."

She glanced at Ralph and Amanda sitting in front of a blazing-hot fire, playing cribbage. She didn't want him out in the cold night.

"No need. I'll be fine," she said, her confident voice belying her anxiety. Since being accosted by that inebriated man, walking alone made her nervous, especially at night. The gun in her cloak pocket gave her small comfort. Could she use it if she had to?

"Happy New Year," she called and stepped outside.

The night was cool and clear and the sky bright with stars. Her breath came out in white plumes. After giving her sister a final wave good-bye, she shoved her hands into the cloak's deep pockets for warmth.

With a heavyhearted sigh, she started for home.

Laughter wafted from a nearby house, along with snatches of a song. Someone was playing "Auld Lang Syne" on a piano, and in the distance she could hear the high-pitched sound of a fiddle. Someone anxious for the new year to start set off a firecracker. A bright light flashed overhead, followed by a loud boom that set off a chorus of barking dogs.

The whole world seemed to be in a partying mood. Never had Meg felt so utterly alone, and her feet dragged as if attached to a ball and chain.

Halfway down the block, a tall form stepped out of the shadows. Halting in her tracks, she slipped her hand into the cloak's deep pocket where she kept her gun.

"W-who's there?" she called.

❧

"Miss Lockwood, is that you?"

Relief whooshed out of her, and she pulled her

hand out of her pocket. She'd recognize that strong baritone voice anywhere.

"Mr. Garrison!"

She hadn't seen him since the day he questioned her in court. He had only been doing his job, and she tried not holding that against him, but it was hard. Especially tonight when she felt so emotionally vulnerable. He knew things about her that few people knew, and worse yet, all unknowingly, he made her feel and think things that shook her to the core.

"What…what are you doing here?" Somehow she managed to conceal her mixed emotions behind a calm voice.

"I live here," he answered, moving into the amber circle cast by the gas streetlight. She glanced at the imposing house behind him. It was the only structure on the block not blazing with light. "You live at Mrs. Abbott's boardinghouse?" Why on earth? There were other boardinghouses on the street with less scandalous pasts.

As if reading her mind, he flashed a smile. "Worried about my virtue, are you?"

Feeling her face grow warm, she was grateful for the dim light. "Certainly not. I was just…wondering why you aren't throwing your hat over the windmill like everyone else."

He tilted his head. "You're not. Is your father—"

"He's fine health-wise. I'm just not in a celebratory mood."

"Guess that makes two of us."

She studied him. Rather than hide his good looks,

the dim yellow light emphasized his fine chiseled chin and handsome broad forehead.

"Why is that, Mr. Garrison?"

"Grant," he said.

"I'm sorry—"

"The trial's over except for the verdict. We can stop with the formalities." When she failed to respond, he added, "You aren't still harboring ill feelings toward me, are you? For what happened in court? I wasn't too rough, was I?"

"Rough enough," she said.

"I only did what I had to do."

She bit her lip. She had every reason to be wary of him. Still, tonight she was in desperate need of someone to talk to, even one as suspect as him.

"In that case, you can call me Meg."

"Meg." He made her name sound more prominent, more significant than it really was.

"You still haven't told me why you're not out celebrating," she said. A handsome man like him wouldn't have any trouble attracting female companionship. It was a wonder that Sallie-May hadn't charmed him yet. She must be losing her touch.

"I guess you could say I miss home and spending the holidays with my family back in Boston. Normally at this time of year, there's snow on the ground. I miss that too."

Meg shot him a puzzled glance. What an odd thing to say. It had only snowed once in Two-Time that she recalled, and it had created a horrible, sludgy mess that took days to clear away. It was hard to imagine anyone missing snow.

"I've never been outside Texas," she said. Was that the source of her recent discontent? "Do you think I would like Boston?"

Elbow on his crossed arm, he tapped his chin. "I'm afraid Boston would be too confining for you. The ladies there spend most of their time at tea parties and quilting bees. You'd probably be bored to death."

Surprised that he knew that about her, she studied him a moment before asking, "What family do you have there?"

"Three brothers, two sisters, and more nieces and nephews than I can count."

"Yet, you came here to be with another sister."

"Mary was my twin. Unfortunately, by the time I got here…" A muscle clenched at his jaw. "I spent Christmas with my sister's husband and three children. This was a hard year for them. For all of us."

"It must have been," Meg said, wishing she could think of something to say to ease the pain so evident in his voice.

"Perhaps I should have studied medicine. Maybe then I could figure out a way to keep women from dying in childbirth." His voice was thick, as if coming from the deepest part of him.

His grief was like a magnet, drawing her hand to his arm. It was a bold gesture for a woman to make, but it felt as normal and right as reaching out to a child.

"How old are the children?" she asked.

"Jason's nine, Michael's six, and the youngest, Jennifer, is four."

Meg sucked in her breath. "I'm so sorry." It was hard to imagine losing one's mother so young.

Grant covered her hand with his own, the warmth traveling up her arm. "They say time heals all wounds, but they never say how much time it takes."

She pulled her hand away, but only because his touch was doing strange things to her. "My mother said that each heart has its own clock."

He tilted his head. "If that's true, I think mine must have stopped the day I learned of my sister's death."

Meg let his words hang for a moment before asking, "What was she like? Your sister?"

Grant gave her an odd look, and she feared having overstepped her boundaries.

"You're the first one to ask me that," he said. "Thank you." She heard his intake of breath. "Most people quickly change subjects upon learning of my loss."

Not sure what to make of this unpredictable man, Meg gazed up at him while he spoke lovingly about his sister and growing up together in Boston.

"She was funny and clever." He chuckled before adding, "Come to think of it, she would have probably given that dogcatcher a bad time too."

"I wish we could have met. I know I would have liked her."

Grant nodded. "My sister had a difficult pregnancy and wasn't able to spend much time in town. She still wrote glowing letters about Two-Time. Talked me into coming here. Said it would be the perfect place to practice law." He rubbed the back of his neck. "But I'll be hanged if I can figure out what she found to like. Never have I looked so far to see so little."

Meg laughed. "Texas takes some getting used to,"

she said. "But it has a big heart. You just have to know *where* to look."

He angled his head. "So tell me, what would I see if I did know where to look?"

She thought for a moment. "In the spring, you'd see fields of bluebonnets blooming upon the rolling hills. You'd also see buffalo with orange calves and—"

"Orange?"

"That's what color buffalo are at birth."

"Ah." He tilted his head. "And in the summer? What would I see then?"

Meg told him about her favorite swimming hole and the Independence Day dance at the Lazy M ranch. "In the fall, you'd see maple trees dressed in red and gold. And, oh yes, purple skies."

"Is that what you think my sister liked so much about Texas?" he asked. "Orange calves and purple skies?"

"I reckon she liked those just fine, but I'd bet my boots it was the people she liked best."

Grant arched an eyebrow. "Would those be the feuding, opinionated people? Or the gun-toting people with short fuses?"

She laughed.

He gave her a crooked smile. "What's so funny?"

"Folks 'round here would be surprised to hear you describe them that way."

"Oh? And how would you describe them?"

Meg thought for a moment. "I'd say we're an independent lot with strong beliefs and hearts as wide and deep as the ocean. Actually, the name *Texas* is from an Indian word meaning *friends*."

He arched his eyebrows. "Are you sure it doesn't mean feuds?"

"No, I'm pretty sure it's friends," she said. "Maybe one day you'll come to see us as we really are."

Grant opened his mouth to say something but then stopped, his head tilted toward the sound of bells pealing out the hour of midnight—Lockwood time.

She'd offered to ring the bells so that her father wouldn't have to, but he would have none of it. He'd rung in the new year for more than fifteen years and had no intention of stopping now, bad heart or not.

Fireworks lit up the sky, and the sharp, popping sounds of gunfire rattled the air.

"Happy New Year, Meg," Grant said.

She smiled up at him, amazed to discover her depression gone. Also gone was her earlier reserve. "Happy New Year, Grant."

He stepped away from the lamppost, and she caught the sweet fragrance of bay-rum hair tonic. "I don't know how it's done here, but in Boston, if you don't kiss someone at midnight, it means a year of loneliness ahead. Would you mind if I kiss you?"

Twenty-two

MEG STARED UP AT HIM. HE WANTED TO KISS HER?

"On the cheek," he explained.

Her pulse quickened, and she swallowed hard. "Th-that would be fine," she stammered. If a single kiss was thought to ward off loneliness, who was she to argue?

Grant moved his hands to her waist, and she angled her face to the side. Just before his lips touched her cheek, she changed her mind and turned her head to tell him as much.

"I don't think—"

Her words were crushed the moment his mouth found hers, the tolling bell and booming skyrockets urging them on like the crack of a whip on a team of horses.

The warmth of his lips quickly melted the last of her resistance, and warm currents rushed all the way down to her toes. A knot of shivery feelings exploded inside, matching the fireworks overhead and shattering her calm.

The hands at her waist were firm, his mouth insistent. Fingers pressed against his chest, she absorbed the impact of his hard muscles through her palms.

Feeling suddenly emboldened, she rose on tiptoes and slipped her hands up his chest and around his neck. Pulling him closer, she ran her fingers through his hair and met his kiss with equal ardor.

Did this man ever know how to kiss! Even more shocking was her own eager response. Where had this new brazen and passionate self come from? They were both out of breath by the time he pulled away.

She wasn't sure when the actual bells stopped ringing, but the deep gongs still seemed to echo through the pounding of her heart.

"I-I didn't mean for that to happen." His whispered voice caressed the shell of her ear like velvet, sending warm shivers down her neck. "I just meant to kiss you on the cheek. Honest."

"Perhaps an anatomy lesson is in order," she whispered back, her voice thick with emotion.

He laughed, breaking the tension between them, and moved his hands away from her waist. "I told you I should have studied medicine."

They stood staring at each other for a moment before looking away, she to gaze at the smoke veiling the stars, he to pull out his watch. Holding it to the light, he thumbed the case open.

"We have exactly thirty-eight minutes till midnight strikes again." Snapping the lid shut, he slipped the watch back into his vest pocket. His heated gaze locked with hers. "So what do you say about celebrating New Year's with me a second time?" His voice was husky and, more than anything, persuasive.

Her mouth went dry. "A s–second time?"

"If one kiss will ward off loneliness for the year, who's to say what two would do?" When she hesitated, he added, "I think it only fair to warn you that next time I won't be aiming for your cheek."

Her breath caught in her throat, and her knees quivered. His eyes, his voice, his very essence beckoned. It was all she could do not to fly into his arms and start the second New Year early.

Grant tilted his head. "So what do you say?"

She wanted to say yes. *Yes, I'll celebrate a second New Year with you.* But something held her back—a voice in her head. His voice. *What about dancing, Miss Lockwood? Were you too heartbroken to dance?*

And what about kissing?

She stepped back, a soft gasp escaping her parted lips. Had kissing her been a trick? Something to use against her? A way of persuading the judge to rule in his client's favor?

"I–I better go," she said, her voice barely a whisper.

He stepped forward, his hand extended as if he were asking her to dance. "Don't go… If you prefer, we'll just talk."

Meg's heart knocked against her ribs. She wanted so much to stay—and not just to talk. She wanted to feel his lips again. To feel his closeness. To feel his heart beating next to hers as if they beat as one.

If only the voice in her head would go away. *And what about kissing, Miss Lockwood? Were you too heartbroken to kiss?*

"I–I have to go."

"Are you sure?"

She wasn't sure of anything. Certainly not his motives. At the moment, she wasn't even sure of her own feelings. "Yes."

"I'll walk you home—"

"No!" She shook her head and backed away. She didn't trust herself with him another moment. "No need." She turned and fled, her feet pounding the hard-packed ground and tears of confusion blurring her vision.

❧

Grant called after her. "Meg, wait."

Even as he called her name, his mind was in a whirl. What in blazes just happened? What had come over him? And why did she run away?

Had he been too forward? Too pushy? Too presumptuous?

It wasn't like him to lose control. He'd only meant to give her a genial peck on the cheek. A friendly gesture between two lonely souls on a night when everyone else seemed to be having a good time.

Never had he intended to kiss her full on the lips. He could still smell the fragrance of her hair, her skin. Feel the softness of her breath. Recall in stunning detail the way she'd responded to him. The way she'd kissed him back...

He grimaced. What was wrong with him? Where was his head? It wasn't like he was new at this sort of thing. There'd been women in the past. Several in fact, thanks to his matchmaking mother and sisters. But none had been as intriguing as Meg, or as tempting. And none had made him break his previously rock-solid rule against mixing business with pleasure.

Not good. Not good at all. Kissing her was wrong, all wrong. He was still Tommy Farrell's lawyer, and that meant he was obliged to act professionally at all times. His client deserved no less. Kissing the plaintiff was inexcusable. What if she went to her father? Her lawyer? What if Barnes went to the judge? One moment of madness could cause Grant to lose his client's case and ruin his reputation as a lawyer.

The last was the least of his worries. Grant wasn't even certain he planned to hang around after the trial. Meg could talk up Texas till the cows came home, but settling down here permanently was the furthest thing from his mind. The town was too wild for his liking, the people too ornery.

Even more worrisome was that something about Two-Time made him act unlike himself. Maybe it was the water. Maybe it was the air. He didn't want to think it was Meg Lockwood.

Mr. Garrison, did you or did you not kiss the plaintiff?

I did, Your Honor.

And did you or did you not enjoy it?

Enjoy it? Yes, I enjoyed it. And if I had it to do over, I would willingly and gladly kiss her again.

❧

Upon reaching home, Meg grabbed hold of the porch railing and gasped for air. She was breathing so hard she could hardly move, and her knees threatened to cave in.

Oh God. What is happening to me?

The light in the window indicated Mama was still up, no doubt waiting for Papa to return from ringing in the new year.

Meg didn't dare let either parent see her. Not like this. Not while her whole body was on fire. Not while her mouth still burned with the memory of Grant's kiss.

The sound of whistling and the click of the front gate announced her father's return. She drew back into the shadows and held her breath until he entered the house with a stomp of his feet.

Pressing her fingers against her still-burning lips, she closed her eyes. Never before had she been kissed like she'd been kissed tonight. Certainly not by Tommy.

Nor had she imagined that a kiss could be so all encompassing. And yet…leave her aching for more. Much more.

If time could be measured like so many lengths of calico, as Papa believed, why did minutes seem like seconds whenever she was with Grant? Only to feel like hours when they were apart?

And why did time always move forward like an arrow heading for some distant target? Why couldn't it go in reverse?

So what do you say about celebrating New Year's with me a second time?

She paced back and forth on the dark porch. She thought of a dozen reasons why she couldn't, shouldn't, didn't dare return for a second helping of those heavenly soft lips.

He was a fancy big-city lawyer, and she was just a small-town girl. He'd gone to a prestigious school, and she'd barely made it through the one-room school-house on the edge of town. He'd seen things she never hoped to see and knew things she couldn't even guess at. What would a man like him see in the likes of her?

Kissing her had been a trick. Something to use against her. That was the only thing that made sense. Even now, Grant was probably on the way to wake the judge and tell him what had happened. What the so-called heartbroken jilted bride had done this time.

And yet...

This was the same man who had prevented the embarrassing contents of her hope chest from being exposed in court. Who'd paid for a young boy's gift to his pa. Showed concern for her father. Would such a man turn something as personal as a kiss against her?

If I had someone like you...

The memory of his words only increased her confusion and made her uncertainty more pronounced. *Go back to him. Don't go back...*

The more she debated the pros and cons of returning to him, the weaker her resolve to stay away became. Grant had always been open and honest with her. Would such a man stoop so low as to use a New Year's kiss against her in court? No, a thousand times no!

A tingle of excitement raced down the length of her. Anticipation burned through her like wildfire and made her want to throw off her cape. Maybe if she hurried, he would still be outside, waiting. If she hurried, perhaps she could reach him before the Farrell bell began to ring. That way she could enjoy the full twelve strokes of midnight nestled in his arms.

In her hurry to leave the shadows, she knocked

against a small table, and a potted plant crashed onto the wooden porch.

The door flew open, and her father's large, bulky form was outlined in the doorway.

"Meg, is that you?"

Her heart sank. "Yes, Papa."

"Well, come in before you catch your death of cold."

Meg glanced down the street toward the boarding-house, but it was too dark to see much beyond the streetlight. Worse, Farrell's bell began to ring, the first stroke piercing through her like an arrow. Fireworks exploded overhead, sending a shower of sparks flying in every direction like little pieces of her heart.

Swallowing the lump in her throat, she followed Papa inside on leaden feet.

Twenty-three

A CROWD WAS ALREADY WAITING OUTSIDE THE courtroom when Meg and her family arrived that Monday morning in early January.

The chaos was like a circus. All that was missing were Colonel Tom Thumb and P. T. Barnum's traveling menagerie. Drummers hawked everything from peanuts to hot buns, and one man stood on a soapbox proclaiming the end of the world.

The spectacle, bad as it was, hardly affected Meg. While everyone else anticipated the reading of the verdict, Meg was looking forward to seeing Grant again. She hadn't been able to think of anything else since New Year's.

Her only regret was not going back to him that night. Foolish, foolish girl! How could she possibly have thought he would do something as underhanded as using her kisses against her in court? A fine, honest man like that!

Now if she could just figure out a ladylike way of letting him know she was interested. Maybe Miss

Lonely Hearts would have some ideas in that regard. The thought brought a smile to her face.

"You certainly look confident," Josie said in a hushed voice by her side. "Do you know something about the judge's ruling that rest of us don't?"

Meg forced her mouth to turn downward. "No, of course not." She cleared her voice. "I was just… eh…thinking about New Year's. I had a great time at your house."

Josie's eyebrows rose. "You certainly didn't look like you were having a good time."

"I did, Josie. Really, I did."

Her assurances were met with a dubious expression. "Meg, I just want you to know that whatever happens today—"

"Oh, look, there's Tucker." Meg waved to him. "I'll be right back." She quickly moved away from Josie's scrutiny.

The boy raised a newspaper over his head and yelled, "Readallaboutit. The jilted bride ruling due today!" He grinned as she approached. "Hello, Miss Lockwood. Wanna newspaper?"

"No, thank you, Tucker. I already saw the morning paper. I just wanted to ask how your pa liked his watch."

"He said it was the best gift he ever got."

"That's wonderful, Tucker. I'm so glad."

The smile died on her face the moment she spotted the editor of the *Two-Time Gazette* barreling toward her.

He barely reached her before the questions began spewing out of him. "Do you think the verdict will go in your favor?" He held his pen posed, ready to jot down some scandalous quote she would never think of saying. "And what about—"

Ignoring the man, she shouldered her way through the crowd. Win or lose, Meg didn't care. She just wanted it to be over so she and Grant could finish what they started on New Year's Eve. Hand held in front of her face to ward off the blinding camera flash, she accidentally bumped into Grant.

He steadied her with a hand to her elbow, and it suddenly felt as if no one else existed but the two of them.

His gaze dipped to her lips for a moment before meeting her eyes. It didn't seem possible, but it felt like she had just been kissed again, and her heart responded in triple time.

"You all right?" he asked.

She smiled up at him, but before she could answer, the newspaper editor stepped between them, forcing him to release her arm. "What do you think the chances are of a favorable ruling?" he asked, posing the question to Grant.

Grant shot Meg an apologetic look before turning to the editor. She walked away before hearing his answer. Naturally, as Tommy's lawyer, he would have to speak in favor of his client. Just as Barnes conveyed a winning attitude to one and all. Neither side wanted to show doubt or weakness.

"I'll put my money on the jilted bride," someone yelled out.

"The judge's gonna rule for Farrell," shouted another. "Mark my words. Any man smart 'nuff to run away from a marriage trap deserves to win in my book."

Meg turned right, then left, but every way was blocked.

Josie appeared by her side. "Don't pay any attention to them." She took Meg by the arm and steered her through the crowd.

"Meg!" It was Tommy. "We need to talk."

Josie warded him off with an open hand. "This is neither the time nor place." She practically pushed Meg into the courtroom.

"Good luck," Josie whispered.

"Thank you." While her sister grabbed two empty seats in the gallery, Meg hurried up the aisle and took her place between Barnes and her father.

"Ah, there you are," Papa said. In a softer voice he added, "Can't wait to see the look on Farrell's face when he finds out he has to pay for the trouble his son caused."

Her stomach knotted. She'd been so wrapped up in her own joyful thoughts that she'd forgotten what was at stake. A win for her would be disastrous for the Farrell family, and that was the last thing she wanted.

She turned to Barnes. "Do you think Papa's right? Do you think the judge will rule in our favor?"

Barnes lifted his shoulders. "I gave up trying to guess which way the legal wind would blow years ago." Fortunately, his voice had returned during the holidays and he sounded like himself again. "We'll just have to wait and see."

The sudden roar of the crowd signaled the opening of the door, and Meg glanced over her shoulder. Grant had entered the courtroom, his presence filling the room like water filled a glass.

She quickly turned to face the front. Squeezing her eyes shut, she forced the memory of New Year's to the back of her mind, knowing full well the reprieve would only be temporary.

Waiting until after she thought Grant was seated, she chanced a glance at the defense table. With his stern, businesslike demeanor, he hardly looked like the same man who had melted her heart with one searing kiss.

Her father moved restlessly by her side. "Where in blazes is Amanda?"

"I think she had something to do," Meg said. She'd insisted that her sister attend a suffragette rally in Austin. Amanda had her heart set on it, and Meg saw no reason why she shouldn't go.

"Something to do?" Her father's eyebrows rose like two half moons. "What could be more important than being here today to celebrate?"

"Shh, Papa."

Spectators streamed into the courtroom, and soon, the seats were all taken, requiring latecomers to crowd in back or stand outside and hang through open windows.

"All rise," called the bailiff, and shuffling feet replaced the buzz of voices.

The judge walked in, his judicial robe trailing behind him like a flock of black birds. He took his place behind the bench and, with a single curt nod, motioned everyone to sit.

An expectant hush settled over the crowd as they waited for him to announce his decision—and wait they did. Judge Lynch was center stage, and he wasn't in any hurry to relinquish the spotlight. As such, he went to great lengths to explain how he had reached his decision. He spoke in legal terms that no one save the two lawyers could possibly interpret, but his message was clear to one and all. No one, with the possible exception of Abraham Lincoln, had ever had to make such a difficult decision.

Her father fidgeted. "In the name of Sam Hill, would the man get on with it?"

"Shh, Papa."

The hourglasses had long since run out of sand, and still the judge kept talking. "In my opinion, there is nothing as reprehensible as the law that permits breach-of-promise suits. Nor is there any law open to more abuse. Marriage is not a business and should not be regarded as such."

The judge paused to take a sip of water. "Having said that, I have to rule on the facts of the case. And the fact is that the accused did indeed lead the plaintiff to believe—"

Tommy jumped to his feet so quickly that his chair fell backward and crashed to the floor. A collective gasp filled the courtroom as all eyes turned to him.

"I never should have walked out on you!" Tommy shouted in a high, thin voice. "I'll marry you, Meg!"

Twenty-four

CONFUSION FOLLOWED TOMMY'S OUTBURST. MEG didn't know what to say, what to do, which way to turn. Barnes seemed equally befuddled. Papa just looked thunderstruck.

"What? What?" The judged reached for his hearing horn and stuck it against his ear. "What did you say?"

"I said—"

The rest of his sentence was drowned out by the buzz of spectators, which quickly turned into shouts of approval.

"He says he wants to marry her!" someone yelled out the window to the crowd waiting outside.

A peeved spectator in the back of the room took exception. "Hey, that's not fair! I have money riding on the judge ruling for the defense."

Grant rose to his feet. "Your Honor, I request—" The rest of his sentence was drowned out by whoops and hollers.

Lynch banged his gavel. "Order. Order in this court!"

Ignoring the judge, Tommy's father popped up and pointed his finger at Papa. "Lockwood," he yelled.

"You let your daughter marry my son, and I'll agree to a one-time town."

Thunderous applause and the stomping of feet followed his outburst.

"Order!" the judge bellowed. "There will be no showdown!" His pleas went unnoticed. Applause and shouts of approval drowned out both the judge's voice and the pounding of his gavel.

The blacksmith pumped his fist in the air. "It's about time. That's all I gotta say. Let's get these two young'uns married off so we can all live in peace."

"Hear, hear," shouted a man sitting next to him.

Not to be outdone, the mayor stood, his head encircled by blue smoke from his cigar. "I think that's a fine idea," he said. "What do you say, Lockwood?"

All eyes turned to Meg's father, whose face was as stoic as rock. "My daughter might not wish to marry—"

"Why wouldn't she wish to marry him?" someone bellowed. "If she's as heartbroken as you say she is, she'll welcome Tommy's change of heart."

Aware that everyone's attention had now shifted to her, Meg felt her heart pounding against her ribs. Her gaze sought Grant's. *Losing, Miss Lockwood? I'm afraid that's something of which I have no knowledge.*

She gasped for air and willed Grant to do something, say something. Much to her dismay, he remained seated and in conversation with his client. Had he planned this all along? Planned for Tommy's last-minute change of heart, should things start to go her way? She didn't want to believe it of him, but what else could she think? He'd made no secret about his feelings, about how much he loathed breach-of-promise suits. But never did she dream that he would go to such lengths to keep the judge from ruling in her favor.

"I-I…" She cast a pleading look at Barnes. *For goodness' sake, don't just sit there. Do something!*

"The lady says yes!" someone shouted, and the courtroom erupted again with shouts of joy.

"Order!" The judge's incessant banging finally gained control. "Counselors." He gave his bench another whack of his gavel and rose like a raven about to take flight.

"In my chamber. Now!"

❧

Meg walked out of the courtroom in a daze, only to find a noisy celebration in full swing. Two feuding families were about to join forces through marriage. At long last, the town would be united under one time zone.

Bells pealed out, the Farrell bell joining forces with the church bells to create a cacophony never before heard in the town. The Lockwood bell remained silent.

Sallie-May pushed her way through the throng of people. "Oh, Meg. I'm so sorry—"

She said more, but her voice was drowned out by the revelers.

Tommy caught up to Meg, and the crowd corralled them in a tight circle. Meg felt like her whole life was spinning out of control. A wooden puppet controlled by strings couldn't have felt more helpless.

The newspaper editor plied them with questions. "How did it feel when he proposed a second time?"

"Well, I—" She looked at Tommy, and he looked at her. "I was surprised," she murmured. *Surprise* didn't even begin to describe how she felt. *Tommy Farrell, I'll kill you. I swear I will!* Announcing his intention to marry her in court at the last possible moment was almost as bad as leaving her at the altar. Worse!

"When's the wedding?" someone called out.

"We haven't set a date yet," Tommy said, wiping beads of perspiration off his forehead with the back of his hand.

The minister interrupted. "I say we get these two young people married off as soon as possible. How about this weekend?"

Much to Meg's dismay, the celebration seemed to last forever. She just wanted to go home and hide. If it was possible to fall through a hole in the ground, she would have gladly done so, but never had the ground beneath her feet felt more solid.

Grant walked out of the courthouse. The crowd closed in around him like ants at a picnic. Folks patted him on the back and offered congratulations.

Meg felt a heavy weight crushing down on her.

So this *was* Grant's doing. She should have known. A big-city lawyer like him was bound to have a clever plan up his sleeve. He would do anything rather than lose a case.

So when did you think up the plan? Before we kissed? Or after?

His gaze met hers. His face was inscrutable and his dark eyes even more so, letting nothing in and even less out. After a moment, he turned and vanished amid the crowd of well-wishers. Had he physically trampled on her heart, it couldn't have hurt more.

∽

The sheriff stepped out of his office just as Grant rode past on his horse. "Why, you sneaky dog, you," he called after him. "Congratulations."

Ignoring him, Grant urged Chester into a full gallop.

People actually thought that Tommy's courtroom shenanigans had been a legal trick.

As if he would agree to such a thing. He still couldn't believe Tommy had acted on his own. Grant hadn't thought the young man had it in him. Even more surprising, Meg seemed to go along with it.

He'd obviously attached more importance to their New Year's kiss than she had. How could he have been so wrong?

He was so focused on his thoughts that at first he didn't see the widow Rockwell dragging a small table across the street. When he did, he was tempted to keep going, but she looked so weary that he didn't have the heart.

Dismounting, he tethered his horse to the fence. "Here, let me help you with that."

The woman's face melted into a grateful smile. "Thank you, Mr. Garrison. Much obliged."

He picked up the table and hauled it across the street. "Didn't we move this yesterday?"

She looked blank. "Was it just yesterday? Why, I guess it was." She pulled her shawl tight around her shoulders. "Which house do you think I should live in?"

"Beats me," Grant said. "They both look the same." In truth, the houses were identical down to the blue trim.

She pointed to the stairs at the side of one house. "As a child, my husband slept upstairs in the loft."

Her eyes glazed over, and a look of confusion crossed her face. "Or was it that house?"

Grant suddenly realized that the woman wasn't off her rocker, as he had supposed; rather, she was grieving, and that was something he knew about.

Recalling how good it had felt to talk to Meg about his sister, he said, "Tell me about your husband, Mrs. Rockwell."

The woman looked surprised and then pleased. "You want to know about my Charley?"

"Yes, and I'll tell you about Meg."

"Who's Meg?"

"What?"

"You said you'd tell me about Meg. Was she your wife?"

"No, no, I mean…" Grant shook his head. Where was his brain? "I meant to say Mary, my sister. I'll tell you about her."

But even as he spoke about his beloved twin, his mind kept drifting back to Meg.

❧

"I can't do this!" Meg cried out, hands planted on her waist.

At long last, she and Tommy had managed to escape the crowd of well-wishers. Now it was just the two of them, facing each other on her front porch like two combatants.

"I hafta marry you, Meg. Don't you see? It's the only honor'ble thing to do."

Tommy looked like he'd just been in a fight. Shirttails hanging over his trousers, he'd somehow managed to lose his bow tie, and his spiked hair stood on end as if it had been combed with an eggbeater.

"Don't talk to me about honor. If you were all that honorable, you would never have left me at the altar in the first place!"

"I don't blame you for bein' riled. If I was you, I'd be mad too."

"*Mad* doesn't even begin to describe how I feel!" She threw up her hands. "You knew the judge was about to rule in my favor. That's the only reason you agreed to marry me."

Tommy grimaced and raked his fingers through his hair. His shoulders drooped along with his expression. "Meg...the only way my family can come up with ten grand is if we sell the shop and mortgage the house. Even then"—he shook his head—"that won't even begin to pay for legal fees."

"Oh, Tommy, no. You can't do that."

"If I don't marry you, my family will end up at the county poor farm."

She felt trapped. Worse, she felt sorry for him. For the whole Farrell family. "I don't want your money, Tommy. I don't."

"It doesn't matter. The judge said if I don't marry you this time, I better come up with the big bucks else he's throwin' me in jail."

"Oh dear goodness." Her heart rose to her throat. "He can't do that."

"He's the judge. He can do anythin' he wants."

Her mind whirled. There had to be a way. "I'll have Papa talk to him. Tell him we don't want the money."

Tommy shook his head. "The judge made his

rulin'. There ain't nothin' we can do. 'Sides, everyone is countin' on the Farrell-Lockwood feud comin' to an end."

He was right. It was no longer just the two of them affected. It was the whole town. How did life become so complicated?

"What did Grant…uh…your lawyer say?" If Tommy noticed her slip of tongue, he gave no indication.

"He said that marryin' you was the only way out."

Tommy only confirmed what she already suspected, but still Meg felt her heart squeeze tight. "He…he said that?" So he *had* planned this all along. The kiss was just a…what? A ruse? A game? A way to keep her distracted?

"Don't look so horrified, Meg. You make it sound like marryin' me is the end of the world."

That's exactly what it felt like, but she didn't want to say as much. "What…what about Asia and the Pacific Islands?"

Tommy shrugged as if his dreams were of no consequence, but the faraway look in his eyes told her otherwise. "It won't be so bad. I'll be a good husband to you, Meg. I swear. I'll never stray, and I won't cause you any more problems. Maybe one day, we can go the islands. Just you and me."

She tried to breathe, but something like a boulder was lodged in her chest. This whole mess was partly her fault. If only she'd known her true feelings from the start. She loved Tommy, she did, but now she realized that love was more like for a brother than a lover.

"I don't know, Tommy…"

"We don't have to go to the islands," he said,

misunderstanding her hesitation. "We can go to Paris or Ireland or even Italy."

The more he talked, the lower Meg's spirits fell. Her feelings for Tommy had never caused her to lose sleep or stop eating, not even when he'd left her at the altar. Not like the people who wrote to Miss Lonely Hearts. She'd experienced none of the tortured misery of a broken love affair as described in the letters. None of the heartache.

If she could force herself to love Tommy as he deserved to be loved, she would gladly do so. But the heart had a mind of its own, and the most anyone could do was follow.

Of course, that didn't mean she had feelings for anyone else. Certainly not for Grant. Not now. Not after he'd thrown her under a train, so to speak, rather than lose his case.

"There's somethin' else," Tommy said, staring down at his feet.

She gulped and knotted her hands by her sides in an effort to brace herself. Something in his voice told her that things were about to get a whole lot worse.

"What is it, Tommy?"

He looked up. "Judge Lynch is only in town for another week."

She frowned. "So?"

"That means that I have seven days to come up with ten grand or—"

Her stomach turned over. "Or...or what?"

"Marry you."

Twenty-five

JOSIE'S DOOR OPENED TO MEG'S KNOCK.

"Oh, Meg. Come in." Josie took Meg's hand and pulled her inside. "Are you all right?"

Meg gave a wooden nod. "As all right as I'll ever be."

Josie closed the door. "Come. Amanda's here, and I made us tea." She led the way into the kitchen.

Amanda didn't even wait for Meg to sit before bombarding her. "What is this I hear about you marrying Tommy? Everyone in town is talking about it. Are you out of your cotton-picking mind?"

Meg pulled out a chair and sat. "No. I mean yes. I mean I don't know."

Amanda leaned forward on crossed arms. "What do you mean, you don't know?"

Josie filled Meg's cup. "It's not her fault." She set the teapot on the table. "Tell Amanda what happened in court."

Meg sighed. "The judge was just about to give his ruling—"

"And he was about to rule for Meg," Josie interjected.

Meg reached into her sleeve for her handkerchief.

"That's when Tommy jumped up and said he wanted to marry me."

Amanda sat back, aghast. "And you accepted?"

Josie answered for her. "Meg had no choice. Not after Mr. Farrell and Papa agreed to make Two-Time a one-time town, but only after the wedding."

"What else could I do but say yes?" Meg asked. Everyone counted on the feud coming to an end, but that wasn't all. She then explained the impossible position Tommy was in. Had put her in. Grant had put them both in. "If we don't marry, his family will be in financial ruin. I don't even know if they can raise ten grand. Either way, we have less than a week to get married."

"A week!"

Josie nodded. "That's all time the judge will give them."

Meg sighed. "I asked Barnes to talk to him, but it was no use. The judge said we already have the fixings for a wedding, so there was no reason for delay."

Josie squeezed Meg's hand. "He also said that the sooner our two families are joined through marriage, the sooner the town's clocks could be synchronized."

"What does Papa say?" Amanda asked. "You know how he feels about Tommy. About the whole family. Surely he disapproves."

Meg dabbed at her eyes. "He agrees with the judge's decision."

"What!" Amanda's gaze darted from Meg to Josie and back again. "But he never wanted you to marry Tommy in the first place. He's never had a civil word to say about him. What made him change his mind?"

"He says my reputation is ruined. And he's right—it is. Who would want to marry me now after everything that's happened?"

Meg's thoughts traveled back to New Year's Eve. Grant sure hadn't made her feel like damaged goods that night. What a fool she was! Would she ever be able to trust another man?

"Oh, Meg," Josie said. "I'm sure some nice man will come along and see you for the wonderful, loving woman you are."

"I'm not so sure about that." Meg sighed. "Every man in town thinks I'll sue at the drop of a hat. Why, just the other day Mr. Harrison refused to sell me a bar of that new Ivory soap. Said he didn't want me suing if it didn't float."

Amanda made a face. "Trust me, you don't need floating soap, and you certainly don't need a man. Women have more choices today than poor Mama had. Marriage is no longer a woman's only option."

"Maybe not," Josie said, "but there are still more good reasons for getting married than not."

"Like bringing a town together," Meg added. If nothing else good came out of this marriage, at least she could take comfort in that.

Amanda wrinkled her nose. "And Papa agreed to the town having only one time?" she asked, looking as doubtful as she sounded.

"He didn't have much choice," Josie said. "I, for one, will be happy to see the end of this silly feud."

"Don't count on it." Amanda took a sip of tea before adding, "The clocks might change, but Papa's attitude won't. He doesn't see much beyond his own nose. Nor does he understand how his stubbornness affects others."

Meg's heart sank. What if she married Tommy and nothing changed? What if the town remained as divided as ever?

"We still don't know what caused the feud in the first place," Josie said.

"And probably never will," Meg added.

Josie regarded her with a worried frown. "Are you okay with this, Meg? Marrying Tommy?"

"It's for a good cause." Meg heaved a heavy sigh. Maybe given time, she and Tommy would come to love each other like a proper married couple should.

Amanda rolled her eyes. "And you make fun of my causes. At least I'm not required to change my name or kowtow to a man."

Josie's brow creased. "Meg, you didn't answer my question."

Meg took a deep breath. She didn't even know how to answer. "I did want to marry him at one time, but so much has happened. I just don't feel the same as I once did."

"Oh, Meg." Josie shook her head. "That's no way to start a marriage. What are you going to do?"

"I don't know," Meg said and looked away. "I just don't know."

Twenty-six

MEG STOOD IN FRONT OF THE MIRROR IN THE CHURCH anteroom, dressed in her wedding gown. Mama had done an amazing job of mending the tear, and it was almost invisible now. Too bad hearts couldn't be as easily patched.

It had been the longest week of Meg's life, and the shadows beneath her eyes attested to the fact that it had also been the hardest. Her sisters and Mama had left the room to take care of some last-minute preparations. Meg was grateful to be alone, though her thoughts gave her no comfort.

This was her wedding day, and she felt…what? Nervous? Anxious? Sad? Disheartened? Actually, she would settle for any of those feelings. But all she felt was numb.

She went through the motions with little thought or care. It was like everything was happening to someone else.

Following a quick tap on the door, her father's head popped in.

"Tommy's here," he said.

Meg tried not to let her dismay show. Any hope of him leaving her at the altar a second time was now gone. The sharp edge of guilt ripped through her. Tommy had done everything possible to make up for all the trouble he'd caused. He'd apologized, not just once but several times during the last few days. So why was she still holding a grudge, if that's what it was? Why did she feel so utterly trapped?

"He's early," she said, the words like acid on her tongue.

"He's not early at all," Papa said. "He's right on time. *Lockwood* time. Guess that means he plans to go through with the wedding. Got a minute?"

"Of course."

He pushed the door open all the way and stood gazing at her, a suspicious gleam in his eyes. "You look beautiful. Just like your mother did on her wedding day." He stepped into the room carrying a box and closed the door with a backward thrust of his foot.

Meg forced a smile. "And you look so handsome."

His tie was crooked and his hair slightly mussed, but somehow that made him look all the more endearing. It was easy to blame her father for the whole terrible mess, but the truth was she was equally at fault. Papa had warned her from the start to stay away from Tommy, insisting he was nothing but trouble. Had she not been so mule-headed, she might have listened. Instead, she'd rebelled by imagining her feelings for Tommy were more intense than they really were.

"I wanted to give you your wedding present. It just arrived from France." Setting the box on a chair, he pulled out a gold clock and placed it on the mantel.

"Oh, Papa. It's beautiful. But..." She checked her pendant watch. "But the time is wrong." It was running fast.

"Not wrong, my pet. That's the time that Farrell and I agreed upon. It's the standard time set by the Harvard College Observatory, adjusted by longitude and latitude. We're now running ahead of the sun." He shook his head. "God forgive us."

Meg flung her arms around her father's neck, and he got all red in the face. She pulled away. "Does this mean that you and Farrell have made up?"

A look of disgust crossed his face. "Let's not go overboard. We agreed to synchronize the town's clocks, that's all." He forced her to look at him with a finger to her chin. "Isn't that enough?"

She pulled away. "I'm going to be a Farrell, Papa." If that wasn't enough, she and Tommy planned to live with his parents for at least the first year of their marriage.

He rolled his eyes. "Don't remind me."

"Papa!"

"All right, all right. Not another disparaging word about the Farrells will pass through these lips."

She laughed. She couldn't help it. "That will be the day."

He laughed too.

She grew serious. "Papa." She knew better than to pursue the subject, but she couldn't seem to help herself. "What happened to make you and Mr. Farrell hate each other?"

He heaved a sigh. "Meg, we've been over this before."

"But you've never answered my question."

Her father's face darkened. "Why do you keep pushing it, Meg? Nothing that happened in the past affects you."

"Oh, but it does, Papa. Don't you see? It affects this whole town. Our families not talking will affect every holiday, our children…"

At the mention of children, her father grimaced. The thought of sharing grandchildren with his nemesis was evidently a hard pill to swallow. "I'll see that it doesn't. I just want you to be happy."

That's all she wanted too, but she didn't know if that was possible now. Tommy didn't make her heart flutter. Not the way Grant Garrison did when he kissed her. She drew in her breath. Why did the memory continue to haunt her? She now knew the kiss had meant nothing to him. That she meant nothing to him. So why keep obsessing over it? And on her wedding day, no less.

"All right. Have it your way." She started for the door.

"Where are you going?"

"To find Tommy's father. If you won't tell me the reason for the feud, maybe my future father-in-law will."

He threw up his hands. "For the love of Pete. What has gotten into you?"

"I mean it. If you won't tell me, I'll insist that Mr. Farrell does." In a softer voice she added, "You owe me that much, Papa."

Her father's shoulders sagged, and he rubbed his hands over his face. Finally he said, "What I'm about to tell you stays in this room. You're not to breathe a word of this to anyone. Do I make myself clear?"

She stilled. "I won't. I promise."

He glanced at the clock as if hoping for a reprieve. When the clock remained silent, he began, "Farrell was in love with your mother. And she was in love—" He stopped as if the mere effort of saying the words was too much for him to bear.

Meg's breath caught. Mama and Mr. Farrell? It didn't seem possible. "But…but she married you."

"Only because…she had to."

It took a moment for the meaning of his words to become clear. "You mean you and Mama—"

When he made no effort to correct her, she shook her head in disbelief. Mama was so upright and moral—the perfect lady. Never had Meg heard her say an unkind word or known her to do anything improper. It was unthinkable.

"Don't blame your mother," her father said as if guessing her thoughts. "In my youth, I was quite irresistible."

"You're still irresistible today, Papa." The hair at his temples was more white than brown, and his waist was as wide as his shoulders, but he still cut a debonair figure, especially today in his dark suit.

This brought a shadow of a smile to his face. "Ah, dear daughter. And I thought you would hate me if you knew what I'd done."

"I could never hate you, Papa." Her mind whirled. "Does…does Josie know?"

A shadow of regret crossed his face. "I'm in the clock business. How can I tell my oldest daughter that her father timed her birth so poorly?"

"So your feud with Mr. Farrell started over Mama?"

"Once your mother found out she was in a family

way, she had no choice but to marry me." His voice broke, and a look of unbearable pain etched his face.

Meg had always felt closer to her father than her mother—it was easier to relate to her father's many faults than her mother's calm perfection. But now she felt her alliance shift. Had her mother really loved another man all her life? Did all that grace and loving devotion hide a broken heart? Had her mother sacrificed her happiness for the greater good? Much as Meg was about to do...

"I love your mother very much," he said, as if guessing her thoughts. "I don't know what I'd do if I lost her."

"But Mr. Farrell is married. He would never... Mama would never—" Something suddenly occurred to her. "That's why you've kept this town divided all these years. To keep Mama away from Mr. Farrell."

It was hard to believe that a forty-minute time disparity could create such a wide gap between people, but it had worked like a charm. Small differences often led to great disputes.

"I'm not perfect." He suddenly looked every bit his age. "I know that's hard to accept."

"It's not as hard as you might think, Papa," she said without irony.

He shrugged. "Now that you know, does it change anything?"

Yes, it did. It changed everything. It was like waking up and suddenly finding out she belonged to a different family. She looked at her father now like one might look at a stranger.

"Papa, you agreed to put the feud to rest as a wedding gift."

"I agreed to standard time. That's all I agreed to. I won't have my daughter living under Farrell time."

"Please, Papa. We need to bring the town together. The only way we can do that is by putting all the clocks in synchrony. The emotional ones as well as the physical ones."

"Sorry, Meg. What you ask of me…" He shook his head. With that, he turned and left the room.

Twenty-seven

SHAKEN BY THE CONVERSATION WITH HER FATHER AND all he'd revealed, Meg slipped out through the side door of the church. She needed air. More than that, she needed to think. Mama and Mr. Farrell? She still couldn't believe it.

The bare-limbed trees offered no reprieve from the white sun that glared down on her like a scolding parent. The brisk air did little to cool her flushed face. In the distance, a train wound its way to the depot like a metal snake, the shrill whistle echoing the silent cry of her heart.

She walked out of the church to the cemetery, holding the hem of her wedding gown just above her satin slippers. Everything she'd thought she knew about her parents was false. It was as if her whole world had been turned upside down.

Her eyes filled with tears as she stumbled blindly between the headstones. Her mother had done the noble thing by marrying the father of her child. But was it the right thing to do? Might not the town have been better off if her mother had followed her heart instead?

The thought held her frozen to the spot. How could something that happened more than twenty years ago have such a profound impact on the present?

A sob rose in her breast. Not that long ago, she had wanted to marry Tommy. It seemed like the natural progression of a friendship that had spanned almost a lifetime. But now marrying him seemed so terribly, utterly wrong…

For most of her life, she'd done what was expected of her. She seldom felt compelled to fight convention. Not like Amanda. So why did she feel this sudden need to flee? Maybe…she was still angry at Tommy for leaving her at the altar the first time. Yes, that was it. That had to be it.

But he was there at the church now, waiting for her. That had to count for something, didn't it? She loved him before, or at least thought that she had. Maybe in time she could learn to love him again.

Moving blindly along the path, she ended up in front of a gray headstone. It marked the grave of Grant's sister.

She blinked away the vision of Grant standing here the day they'd first met, but that only left room for other visions of him. Other memories.

So what do you say about celebrating New Year's with me a second time?

Oh, how she wished she'd followed her heart. Things not done were always the most regretted. The words not said to a loved one. A missed opportunity for kindness. An action not taken.

She imagined herself in her golden years rambling on about the kiss that got away, much like Old

Man Johnson and his fish tales. Wondering, always wondering—would Grant's second kiss have been as delightful as the first? Would it have lived up to the promise in his eyes or satisfied the gnawing hunger inside her?

In an effort to bury her thoughts once and for all, she stared at the simple gravestone. The inscription read: *Mary Garrison Simpson—beloved wife, daughter, sister.*

On impulse, she pulled a flower from her hair and placed it on the grave.

Beloved wife.

Would anyone ever think that of her? Would Tommy?

"Meg?"

Recognizing Grant's voice, she looked up, and it was as if the earth suddenly stopped turning.

No, no, no. She had no right to feel this way—as if the very heavens had opened up. Not after the trick he pulled in the courtroom. Not while another man waited for her in the church.

He glanced down at the flower on his sister's grave, and his gaze traveled up Meg to meet her eyes.

It was then that she noticed he was carrying a carpetbag, and her heart sank.

❧

Grant stared at the vision in front of him and felt a squeezing pain in his chest. Had his heart been caught in a vise, it couldn't have hurt more.

Meg looked even more beautiful than she had the day he'd first set eyes on her all those weeks ago. She wore the same dress—the dress that cost an astounding two hundred and fifty-nine dollars and was worth every penny.

She had been angry when first they'd met. Today he saw…what? Not happiness. Not joy. Not like when she had danced in the street. Or on the night he'd taken her in his arms and kissed her. Instead he saw hurt, confusion, maybe even panic, and his heart jolted with alarm.

"Are you all right?" he asked.

She blinked as if holding back tears. "I'm fine," she said with a wave of dismissal. Her gaze dropped to his carpetbag, and he heard her intake of breath. "You're leaving?"

He nodded. "On the next train."

Her eyes sought his, and he detected accusatory lights in their depths. "B-but why? Is it because you miss Boston?"

It's because I had the misfortune of falling in love with you. But he couldn't say that. Not while she stood in her wedding gown ready to marry another man.

"I don't think this is the place for a big-city lawyer like me."

Meg moistened her lips, and he recalled the taste and feel of those lips on his.

"I guess you never did find out what your sister saw in the town," she said.

His gaze dropped to the single white flower on his sister's grave. "Nope, never did."

For a moment they stared at each other without speaking. Grant's mind traveled back to New Year's Eve. Did he really hold her in his arms? Devour those pretty, soft lips? Did she really kiss him back?

The memory felt so real and yet…it also seemed like a dream.

"I wish you and Tommy much happiness."

She looked at him through misty eyes. The words trembling on her lips remained unspoken until at last they fell away, never to be revealed.

Organ music drifted through the open door of the church. Buggies, carriages, and wagons were parked on the street in front. No doubt the church was packed with wedding guests.

A distant train whistle reminded Grant of the time. "I better go. I have a train to catch." *And if I don't leave, I'm likely to do something completely off limits… Something that both of us will end up regretting.*

Her sister Josie beckoned from the steps of the church. "Hurry, Meg. It's almost time."

"I'll be right there." Meg turned back to him. "I guess this is good-bye." Her voice was cool, distant, so unlike the warmth he remembered from other occasions. From New Year's Eve…

"Guess so," he said, unable to say anything so final.

He watched her walk away, and it felt as if she had taken a piece of his heart with her. "Meg!"

She stopped and turned. She stood a short distance away in a cloud of satin with the sun at her back, in her hair. The vision would forever be engraved on his heart. Whether that would be a curse or a blessing, only time would tell.

Grant took an unsteady breath. The three little words he wanted to say stuck in his throat. "Be happy," he managed at length.

There was nothing left to say; nothing else he dared

say. With a heavy heart, he placed a hand briefly on his sister's tombstone. Part of his past was dead to him, and at that moment it seemed like the future was too. He started along the path leading out of the cemetery, the longest walk of his life.

"Grant!"

He whirled around, and his heart thudded.

"I almost came back," she called softly. "On New Year's Eve. I almost came back to celebrate a second time."

He stared at her. Why was she telling him this now? To punish him for kissing her? To torture him? To make him feel worse than he already did?

"I'm glad I didn't," she said, the words like arrows to his heart.

Her gaze locked with his just as the church bells pealed from the tower. And just like that she was gone—gone to become another man's bride.

Twenty-eight

MEG STARED IN THE MIRROR WHILE MAMA FUSSED over her, but all she could see was the look on Grant's face when she told him she'd almost returned to him.

He'd looked stoic, unmoved, as if she had simply pointed out the weather. If she hadn't believed it before, she now knew it without a doubt—she meant nothing to him. The kiss they'd shared held no meaning. At least not for him.

At that moment in the cemetery, she'd hated him. Hated him for making her feel things she never wanted to feel. Hated him for fooling her with his kindness. Hated him for making her feel more like herself in his presence than she had ever felt before.

And so she'd lied. Said she was glad. Yes, she'd wanted to hurt him. Hurt him like she was hurting. But he didn't even offer her that satisfaction. Instead, he'd just gazed at her, seemingly indifferent and unaffected.

"Hold still," Mama said. "You're as wiggly as a kitten."

Mama caught Meg's gaze in the mirror and frowned. "Why so sad? You should be happy."

Not wanting Mama to worry, Meg forced a smile. "I'm just nervous."

Mama put the hairbrush down. "That's how it should be."

Meg frowned. "How can you say that?"

Mama ran a knuckle along Meg's cheek. "Nervousness shows how deep your feelings are, and that you're taking this marriage seriously."

Meg grimaced inside. Mama always assumed the best in people, the best in her daughters, and turned a blind eye to another's faults. No doubt she would be shocked if she knew the real cause of Meg's misery.

Mama stepped back and reached for the wedding veil. Lifting it over Meg's head, she lowered it gently onto the floral wreath and fluffed out the Brussels lace. "There. You look perfect. Don't you agree, girls?"

Amanda made a face. "If you don't mind looking like frosted cake. As for me and Josie"—her mouth puckered as she stared down at her own rose dress— "we look like we're wearing lampshades."

Mama frowned. "Amanda, of all the things to say."

"It's true, Mama. I don't know why women dress in silly gowns and veils just to get married." She glowered at Meg. "And insist that their sisters do likewise."

"It's tradition," Mama said.

"Tradition has nothing to do with it." Amanda rolled her eyes. "They're simply doing what Queen Victoria did. I guess we should be glad she didn't marry in the altogether."

"Amanda, really," Mama scolded. "Such talk. In a church, no less."

Josie tucked a curl behind her ear. "And what, may I ask, will you wear on your wedding day?"

Amanda gave her head a toss. "If I were to get married—which of course I have no intention of doing—I would walk down the aisle in a cracker barrel and insist my bridesmaids do the same."

Normally, such silly chatter would make Meg laugh, but not today. She didn't feel much like laughing or even smiling. If only her heart didn't feel so heavy. If only she could breathe… Whoever invented the corset deserved to be shot. Whoever invented love…

She closed her eyes. Not love. What she felt for Grant couldn't be love. She refused to let it be love. Yes, she was sorry to see him go. Yes, she had hoped for a different reaction when she called out to him. Certainly she didn't expect him to just stand there and stare.

Had he given the slightest indication he regretted how the trial ended, regretted the part he'd played in her unhappy ending, she would have…what? Thrown herself into his arms? Forgiven him?

As much as she hated thinking herself capable of leaving Tommy at the altar as he had left her—and letting down the whole town to boot—she would gladly have done so and more. All it would have taken was one encouraging word from Grant.

She cringed. Oh dear goodness. What a thought. On her wedding day, no less. A knot formed in her throat, and her corset cut into her as she tried to inhale.

A knock at the door brought her back to the present. Papa popped his head into the room. "It's time," he announced.

Mama checked Meg over once again, straightening the satin bow on her bustle and smoothing her veil. Meg watched her like one might watch a stranger. *Oh, Mama, did you feel like this on your wedding day? Were you in love with another man? Did it feel like your heart was breaking? Did you think you wanted to die?*

Mama stepped back, her eyes misty. "You make a perfect bride," she said.

No, not perfect. She was anything but perfect. *Oh, Mama, if you only knew...*

Josie and Amanda reached for their bouquets. Luckily, the pink and white ranunculus and dianthus from Mama's winter garden were in full bloom. The flowers were tied with a pretty white bow.

Papa walked up to Meg. With a gentlemanly bow, he crooked his elbow. "Ready?"

Meg gave a slight nod. Holding her own bouquet in one hand, she slipped her other hand through the circle of his arm. Her corset squeezed her middle and her shoes pinched her feet, but nothing hurt as much as the stabbing pain in her heart.

Josie stepped out of the room first, and Amanda followed.

Walking by her father's side on wooden feet, Meg closed her eyes. *I love Tommy, I do. Everything will be all right, and I'll be the best wife I can possibly be—just like Mama.*

If it kills me!

❧

Papa led Meg out of the anteroom and walked her to the chapel. Her legs threatened to buckle, and she felt sick to her stomach. Worse, her lungs battled with her corset for nearly every breath she took.

The organ music swelled as they drew closer to the open doors of the sanctuary. Never had the church been so packed. The trial and all the publicity that followed had made Meg's second wedding a not-to-be-missed event. Even people who wouldn't normally be caught dead in a house of worship were on hand, sitting on the edge of their seats as if the pews were made of nettle.

In contrast, Sallie-May looked perfectly at ease, batting eyelashes and all, having planted herself next to one of the richest cattlemen in Two-Time.

The organ played the "Wedding March," and rising, the guests turned to face the back of the church. Meg entered by her father's side.

Reverend Wellmaker and Tommy stood in front of the altar. Tommy made a handsome groom in his black suit, even with his crooked bow tie.

"Here we go," Papa said, patting the arm clinging to his. They started down the aisle, and the slippers on Meg's feet felt like they were cast in steel.

Halfway to the altar, she pulled her arm away. "Stop, Papa," she whispered.

He froze in his tracks. "What's wrong? What's the matter?"

"I need to talk to Tommy."

"Now?" Her father stared at her. "You need to talk to him *now*?"

"It's important." She needed Tommy's assurances that this was the right thing to do. Was he having similar feelings of hopelessness? The same growing panic? Was this how he'd felt when he left her at the altar that first time?

"Great thunder, can't it wait until after you're man and wife?"

"No, Papa, it can't wait. That would be too late."

"What could possibly be so important?"

"I can't tell you. I just need to talk to Tommy." Maybe she just had cold feet. Perhaps every bride felt this way walking down the aisle. Maybe nervousness was a good thing, like her mother said, but she had to make certain.

"For the love of…"

While Meg and Papa stood arguing, the organist played louder, as if trying to drown out their escalating voices. Wedding guests craned their necks, and a buzz of whispers rippled from the front of the chapel to the back.

What is it? What could be wrong?

Josie and Amanda, standing on either side of Tommy, glanced at each other and shrugged. Seated in a front pew, Mama whispered something to Ralph. Finally, the minister hurried up the aisle to see what was causing the delay.

Reverend Wellmaker's eyes looked grave behind his spectacles. "Is there a problem?"

"My daughter wishes to speak to her fiancé," Papa explained, his tone edged in exasperation.

The minister's eyebrows knitted. "Now?"

"Yes, now," Papa said, forgetting to lower his voice.

The preacher looked a bit startled but nodded. "Very well." He motioned for the anxious-looking bridegroom to join them.

Tommy hurried up the aisle. "What's the matter? What's wrong?"

Meg resisted the urge to straighten his crooked bow tie. "I'm not sure we're doing the right thing," she said, keeping her voice low so the guests couldn't hear.

He grimaced as if in pain. "You know I have to marry you. The judge—"

"I don't want your money."

"I know, but it's not just the money. You know everyone is dependin' on us to end that stupid feud. If we don't get married, the town will always be divided by time, and you know what a mess that is."

Meg curled her hands by her side. He'd only confirmed what she already knew; there was no way out. "It's just that…you want to do other things, and so do I."

"Are you saying you don't want to marry me?" he asked, forgetting to whisper.

His shocked reaction surprised her. Apparently, he'd forgotten that the whole mess started because *he* didn't want to wed *her*.

"Is that what you mean?" he asked when she failed to answer.

Meg reminded him to keep his voice down with a quick glance at the curious onlookers.

Oh God, she mustn't think of Grant. Not now. Not ever. "But of course I'll marry you," she said too quickly and looked away.

He hesitated. "Meg, I know this has been really hard on you. I'll make it up to you, I swear—"

Tommy's father shot up from the front pew.

"What's going on?" he demanded, storming up the aisle toward them.

The organist stopped playing, and all eyes were fixed on the little knot of people in the center aisle.

Papa glared at Farrell. "My daughter has something she wants to say to Tommy."

Farrell glowered back. "This better not be one of your tricks, Lockwood. You made a deal, and I expect you to stick to it."

Papa's face flushed furiously. "This is between the bride and groom, so don't go dragging your lariat where it don't belong."

Mr. Farrell's nose was practically on Papa's chin, his balding head shaking with righteous indignation. "I'll put my lariat any danged place I please. And furthermore—"

Tempers rose along with heated voices. Meg tugged on her father's coat. "Papa, please!"

Oh dear goodness! What had she done?

Mama raced up the aisle, followed by Josie and Amanda.

"Henry!"

With Josie's help, Amanda tried pulling Papa away. Refusing to budge, Papa and Farrell continued to spew insults as if competing in a one-upmanship contest.

"You're nothing but a dang—"

"Why, you—"

Mr. Farrell advanced. Tommy grabbed his father's arm, but it was too late. Mr. Farrell's fist shot out, missing Papa by a mile and Reverend Wellmaker by mere inches.

Papa staggered backward, a surprised look on his face.

Meg covered her mouth in horror and turned to her brother-in-law. "Please make them stop."

Affording her a sympathetic look, Ralph laid a firm hand on Papa's shoulder. "Let's all go outside and discuss this calmly…"

His unruffled manner and reasonable voice was no match for the years of pent-up emotions that had suddenly come unleashed. Paying him no heed, Papa pulled away and barreled toward Farrell headfirst.

The moment Papa made contact, the wind whooshed out of Farrell. "*Oomph!*" The two of them fell to the floor in a hopeless tangle.

"Oh no!" Meg cried. She grabbed hold of Tommy's arm. "Do something. Make them stop!"

Before Tommy had a chance to act, a loud boom shook the building to its foundation. The explosive sound rattled the stained glass windows, and a gas light fixture crashed to the floor.

Panic filled the church. Women screamed, and some guests fell to their knees in prayer. Others scrambled to climb over pews and each other.

Ralph whirled around to face the double doors in back, along with several other men. "Sounds like it came from the train depot."

Meg's heart flew to her throat. *Oh no! Grant…*

Dropping her bouquet, she ripped off her veil and joined the throng racing out of the church.

Twenty-nine

UNBELIEVABLE CHAOS GREETED MEG AND THE OTHERS at the train depot. People ran in every direction, doctors carrying black bags converging on the center of the mess.

Eyes burning from the smoke, Meg stared at the tangled mass of steel in horror. Two trains had collided, one rear-ending the other. The first locomotive remained upright, but several carriages tilted at sharp angles. The back of the train, including the caboose, coiled around itself like a snake about to strike.

The second train had fared worse. The engine lay completely on its side, and the rest of the train fanned into a tangled heap parallel to the twisted tracks. Smoke poured out of its collapsed smokestack, and men rushed by with buckets of water.

"Grant!" Meg picked her way through the confusion, stepping over pieces of steel and broken glass. Steam blasted out of a toppled black dome. Already, dazed passengers were being pulled out of the wreckage. Some victims were able to walk; others had to be carried out. Many had head injuries, while several had bloody arms and other wounds. One poor man's leg was bent into an L shape.

Shouts rang out. "Over here! Over here."

Children's cries mingled with the excited voices of rescuers and the hollow groans of the injured.

"The train came too early," someone shouted.

"No, the other one left too late."

Seeing Grant sitting on the side holding his head, Meg let out a cry of relief and ran to him, calling his name.

But the man looking up at her wasn't Grant. Didn't even look like him. He was much older and had a full beard. He clutched at her satin skirt, leaving a smear of blood behind. A wide gash gaped open across his forehead.

Meg looked for someone to help him, but the rescuers were all occupied elsewhere. Forcing herself to remain calm, she glanced around for something to stem the flow of blood. Unable to find anything, she tried tearing a piece of fabric from her wedding gown, but it wouldn't give. She had better luck tearing a square of cotton off her petticoat.

Ever so gently, she pressed it against the man's head. "Hold this," she said.

Eyes glazed, he lifted his hand to the soft fabric.

After making him as comfortable as possible, Meg stared at the horror around her. It was a nightmare, like a war zone.

"Help me, miss," someone called. It was an elderly man with blood-soaked trousers.

Meg dropped to her knees by his side. "Do you have a knife?"

He gave a weak nod of the head. "Boot."

His knife was what was commonly called an Arkansas toothpick. Gripping it in her hand, she carefully cut away his trouser leg, revealing a deep gash. He was losing a lot of blood, so she cut a thin strip of fabric from her petticoat and tied it high around his leg as a tourniquet.

Spotting a doctor, she waved him over. "We need you over here."

One by one, she helped make dazed and wounded passengers as comfortable as possible. She calmed small children and their traumatized parents. She cut bandages and tourniquets from her petticoat with the knife and, when she ran out of fabric, started on her wedding dress. Soon her skirt hung about her in tatters, the bodice smeared with blood. Still, she kept going while she searched the crowd for Grant. But there were too many people and too much confusion to see beyond a few feet.

Somewhere she'd lost a satin slipper and didn't even know it until she stubbed her toe.

"Meg, over here!" Amanda called, waving both hands above her head. She and Josie were frantically helping a young woman heavy with child.

"I think the baby is coming," Amanda cried. The woman's anguished face confirmed it.

Meg felt a moment of panic. She knew nothing about birthing, and neither did her sisters. "I'll fetch a doctor."

She hastened away. The entire town seemed to have turned out to help. Friends, neighbors, and enemies worked side by side. She caught a glimpse of Tommy and his pa atop a carriage car lying on its side, struggling to pull an injured man out of a train window.

The doctors were all occupied with the injured and too busy to respond to her pleas for help. Finally, Meg spotted Mrs. Connor, the town midwife, rocking a crying baby.

Jostling through the crowd, she reached the woman's side. "Please," she shouted to be heard above the infant's wails. "There's a woman about to give birth. Over there by the baggage room."

Mrs. Connor shoved the baby into Meg's arms and hurried away.

Meg looked down at the tiny red face. Girl or boy? She couldn't tell. "Where's your mama, eh?" She placed the infant on her shoulder. Rocking the child back and forth, she talked in a soothing voice. The infant stopped crying and fell asleep.

Sometime later, a woman's shouts reached Meg's ears. "Where's my baby! Anyone seen my baby?"

The woman was pretty badly bruised, with one leg in a splint, but when Meg gently placed the child in her arms, she managed a cry of pure joy.

"Thank you, thank you," the woman whispered in an emotional voice and promptly burst into tears. "Thank you."

Leaving mother and child, Meg turned just as a doctor finished putting a victim's arm in a splint. Only the top of the man's head was visible, but the sight of blond hair was enough to tell her it wasn't Grant.

The smell of oil, coal, and creosote ties made Meg feel dizzy, and her stomach churned. The early throes of panic that had swept the station had now given way to confusion.

Hours passed. Dusk fell, and the cool air turned frigid. A wagonload of blankets arrived, and Meg gathered an armful to distribute to the victims, saving a couple for the woman in labor.

When it looked as if that time had arrived, Meg and Amanda held up a blanket to provide a measure of privacy for the expectant mother while Josie assisted the midwife.

"Push," Mrs. Connor ordered. Amazingly she was able to stay calm, as if delivering a baby under such dire circumstances was a normal occurrence.

The young woman's screams could be heard over the shouts of rescue workers, sending chills down Meg's back. Nearby, the woman's injured husband struggled to sit up, and Meg rushed to his side. The young father's leg was wrapped in a blood-soaked kerchief. He looked in worse condition than his laboring wife. His face was pale, and his eyes were round in fear.

"Is she gonna—"

Meg assured him with a nod and a smile. "She's in good hands."

After what seemed like forever but was really only minutes, Mrs. Connor sang out, "You have a baby boy." The happy news was followed by a baby's thin cry, which brought smiles all around.

"A son?" The father looked like he never heard of such a thing.

"Yes, yes," Meg assured him. "You have a beautiful son."

Tears filled his eyes. "Is…is he all right?"

Meg laughed. "I'd say anyone with lungs like that is more than all right."

The father's wide smile warmed Meg's heart. "Well now…"

While the midwife attended the needs of the child's weary mother, Josie wrapped the infant in a blanket and placed the small bundle in his father's arms.

Meg watched with a worried frown. Josie's and Ralph's three-year marriage had failed to produce a child, but nothing in her sister's manner suggested anything but delight for the young couple. Josie's ability to put her own feelings aside to embrace another's happiness was something to be envied.

Meg stared at father and son through misty eyes. Their new connection was the most beautiful sight she had ever seen. Even Amanda had a suspicious gleam in her eyes. Never had Meg seen her younger sister look so fiercely engrossed without holding a picket sign.

Since Mrs. Connor had everything under control, Meg walked the length of the depot, winding around the wounded and dodging carts and workers, stopping to help anyone in need. The whole time she worked, her eyes, her heart, her soul searched for Grant.

God, where is he? She'd seen many miracles here today. Was it too much to hope for yet another?

Thirty

MEG COULDN'T REMEMBER EVER FEELING SO EXHAUSTED. Her muscles were sore from helping to lift the injured into wagons. Her eyes watered from the smell of smoke and heated steel. She was cold, so very, very cold, her fingers frozen to the bone.

Her wedding gown was completely ruined. Not only was it ripped to shreds, but it was also splattered with blood. Even Mama's expert sewing skills couldn't repair the damage this time. Several inches of fabric were missing from her hem. The bow from the top of her bustle had been made into a splint for a young man's injured leg. The sleeves of her dress had become bandages.

Shivering, she blew on her hands, praying she'd find Grant at last. And then she saw him on the other side of the depot. Just like that, her misery disappeared.

All at once, she was moving, her frozen feet barely skimming the wooden platform. She called his name and he turned, his face seeming to light up at the sight of her. Or maybe it was just a trick of the eye.

She was tempted, so tempted, to toss propriety to the wind and throw her arms around him. Instead, she touched his bloodied hand. He was coatless, his shirt splattered with blood and the sleeves rolled up to his elbows.

"You're hurt."

"No." His fingers encircled her wrists, stopping her probing search for his injury. "I wasn't on the train."

She gazed up at him, her heart so full of relief and thanksgiving that she thought it would burst. "What?"

"It's not my blood. I wasn't on the train—"

A million questions flitted through her mind, but before she could get the words out, a male voice called, "We need help!"

Grant glanced over his shoulder. "Be right there." He turned back to her, his face suffused with concern. "Your dress…"

Suddenly aware that his fingers were still pressing into her flesh, she pulled her hand away. Blushing beneath his steady gaze, she lowered her eyes.

"I-I must look dreadful."

No sooner were the words out of her mouth than she regretted them. How could she worry about appearances when so many people were hurting? Nevertheless, she reached up to smooth her hair. The pins had fallen out, and locks tumbled down her back in tangled curls.

"You look—" He wagged his head as if shaking away whatever he had been about to say. "You're cold," he said instead, his voice husky.

Arms crossed in front, Meg hugged herself to ward off the chill. "It doesn't matter." Knowing he wasn't injured put her mind at rest so she could concentrate fully on the wounded passengers.

"Here." Grant pulled off his vest and wrapped it around her shoulders. "It's not much, but every little bit helps."

"Thank you." The manly smell of bay-rum hair tonic, sweat, and leather all but erased the metallic odor of blood. But it was the warmth left by his body that made her limbs tremble and her emotional barriers waver.

"Meg…" His gaze clung to her face. "Your wedding day. It was ruined…"

The reminder of his courtroom trick slammed into her, and she sucked in her breath. There wouldn't have been a wedding had he not done what he did, told Tommy what he had. Hurt unlike anything she'd ever known threatened to overwhelm her. Balling her hands into fists by her sides, she fought for control. This was neither the time nor the place to vent such thoughts.

"Go," she said, her muffled pain sounding like bitterness. "They need you."

Grant tilted his head in a frown. "Are you sure you're okay?"

Refusing to give in to tears, she looked away. "Just go."

He hesitated for a moment before vanishing into the milling crowd.

❦

Meg immediately recognized the young boy lying on the platform, and the shock of icy fear gripped her. Dropping to his side, she shook him gently on the shoulder.

"Tucker," she cried. "Tucker, wake up!"

He was one of the injured still waiting for medical attention. He wore no coat and only a thin shirt.

She shook him again, and this time, his eyes fluttered open. Air rushed out of her lungs. He was still alive. Thank God. He'd lain so still and looked so pale that for a moment she thought…

She pushed his hair away from his face and felt a lump on his forehead.

His newspaper bag was still slung across his body. It was common practice for local newsboys to sell papers on trains during depot stops.

Ever so carefully, Meg lifted the canvas bag over his head and pulled out a single newspaper, all he had left. She then folded the bag to make a pillow for his head.

"There you go. How's that?"

Tucker's eyelids drifted downward.

She glanced around, hoping to spot someone passing out blankets, but no such luck. Some of the poorer families in town placed newspapers in shoes and coat linings for warmth, and this gave her an idea. Spreading the newspaper over him, she tucked the ends beneath his small, still frame. She pulled the vest from her shoulder and placed it over the newspaper.

"Meg…"

At the sound of her father's voice, she lifted her head.

Still dressed in his wedding attire, Papa pulled off his coat and spread it over the boy.

Anger unlike any she had ever known welled up inside her. "You did this!" she cried. She indicated the chaos around them. "You and your stupid feud!"

Biting back tears, Meg felt her body tremble.

Her father's pale, haggard face elicited no sympathy. Instead, angry words bubbled out of her like lava from a volcano.

Papa looked stricken. "I never meant for any of this to happen."

She let out a sob. "But it did. It did!" Had it not been for the time confusion, the first train would have been long gone before the second train arrived. "And all because of Mama—"

"What about me?"

At the sound of her mother's voice, Meg swung around. Mama looked exhausted, her lips tinged blue from the cold. Her usually perfectly coiffed hair had come undone, and strands of fine hair fell around her face. Splotches of blood marred her green velvet dress.

"What about me?" her mother repeated, this time louder, but she was looking at Papa, not Meg.

"Nothing, my dear," Papa said. "Meg is just…upset."

Meg looked down at the boy. Tucker was still breathing, but he remained deathly still. Something inside her snapped. *Oh no, Papa. Not this time. We're not playing that game ever again!*

Fighting for control, she rose unsteadily to her feet and faced her mother. "I know, Mama. I know everything." It wasn't the place to air the family's dirty laundry, but it couldn't be helped. The Lockwood-Farrell feud had caused enough damage through the years—far too much—and it had to stop.

Her mother stared at her. "What do you know?"

"I know about you and…and Mr. Farrell." No sooner were the words out of Meg's mouth than she regretted them.

"Meg, please—" her father began, but her mother cut him off with a shake of her hand.

"What are you talking about?"

"I told her that you had feelings for him," Papa said. "That you loved him."

Mama stared at him, dumbfounded, and for a moment, no one said a word. When at last Mama spoke, her voice sounded distant. "What gave you that idea?"

When Papa failed to respond, Meg answered for him. "He said the only reason you married him was because you were in a family way."

Mama's jaw dropped. For a moment, the three of them stood so still that it was as if they were caught on an artist's canvas. Even the shouts of workers and the groans of the injured failed to penetrate the icy stillness that followed.

Finally, her mother pulled her gaze from Meg and turned to face Papa. "You said that?"

Papa took a step toward her, but Mama backed away. "All these years..." Raw hurt glittered in her eyes. "All these years... Is that what you thought?"

Papa rubbed his forehead. "What else could I think?"

"What else?" Her mother's voice quivered. "What *else*?"

"Mama, forgive me," Meg pleaded. "I shouldn't have said anything—"

"Hush, child. This is between your father and me!" Meg hardly recognized her mother's harsh voice.

Papa flung out his hands in that helpless way he did whenever he fell out of Mama's good graces. "I saw you," he said.

"You *saw* me?"

Papa nodded. "The night of the summer ball. I saw you in his arms."

Her mother pressed her hand to her forehead as if forcing a long-lost memory to surface. "What you *saw* was one friend helping another." Her hand dropped to her side, and her nostrils flared. "That was the night he told me he was in love with Deborah. I encouraged him to tell her how he felt." Deborah was Mr. Farrell's wife.

Papa frowned. "Are you…are you saying you never…? That he never…?"

Mama gestured to the wreckage around them. "You mean all this is because you saw me comforting a friend twenty-some years ago?"

Papa tried to explain, but Mama backed away, shaking her head.

"All these years, I thought the feud started because he opened up a clock shop, just like you did."

"It wasn't that." Papa reached out to Mama, his voice filled with remorse. "I honestly thought you and he… Will you ever forgive me, my love?"

"Forgive you? How can I? How can anyone?" Mama glanced at the young boy at Meg's feet and stormed away.

"Elizabeth, wait!"

But before he could chase after her, one of the rescue workers called to him. "I need a hand over here."

Papa glanced in Mama's direction, hesitated, then spun around to help pull an injured man out of the wreckage.

Recalling the look on her mother's face, Meg

blinked back tears and pressed a hand to her mouth. *Oh God, what have I done?*

A rustle of paper drew Meg's gaze downward.

The boy stirred, but his eyes remained shut. She dropped to her knees. "Tucker. Wake up."

Tucker's eyes flickered open, but it took a moment before he could focus. He looked confused, disoriented. "What happened? Where am I?"

Meg pressed a hand gently to his cheek. The lump on his forehead was now the size of an egg. "You were in an accident. A train accident."

"Am I going to die?"

"Certainly not," she said and tapped him gently on the nose.

No sooner had she voiced the words than she caught sight of Tucker's father. Jumping up, she waved her hands to gain his attention.

"Mr. Malone! Over here!"

Mr. Malone hurried to her side. Spotting his son, he fell to his knees, tears of relief rolling down his red, beefy face. "Tucker."

He cradled the boy in his arms, rocking him back and forth. "I was out of town and didn't know about the train crash till a short time ago."

Dr. Stybeck joined them, black bag in hand. He looked tired, the bags under his eyes the size of plums. Mr. Malone set his son down and moved away so the doctor could conduct his examination.

Meg patted the father's back. "He's strong and will soon be as good as new."

She wished she could say the same for Mama and Papa. She caught her lip between her teeth. Her dearest wish had been that the Lockwood-Farrell feud would finally end, and it looked like at long last it might.

But at what cost?

Thirty-one

AT NEARLY MIDNIGHT, SOMEONE SHOVED A CUP OF coffee into Grant's hand. The beverage was bitter, but the warmth was welcome. He wrapped his frozen fingers around the heated cup.

He hadn't seen Meg for hours, but now that the crowd was thinning, he looked for her again.

Maybe she'd gone home. He certainly hoped so. This was no place for a woman. It was no place for anyone, honestly, and he'd now seen enough blood to last a lifetime. Miraculously, there were no deaths, just broken bones, mild concussions, and the expected cuts and bruises.

Some of the injured had been carried away and placed in the back of wagons. Several victims were even able to walk the short distance to town. Given the condition of the trains, that was saying something.

Still, it could have been so much worse. The fact that the second train entered the depot at a reduced speed had helped to lessen the impact.

A few minutes earlier, and Grant would have been on that train. At the very last minute, he'd changed his mind about leaving town. No sooner had he led his horse out of a boxcar and away from the tracks than the accident occurred.

Shuddering, he could still recall the horror of hearing the rumble of the second train as it slid into the station. The shrill whistle sounded like a scream. Or was that his own scream he heard?

The impact had shaken the ground and practically knocked him off his feet. His horse had reared back on his hind legs, and it was all Grant could do to hold on to him. The grinding and buckling of steel seemed to go on forever. It was as if time had suddenly stood still.

Pushing the memory away, he stepped aside to let two volunteers carrying an injured man pass by. Cots had been hauled from the nearby deserted fort and set up in the church and saloons. Anyone with a room to spare agreed to take in guests, and others had been sent to the hotel. In a surprising act of generosity, the proprietor had donated several rooms to the wounded, free of charge.

Earlier, he had seen Mr. Malone carry his boy away. Grant hadn't even known Tucker was on one of the trains. Fortunately, the lad didn't look seriously injured.

Grant leaned against a wooden post. Volunteers were still checking the wreckage for more victims, but right now, it looked like the worst was over. It was the first real breather Grant had had since the initial crash.

Overhead, the sky was dark and starless, but the light from dozens of lanterns flooded the area. Tiny moths flitted around the shiny glass globes.

Grant watched Old Man Crawford and his

bagpipe-playing neighbor carry a man to one of the wagons. For once, they weren't shouting at each other.

The mayor stopped to help an elderly man to his feet. The dogcatcher, Mutton, used his snare pole to retrieve a child's rag doll from the rubble. The owner, a little girl of maybe two or three, was all smiles when he presented it to her.

Grant had often wondered what his sister found to love about Texas. He'd laughed when Meg suggested it was the people.

Would those be the feuding, opinionated people? Or the gun-toting people with short fuses?

No feuds at the moment. No guns either. Even Farrell and Lockwood were working together like congenial neighbors. Maybe his sister had been on to something after all.

Grant swallowed the last of his coffee and pulled away from the post, careful to step around the injured waiting to be transported.

Spotting Meg, he felt his heart skip a beat and paused a moment to gather his wits.

She was on her knees spooning hot soup into the mouth of a matronly woman. Just the sight of her lifted his fatigue. Her face pale, she looked tired and in worse shape than some of the victims. He longed to go to her, longed to take her in his arms and carry her away from this mess. Take her somewhere safe. But he had no right to such thoughts. No right at all, because she was now another man's wife.

Still, he couldn't bring himself to walk away. No doubt she could use a hot cup of coffee.

He stepped into the baggage room where food

and beverages had been set up, but already the coffee was gone. Leaving his empty cup behind, he walked back outside.

Something caught his eyes on the wooden platform. A satin slipper, the kind worn by brides... He bent to swoop it up. It felt soft to his touch and reminded him anew of all the things about Meg he had come to know and...yes, even love. Her loyalty to her family. Her concern for animals. Her wit and laughter. Her smile and...

He didn't want to think about the rest. Somehow he had to find a way to put such memories out of his mind, not only now, but forever.

Shaking away his thoughts, he threaded a path through the crowd, anxious to return the dainty slipper to its owner.

Meg looked up when he approached and then turned to spoon more soup into an elderly woman's mouth. He recognized the woman from church as Mrs. Ashley. Her snowy-white hair matted with blood, she pressed her trembling hands together. Whether from cold, delayed shock, or old age, Grant couldn't begin to guess.

He waited for Meg to look at him again, and when she didn't, he frowned. She seemed to be purposely ignoring him. Had he only imagined her concern earlier when she thought he was injured?

"I found your shoe," he said. The toes that peeped though her tattered stocking looked almost blue with cold.

"Much obliged." Without looking at him, she dipped the soup spoon into the bowl.

"I believe there's a certain procedure for returning a lady's slipper." God forgive him, but he was having a hard time thinking of her as another man's wife.

At last, she lifted her gaze to him, her eyes dark and unfathomable. "Is that so?"

"Absolutely." He dropped to one knee and reached beneath the tattered hem of her gown for her ankle. She tried pulling her foot away, but he wouldn't let go. He held her foot for a moment to warm it before slipping on the satin shoe.

Mrs. Ashley spread her parched lips. "Just like in the fairy tale."

"Yes, well…" Meg pulled her foot away, a look of annoyance on her face. She raised a delicately shaped eyebrow. "What's so amusing?"

Grant hadn't even realized he was smiling. "I think I know what my sister found to like about Two-Time." He indicated the dozens of volunteers still checking the twisted wreckage for possible victims. "You were right. It *was* the people."

Something flickered in the depth of her eyes—a memory? "Maybe some good came out of today after all," she said.

"Maybe." Did he only imagine a thawing in her manner? A softening of her eyes?

"Does that mean you plan on staying?" she asked, guiding the spoon into the woman's mouth.

Before he could answer, Meg's sister Josie appeared at her side. "We're ready. Tommy's waiting to take us all home."

"I'll be there as soon as I see Mrs. Ashley into a wagon," Meg said.

She set the bowl down and helped the widow to her feet. Mrs. Ashley paled and swayed slightly. Fearing she might fall, Grant took her other arm. His gaze locked with Meg's for a moment before they both looked away.

Together, they walked Mrs. Ashley to one of the many wagons waiting to take survivors to town.

Grant guided the woman's slight frame up a wagon ramp and onto the hay-covered bed. Meg managed to find a spare blanket. He helped her unfold the woolen cover and spread it over Mrs. Ashley's prone body. He accidentally touched Meg's soft hand and didn't pull away as quickly as he should have. Their gazes held, and his heart beat faster. Something like a light passed between them before Meg turned to the widow.

"Are you warm enough?" she asked in a thin, breathless voice.

The elderly woman reached up to pat Meg's arm. "I'm fine, thanks to your good care. Now go home. You look flushed, and you've done enough."

Meg hesitated. "Are you sure you'll be all right?"

"I'll stay with her," Grant said.

Meg gazed up at him, lips parted. Mrs. Ashley was right; Meg's cheeks did look red. Because of him? Did that mean he affected her every bit as much as she affected him? A flash of unbelievable joy rushed through him, but was quickly followed by a feeling of utter despair and self-loathing. She was a married woman, and he had no right—no right at all—thinking such thoughts.

"Her son lives in Austin," Meg was saying. "He should be notified."

Grant swallowed hard and managed a wooden nod. "I'll take care of it."

Meg needed to go home. She looked dead on her feet. This time, he detected gratitude on her face, but it still required more of Mrs. Ashley's assurances before she finally agreed to leave.

Grant watched her walk away and join her new husband. Tommy wrapped a blanket around Meg's shoulder. Arm around her, he led her away just like any loving spouse would do.

Feeling a crushing blow, Grant stood by the wagon, holding Mrs. Ashley's parched hand in his own and wishing it was another hand he held.

"Such a pretty young thing," the widow said, her voice splintered with fatigue.

"Yes, she is."

The faded old eyes seemed to reach into the very depths of him. "Too bad real life isn't like a fairy tale."

❧

After dropping Josie off, Tommy pulled up in front of Meg's house and set the carriage brake.

Amanda climbed out of the backseat and, with a weary wave, headed up the walkway to the porch without waiting for Meg.

Meg started to follow, but Tommy stopped her with a hand to her arm. "Meg, wait. We need to talk."

"Not tonight, Tommy. It's been a long, hard day and—"

"Please, Meg…" Releasing her, he scrubbed his face with his hands. "I'm sorry that our weddin' was ruined again."

She slumped back in her seat. In the dim gas street-light, Tommy looked haggard, his hair mussed along with his clothes.

"Not your fault."

He dropped his hands. "I've been thinking about what you said in church."

She hardly had the strength left to hold up her head. "We'll talk some more…tomorrow."

He tapped his fingers on the seat rail. "You don't want to marry me, do you? Admit it."

Running her hands up her arms for warmth, she tried to think of a way to explain, a way that sounded less hurtful. It was no use. She was too tired to form a lie or even to choose her words.

"No," she said, grateful that honesty required so little energy.

He rested his head on the back of his seat. "Because I left you at the altar? Is that it?" He lifted his head. "You wanted to get back at me."

Pained that he would think such a thing of her, she shook her head. "Oh, Tommy, no. It wasn't because you left me. It was because I-I realized you were right. The two of us getting married would be a mistake. We're very different and don't even want the same things. It just took me longer than you to realize it."

That was true as far as it went, but how could she tell him the rest? How could she tell him that she was in love with someone else? With Grant.

Oh, sweet heaven. She was even too tired to lie to herself.

"You sure picked a funny time to decide that," he said, his voice tight.

"And you didn't?"

He grimaced. "I never meant to hurt you, Meg. You're the best friend I ever had."

"I know." A lump formed in her throat. "You're mine too. I'm going to miss you something awful. Promise me you'll write. No matter where in the world you go."

He made a face. "Fat chance of me goin' anywhere now. If I don't come up with ten grand, I'll be writin' from the iron-bar hotel."

"Oh, Tommy!" She'd completely forgotten the judge's ruling. The canceled wedding would cost Tommy dearly, and it was all her fault. "There's got to be another way." She couldn't let her best friend go to jail!

He let out a sigh. "If there is, let's hope my lawyer finds it. But I have to be honest. It don't look good."

The mere mention of Grant made her ache inside, and she looked away. How she hated her traitorous heart, hated feeling so out of control. Why couldn't she love the man she wanted to love? Why did her heart dictate that she had to love another?

For the longest while, neither of them spoke, each lost in their private thoughts.

Tommy broke the silence. "If I go to jail, will you visit me?"

"Of course I will," she said. "I'll even sneak a file to you."

He laughed. "'Member the time I had to stay after school for truancy? You released a mouse in the classroom so that I could catch it and look like a hero in the teacher's eyes."

Meg did remember. "It worked, didn't it?"

"Yeah, and I never had to stay after school again after that."

"No, and the other kids were mad because you practically got away with murder."

The memory made her feel worse, because it only reminded her of the close friendship they'd shared through the years and had almost ruined with two ill-advised weddings.

"Papa sure did make a mess of things, didn't he?"

"Not just your pa. Mine too," Tommy said. "I only wish I knew what started the feud in the first place."

Not wanting to betray her father's confidence, Meg hesitated. She and Tommy had discussed that issue numerous times, and he was just as puzzled as she had been. It didn't seem right to keep what she now knew to herself. Their fathers' feud had affected him every bit as much as it had affected her, and he deserved to know.

"Papa thought my mother and your father…"

Tommy stared at her in astonishment. "Are you sayin'…?"

She shook her head. "He was wrong. There was never anything between them. Pa knows that now."

"But all these years—"

"I know, Tommy. I know. They were once good friends, just like you and me."

"Swear that nothin' like that will happen to us," he said with earnest intent. "That we'll always remain friends, no matter what."

Managing a weak smile, Meg patted him on the arm. "I promise." She shivered in the damp night air. "I-I'd better go. It's late, and we both need to get some sleep." She climbed out of the wagon and dragged herself up the path to the porch.

"Meg," he called, his voice a whip in the cold night air.

She turned. "What is it, Tommy?"

"You sure did make a fine-lookin' bride."

She smiled. "And you made a fine-looking groom." With that, she turned and walked into the house.

Thirty-two

THE MORNING FOLLOWING THE TRAIN CRASH, MEG raced down the hall to Amanda's room. Shoving her arms in the sleeves of her dressing gown, she grimaced with every move. Her muscles were sore, and it felt as if someone had stuck a knife in the small of her back. To top things off, she had a king-size headache. She'd hardly slept a wink, but her aching bones and sore muscles were the least of her worries. Every time she'd closed her eyes, the horrible images of the train wreck flashed into her head.

Not bothering to knock, she burst into the room. "Wake up, Mandy. We need to talk."

Amanda lifted her head from the pillow and regarded Meg through buttonhole eyes.

Meg yanked open the draperies, and the early-morning light fell across the bed like a blazing sword.

Amanda groaned and reached for the mechanical clock on her bedside table, bringing it to her squinting eyes.

"It's not even seven," she said in a foggy voice. Amanda preferred nights to mornings.

"I know, but this is important."

Replacing the clock, Amanda sat up and yawned. "It better be." Her eyes widened as if something suddenly occurred to her. "Papa…?"

"He's fine. At least health-wise, but Mama left."

Amanda rubbed her forehead as if trying to make sense of Meg's words. "What do you mean, left?"

"I mean she left Papa. She moved in with Josie and Ralph."

Amanda blinked and suddenly looked wide awake. "But…but why?"

"Mama blames Papa for the train wreck." Meg left out the part she had played in their parents' problems. "It was a new engineer, and he got confused about the time." According to the morning paper, his watch had stopped. When he asked a passenger for the time, he was given Farrell time instead of train time. "He was late leaving the depot."

Amanda shook her head, and her tangled blond hair fell down her back. "I can't believe it. I mean, Mama and Papa. They were meant to be together. Like…like oil and water."

"Oil and water don't mix," Meg said, pulling the ties of her dressing gown together.

"You know what I mean." Amanda threw back the covers and swung her feet to the floor. "What are we going to do?"

"I don't know. But we have to think of something." She turned toward the door. "Get dressed, and we'll see what Josie has to say."

"What about you? Your wedding?"

Meg's hand froze on the doorknob. Had it only

been a day since that nightmare of a wedding? So much had happened since that it seemed like a lifetime ago.

"It's over," she said. "Tommy and I won't be getting married." She then left the room, her thoughts flying in a dozen different directions. What would happen to Mama and Papa? Tommy too? Would he really have to go to jail? If Grant had another rabbit in his hat, he better pull it out—fast!

⁂

Grant opened his eyes to a stream of sunlight and groaned. He felt like he'd been thrown from a horse and trampled. He couldn't have hurt more if he'd actually been in that train wreck.

A half-dressed woman loomed over him. He rubbed the grit from his eyes and looked again. This time, the painting of Mrs. Abbott came into focus, releasing a flood of memories.

What seemed at first a nightmare had turned out to be true. The train crash. The injured. Meg…

He rubbed his bristled chin. His mouth was lined with cotton, and his head throbbed.

By the time he'd arrived at the boardinghouse, his landlady had already given his room to one of the train victims. She gave him a choice: bed down with her or take the brocaded sofa in the parlor. He picked the lesser of two evils. Though his aching back could probably argue the fact.

Grimacing, Grant stretched his cramped legs and almost knocked over a fringed lamp with his foot. He finally unwound himself enough to plant his feet on the floor. He reached into his carpetbag for a fresh pair of trousers and a clean shirt.

Hand on his back, he straightened his spine like an arthritic old man rising from a chair and then dressed.

No sooner had he buttoned his shirt than Mrs. Abbott entered the room, voice first. "Ah, you're awake. Breakfast is almost ready. Would you like some hot coffee?"

"Yes, please." His voice rattled in his throat. "The stronger, the better."

Without bothering with shoes, socks, or combing his hair, he joined her in the dining room.

She tossed a nod toward the oak sideboard. "I emptied your pockets. Your clothes are soaking in a bucket of water, but I don't know that we can get all that blood out."

He glanced at his money clip, pocket watch, and unused train ticket. "Much obliged."

He waited for Mrs. Abbott to fill his coffee cup before seating himself at the table. She tottered into the kitchen, her voice floating back to him.

"None of the other boarders have come down yet."

The grandfather clock in the parlor told him it was a little after ten. On a normal weekday, most of the others would have left by now to open shops and other businesses, but no one got much sleep last night.

Realizing suddenly that his landlady was staring at him as if expecting him to say something, he nodded. "It's just lucky no one died."

"I'll say." She poured herself a cup of coffee and sat at the table opposite him. "It's a cryin' shame about the Lockwood weddin' though."

A stabbing pain shot through him. "You…you were there?"

"'Course I was. Wouldn't miss it for the world. And I have to tell you, I never saw anything like it in my life."

He took a long sip of coffee. He didn't want to hear about Meg's wedding. Didn't want to think about it.

"Now the poor girl's got to do it all over again."

He lowered his cup. "Do what?"

"Why, get married of course."

He froze. "Are you saying Farrell left her at the altar again?"

"Oh no, nothin' like that. He was there all right. Lookin' all spiffy and serious as a Baptist preacher. But…" She shrugged.

Grant set his cup on the saucer. "Go on."

"When Miss Lockwood started down the aisle…" Mrs. Abbott clapped her hands to her chest. "I have to say, she was the most beautiful bride you ever set your eyes on. What a dress…"

She went into great detail describing the dress Grant was all too familiar with and forcing him to interrupt. "Are you saying that the train crash stopped the wedding?" He hated to be rude, but a man had only so much patience.

The question rendered her silent for a moment. "It wasn't just the train crash. But not to worry. I'm sure they'll have another weddin'. You know what they say? The third time's the charm."

Grant stared at her, not sure he'd heard right. "What do you mean it wasn't just the train crash? Why didn't they go through with the wedding?"

"I don't rightly know. One minute she was walkin' down the aisle…"

"Yes, yes, go on."

"Then suddenly she stopped."

Sitting forward, he grabbed hold of the table. "Why? What made her stop?"

"Beats me. All I know is that she and her pa started arguin'." Mrs. Abbott rolled her eyes. "You won't believe how they carried on. In church, no less. Mr. Farrell…" She shook her head.

For mercy's sake, would she get on with it? "What about Mr. Farrell?"

"Why, he jumped into the fracas and so did the preacher. Have you ever heard anythin' so shockin' in your life? Before you knew it…" She rubbed her forehead as if the memory was too much for her to bear. "Haven't seen a brawl like that since I was in my prime. You won't believe the way men used to fight over me. I remember the time that this handsome Texas Ranger drifted into town… 'Course, back then, they didn't call them Rangers. They called them minutemen or some such thin'. Anyway, as I was saying, this handsome man—"

"Let me get this straight. You're saying that Miss Lockwood didn't marry Mr. Farrell."

Mrs. Abbott blinked. "How could she? Before the fight broke up, the train crashed."

Grant sat back. His heart pounded, and hot blood shot through his veins. *Meg isn't married.* It shouldn't matter to him, but it did. It mattered more than words could say.

Meg isn't married.

He jumped up and made a dash for the door.

"Aren't you gonna to eat your breakfast?" Mrs. Abbott called after him.

He stormed outside without answering her.

Meg isn't married…

❧

Grant shot through the gate at the end of the walkway and barreled down the road. He stepped on a sharp rock and cursed himself for not putting on shoes and socks.

He hobbled past Mrs. Rockwell, who was dragging a chair across the street. Cowboy streaked by chasing Mr. Ferguson's dog. Mr. Crawford hung out of his upstairs window shouting at his neighbor.

"Dad-blame it. Do you know what time it is? I'll kill you dead. I swear I will!"

One would never guess that the two men had worked side by side the previous night in perfect harmony.

Grant made a beeline straight down the middle of the narrow lane. He didn't even flinch when gunfire rent the air. Nor did he slow when Mr. Sloan crossed his path chasing the Johnson boy.

"You come back here, you young whippersnapper. Those are my carrots you stole…"

Reaching the end of the block, Grant jogged up the two steps leading to the Lockwood front porch and pounded on the door.

Seconds later, Meg opened the door and his already-racing heart skipped a beat.

"Grant." Her luminous eyes rounded. "What… what are you doing here?"

After a halfhearted effort to tuck his shirt inside

his trousers, he raked his hand through his hair but doubted it did any good. He looked anything but his usual conservative Boston lawyer self. He hadn't even shaved, for crying out loud.

Meg glanced over her shoulder and stepped outside, closing the door behind her. She stood so close he could see the gold flecks at the tips of her lush eyelashes. She couldn't possibly know what she was doing to him, how her nearness made his heart turn over and made every part of him ache to take her in his arms.

She was dressed in a floral print skirt and white lace shirtwaist tied at the neckline with a pretty blue bow, but she looked pale and distraught.

Alarmed, Grant stepped forward. Had she been crying? "Are you all right?" he asked.

"Just…a family problem," she said, though her voice, her face, suggested much more. Her forehead creased, and her gaze dropped the length of him. "Is something wrong?"

"Wrong?" No, nothing's wrong. Not now that he knew she wasn't wed. *Except that I'm standing here in bare feet and feeling perfectly ridiculous.* "I'm here on… on business."

He couldn't bring himself to tell her why he was really here. Not till he knew the full story. Knew why she had stopped her wedding, and if he had even the remotest chance of winning her heart.

She pulled her gaze away from his feet. "Business?"

Grant rubbed his bristly chin and groaned inwardly.

She moistened her lips. "Did anyone…" Her forehead furrowed. "Did everyone make it through the night?"

He nodded. "Far as I know."

"That's good news." Meg pressed a hand to her chest. "You said you were here on business. Is it about Tommy?"

"Tommy?" It took a beat for him to remember who the heck Tommy was. "Oh, you mean Tommy Farrell." His client. And the man she didn't marry.

"None of what happened was his fault," she said. "Surely the judge will take that into account."

"Before I talk to the judge, I need to know what you plan to do."

She frowned. "I'm sorry…"

Grant momentarily lost himself in the turquoise depths of her eyes. "When do you plan to reschedule your wedding?"

She shook her head. "It's over. We won't be getting married."

His heart practically leaped out of his chest. "Why? Why won't you marry him?" *Is it because of me? Is it because our kiss still haunts you as it haunts me?*

"Tommy has other things he wants to do, and so do I."

He stepped forward. "Like what? What other things?"

"Just…things," she said vaguely.

He stopped short of taking her in his arms, but only because a horse and wagon drove by. A man seen hugging an unmarried woman in broad daylight would appear ill-mannered, even by Texas standards, and wouldn't the editor of the *Two-Time Gazette* have a field day with that! Grant could see the headline now: BAREFOOTED LAWYER ACCOSTS JILTED BRIDE.

Meg gave her head a slight toss. "So, you see, your plan didn't work."

"Plan?" He stared at her, trying to make sense of the hurt he heard in her voice and saw in her eyes. What plan? Before he could make sense of it, she confused him further by placing a beseeching hand on his arm.

"Please…you mustn't let Tommy go to jail." She pulled her hand away, leaving behind the burning memory of her touch. "I won't marry him, and I don't want his money."

It shamed Grant to realize that he hadn't given a thought to how her decision would affect his client. "I can probably talk the judge into giving Tommy more time to meet the demands of his sentence, but…I'm afraid that's all I can do. Lynch's mind is made up."

He heard her intake of breath, but she said nothing.

"May I ask you something?"

Her chin inched up a notch. "Of course."

"You said something in the cemetery…about New Year's. That you almost came back to celebrate a second time."

Her cheeks reddened, and she looked away. "I felt sorry for you. Your sister…and you being away from home and all."

He stared at her, stunned. "You…you felt sorry for me?" Was that all it was? Pity?

There were many reasons for kissing someone, but pity had to be the least desirable.

Her gaze met his. "I can't imagine being away from family," she said. "Especially during the holidays."

The dogcatcher's wagon rumbled by. Another gunshot sounded. A dog barked. The earth continued to turn, and yet…it felt like the end of the world. His world.

"I better go." He turned abruptly.

Meg called after him. "Please, Grant. Don't let Tommy go to jail. I do love him, you know."

With those crushing words ringing in his head, he stalked away.

❧

Meg watched Grant stride down the middle of the street. Not even his unkempt appearance could hide his male appeal.

She should never have said she'd felt sorry for him. She knew it even before she saw the stricken look on his face. What she'd really wanted to say was that she'd felt the depth of his grief and loneliness that New Year's Eve and had wanted to soothe his pain.

That was the God-honest truth as far as it went, but there was more. Much more. The moment their lips met, it was as if the whole world had been created for the sole purpose of bringing the two of them together.

But she couldn't say that, not quite that way. It seemed too personal. Too intimate. Too close to the heart.

She forced herself to breathe, but it did nothing to relieve the pain. How was it possible to hurt so much without a physical wound? Nothing written in the Miss Lonely Hearts column compared with the misery that cloaked her like a shroud. This only added to her guilt.

Tommy agreed that marriage was not right for them and didn't blame her for anything that had happened. Would he have been so understanding if he had known she was in love with another? In love with Grant?

She'd tried fighting it, denying it, but she could no longer ignore the truth. The train wreck had made certain of that. She'd known it in her terror. Fearing that Grant was injured or even dead made such pretenses fall by the wayside. Just the mere thought of not seeing him again had been more than she could bear.

Oh yes, she loved him. Loved him even though he'd let her marry another man rather than lose a case. Even though he'd betrayed her in the worst possible way.

How could she love such a man? The answer came from the whispers of her heart. Oh dear goodness. Given all the good qualities she knew he possessed— his kindness and compassion—how could she not?

Thirty-three

MEG COULDN'T STAY ANGRY AT PAPA FOR LONG, no matter how hard she tried. The truth was, he worried her. Never had she seen him in such bad shape. Since Mama left, he'd walked around the house like a lost puppy. Meg prepared his favorite meals, but he only picked at his food. His face already appeared gaunt. Shadows skirted his eyes, and a network of deep lines made his skin resemble drought-parched ground.

The meticulous schedule he'd always followed fell by the wayside. Suddenly time seemed to hold no meaning for him. He arrived at the shop late and left early. He slept in fits and starts.

Late that Friday night, she heard him pacing the floor. Unable to sleep herself, she drew on her dressing gown and ran to his room with bare feet. She knocked on his bedroom door and, when he didn't answer, cracked it open. A sliver of light spilled into the dark hall.

"Papa?"

He turned to stare at her, his face haggard and his sunken eyes red. "How could I have been so stupid?" he muttered as if talking to himself.

She entered the room, closing the door behind her. She hated seeing him so distraught when he had always been so robust and strong. As a child, she'd thought he was a giant who could do no wrong. He'd taught her how to stand up for herself against school ruffians and walked the floor with her whenever she was hurt or feverish.

She was only five when he taught her how to adjust the grandfather clock in the parlor. She was so short that she had to stand on a stool to reach the pendulums, but he'd patiently instructed her until she could do it herself.

Though they'd had their share of battles through the years, never once did she doubt his love for her.

Now the tables had turned, requiring Meg to comfort him. Taking him by the hand, she led him to the chair in the corner where Mama liked to read, a mistake she realized as soon as he was seated.

The sweet fragrance of lavender perfume scented the air, bringing visions of her mother to mind. On the table next to the chair, a pearl earbob lay beside the book of poetry Papa had given Mama on their last anniversary.

Meg knelt by her father's side, holding his hand as he'd held hers so many times in the past.

"You're not stupid, Papa."

"People could have been killed."

"That's true, but thank God nobody was." She wasn't normally one to believe in miracles, but the lack of serious injuries had made a true believer of her.

"Your mother has every right to hate me."

"She doesn't hate you, Papa." Mama didn't have it

in her to hate anyone. "She's just hurt. Give her time, and she'll come around."

He stared at the palms of his hands. "I can fix every timepiece that was ever made with these hands."

"I know, Papa. I know."

"But I can't fix the damage that has been done. Not to your mother. Not to this town."

"Yes, you can, Papa. By ending the feud and changing the way we keep time."

"The only way that can happen is if I agree to Farrell time. But that's based on some ridiculous formula that's scientifically invalid. My father and grandfather would turn over in their graves."

"But at least that would bring peace to the town."

He frowned. "But it wouldn't solve the train problem. They would still be running on a different time schedule. There could still be more accidents."

"Surely the train wreck made Mr. Farrell realize that things can't go on as they are."

Papa sighed. "All because of me, his son must cough up ten grand or face jail. Do you think Farrell would agree to anything I have to say?" He shook his head.

"You must try, Papa."

Even as she said it, she knew the chasm between the two men was too wide to bridge. As a child, she'd believed her father could do anything, but now she harbored no such illusions. The hardest thing about growing up was learning to accept parents as the flawed people they really were, warts and all.

She laid her head on his lap, her heart heavy. "They say time heals all wounds, Papa."

"Not all of them, Meg. Not all."

❦

Things didn't fare much better at the shop the following Monday. Papa spent the better part of the morning staring at his tools as if trying to recall their purpose.

Meg tried her best to keep the shop running efficiently, while at the same time assisting customers. It didn't help that sleep, if it came at all, was fitful and filled with disturbing dreams—mostly about Grant, but also the train wreck.

Monday was clock-winding day, and the chore fell on her shoulders. Some clocks required tiny bronze keys. Others had metal cranks that had to be inserted onto winding points. Grandfather clocks were outfitted with weight chains that needed to be pulled down individually. Clocks that chimed on the quarter hour had more gears and therefore more winding points than clocks chiming only hourly. The tyranny of time knew no end. Along with the winding, hands had to be adjusted to accommodate the earth's movements. The sun rose farther in the north in the summer than it did in the winter, and that meant tiny adjustments had to be made throughout the year.

The complicated routine kept her hands busy but did nothing for her troubled thoughts.

Worry about Tommy and his family had made her toss and turn through the night. Besides that, she was so worried about Papa that she could barely eat. He just wasn't himself.

Though he loved debating politics, religion, and any other controversial subject, he didn't even bother to voice his opinion when Mr. Monroe objected to the proposed building of the Panama Canal.

"Makes no sense cutting across Panama," Monroe argued, trying to get a rise out of Papa. "Any fool reading a map can tell you that Nicaragua is the wiser choice."

"With all its volcanoes?" Meg asked, hoping to pull her father into the conversation, but her efforts failed. Soon even Mr. Monroe gave up and left.

At times it was necessary to repeat something before Papa would respond or answer a question. Even then, his answers were vague or incomplete. Sometimes he would stop talking midsentence, as if forgetting what he had been about to say.

Clocks in for repairs sat neglected on shelves. Meg had watched her father enough times to know how to take clocks apart and clean and oil the works, but some clocks needed more. They needed her father's expertise.

Meg tried to maintain a cheerful attitude, as much for her father's sake as their customers', but it was hard. No one but family knew that Mama had moved out of the house, and Meg hoped to keep it that way.

Fortunately, Papa mostly stayed hidden in the back of the shop. This relieved her of having to explain his inattention and his disheveled appearance. It also kept him out of gossip's way.

As did everything else in town, last week's train wreck caused much controversy. Some townsfolk blamed Papa for the train wreck, but Farrell took equal blame. Others claimed that the railroad should take full responsibility for not adhering to its own time schedule.

Meg's reputation was a whole different matter. She saw the looks and heard the whispers that were still all over town. *Better watch what you say in front of her. Don't promise her anything, or you might end up in court.*

Many thought she had halted her wedding to get even with Tommy for leaving her at the altar. As if she would do such a thing! Thanks to the *Gazette* though, she was no longer known as the "jilted bride." She was now referred to as the "avenging angel."

Even with all of that, it wasn't just the gossip that kept her close to home and shop. She feared bumping into Grant. She even stayed away from church on Sunday, knowing he would be there. Each time they met, the sight of him made forgetting him— forgetting all that they shared—that much harder.

There were many types of silence. Some, like the silence of nature, were comforting and restful. Some were empty and hollow, like the silence of death. But the worst silence of all was the silence of the human heart.

Thirty-four

MEG COULD HARDLY FIND A PATH TO JOSIE'S DOOR FOR all the pots of poinsettias and white ranunculus. The heady scents made Meg want to sneeze, and she pulled her handkerchief out of her sleeve. The last time she had seen so many flowers in one place was at a funeral.

"What's all this?" she asked when Josie answered her knock.

Josie rolled her eyes. "Papa. If Mama doesn't forgive him soon, I fear there'll be no more flowers left in all of Texas."

"Is Mama here?"

Josie nodded. "Come in."

The smell of freshly baked bread teased Meg's nose as she followed Josie into the kitchen. Mama was sitting at the table. Setting her needlepoint aside, she stood and greeted Meg with a smile and a hug.

"Have some tea," Mama said, taking her seat again.

Meg pulled out a chair opposite her. It had been more than two weeks since Mama moved out, but you would never know it by appearances. She looked calm and beautiful, as always. Not a good sign. Papa was a wreck, but her mother looked close to her usual self. Only the slightest shadows beneath her eyes suggested otherwise.

"You must come home, Mama. Papa misses you. We all do."

A frown flitted across her mother's forehead. "Did your father put you up to this?"

"He doesn't even know I'm here."

Mama gave her a slanted look before picking up her stitchery, but said nothing.

"Mama, please…"

Mama stabbed the fabric with a needle. "Meg, I know you mean well…"

"I just want our family back together again. Is that so wrong of me?"

Mama's hand stilled. "Even after what your father put us through? The trial? The train wreck? People could have been *killed*. If that's not bad enough, he ruined your wedding—and in church, no less. How can you forget what he did?"

Meg wanted to forget about the wedding. About *both* weddings. "Papa feels bad. You should see him, Mama. You wouldn't recognize him. He hardly eats and doesn't sleep, and he let all the clocks run down at the house."

As a child, Meg had hated the myriad of clocks that adorned the walls of the parlor and dining room. Hated how the bells and chimes kept urging her on. *Ticktock, bong, bong, cuckoo…* Time for school. Time for church. Time for this and time for that. Hurry, hurry, mustn't dawdle.

It seemed as if the sole purpose of time was to prove

one's limitations. She was always running late and could never rise to the challenge posed by the mountain of ticking clocks. There was never enough time to leisurely ponder the universe or contemplate the mysteries of young womanhood. There were always chores to be done, lessons to be learned. Wasting time was thought to be the eighth deadly sin. How strange that the thing that could cause such anxiety was thought to heal all wounds!

Mama's mouth drooped at the corners, and she suddenly looked tired. She jabbed the needle into the fabric and set the hoop on the table.

"I've been married to your father for a good many years. Since before the war… To find out that he doubted my love all this time, that the feud, the train wreck…all that was because of me." Shaking her head, Mama drew in her breath. "How can I forgive him for that?"

Meg exchanged a look with Josie. How much did her sister know about the circumstances of her birth? She drew her gaze back to her mother. "It wasn't you he didn't trust. Papa didn't trust himself. He didn't think himself worthy of you." Growing up, Meg would never have guessed that behind all Papa's swagger and bluster beat the heart of an insecure man. Even as she said it, the idea was hard to believe. "Don't you see, Mama?"

"No, I don't see." Elbow on the table, Mama placed a hand on her forehead and rested her head. "All he's ever been interested in is controlling time. I've had it up to here with his clocks and watches and bells and…"

"That's just his way of trying to look bigger and more important in your eyes," Josie said.

It was a surprising insight and one that Meg hadn't even considered. But isn't that how she wished she could look to Grant? Like one of those sophisticated women back east who could play the piano, wear French fashions, and read important books. How foolish to think that a plain, small-town girl like her could capture the heart of a man like him!

"That's…that's ridiculous."

"Mama, listen to me." Meg reached for her mother's hand. "Papa thought you married him because you had to." She clamped her mouth shut and glanced at Josie.

As if guessing her thoughts, Josie laid a hand on her shoulder. "I know, Meg. Mama was expecting me when she married Pa."

Meg drew her hand away from Mama and stared at her sister. "How did you—"

"When Grandmama died, she left us the family Bible. One day, I happened to notice the date of Mama and Papa's wedding written inside."

Mama nodded. "Your grandmother wrote my wedding date in the Bible before she knew I was expecting. How did *you* know?" she asked Meg.

"Papa told me. He feels guilty about what happened and blames himself."

Mama shook her head. "He has a lot to blame himself for, but not that. I take equal responsibility for what happened all those years ago." She reached for Josie's hand. "It was the best mistake I ever made."

Josie leaned over to kiss her mother on the cheek. She then turned to the steaming kettle on the stove.

Mama's eyes glazed over, as if she were traveling back through time. After a moment, a soft smile curved her mouth. "You should have seen your father when he was young. He was such a handsome man. I was afraid when he went to war that he'd come back broken like so many others, but he didn't. Instead, he got this town moving again. He brought us together by ringing his bell every hour. It made us laugh, but it was also a reminder that none of us were alone in this world. We were part of a community."

"Mama, how can we get Mr. Farrell and Papa to stop fighting?"

Her mother sighed. "Sometimes a feud becomes bigger than the people involved. I'm afraid that's what happened here." Her eyes filled with tears.

"Oh, Mama. Please don't cry," Meg said, even as her own eyes watered.

Josie rushed to join them, tears spilling down her cheeks, and the three of them sat around the table bawling like babies.

After a while, Meg calmed her weeping and rubbed her eyes with the palms of her hands. "Tell me what Papa has to do to make you come back."

Mama brushed away her tears with her fingers. "The one thing he's totally incapable of doing. The one thing his pride won't let him do. Make peace with Farrell."

༄

Grant left the jailhouse and mounted his horse. Kidd's hanging had been postponed for the holidays, and now the train wreck had caused another two-week delay.

Every able body had been needed to clear the tracks, leaving no one free to assemble the portable scaffold. That made the criminal the only one in town, other than doctors and salvage workers, to benefit from the crash.

Turning down Jackleg Row, Grant reined in his horse. A line of people waited in front of his office. What's more, similar lines snaked up to the doors of the other legal offices on the street.

What the—?

The answer to his question came moments later, after he dismounted.

"You Mr. Garrison?" asked a man with his arm in a sling.

"Yes, that's right."

His answer made everyone start talking at once. Grant signaled for them to stop. "Please, one at a time." He pointed to a thin man with a bandage on his head. "What can I do for you?"

The man spit out a wad of tobacco. "We're all here for the same reason. To sue the railroad."

Of course. Grant should have known. An accident of that magnitude was bound to tie the court up in litigation. "Let's go inside."

Unlocking the door to his office was like opening the floodgates. He almost got knocked over as people stampeded past him.

His books were still packed, and cartons towered in the corner of the room. A local shipping company had been paid to take them to the depot on the fatal day of the train crash, and it had taken them several days to return the boxes to his office, fortunately with little damage.

Grant regarded the group with mixed feelings. Given the inefficiency and time-consuming chore of filing individual lawsuits, he explained the concept of group litigation. It would have been easier to explain politics to a two-year-old.

"I don't understand. Why can't I file my own lawsuit?" one man on crutches demanded to know.

"You can. But you can accomplish the same thing by doing it as a group. Especially since some of the victims have already left town and won't be around to testify."

"Are you sayin' we hafta share the settl'ment?" another asked.

"Yes, but it will be a far larger settlement than if you file individually."

On and on the questions came, like a pump spitting out single drops of water. It took all morning and a portion of the afternoon to convince everyone that group litigation was best.

No sooner had the last client walked out of his office than Grant sank back in his chair and stared at the stack of paper on his desk. Now that Judge Lynch had left town, paperwork had to be dispatched to the county offices via mail or telegraph, causing yet another delay.

Judge Lynch did grant Tommy a ten-day extension to get his money together and pay the Lockwoods, and the judge had also surprised Grant with a proposal. He'd asked if Grant would be interested in serving on a committee to form a Texas bar association to promote the uniformity of legislature and uphold the honor of the legal profession.

It was an intriguing idea and one that Grant would

normally jump at, but he wasn't sure how long he planned to stay in town. He had a better feeling for Two-Time since the train wreck, though on the surface nothing had changed. Daily disputes with fists, firearms, or bluster were the norm.

Still, knowing how everything—even feuds—was forgotten in the face of trouble made the town's peculiarities easier to bear.

As for Meg…

No matter how hard he tried putting her out of his mind, memories kept popping up with annoying regularity. Sometimes he woke in the dead of night to the sound of her laughter. At other times he'd be thinking of something else entirely when a vision of her suddenly clouded his thoughts.

He grimaced as he recalled the last words she'd said to him. *I do love him, you know.*

He couldn't imagine anyone throwing that love away for a bunch of tropical isles. Tommy Farrell was a fool. But then, so was Grant for pining after a woman who had made it clear she had no interest in him whatsoever.

Business had started booming, and he was tempted to stay, but how could he? Every time he gazed out the window, he searched for her. Even worse, the hourly ring of the Lockwood bell reminded him of New Year's. Staying in this town would be nothing short of torture.

The door swung open, bringing him out of his reverie, and in walked Tucker.

Grant turned his swivel chair around to face the boy straight on. "Hi, Tucker. What can I do for you today?"

The swelling had gone down on Tucker's forehead, and only a slight blue mark appeared between strands of hay-colored hair. "I want to sue the railroad."

Grant folded his hands across his middle. Tucker had no way of knowing he would be included in the collective lawsuit. "Is that so?"

"Yeah, and since you're my lawyer, I figured you'd know what to do."

"Your law—" Grant rubbed his chin. He did say once he was the boy's lawyer, no denying that. He pointed to the chair. "Sit." The boy had gumption, that's for sure. In some ways Tucker reminded him of himself at that age. He waited for Tucker to be seated, then replied, "I'll handle your case." And because the boy looked so earnest and determined to file the lawsuit himself, Grant added, "But it'll cost you more than a quarter."

Tucker dug into his pocket. "That's okay. I can afford it. See..." He held out his hand. "This time I have two quarters."

❧

Meg arrived home after work to find Josie waiting on the Lockwoods' front porch.

"Everything all right? Is Mama...?"

"Mama's fine. Papa home?"

"No, he's still at the shop. Why?"

"I need to talk to you and Amanda. Is she here?"

"I don't know." Meg walked into the house and called up to the second floor. "Mandy!"

Amanda appeared at the top of the stairs with a mop in one hand and a kerchief on her head. Meg couldn't recall ever seeing her sister look so domesticated. Since Mama left, it had fallen to Amanda to tackle the regular household chores, which put her in a perpetually bad mood.

"What is it?" she snapped.

"Come on down. Josie's here."

Meg led Josie to the parlor where Amanda joined them, mop still in hand. "What's going on?" she demanded. "When's Mama coming home?"

Josie sighed. "I don't know. She still refuses to talk to Papa. She won't even talk to me about it."

Meg felt wretched, the burden of guilt almost too much to bear. If only she'd kept her big mouth shut.

"I have something you both need to see." Josie waved an envelope. She opened it and pulled out a folded sheet of paper. The paper crinkled as she unfolded it and began to read.

"Dear Miss Lonely Hearts…"

Amanda tossed the mop to the floor. "I'm working my fingers to the bone, and you come over here to read a dumb letter?"

Meg didn't blame Amanda for being upset. With their family falling apart, why should they care about some stranger's stupid problems?

"Hear me out," Josie pleaded and continued reading.

"Dear Miss Lonely Hearts,

"The love of my life has left me, and I don't know what to do. I'm afraid I might have lost her for good.

I've begged for forgiveness, but she won't listen. She won't even talk to me. I'll do anything you say to get her back.

"Sincerely,
"An Old Fool."

Amanda rolled her eyes. "Old fool, indeed! Anyone who writes to strangers for advice should be shipped off to the lunatic asylum."

Josie waved the letter in both her sisters' faces. "Do you know who wrote this?"

Meg shook her head. Why was Josie being so persistent? "No, and I don't care—"

"Papa."

Meg's back stiffened. "That's…that's ridiculous. He would never write such a letter."

"Take a look."

Snatching the letter from Josie, Meg read it for herself while Amanda peered over her shoulder. "It can't be…" But it was. She would recognize her father's big, bold handwriting anywhere.

For several moments no one spoke, the silence broken only by the steady cadence of ticking clocks.

"Do…do you think he knows you're Miss Lonely Hearts?" Meg asked at last.

Josie shook her head. "There's no way he could know unless one of you told him."

"Not me," Amanda said.

"Me neither," Meg said. "What are you going to do?"

Josie plucked the letter out of Meg's hand. "Answer him, of course."

Meg chewed on a fingernail. Papa writing to Miss Lonely Hearts? That was crazy. It could only be the act of a desperate man. That just underscored the seriousness of the problem.

Amanda pulled the scarf off her head and tucked it into her apron pocket. "But how will you answer him? What will you say?"

"That's why I'm here. I was hoping between the three of us we could come up with the right words."

Meg frowned. Josie had never before asked for help with wording. She always knew what to say, what to write.

Amanda placed her hands on her hips. "Papa won't even take advice from us. What makes you think he'll do anything Miss Lonely Hearts tells him to do?"

Josie tucked the letter into her purse. "Like I told you before, people who write know in their hearts what they have to do. They're just asking for permission to do it."

"Is that what you think Papa's doing?" Meg asked. Asking for permission from someone didn't seem like something he would ever do, but then, he hadn't been himself since Mama left.

"I'm willing to bet on it," Josie said. "All we have to do is figure out a way to give it to him without making it look too obvious."

"How are we going to do that?" Meg asked. "We don't even know what he wants permission to do."

"That's why the wording has to be vague, yet clear."

Amanda rolled her eyes. "No contradiction there."

Josie pulled a pencil and notebook out of her purse. "We know that the only way Papa can get Mama back is to end that stupid feud. *That's* what we have to give him permission to do. The rest is up to him. So put on your thinking caps."

Meg plopped herself down on the sofa and crossed her arms. Something told her it was about to be a very long night.

Thirty-five

JACOB KIDD LOOKED UP FROM HIS JAIL CELL AND greeted Grant with a grunt. "'Bout time you got here."

Noticing another prisoner in the next cell over, Grant did a double take. He recognized Meg's younger sister, Amanda, even before he got a good look at her face. She didn't look much like Meg, except for the turquoise color of her eyes, but that was enough. More than enough to trigger the painful memories as well, and take his mind to places he didn't want to go.

Banishing his wayward thoughts, he doffed his hat. "Miss Lockwood." He then turned and focused on his client. "Got here soon as I could. What's so urgent?"

Every time Kidd was scheduled to hang, something happened to postpone it. The man had more lives than an alley cat.

"I wanna sue the county."

"Sue the count—" Grant lifted his eyebrows. Suddenly everyone in town was sue-happy. All this sudden interest in litigation was turning Two-Time into a miniature version of Boston. Even shopkeepers had queried him about the possibility of suing the railroad for crash-related loss of business.

"What for?"

"Breach of promise."

Grant glanced at Amanda Lockwood sitting on the edge of her cot. "Are you saying that someone promised to marry you?"

Kidd looked perplexed. "Marry me? Whatcha talkin' about? They failed to hang me. That's what!"

"Let me get this straight." Grant rubbed his chin. "You want to sue the county for *not* hanging you?"

"And for undue duress. That's a legal term, right?"

"Are you saying you were mistreated?"

"Of course I was mistreated. They walked me clear to the gallows, blindfolded me, put me in a necktie, and then took off."

Grant shook his head. "So what you're saying is that they left you hanging, so to speak."

"Yeah, and it coulda caused me great throat trouble." Kidd pushed his lips out in disgust. "By the time the sheriff came back, no one could find the hangman. So they hauled me back to jail."

Grant rubbed his forehead. "You are aware that there was an emergency. People were hurt."

"Heard something about that, but that don't change nothin'. When they say they're gonna hang a body, that's what they oughta do."

"It could take weeks before your case comes to trial. Months." Grant wasn't even sure he would still be in town.

"Months, eh?" Kidd's eyes glittered, and Grant could almost see the wheels turning in his grizzly head.

"Are you saying you don't want to handle a lawsuit for a condemned man?"

"Unless you have family, I don't see the point," Grant said. "Win or lose, you'll still be dead."

"Hmm. I see what you mean. Guess the judge is gonna have to give me one of those whatchamacallits."

"Do you mean a stay of execution?"

"That's the one. So whatcha say?"

Grant had successfully initiated such stays, but filing one so the prisoner could sue the authorities? No judge in Boston would allow such a thing. But this was Texas, and that was a whole different animal.

"I'll see what I can do."

"You do that," Kidd said and smiled.

Grant started to leave, but then stopped. "What are you in for this time, Miss Lockwood?" he asked.

"Theft."

Grant lifted his eyebrows.

"She let all of them dogs loose," Kidd said.

"Dogs?"

"The ones in the dogcatcher's wagon."

She sniffed. "Yes, and I'll do it again if I have to."

Even in her indignant state she reminded him of Meg, and it wasn't just the color of her eyes. It was the way she wrinkled her nose and moved her head. He could almost hear Meg's voice, see her dancing, imagine her in his arms. *Happy New Year, Grant.*

"Mr. Mutton has no right locking up licensed dogs!" she added.

Startled out of his reverie, Grant rubbed his chin. "I quite agree." He hesitated. "Gather up your belongings. Soon as I post bail, you'll be free to go."

Kidd gazed through the bars at Miss Lockwood. "See, whad' I tell you? For a big-city lawyer, he ain't so bad."

～

Meg whisked her feather duster from clock to clock with a worried frown. She eyed the morning newspaper still on the counter where Tucker had left it earlier. Today was the day that Papa's letter to Miss Lonely Hearts was scheduled for publication.

Usually her father had read the paper by now. What was taking him so long? And what if, for some reason, he neglected to read it?

With a quick glance in back where her father was working, she opened the morning paper and quickly turned to Josie's column. Papa's letter was there all right, in living black and white.

Her gaze scanned down to Josie's reply.

Dear Old Fool,

> *It sounds like your ladylove needs more than mere words. She needs to hear the bells of sincerity, but only you know how to ring them. He who rules time has the power, and the power is in your hands. As Lord Byron so wisely said, "Time is the corrector where our judgments err."*

Meg refolded the paper and laid it back on the counter. Was Josie's message too subtle? Papa wasn't one to pick up on nuances. Still, Josie insisted that Papa knew what he had to do, but did he? More importantly, could he?

She reached for her feather duster.

The door swung open to a jingle of bells. Grant strolled into the shop, his presence affecting every cell in her body. Mouth dry, she laid her duster on the counter and wiped her damp hands on her skirt.

She hated, absolutely hated, that despite everything that had happened, he was still able to control her breathing—control her very heartbeat. If that wasn't bad enough, he invaded her deepest thoughts. Even sleep offered her no relief because he was a constant presence in her dreams.

Grant pulled off his hat and acknowledged her with a wary nod as Tommy entered behind him.

Grant looked very much the eastern lawyer today, smart, clever—a man who would do whatever necessary in a court of law to wield his idea of justice. Use whatever means…

How he must resent the way things had turned out with Tommy, resent her for ruining his clever plan.

Such were her thoughts that she hardly paid any attention to Tommy until he slapped something on the counter, startling her.

It was a check for ten grand. "Right on time," he said.

Meg stared at all the zeroes on the check. "Where did you get that much money?"

Tommy's lips thinned. Dressed in his usual dungarees, red hair standing on end, he didn't look like the same man who'd sat in court or waited for her at the altar.

"Pa mortgaged the house and took loans out on the business."

Meg's heart sank. "Oh no. Tommy, I'm so sorry. I never meant…" Her eyes filled with tears.

Tommy never did like seeing her cry, and today was no different. "It's okay, Meg," he said, dropping the accusatory tone of his voice. He reached across the counter to take her hand in his. "I don't blame you." With his free hand, he checked his pockets for a handkerchief and, as usual, came up empty. "I'll find a way to pay Pa back. I will. I'll even pay back the money borrowed from Mr. Garrison."

Sniffling, Meg pulled her hand from his and palmed away a tear. Grant had loaned him money?

Grant appeared by Tommy's side with a clean handkerchief. Taking it from him, Meg quickly looked away. She wanted nothing from Grant, but declining his handkerchief seemed rude.

"Thank you," she said, her cool voice hiding her inner torment.

Grant stepped back without a word and resumed his stance by the door.

Dabbing at the moisture on her cheeks, she stared at the check on the counter. "Oh, Tommy. That's a lot of money. It will take years to pay it back."

"Maybe not. There's gold in Alaska. Heard there're riches to be found. Lots of them." He was obviously trying to make her feel better, but the thought of him working as a miner had the opposite effect. Tommy avoided physical labor like smallpox.

As if guessing her thoughts, he added, "It's not exactly the Pacific Islands, but it's somethin'."

"I feel terrible."

She glanced at Grant, but his stoic face gave no clue to his thoughts.

Tommy said something, but when she failed to

respond, his glance swung back and forth between her and his lawyer. "Meg?"

She blinked. "I'm sorry…"

He gave her a funny look. "I said I need a receipt to show the judge."

"I'll write you one," Papa said, emerging from the back of the shop. He then pulled a receipt book from a drawer, along with a pen and bottle of ink. After scribbling out a receipt for ten grand, he signed and dated it and slid it across the counter.

Tommy took the receipt without a word and tucked it into his pocket. "Meg, don't look like that. It's not the end of the world. Honest. I'll write and let you know how I'm doing. Bet you never got a letter from Alaska."

"No, I never did. And I'll write back. I will, Tommy. I promise."

He gave her a lopsided grin and turned to the door where Grant stood holding it open for him.

"Wait," her father called. "You forgot something."

Both men turned, Grant with his hand still on the doorknob. Eyebrows arched, Tommy tossed a questioning glance at Meg before switching his attention to her father.

"What did I forget?"

"This." Papa tore the check into a dozen pieces and tossed them into the air. The little scraps of paper fluttered to the floor like falling snow. Meg's mouth dropped open.

Tommy stared at the scraps of paper, his eyes round. "Does this mean…?"

"You've got your receipt," Papa said. "That's all

the judge needs to see. Now get out of here. We've got work to do."

Tommy turned to Grant. "Is…is this legal?"

Grant shrugged. "Don't know what you're talking about. Never saw a thing." With that, he walked out of the shop.

"Whoopie!" Tommy leaped up and slapped the doorframe before racing outside. "Pacific Islands, here I come!"

Grinning, Meg flung her arms around her father's neck. "What is this?" he asked, his gruff voice belying his pleased look.

"This, Papa, is my way of saying I love you." She pulled back. "That was a very good thing you did. I'm sure Mama would agree."

"Don't count on it, Meg." He picked the newspaper off the counter, tucked it under his arm, and shuffled into the back room.

Meg balled up the handkerchief in her hands— Grant's handkerchief—and this time there was no stopping the tears.

Thirty-six

MEG LEFT THE SHOP LATER THAT DAY, AHEAD OF HER father. She was so busy pulling on her gloves that she failed to notice Grant until she practically plowed into him.

Stopping short, she dropped her glove. "Y-you startled me." She fought to rein in her galloping senses, but it would have been easier to stop a herd of stampeding cattle with one hand. "What are you doing here?"

He bent to retrieve her glove. Straightening, he handed it to her. "I came for answers."

She wiggled her fingers into the silky depths. "What do you mean? What kind of answers?"

He grabbed her firmly by the arm and pulled her out of the path of passersby. He was so close that his warm breath mingled with hers, so close she was sure he could hear her pounding heart.

"What did I do to make you so angry at me?" he asked, his voice a low rumble in her ear.

"I'm not angry."

He cupped her chin in his hand and lifted her face to his. "No? Well, you could have fooled me."

She glared at him. "If you would kindly step aside."

"Not till you answer my question."

"I have nothing to say to you." She pushed his hand away, and all the anger, resentment, and—more than anything—pain buried in her heart broke free.

Suddenly she had a lot to say indeed, and words spewed out of her in a rush. "I thought you would use New Year's against me in court. So what went wrong? Did my *wanton* behavior fail to sway the judge? Did—"

"You thought I would use…what happened between us?" He looked clearly aghast.

Her cheeks flared, but she refused to look away. "Dancing, laughing, and flirting, Miss Lockwood?" She threw his words back at him like darts on a target board. "Were you too heartbroken to kiss?"

He stared at her in disbelief. "You think that's why I kissed you?"

"Yes, but it didn't work, did it? That's when you decided to make Tommy agree to marry me so that Papa would have to drop the suit."

"You think that was my doing?" Grant sounded incredulous. "I didn't have a clue what was on his mind until he spoke up in court. And if you think for one moment that I would use New Year's"—his eyes glittered with anger and maybe even hurt—"you don't know me."

She searched his face. He certainly looked sincere. Sounded it too. "But the *Gazette* said—"

His nostrils flared. "And you believed that piece of yellow journalism?"

She caught her breath. "It wasn't just the *Gazette*. Everyone's been saying—"

"I don't give a—" He raked his fingers through his hair and lowered his voice. "What happened in court was all Tommy's doing. I had nothing to do with it. I would never—"

She felt a stirring of hope inside. "Never what?" she whispered.

"I would never advise a client to do something that was clearly a mistake."

It wasn't the answer she'd hoped for, or even wanted to hear. "But Tommy said—"

Grant's lips thinned. "What? What did he say?"

"He said you told him that the only way out of paying the money was to marry me."

"It's my job to tell a client the facts, and that's what I did. I certainly didn't encourage him, if that's what you think."

Her mind reeled in confusion. "If…if that's true—"

"It's absolutely true!"

She caught her breath. "Then…then I owe you an apology."

He studied her as if to determine her sincerity. "Just so you know, what happened on New Year's was between you and me. No one else. I've never stopped thinking of it. Nor have I stopped wishing you had come back for more."

His words were like warm, gentle waves washing away her deepest pain. "Oh, Grant," she whispered when at last she could find her voice. "I…I'm so sorry for…for misjudging you."

His gaze clung to hers. "You said you loved him."

"I do. We've been through so much together. I love him only as a friend. It can never be anything more than that."

He moved closer. "Are you saying—?"

She nodded, and her eyes filled with tears. There was so much she wanted to tell him, so much she needed to say, but a knot of emotion sat heavy like a rock in her throat. Swallowing hard, she gazed up at him, her love so great it felt as if her heart was about to burst.

"Grant, you're the only one I ever truly loved. I know that now."

He caressed her face tenderly. "Oh, Meg, you don't know how happy I am to hear you say that. I've never loved another woman like I love you."

Joy unlike any she'd ever known filled her heart, and a warm glow flowed through her. "Oh, Grant, I—"

"Meg!" At the sound of her father's sharp voice, the two of them drew apart. Papa stood a short distance away, motioning to her. "Time to go home."

She hesitated. "Coming, Papa." She turned back to Grant. "I have to go."

"Meet me later."

She glanced at her father's stoic expression, and her heart sank. His low opinion of Grant couldn't be plainer if he'd shouted it from the rooftops.

She felt as if she was being pulled in two different directions. Papa needed her, but her heart belonged to Grant. He was worth fighting for—and she planned to do just that, but not yet. Not while her family was still broken. Not while she had another battle on her hands.

"I can't," she whispered, beseeching him to understand. "Not yet…"

His dark, earnest eyes sought hers. "When?"

"Soon," she whispered. She backed away and turned to join her father. She glanced at Grant over her shoulder. "Forgive me," she mouthed. *Please, please forgive me.*

Thirty-seven

FOR TWO DAYS NOTHING HAPPENED. MAMA DIDN'T come home, and so far, Papa had not made any progress in winning her back.

That night, Meg was beside herself with frustration and could hardly concentrate on the novel in her hands. Why, oh why couldn't her parents settle their differences? She wanted her family whole again, but that wasn't the only reason for her impatience.

Grant had asked her to meet him, and the longer she stayed away, the more her doubts increased. She'd asked him to wait, but would he?

If I had someone like you…

The memory sent a warm flush to her face but did little to erase her uncertainties.

Tomorrow would make three days since they'd last met, and he'd made no attempt to see her. That hardly sounded like a man in love, or even one mildly interested. Had she misread the promise in his eyes? The longing in his voice?

Somehow Grant staying away was worse than

being left at the altar. Far worse. Papa was fighting for Mama. Why wasn't Grant fighting for her?

The grandfather clock sighed, and a chorus of chimes, cuckoos, and bongs announced the hour of ten. Meg placed her book on the end table. It looked like nothing would happen tonight, so she might as well go to bed. Josie's letter had failed to get the desired results. Now what?

Rising, she stretched and reached for the lamp switch. Something made her perk up her ears, and her hand froze. Was that…?

She strained her ears, but there was no mistake. From the distance came the distinctive sound of the Lockwood bell. Her breath caught in her lungs. The bells never rang after dark unless it was New Year's or an emergency.

Amanda called from the top of the stairs. "What happened? What's wrong? Where's Papa—"

"Isn't he in his room?"

"No."

Meg didn't know what to think. When did Papa leave the house? "We better see what's going on."

Amanda practically fell down the stairs in her haste. Meg reached the front door first. Pulling two cloaks from the wall hooks, she tossed Amanda hers and dashed out the door.

"Hurry!"

The cool, clear air carried the sound over the sleepy town, and already neighbors were pouring out of the houses and onto the street. Those who had already retired for the night stuck their heads out of second-floor windows, mobcaps tied on, and inquired of those below. "Is it a fire?"

That was always the worst fear, but far from the only one.

"Maybe somebody tried to rob the bank."

"Do you think the prisoner Kidd escaped?"

Running feet pounded the street as people rushed toward town, some carrying lanterns that swung back and forth like shiny sabers.

Meg reached for Amanda's hand so as not to lose her in the crowd. Why would Papa ring the bell at this time unless something was terribly wrong?

She searched the crowd for Grant. Had he heard the bells? Would he ignore them? Or would he, like all the others, rush out to see what the fuss was about?

The crowd spilled onto Main like floodwaters, hundreds of feet pounding the ground. Since there was no traffic, they filed down the middle of the street.

"I don't see any smoke," someone called out.

"Maybe the sheriff will know something."

But neither the sheriff nor his deputy was in the office, and the crowd kept going. They swept en masse by the hotel and Farrell Jewelers, and continued on past the gun shop and the general store.

The bell grew louder and seemingly more urgent as they neared the Lockwood Watch and Clockworks shop.

Meg lost Amanda in the confusion. Hoping to spot Josie or Ralph, she craned her neck, but it was hard to pick out any one person in the mob, even someone as tall as Grant.

The memory of another time—another ringing of the bell—came to mind, and it was all Meg could do to breathe.

Happy New Year, Meg.

The crowd reached the clock shop where Papa stood tugging on the bell rope with all his might. T-Bone stomped up to Papa and pointed a threatening finger. For once, he wasn't wearing his butcher apron. Instead, he was dressed in a white nightshirt that made him look almost ghost-like.

"You better have a good reason for dragging us out of bed in the middle of the night, Lockwood!" T-Bone said, ripping the bell rope out of Papa's hands.

"Yeah," yelled Blacksmith Steele.

Fists pumped the air as several men, including the dogcatcher and the mayor, crowded around her father. Papa had always seemed big and strong—invincible, even—but in the midst of the angry mob, he looked surprisingly vulnerable.

Meg waved her arms. "Stop, please. Everyone!" Her voice was drowned out by the angry shouts around her.

Trying not to panic, she glanced around. Where was her brother-in-law? The sheriff? Even Tommy. *Oh, Grant, why aren't you here? You would never let anyone hurt Papa…*

Her hand brushed the side of her cape, reminding her of the gun in her pocket.

She hesitated, but the shouts only grew louder, the threats more serious. T-Bone shoved Papa and yanked the rope out of his hands.

She pointed the gun at the rooftop, squeezed her eyes shut, and pulled back on the trigger. When nothing happened, she cocked the hammer. This time when she pulled the trigger, the gun practically exploded in her hand. Crying out in alarm, she dropped the weapon, and it fell to her feet.

Silence followed the report, and all eyes turned to her, even Papa's. The crowd backed away, leaving her alone in the center of a circle.

T-Bone dropped the bellpull and gaped at her. Things might have ended there, had Papa not grabbed the end of the rope and resumed ringing the bell.

Just when things seemed about to grow ugly again, Sheriff Clayton pushed his way through the mob. "Don't move, any of you," he yelled. He stalked up to Meg and picked her weapon off the ground where she'd dropped it. "What's the meaning of this?"

Before anyone could answer, another bell rang—this one a distance away. The Farrell bell.

The sheriff whirled around. "What the—"

A hush settled over the crowd, followed by a nervous buzz. The Farrell and Lockwood bells ringing together in the dead of night? Never before had such a sound been heard. What could it mean?

"The world must be coming to an end," a voice shouted.

T-Bone cursed. "If it is, I wish it would hurry. I ain't got all night."

Meg suddenly spotted Mama standing between Josie and Ralph. She looked as puzzled as everyone else.

Papa stopped ringing the bell and wrapped the rope around its hook. He then faced the hushed spectators. "Ladies and gentleman," he said. "I'm sure you all want to know why I brought you here."

"You better have a good expl'nation!" Sheriff Clayton growled. "Or I'm runnin' you in for disturbin' the peace."

"Then you'll have to run us both in," a voice sounded from behind.

Spotting Mr. Farrell, Meg's hopes soared. Could this possibly be the good news she and her sisters had been waiting to hear?

People stepped aside to let Farrell through, and he joined Papa in front of the shop. The two men standing side by side without fighting was a rare sight indeed. The mob grew so quiet that the sound of moths could be heard butting against the gas streetlight.

Farrell lifted his voice. "Lockwood and I have an announcement to make."

Papa nodded. "Starting tomorrow at precisely twelve noon and twelve-forty, the town of Two-Time will become a one-time town. We will follow standard time as set by the railroad so that there will never be another accident."

Meg's jaw dropped. How did Papa ever get Mr. Farrell to agree to such a thing?

Her father continued speaking, but whoops and hollers drowned out the rest of his statement. No one cared about details. Let the two jewelers work that out. Tonight was the time to celebrate.

No one wanted the occasion to end. People stayed to talk to friends and neighbors about the wondrous event that would forever change their town. Before long, fiddle music filled the air, along with Mr. McGinnis's dreaded bagpipes. Young people started dancing, and a few older folks followed along. A group of mariachi players eventually appeared, strumming guitars.

Amanda nudged Meg's arm. "Oh, look!"

Meg turned just in time to see Mama throw herself into Papà's arms.

⁓

Moments later, Meg chased after Tommy's father as he headed down Main.

"Mr. Farrell!" she called.

Turning, he waited for her to catch up. "Meg."

"I just wanted to say thank you."

"Don't thank me. Thank your pa for tearin' up that check. Sure took a burden off the family."

"I'm sorry we put you through all that," she said.

Mr. Farrell ran his hand over his shiny bald spot. "Tommy had it coming to him. He should never have left you danglin'."

"Is that why you agreed to the time change? Papa tearing up the check?"

"That was part of it. I was also afraid he'd lost his mind." His jowls quivered beneath his beard. "He kept bangin' on my door yellin' somethin' about Lord Byron. Whoever he is."

Meg smiled to herself. So Josie's column did do some good.

"I finally opened the door, and that's when your pa told me everythin'. Just want you to know, there never was anythin' between your ma and me."

"I know that, and Papa knows it now too."

"When the wife found out Elizabeth left him, she got it into her fool head to do the same to me."

Meg stared at him. "Mrs. Farrell left you?"

"That she did. Said she wouldn't come back till Henry and I solved our diff'rences."

Meg couldn't believe her ears. Just wait till Amanda heard about this! Gaining the right to vote and marching for a cause was one way women could exert power, but it was by no means the only way. Mama and Mrs. Farrell together had done what no one else in town had ever been able to do—they'd brought an end to the Lockwood-Farrell feud.

"Do you think you and Papa can be friends again?"

Mr. Farrell shrugged. "You and Tommy are still friends. Guess that means anythin's poss'ble."

Mrs. Farrell called to him, and Mr. Farrell's face lit up. It was clear that he loved his wife very much and was glad to have her back.

"I better go. Thanks to your pa, I have a whole bunch of clocks I've got to reset tomorrow." He turned. "Dang it," he muttered. "Why'd it have to be railroad time?"

No sooner had Mr. Farrell vanished into the crowd than someone grabbed Meg by the arm and twirled her around.

Startled, she gasped. "Grant!"

He laughed. "Is that why you couldn't meet me? Because you were trying to get your father to end the feud?"

"Something like that," she said.

His expression suddenly grew serious. "I knew you had something up your sleeve." His gaze intensified. "You asked me to wait, and I decided to give you till the weekend before I broke down your door. Do you think your father would have sued me for destruction of property?"

"At the very least," she said and laughed. She then

told him everything that had happened. He chuckled when she got to the Miss Lonely Hearts letter.

"I remember that letter. My landlady had a devil of a time trying to figure out who wrote it. I think Lord Byron threw her."

She laughed. "It confused Mr. Farrell as well."

His eyes sparkled. "If I ask you to dance, will you think I'm up to no good?"

Heart pounding, she smiled up at him. "Are you?"

"Absolutely."

Joy unlike anything she had ever known rushed through her, and much to her dismay, she burst into tears.

A look of horror crossed Grant's face. "I didn't mean to upset you," he said, reaching in his pocket for his handkerchief. "If you'd rather not dance—"

"I want to," Meg said, taking the offered handkerchief. "I'm just so h-h-happy." Mama and Papa were back together, the feud was over, and here she stood with the man she loved more than anything else in the world. What more could she ask for?

He stared at her all funny-like. "Do you always cry when you're happy?" he asked.

"Nope. This is the first time." And with that, the tears streamed freely down her cheeks.

After a good cry on Grant's shoulder, Meg returned his handkerchief. They stood only a foot apart, but even that short distance seemed too far.

"I'm ready to dance now," she said, feeling breathless with pleasure. Facing him, she dropped her arms to her sides.

A brass horn joined the violins and guitars, and the

music seemed especially sharp in the cool, clear air. Mariachi music was designed to celebrate the struggles and triumphs of the Mexican people, and tonight the music spoke to Meg's heart in ways it never had before. It spoke of new beginnings.

"I know my way around the dance floor in Boston," Grant said, "but haven't the slightest idea how to dance here."

"It's easy," Meg replied and demonstrated. Swaying her body from side to side, she hammered her heels into the hard-packed soil. Driven not by the music but the smoldering flames in his eyes, she felt as light-hearted as a butterfly.

"Every time you strike with your feet, you must do a backswing like this," she said.

Grant was all arms, legs, and awkward moves. Soon they were both bent over in hysterics. Never could she remember having so much fun.

Finally, after much trial and error, he pulled her into arms, locking her in his warm embrace. He then led her in a slow waltz, gently rocking her back and forth.

Sallie-May giggled as she whirled by in the arms of her new beau, and Meg was happy for her. It was too early to tell, but it sure did look like Sallie-May had finally found herself a wealthy rancher.

"I'm afraid this is more my style," Grant whispered apologetically, giving Sallie-May and her partner a rueful look.

"I like your style just fine," Meg assured him and smiled.

He grinned back. "Do you now?"

Eventually the musicians drifted away, along with the

crowd. Soon it was only the two of them. He led her in a slow dance down the middle of Main, accompanied by a big, bright moon peering through lacy clouds.

Angry shouts wafted from a nearby saloon. The sheriff hauled a handcuffed man down the street toward the jailhouse. A group of rowdies roared out of town on horseback, shooting a barrage of bullets into the air. Madame Bubbles had a scream fest with one of her clients. Two dogs chased a cat into an alley. A drunk walked by, singing at the top of his lungs.

"Glad to see things have returned to normal," Grant teased. "I was afraid that Two-Time was becoming too civilized for my blood."

"No fear of that," Meg replied. "We still know how to put on a good feud now and again."

At long last they stopped dancing, but Grant's hands remained at her waist.

He looked at his watch, and at the stroke of midnight, he asked, "Do you know what today is?"

Head pressed on the strong expanse of his chest, she gave a happy sigh. "It's the day Two-Time will become a one-time town," she murmured.

"It's also January 29."

She looked up at him, not sure what he was saying. "Don't tell me it's your birthday."

"Nope. Better than that." The moonlight had turned his eyes to gold. "I have it on good authority from my Chinese clients that today happens to be the start of the Chinese New Year."

Her heart pounded, and a rush of anticipation coursed through her. "Is...is that so?"

"Yes, it's so." He grinned. "Happy New Year, Meg."

She grinned back. *Well, what do you know?* Two-Time would be a one-time town, but for tonight, it was celebrating the start of a new year twice.

"Happy New Year, Grant." She closed her eyes and puckered her lips.

Laughing, he tightened his hold on her and gently cupped her face. "I like the way you Texas girls think." He brushed his forehead against hers before capturing her mouth with heated lips.

She kissed him back, wishing the moment could last forever. Papa would have a fit, of course. His negative opinion of lawyers in general and Grant in particular was secret to none. That would make this suitor even more objectionable than most.

But tonight—tonight—she didn't care. There would be time enough tomorrow to battle Papa. Tonight, it was all about love…

Thirty-eight

Two days later, Grant entered the jailhouse. "Got good news for you." He stopped. Kidd was still in the cell that he had been occupying for some months now, and Meg's sister Amanda was in the one next door.

Grant doffed his hat. *Here we go again.* "What are you in for this time, Miss Lockwood?"

"Voting in the election for mayor," she said with an indignant toss of the head.

"Ah."

"It's not fair that only half of our citizens get to vote. The *wrong* half, I might add!"

"Can't argue with you there, ma'am."

Kidd rose from his cot and gave an impatient grunt. "You said you had good news."

"Yes, indeed. There's no such thing as either Farrell or Lockwood time anymore. That means if you agree to drop the lawsuit against the county, your sentence will be commuted." It had taken some wheeling and dealing on Grant's part, but the judge finally agreed that leaving Kidd hanging, so to speak, with a rope around his neck constituted cruel and unfair punishment.

"What's that mean, commuted?"

"It means you can forget the gallows. You'll be serving the rest of your sentence in prison."

Kidd's toothless smile split his face in two. "Well, if that don't beat all."

"And there's another choice—tell us where the loot is from your last robbery, and the judge agreed to commute your sentence to only seven years."

Kidd worked his chin up and down, grinding his toothless gums together. "Make it five, and he's got hisself a deal."

Kidd was as predictable as a clock, which is what Grant had counted on. "You strike a hard bargain, Mr. Kidd."

"Yeah, but I coulda asked for four."

"And you would have gotten six." Grant turned and stepped through the open doorway into the sheriff's office. Stopping in front of Clayton's desk, he reached into his coat pocket for his gold money clip and counted out five ones.

"This is for the lady," he said, tossing the bills onto the desk.

"Why you keep doin' that?" the sheriff asked, collecting the money and reaching for the cell key. "Why do ya keep bailin' her out?"

"Let's just say I believe in taking care of family." With that, Grant left the office. Amanda wasn't his sister-in-law yet, but if he could persuade that crazy father of hers to let him court Meg, she would be soon enough. If posting bail for members of that family didn't bankrupt him first.

⤝⤞

Meg stood beneath the tall cottonwood tree and stared at the two yellow eyes glaring down at her from the uppermost branches.

Next to her, the widow Rockwell wrung her hands together. "The poor thing's been howling all night. I don't know what to do."

"I see him," Meg said and lifted her voice. "Come, kitty, kitty."

No amount of coaxing convinced Cowboy to come down this time, not even the bowl of milk his owner had set out for him.

"See? What did I tell you?" The woman looked so upset that Meg felt bad for her.

Someone had left a ladder propped against the trunk, probably the last person to come to the cat's rescue. Meg grabbed hold of the side rails of the ladder to check for stability. She'd been in trouble many times for climbing this tree. In her younger years, she and Tommy often raced to the topmost branches, and nine times out of ten, she'd reached the top first. But that was when bodies were more flexible and fears something to laugh at.

No laughing today. She placed a foot on the lower rung and began climbing.

Mrs. Rockwell called, "Oh, do be careful, dearie. I don't want you falling."

Upon reaching the top of the ladder, Meg grabbed hold of a leafless branch and craned her neck. Cowboy stared back with a look of superiority. She should have known; the pitiful cries were nothing but a ruse.

The only way to reach the cat was to climb to the uppermost branches, something Meg was reluctant to do. She had agreed to meet Grant in town for lunch and didn't want to chance ruining her dress.

She raised a hand. "Come on, Cowboy. I'm not going to hurt you."

Cowboy flipped his tail and hissed, but otherwise stayed put.

Stretching, Meg was able to reach the branch the cat sat on. She grabbed hold of it and gave it a good shake. Startled, Cowboy arched his back and yowled. He then pounced on her shoulder without warning, digging his claws all the way through her dress to her flesh beneath.

Meg lost her footing and cried out. The ladder wobbled and slid sideways. It was only through fast action on her part that she was able to grab a tree limb to keep from falling.

Cat and ladder hit the ground at the same time, leaving her dangling in the air.

"Hold on," Mrs. Rockwell called.

I'm trying, I'm trying…

The branch suddenly snapped in two. Arms windmilling, Meg dropped like a lead balloon.

❧

"You can open your eyes now."

Her lashes flew up at the sound of Grant's voice. She wasn't dead, but she sure was in heaven. Or so it seemed, since she woke up cradled in Grant's arms.

"You…you caught me," Meg stammered, heart pounding so hard she could hardly get the words out.

"You're lucky I happened to be passing by," he growled.

"You can put me down now," she said.

"Can't do that," he said.

"Why not?"

"Because you need a lawyer."

He carried her into one of Mrs. Rockwell's Sunday houses and kicked the door shut with his foot. Only then did he set her down. The tiny parlor and kitchen area was empty except for a single chair.

"What do you mean, I need a lawyer?"

Gazing into her eyes, he pulled a twig from her hair. "Scaring a cat and damaging a tree. You know how touchy these Texans are."

Pressing her fingers to her mouth, Meg feigned concern. "Oh dear goodness."

"And as a witness, I'll be called to testify."

Warming to the game they played, she said, "Whatever should I do?"

"Well..." Grant raked his fingers through his hair. "There's this little law that says a husband can't testify against his wife."

Her already fast-beating heart practically leaped out of her chest. "Is...is that so?"

He stepped closer and handed her a handkerchief.

"What's this for?" she asked.

"I know how you cry when you're happy. So I'm kind of hoping you'll need it in the near future." He paused. "That is, if you don't think I'm jumping the gun."

Her heart stilled. "Why...why would I think that?"

"I'm not sure how they do things here. But where I come from, a man wishing to ask a woman's hand in marriage must first have a serious talk with her father. On the other hand, there is that little matter of the tree, not to mention a traumatized cat."

"I do believe you're trying to blackmail me," Meg said.

Grant lifted his hands above his shoulders. "Guilty as charged. So what do you say? Will you marry me?"

Her heart thudded, but before she could answer, he continued. "The day I fell in love with you"—his voice caught with emotion—"was the first time I saw you dragging your hope chest down the middle of the street."

"That's strange," she said, her eyes burning with tears of pure joy. "For I do believe that was the day *I* fell in love with *you*."

"Is that so?"

"Yes, that's so." Her mouth curved.

Beaming practically from ear to ear, he circled her waist with his hands. "Maybe you better give my handkerchief back, because you've just made me the happiest man alive."

"Are...are you sure you want me?" she whispered. A woman with two disastrous weddings under her belt couldn't be too careful.

"Oh, I'm sure. Never been surer of anything in my life," he said. "The only thing I'm not sure of is how to get your father to approve...if you agreed to be my wife, that is."

"Maybe you should pose that question to Miss Lonely Hearts."

Grant chuckled. "Maybe so." He lifted her chin tenderly. "I love celebrating New Years with you. But celebrating every day for the rest of our lives would be even better. That's how much I love you."

Tears sprang to her eyes. Never had three words meant so much. "Oh, Grant!" And with that, Meg flung her arms around his neck. In case there were any lingering doubts of her intention, she bent her head back and yelled, "Yes, yes, yes, I'll marry you!"

৵৹

A short while later, Meg rushed into the house and found Papa in the parlor fiddling with the cuckoo clock.

Grant wanted to talk to her father himself, had in fact insisted upon doing it the proper "Boston" way. With his fine persuasive skills, he might have succeeded in getting her father's approval, but this was her battle.

It wasn't enough that Papa gave his approval; she wanted his promise that he would never treat Grant as he had treated Tommy. She hated that the happiest day of her life had to be spoiled, but it couldn't be helped.

Papa looked up as she approached. As if sensing something in her manner, he frowned. "Tommy get off all right?" he asked.

She nodded. "Yes, he did." She had gone to the train depot that morning to see him leave on the train bound for California. There he hoped to hop on a cargo ship headed for Asia.

Papa arched a bushy eyebrow. "And you don't mind?"

"No, Papa. We're friends, and that's all we'll ever be."

"You two sure took a roundabout way of figuring that out."

"You're a fine one to talk, Papa. Look how long it took you to know how much Mama loves you. How much she's always loved you."

This brought a smile to his face. "Hard to believe,

isn't it? Your mother could have had anyone she wanted. Thank God she has terrible taste in men."

It wasn't like Papa to disparage himself. "I'm afraid I may have taken after Mama in that regard," Meg said carefully.

He father poked at the insides of the clock. "You're not talking about that jackleg lawyer, are you?"

She moistened her lips. So Papa suspected. "That's exactly who I'm talking about, and I want you to stop calling him that."

The bird popped out of its little house. *Cuckoo, cuckoo, cuckoo.*

Papa adjusted the pendulum chains. "Did you know that cuckoos don't bother raising their young?"

Meg gritted her teeth. *Oh, no you don't, Papa. You're not distracting me with bird talk—or anything else, for that matter. Not this time.*

"Grant is a wonderful, caring man."

For a long moment her father said nothing as he adjusted the chains of the Black Forest clock. "The mama bird lays eggs in the nests of other birds," he said at last. "That way the parents don't have to worry about raising them. They let others do all the work."

"And I love him, Papa. I do." She couldn't believe the relief she felt at finally being able to say those words aloud.

Her father's hand stilled, and he narrowed his eyes. "You sound like you really mean it," he said. "Not like last time."

She stared at him. Was that why he had been so dead set against her marriage to Tommy? Had Papa doubted her love? Had he known her true feelings even before she did? Maybe Papa was better at subtleties than she gave him credit for.

"No, it's not like last time," she said. "And he loves me too."

He turned back to the clock. "I'd make a terrible cuckoo bird." She heard his intake of breath. "I don't like my fledglings leaving the nest."

She blinked. It wasn't the first time of late that he'd admitted to faults, but his confession nonetheless surprised her. Was this new thoughtful and introspective side of him due to some inner milestone? Or had the series of recent scares made him take stock? Whatever the cause, Meg felt grateful.

"Oh, Papa…is…is that why you chased away every boy who ever looked at me?"

"Did I really do that?"

"Yes, Papa, you did. You tried chasing Ralph away from Josie too, until Mama put her foot down. You did the same with Tommy, but he was too stubborn to leave."

He shrugged. "As your father, I have a prescriptive right to look out for your welfare. For the welfare of all my daughters."

"And does your prescriptive right extend to Grant Garrison?"

"You're serious about that scalawag, are you?"

"Yes, Papa, I am."

"Even after the way he grilled you on the stand?"

"He was only doing his job."

He studied her long and hard. "I should warn you that if you decide to marry him, I'll…" He stopped when Mama walked into the room.

Meg glanced at her mother with a beseeching look. "You'll what, Papa? What will you do if I marry Grant?"

"Yes, what *will* you do, Henry?" Arms folded, Mama tapped her foot, her gaze as sharp as her voice.

Papa looked momentarily remorseful, like a child caught stealing cookies. He'd been on his best behavior since Mama moved back home, though his lapses were becoming more frequent as time went by. At the rate he was going, he'd be back to his usual self by next week.

"I promise to behave myself and not mess up her wedding," he managed at last, though judging by the pained look on his face, it caused him great anguish to say it.

"And you'll stop calling him names?" Meg persisted. "And you'll make him feel welcome in our home at all times?"

Papa glanced at Mama's stoic face before splaying his hands. "Whatever you say."

With a cry of delight, Meg flung her arms around his neck and kissed him on his bristly cheek. "Oh, Papa. I want you to come to love him like I do."

"Let's not get carried away," he said in a gruff voice.

"All right, not love him. Like him."

"Hmm. We'll see."

Knowing that was about as much as he was willing to concede, at least for now, Meg pulled away. "I've got to go."

She could hardly wait to tell Grant that they could now shout the news of their betrothal to one and all.

"Okay, but I'm warning you, Meg," Papa said,

determined as always to have the last word. "This better be your last wedding." He looked at Mama and shrugged. "We sure as blazes can't afford another."

Epilogue

THERE WAS NOTHING PEACEFUL ABOUT PEACEFUL LANE that Saturday morning as Meg rushed to keep up with Grant's long strides. He pushed the cart with her hope chest down the center of the dirt road.

The whining sound of bagpipes was met with Mr. Crawford's angry shouts.

Mr. Sloan chased the Johnson boy out of his yard. "Come back! You have no right stealing my carrots!"

Mrs. Conrad was screaming at the goat that had chewed a pair of long underwear off her clothesline.

The big, yellow hound stood with its front paws against a tree barking at Cowboy, who hissed back from the upper branch. Sneaking up behind, the dogcatcher lowered the loop of his snare around the hound's neck. The hound took off running, yanking the dogcatcher clear off his feet.

Farther along, Mrs. Rockwell dragged a table out of one house and headed across the street to the other. Two doors away, Mr. Quincy was yelling at the paperboy, and Grant's own landlady was arguing with the next-door neighbor who had driven his carriage over her flower bed.

"I still don't know why you wanted my hope chest," Meg said. Their wedding was a month away.

Grant made no attempt to enlighten her until he stopped in front of one of the Sunday houses. "What do you think?"

She gazed up at him in confusion. "Think?"

"I'm now the official owner," he said, "and I was hoping you would agree to us making this our first home."

She stared at him in total disbelief. "You bought this house?"

"Had to." He grinned. "It's the only way I could think to save my back. Mrs. Rockwell now owns only a single house. Once she finishes moving into the one across the street, she'll have to stay there. We're not taking in any boarders."

"Oh, Grant!" Meg's heart swelled with joy, and it was all she could do to keep the tears of happiness at bay. "I think this would make a lovely home," she said. "Just as soon as I decorate it with the *household* goods from my hope chest."

Grant's grin practically reached from ear to ear. "I was hoping you'd say that."

He stopped right there in the middle of that not-so-peaceful lane and, in a shocking display of affection, showed her exactly how much he liked her decorating ideas.

Author's Note

Dear Reader,

I hope you enjoyed Meg and Grant's story.

Whether we like it or not, our lives are dictated by time. As irritating as that might seem, it wasn't that long ago that no one really knew what time it was. Early settlers depended on the sun to tell time. When the sun cast the smallest shadow, they knew it was noon or at least thereabouts. The problem was that solar time varies throughout the year. That's because the earth sometimes moves slower or faster around the sun, which meant that sundials had to be constantly adjusted, in addition to being worthless at night or on cloudy days.

It took thousands of years for man to wrestle time away from the sun with the invention of clocks. Clocks solved some of the problems but then created problems of another kind.

Townsfolk often set their clocks and watches by local jewelers. This worked fairly well until a second jeweler moved into town. As stated in the story, some towns did indeed have several jewelers, and no one could agree as to who had the right time.

Noting the problem, an astronomer named William Lambert was the first man in the United States to suggest standard time. He presented his idea to Congress in 1809, but the idea was not adopted.

If you think living in a town with several different time zones was confusing, imagine the chaos for train passengers. If several railroad lines used the same depot, they all installed their own clocks with different times.

Prior to 1883, an estimated hundred different railroad times existed in this country. Train engineers couldn't remember all the different time changes and would often pull out of the depot too soon, causing passengers to miss connections. But that was a lot better than pulling out too late and risking being hit by another train.

Things got so out of hand that railroad officials finally met and came up with the idea of dividing the country into time zones. On November 18, 1883, at precisely noon, all railroad clocks changed to standard time. At first, some objected, and many towns stubbornly held on to the old way of doing things, but eventually the advantages of standard time became clear.

Worshippers arrived at church on time, employees reached counters or desks when they were supposed to, and shops opened and closed on schedule. Order reigned.

It wasn't until 1918 that Congress finally adopted standard time laws based on railroad time (thirty-five years after the fact and more than a hundred years after

Lambert's proposal). The act also included daylight saving as a way to save electricity during World War I. Congress rescinded daylight saving in 1919, and it was reinstituted during World War II. The Uniform Time Act of 1966 standardized the start and end dates of daylight saving but allowed local exemptions.

Hawaii and Arizona (except on the Navajo reservation) do not observe daylight saving time. The last thing residents need in these states is another hour of hot sun.

As for breach-of-promise suits, some states have formally outlawed the practice, but such claims are still valid in nearly half the states. So, bachelors and bachelorettes, do beware.

As for Two-Time, Texas, it's now on standard time, but the story is far from over. There are surprises in store for Meg's sister Amanda, and you won't believe what they are.

Until next time (oops, there's that word again),
Margaret

Read on for an excerpt from

TO WIN A SHERIFF'S HEART

The next book in the A Match Made in Texas series
by Margaret Brownley

One

Two-Time, Texas
1882

COULD SHE TRUST HIM? *DARE* SHE TRUST HIM?

The man—a stranger—looked like one tough hombre. Perched upon the seat of a weather-beaten wagon, he sat tall, lean, and decisively strong, his sun-baked hands the color of tanned leather. The only feature visible beneath his wide-brimmed hat and shaggy beard was a well-defined nose. The beard, along with his shoulder-length hair, suggested he had no regard for barbers. From the looks of him, he wasn't all that fond of bathhouses either.

He'd stopped to ask if she needed a ride. It wasn't as if she had a lot of choices. If she didn't accept his offer, she might have to spend the rest of the day, maybe even the night, alone in the Texas wilderness with the rattlers, cactus, and God knows what else. Still she hesitated.

"Where you headin'?" he asked.

"Two-Time."

"Same here," he said with a gruff nod, as if that alone was reason to trust him.

His destination offered no surprise. Two-Time was the only town within twenty miles. "Why there?" she asked.

Her hometown had grown by leaps and bounds since the arrival of the train but still lagged behind San Antonio and Austin in commerce and population. Most people, if they ended up in Two-Time at all, did so by mistake.

He shrugged his wide shoulders. "Good a place as any."

Moistening her parched lips, she shaded her eyes from the blazing sun as she gazed up at him. No sense beating around the bush. "You don't have a nefarious intent, do you? To do me harm, I mean?" A woman alone couldn't be too careful.

The question seemed to surprise him. At least it made him push back his hat, revealing steel-blue eyes that seemed to pierce right through her. What a strange sight she must look. Stuck in the middle of nowhere dressed to the nines in a stylish blue walking suit.

"Are you askin' if your virtue is safe with me?"

She blushed but refused to back down. The man didn't mince words, and neither would she. "Well, is it?"

"Safe as you want it to be," he said finally. His lazy drawl didn't seem to go with the sharp-eyed regard, which returned again and again to her peacock feathered hat, rising three stories and a basement high above her brow.

It wasn't exactly the answer she'd hoped for, but he sounded sincere, and that gave her a small measure of comfort. Still, she cast a wary eye on his holstered weapon. The Indian Wars had ended, but the possibility of renegades was real. The area also teemed with outlaws. In that sense, it wouldn't hurt to have an armed man by her side. Even one as surly as this one.

"If you would be so kind as to help me with my… um…trunk. I'd be most grateful."

He sprang from the wagon, surprising her with his sudden speed. He struck her as a man who spoke only when necessary. Even then he seemed to parcel out words like he was divvying out food at a county poor farm.

For such a large man he was surprisingly light on his feet. He was also younger than he first appeared, probably in his early thirties. He would have towered over her by a good eight inches had she not been wearing a hat gamely designed to give her height and presence.

Gaze dropping the length of her, he visually lingered on her small waist and well-defined hips a tad too long for her peace of mind.

"Name's Rennick," he said, meeting her eyes. "R. B. Rennick."

A false name if she ever heard one but for once decided to hold her tongue. He was her best shot for getting back to town. He might be her only shot.

"I'm Miss Amanda Lockwood." She offered her gloved hand, which he blithely ignored. Feeling rebuffed, she withdrew it.

The man was clearly lacking in manners, but he had offered to help her, and for that she was grateful.

Thumbs hanging from his belt, he gazed across the desolate Texas landscape. "How'd you land out here, anyway? Nothing for miles 'round."

"I was on my way home from Austin when I…had a little run-in with the stage driver."

He raised an eyebrow. "What kind of run-in?"

"He was driving like a maniac," she said with an indignant toss of the head. "And I told him so." Not once but several times, in fact.

Hanging out the stage window, she'd insisted he slow down in no uncertain terms. When that didn't work, she resorted to banging on the coach's ceiling with her parasol and calling him every unflattering name she could think of. Perhaps a more tactful way of voicing her complaints would have worked more in her favor, but how was she supposed to know the man had such a low threshold for criticism?

She gritted her teeth just thinking about it. "Thought he would kill us all." He pretty near did. The nerve of him, tossing her bag and baggage out of the stage and leaving her stranded.

Mr. Rennick scratched his temple. "Hope you learned your lesson, ma'am. Men don't like being told what to do. 'Specially when holding the reins." It sounded like a warning.

Turning abruptly, he picked up the wooden chest and heaved it over the side of the wagon like it weighed no more than a loaf of bread. It hit the bottom of the wagon with a sickening thud.

She gasped. "Be careful." Belatedly, she remembered his warning. "It's very old."

The hope chest was a family heirloom, and if anything happened, her family would never forgive her. The chest had been handed down from mother to daughter for decades. She inherited the chest after the last of her two sisters wed. Since she had no interest in marriage, she used the chest mostly to store books.

Today, it contained the clothes needed for her nearly weeklong stay in Austin.

He brushed his hands together. "Sure is heavy. You'd have an easier time haulin' a steer."

"Yes, well, it's actually a hope chest." While packing for her trip, she discovered the latch on her steamer trunk was broken. The hope chest was a convenient though not altogether satisfactory substitute. For one, it was almost too heavy for her to handle alone—the most she could do was drag it.

"Don't know what you're hoping for, ma'am, but you're not likely to find it out here."

He spun around and climbed into the driver's seat without offering to help her. "Well, what are you waitin' for?" he yelled. "Get in!"

Startled by his sharp command, she reached for the grab handle and heaved herself up on the passenger side.

No sooner had she seated herself upon the wooden bench than Mr. Rennick took off hell-bent for leather.

Glued to the back of the seat, she cried out, "Oh dear. Oh my. *Ohhh!*"

What had looked like a perfectly calm and passive black horse had suddenly turned into a demon. With pounding hooves and flowing mane, the steed flew over potholes and dirt mounds, giving no heed to the cargo behind. The wagon rolled and pitched like a ship in stormy seas. Dust whirled in the air, and rocks hit the bottom and sides.

Holding on to her hat with one hand and the seat with the other, Amanda watched in wide-eye horror as the scenery flew by in a blur.

The wagon sailed over a hill as if it were airborne,

and she held on for dear life. The wheels hit the ground, jolting her hard and rattling her teeth. The hope chest bounced up and down like dice in a gambler's hand. Her breath whooshed out, and it was all she could do to find her voice.

"Mr. R-Rennick!" she stammered, grabbing hold of his arm. She had to shout to be heard.

"What?" he yelled back.

She stared straight ahead, her horrified eyes searching for a soft place to land should the need arise. "Y-you sh-should s-slow down and enjoy the s-scenery."

Her hat had tilted sideways, and he swiped the peacock feather away from his face. "Been my experience that sand and sagebrush look a whole lot better when travelin' fast," he shouted in his strong baritone voice.

He made a good point, but at the moment, she was more concerned with life and limb.

He urged his horse to go faster before adding, "It's also been my experience that travelin' fast is the best way to outrun bandits."

"W-what do you mean? B-bandits?" It was then that she heard gunfire.

She swung around in her seat, and her jaw dropped. Three masked horsemen were giving chase—and closing in fast.

Two

"OH NO!" SHE CRIED.

"You better get down, ma'am," Mr. Rennick shouted. "They look like they mean bus'ness."

Dropping off her seat, Amanda scrunched against the floorboards. Her body shook so hard, her teeth chattered. "G-give me your g-gun," she cried.

"Know how to use it?" he yelled back.

"N-no, but I'm a f-fast learner!" She pulled off her gloves, which flew out of the wagon like frantic white doves.

Holding the reins with one hand, he grabbed his gun with the other. After cocking the hammer with his thumb, he handed it to her. The gun was heavier than she expected, requiring both hands to grasp. Keeping her head low, she balanced herself on wobbly knees and rested the barrel on the back of the seat. She held on to the grip with all her might. Still, the muzzle bobbed up and down like corn popping on a hot skillet.

Aiming at a specific target was out of the question. The jostling wagon made control impossible. The best she could do was keep from shooting the driver. She wasn't all that anxious to shoot the bandits either. She just wanted to scare them away.

Eyes squeezed shut, she pulled the trigger. The blast shook her to the core, and her arm flung up with the recoil. She fell back against the footrest and fought to regain her balance.

"Good shot!" he yelled, looking over his shoulder. "You stopped your hope-a-thingie from attackin'. Now see if you can do the same with the bandits."

Her heart sank. Oh no. Not the hope chest. Her family would kill her. That is, if the bandits didn't kill her first. Forcing air into her lungs, she fought to reposition herself. The horsemen kept coming. They were so close now she could see the sun glinting off their weapons.

Bracing herself against the recoil, she fired again, this time aiming higher. The wagon veered to the right, and she fell against the side, hitting her shoulder hard. Her feathered hat ripped from its pins and flew from the wagon in a way that no peacock ever did.

"Oh no!" That was her very best hat, and the fact that it landed on the nearest highwayman gave her small comfort. His horse stopped, but the bandit kept going.

"Stay down!" Rennick yelled.

"But my hat…" It was one of the most elaborate hats she'd ever created. The peacock feathers matched the color of her eyes. "I loved that hat!"

"Yeah, well, too bad it didn't return your affection."

Of all the rude things to say. Blinking away the dust in her eyes, she hunkered close to the floorboards and struggled to catch her breath.

The wagon continued to race over uneven ground,

jolting her until she was ready to scream. Just when she thought her battered body could take no more, the wheels mercifully rolled to a stop.

She shot Rennick a questioning look. "W-what are you doing?"

"Seems like our friends deserted us."

She raised her limp body off the floorboards on shaky limbs and flung herself onto the seat, breathing hard. All that was visible in the far distance was a cloud of dust that seemed to be moving in the opposite direction.

Relief rushed through her like a blue norther. "W-why do you suppose they gave up the chase?"

He lifted the gun from her hand and holstered it. "Guess the hat was enough to convince them that whatever chunk change we might have wasn't worth the trouble."

She glared at him. He didn't seem to notice.

Amanda's hair had fallen from its bun, and she did her best to pin back the loose chestnut strands. She brushed the dust off her skirt and rubbed her shoulder.

"You okay?" he asked.

She nodded, though without her hat and gloves she felt naked.

He drank from a metal flask and wiped his mouth with the back of his hand. "Here." He handed her the canteen.

She hesitated before bringing the spout to her mouth. The water was warm and tasted metallic; still, it helped quench her thirst. Pulling a lace handkerchief from her sleeve, she poured a few drops on it before handing the canteen back.

She dabbed her face with the moist handkerchief,

but it offered little relief from the heat. The sun was almost directly overhead, and though still early spring, the temperature hovered in the high eighties.

"Do you mind if I retrieve my parasol from my hope...trunk?"

"I'll get it." Before she could object, he jumped to the ground and walked to the back of the wagon.

She tossed him an anxious glance and tried to remember how she'd packed. Were her intimate garments on the top or bottom of the chest? She'd packed in a hurry and couldn't remember. Shaking her head in annoyance, she blew out her breath. They had almost been robbed, maybe even killed, and here she worried about—of all things—a few pairs of red satin drawers and corset covers.

He returned to his seat with her parasol, his expressionless face giving no clue as to what unmentionables he had seen.

"Much obliged," she said, taking it from him.

He regarded her with curiosity. "What were you doin' in Austin?" he asked.

She opened the sun umbrella, casting a welcome shadow over her heated face. "I was at a Rights for Women meeting."

He made a face. "I should've known." He picked up the reins. "You're one of those suffering ladies."

She leveled a sideways glance his way. "They're called suffragists," she said. "I take it you don't much approve of women having the right to vote, Mr. Rennick."

"I have no objection to women votin'. But it's been my experience that you give women an inch, before you know it, they'll want the whole kit and caboodle."

"Right now all we want is the right to the ballot." She pursed her lips. "Are you married, Mr. Rennick?"

"Nope."

She narrowed her eyes. Had she only imagined his hesitation?

He met her gaze. "What about you? Got any marriage prospects?"

"None," she said, looking away. "And I plan on keeping it that way."

Three

HIS PASSENGER FELL SILENT AS THEY DROVE THE REST OF the way to town, and that was fine with R. B. Rennick. A loner by circumstance, he wasn't even sure how to act in front of a woman anymore. Especially one as independent as Miss Lockwood.

She was something, all right, sitting there all prim and proper in her conservative suit like a trussed up turkey. No one would guess from looking at her that she favored red satin petticoats and matching undertrousers. Recalling the intriguing contents of her hope-a-thingie, his gaze traveled down the length of her. For a woman who had no interest in marriage, she sure did arm herself with enough trappings to catch an army of men if she so chose.

Clearly, she was a woman who could cause a man all sorts of trouble if he didn't watch out. Even so, the way she'd handled herself in the face of danger had earned his begrudging respect.

He also felt sorry for her. It was hot and humid and dusty, the air thick as a wet blanket. She had to be downright miserable but was either too polite or too stubborn to admit it. If he was a betting man, he'd put his money on the latter.

The sun hung low, and shadows ran long by the time they reached Two-Time. The town was larger than he expected. A railroad ran the length of the town, along with a string of saloons. A street two wagons wide separated rows of adobe and brick buildings, each with false wooden fronts. They passed a general store, bakery, gun shop, post office, and barber along with other businesses.

"What kind of name is that, anyway? Two-Time?" he asked. "Doesn't sound like a very trustworthy name for a town."

"It's not what you think," she said. "Until last year, the town had two time zones." She gave him a short history of the two feuding jewelers, including her father, who kept the town divided for years by refusing to agree to standard time.

Rick had little interest in town history. He was more concerned about the lay of the land. "Where shall I drop you off?" he asked abruptly.

She hesitated. "At my father's place. It's two blocks up yonder. At the Lockwood Watch and Clockworks shop."

He tossed a nod toward a knot of people blocking the street. "Looks like trouble."

She craned her neck. "No more than usual."

He raised an eyebrow. Where he came from, trouble didn't usually start till the sun went down. Something about the night made prisoners restless.

The mass of people spilled off the boardwalk and into the street. Traffic had come to a complete stand-still, preventing him from driving any farther. Tugging on the reins, he guided his horse to the side of the road and parked behind a dogcatcher's wagon.

"You can let me off here," she said.

"Sure?" He slanted his head to the back. "Your hope-a-thingie weighs a ton."

"I can manage," she said.

Setting the brake, he leaped to the ground and hauled her chest out of the wagon and onto the wooden sidewalk. This time, he showed more care in setting it down. A chip in the wood the size of a quarter drew his attention, and he rubbed his finger over it.

He heard her gasp and looked up. For an independent woman, she sure did put a lot of stock in that old chest. Or maybe it was the finery inside…

"It's just a bullet hole," he assured her. "Probably passed right through all that satin and lace."

Her slender frame stiffened, and her cheeks turned a most beguiling red. She really was a looker. Especially now that she'd lost that ridiculous hat. The headgear's odd geometric shape would have given even a mathematician a headache.

At first glance, her turquoise eyes had seemed too large for her delicate features and her body too slight to support such an independent spirit. Now that she was in familiar surroundings, she'd dropped her guard, and all the mismatched parts worked together to create a very pleasant whole.

He touched the brim of his hat with the tip of his finger. "Sure you don't need help with your—"

"No, that's fine," she said quickly, avoiding his eyes. "I can manage from here. Much obliged."

He watched the late afternoon sun play with the golden highlights of her brown hair. Why a woman would want to hide such a fine mane beneath a ridiculous bunch of bird feathers was one of the mysteries of life.

She gazed up at him through a fringe of lush lashes. "If you need a place to stay, we passed the hotel back a ways. There're also a couple of boardinghouses in town. Some of them are even respectable."

"In that case, I'll stay at the hotel." He nodded his good-bye and forced himself to turn away, starting off on foot. Since the street was still blocked, there was no sense trying to drive his wagon. He'd come back later to stable his horse. Without the distraction of Miss Lockwood, he could concentrate more fully on the town. This time, he paid particular attention to the location of the bank, the sheriff's office, and the hotel.

This town was everything he hoped for and more. It was large enough for a man to remain relatively unnoticed, yet small enough to escape quickly should a need arise.

All in all, it was a perfect hide-out for a cold-blooded killer.

Read on for an excerpt from
THE LAST CHANCE COWBOYS:
THE LAWMAN
Book 2 in the Where the Trail Ends series
by Anna Schmidt

One

Arizona Territory, October 1882

AFTER SIX MONTHS ON THE STREETS OF KANSAS CITY,
Jess Porterfield had come home. But he might as
well have kept on riding for all the place where he'd
grown up *felt* like home to him. In the relatively
short time that he'd been away, everything about
the Clear Springs Ranch and the town of Whitman
Falls—indeed, the entire Arizona Territory—had
become nearly unrecognizable.

As he slowly rode up the trail that led to his family's
home, he saw the adobe house with its flat roof meant
to ward off the desert heat. His father had built that
house and added to it through the years as the family
had grown. Jess expected to find his mother, two
sisters, and younger brother inside, gathered 'round
the table in the kitchen. He expected to hear laughter
coming from the bunkhouse. He expected to see a
light in the small outbuilding next to the house where
their foreman lived. He planned to corral his horse and
walk past the chicken coop and the plantings of cholla

and barrel cactus and on into the kitchen as if he'd just
come back from checking on the herd.

Instead, the annual party his family always hosted
after the livestock had been taken to market was in full
swing. The courtyard was packed with people—some
he recognized and some were strangers. Everyone
seemed to be in the mood to celebrate…which made
no sense, given that the ranch had been about to fail
the day he left.

Back then the situation had been dire on all fronts.
His father had just died in a freak accident. A drought
that had gone on for over a year threatened to send
the family and the ranch into bankruptcy. His mother
had been so consumed by her grief that she refused
to believe her husband was truly gone. And he was
ashamed to admit he had left his sister, Maria, on her
own to fend off the land-grabbing Tipton brothers,
who already owned most of the land in the territory.

And yet there were lanterns lighting the courtyard
and bonfires where guests gathered between dances to
warm themselves on this autumn night. He had heard
the music from some distance away, and now that he
was closer, he could also hear the laughter and excited
chatter of people enjoying themselves. So who was
throwing this fandango? He half expected to see Jasper
Tipton and his much younger wife, Pearl, playing the
role of hosts. Surely Maria had had to surrender and sell
out. Truth was, his father had barely been hanging on
before he died. But there were some things that didn't
seem right about the atmosphere of the party—like that
their hired hand, Bunker, would never have agreed to
provide the music for a Tipton party. Yet there he was

along with a couple of the other cowboys, stomping their feet in time to the music they produced from a worn fiddle and guitar and banjo. Just like old times.

"Is that you, Jessie Porterfield?"

Their nearest neighbor and Jess's father's dearest friend, George Johnson, waited for Jess to dismount and tie up his horse at the hitching post before grabbing him in a bear hug. "Good to have you home."

"Looks like there might have been some changes since I left," Jess ventured.

George laughed. "Things are pretty much the same, only better. That sister of yours is quite the little businesswoman."

"You don't say." Jess was baffled. Was Mr. Johnson saying that Maria had managed to somehow save the ranch? "So we still own this place?"

"In a manner of speaking. Maria can fill you in, but the short version is that several of the smaller ranchers decided the only way to fight the Tiptons was to beat them at their own game. So we've banded together in a cooperative arrangement. We share the profits—and the debts. We help each other out. 'Course, having just come back from taking the stock to market, we've got a little time to get settled into this new arrangement, but you mark my words, by spring every small ranch in this territory will be holding its own."

So Maria—his sister—had held the Tipton brothers at bay. Their father would be really proud—of her.

"You've got a new foreman," George continued. "A Florida boy—came drifting in here not long after you left. Went to work with the others and everyone's pretty sure that him and Maria will be heading down the aisle before too long."

Jess was aware that several others had spotted him and a crowd was beginning to form as they pushed forward.

"What about Roger?"

"He took off. Some think he might have been involved in that business with your pa. 'Course, there's no proof, and he was a good foreman and all. Didn't get along with the drifter, though—not one bit."

"What business with Pa?" Jess was reeling with these bits of information that made no sense. But George didn't get a chance to answer.

"Jessie!" his younger sister, Amanda, squealed as the crowd parted to let her through. Jess scooped her up and swung her around.

"Look at you," he said, glad for the diversion. "I go away for five minutes and you go and grow up into a real beauty." He set her down and his expression sobered when his other sister stepped out of the crowd. "Hello, Maria."

He saw Maria hesitate as she ran through a range of emotions that went from anger to confusion and wariness. After what seemed like an eternity, she opened her arms to him. "Welcome home, Jess."

As he hugged her, feeling hesitation even in her embrace, they all heard a shrill cry. Jess looked up to see his mother—Constance Porterfield—running across the yard, her skirts clutched in one hand as she reached out for her eldest son with the other. Jess steeled himself to accept the fact that Constance Porterfield was probably thinking he was his father.

When he'd left, she'd lapsed into a fantasy world of unreality, refusing to believe her husband was gone.

But when she reached him, she pushed his hat off and ran her fingers through his hair, brushing it away from his forehead. "Jessie, at last," she said.

She recognized him—surely that was progress. He smiled and bent to kiss her cheek. "Kill the fatted calf, Ma," he said with a laugh. "I've come home."

"To stay?"

"Yes, ma'am."

"Let the dancing begin," his mother shouted, and the band struck up a lively tune as she pulled him into the center of the lanterns that outlined the dance floor.

"You look older, son," she said, frowning as she studied his face closely.

"And you look...better," he replied searching for any sign of the glassy-eyed, distracted woman he'd left behind.

She frowned. "Stop looking at me as if you expect me to start speaking in tongues. I had a rough time of it, but one cannot hide from reality forever." She quirked an eyebrow and he understood that her words were her subtle way of saying that she had not been the only one hiding from reality.

"Well, you're still the prettiest woman around," he countered, reluctant to get into the details of the last several months.

"Prettier than Addie Wilcox?"

Addie—the reason he had gone and one of the reasons he had finally come to his senses and returned. She was the one person he had not yet allowed himself to think about. His intent had been first to settle things with his family and then…

"She waited for you to come to your senses, you know," his mother continued. "Why didn't you at least write to her?"

"I don't want to talk about Addie, Ma. It's you I've come to see." He was glad to see her well again…and sorry that he'd had no part in her recovery. It was, after all, a key reason for his return—the realization that while he was not and never would be his father, the family needed him and he had a responsibility to be there and care for them. Now it appeared they had managed quite well on their own. "How are you feeling?"

She laughed. "Well, if you're thinking that I'm the batty old woman you left six months ago, stop worrying. I needed some time. I'm still missing your father every minute of every day, but now that the culprit who murdered him is in…"

Jess stumbled to a stop. "What are you saying, Ma? He died in an accident and…" Maybe she wasn't better after all. His heart sank.

She heaved a sigh of resignation. "You have a lot to catch up on, Jessie. We've all had to face some hard truths lately."

Jess thought of what George Johnson had been saying when Amanda interrupted—something about there being no proof that their foreman, Roger Turnbull, had been involved in "that business with your pa."

"Murdered?" he said, unable to take it all in. The news shook him to his boots. Could it be true that his father's death had been no accident at all—but cold-blooded murder? He was speechless, first with disbelief and then rage as he tried to think of what signs of foul play he could have missed that day they'd found his father's body on the trail.

"Now you pull yourself together, Jess," his mother ordered as the band hit the final notes of the tune. "The culprit—Marshal Tucker—is in custody at Fort Lowell. This is a matter for Colonel Ashwood and his men to handle, and you need to stay out of it. Is that clear?"

"Tucker? But what kind of beef could he have had with Pa?"

His mother looked away and then back at him. She linked her arm through his, but it was less a gesture of consolation than one that felt as if she was trying to make sure he stayed put. "You'll hear it soon enough, so it may as well be from me. At least then you know you're getting the truth of it. Tucker was working with the Tipton brothers. It appears that he decided to take matters into his own hands when your father refused to sell. I suspect he hoped he would endear himself to the Tiptons with his actions."

He slapped at a biting bug that attacked his neck. Some things, he realized—like the bugs and the dust and the underhanded Tipton boys doing whatever they found necessary to control the territory—did not change. "You're saying they had nothing to do with this?"

"I'm saying there is no evidence that points to that. I am saying that Tucker is in custody and Colonel Ashwood assures me he will be tried and punished to the full extent of the law."

"But what about…"

"Now you listen to me, Jessup Porterfield—I have lost my husband, but I will not lose my oldest son in the bargain. So you just contain that temper of yours and let the colonel handle this. If the Tiptons are involved, then they will be arrested."

"If? Ma, we both know…"

"No, son, we don't know anything. We suspect, but we do not know, so stay out of it and let the federal authorities do their job. If you're so all-fired interested in taking up the law, talk to Doc. With the arrest of Tucker, Whitman Falls is in need of a new marshal. Now about Addie," she added, so smoothly changing the subject that Jess felt his head spinning like the dancers whirling around the courtyard. That seemed to be happening a lot tonight. "The boys just struck up a ranchera and it looks to me like a certain young lady is standing over there itching to get out on that dance floor."

She gave him a nudge and then went off to dance the reel with his younger brother, Trey, who waved and grinned as if Jess had just come back from a day on the range, not six months gone with no word.

His mother couldn't have engineered a better distraction. Jess looked about, dazed, and saw Addie Wilcox tapping her toe in time to the music. She wanted to dance all right. Question was, would she dance with him? After all, he hadn't just left Whitman Falls and his family's ranch—he had left Addie as well.

Well, the one thing he had always been able to count on with Addie was that she would tell him the truth. She would know what had really happened with his father. Of course first he had to get her to speak to him. Addie had a temper that matched his own. And the fact was that he hadn't written her, but dabnabit, he'd sure thought about her and, more to the point, he'd come back because he'd realized that without her, his life was pretty bleak.

He nodded to friends and neighbors as he threaded his way through those watching the dancing. "Welcome home, Jess," he heard more than one of the women say. "Learned your lesson, did you?" He expected he was going to hear that sentiment a lot in the coming weeks. He'd even heard one man mutter, "Well, all hail the prodigal son." It was what he'd expected—and probably deserved—people assuming he'd come running home because he was out of luck and money. He wasn't of a mind to set them straight. He had far more important matters to attend to.

Addie had to be hearing these comments and she had to be aware that he was making his way toward her, although she refused to acknowledge him. Clearly she hadn't changed a bit in the months since he'd left. She was every bit as stubborn and mule-headed as she'd always been. He ought to just turn right around and ignore her. He ought to ask Sybil Sinclair to dance and see how Addie liked that. He ought to do half a dozen things, but he didn't.

"Evenin'," he muttered, sidling up next to her. He kept his eyes on the dancers. "Good to see Ma looking better," he added.

"No thanks to you," she replied as she took up clapping her hands in time with the beat of the music.

He bristled. Addie had this way of saying exactly what was needed to get under his skin. "Meaning what?"

Of course, he knew what she was saying. *The prodigal son.* He'd seen more than one person's lips murmuring those words as they had watched his mother come running to welcome him back—as she had enfolded him in her embrace.

"I asked you a question, Addie."

"Rhetorical, I'm sure." She kept right on clapping and tapping her toe, smiling at the dancers as they passed by.

"Don't you go throwing around those fancy words with me, Dr. Wilcox."

"And don't you go playing like you're some uneducated country bumpkin, Jess Porterfield. You owe that much respect to your parents, who made sure all their children got a solid education." Her smile tightened. "Besides, I'm not a doctor for real—not yet."

He had to clench his fist to keep from touching her bare forearm below the lace trim of her sleeve, comforting her as he had in the past whenever she got discouraged. "You wanna dance or not?" he grumbled instead, holding out his hand to her.

Just then, the music finished on a crescendo and everybody applauded. "Looks like your timing is perfect, as usual," she said. She turned to go but was prevented from moving by the throng of dancers leaving the floor in search of some cider to quench their thirst.

Jess decided to try a different tactic and moved a step closer. "Ma hinted that I ought to apply for the marshal's job," he said. "Your pa being head of the town council and all, do you think he might…"

She wheeled around and looked directly at him for

the first time since he'd come riding up to the ranch. She was staring up at him, her dark brown eyes large with surprise behind the lenses of her wire-rimmed glasses. "Are you serious? Why would Papa trust you? Why would any of us living in town trust you not to up and leave again?" Her eyes filled with tears.

"Addie, I had to…I never meant…"

Her mouth worked as if finding and then rejecting words before she could spit them out at him. She held up her hands to stop him from saying anything more before she brushed past him, losing herself in the crowd. He glanced around to see others looking at him. Obviously they had witnessed the scene and were now passing judgment, as they always had. Well, he would show them. He would show all of them—even Addie. Especially Addie.

The question was how. He could hardly take over here at the ranch. From the talk he'd had with George Johnson, it sure seemed like Maria had done a better job than he would have thought—or than he could have done—managing things. In spite of the attempts of the Tipton Land and Cattle Company to buy out all the smaller ranchers in the area, including—no, especially—theirs, Maria had found a way to hang on.

So maybe he should think more seriously about applying for the lawman's job. After all, even though a local marshal had no jurisdiction over crimes that took place outside the town's borders—like the murder of his father—it would be a way he could look into the matter without raising suspicions. As head of the town council, Addie's father, Doc Wilcox, would be the one to hire a new marshal.

That gave Jess pause. No doubt Doc would be as down on him as Addie was, so why bother? On the other hand, he needed work—work that would give him the time and the cover he needed to solve his father's murder by tracking down the real killers.

The town was in need of a new marshal. And why wouldn't Addie's father hire him? He'd make a fine marshal. After all, how hard could it be?

"Hello, Jess."

Jess looked around to find Sybil Sinclair gazing up at him. "I was on my way to get some punch," she said, "but…"

"How about we enjoy this waltz first?" Jess offered her his arm the way his mother had taught both her boys a gentleman would escort a lady and led her onto the dance floor.

❧

Addie could not for the life of her figure out why she continued to allow that man to get to her. Why couldn't she be more like Jess's younger sister and her good friend, Amanda—calm and sophisticated? She searched the gathering for Amanda, but hesitated when she saw her friend surrounded by the usual trio of admirers. Amanda had been planning this party for weeks now. She certainly deserved to enjoy herself and not have to sympathize with Addie. Besides, Jess was Amanda's brother, newly returned to the fold from his travels following his father's death—a death everyone now knew had not been the accident they'd first thought.

She stopped dead in her tracks. Her hand flew to her

mouth. What was she thinking? Maybe Jess had over-heard some of the talk. Maybe that was why he was talking about applying for the marshal's position. After all, Jasper Tipton had built that big house in town to please his bride, Pearl, and his brother Buck lived there as well. While the local marshal had no jurisdiction outside the town limits, Jess might just think the fact that the Tiptons resided in town opened the door for him to go after them—and more than likely he would get himself killed in the bargain. Her mind raced as she tried to think the issue through from every side.

"This is not one of your medical cases," she mut-tered to herself. "This is Jess." And when it came to figuring out what Jess Porterfield might be thinking, she fully appreciated that logic was not part of the process. She was still mad at him for leaving all those months ago, but that didn't mean she didn't care about him, and, knowing his temper, he was bound to get into trouble.

With a sigh, she headed off to find her father. Maybe he could talk some sense into the man—the man she had fallen in love with, planned a future with and then rejected. But as she moved through the throng of party guests, pausing now and then to exchange a greeting, it wasn't her father she saw.

It was Jess.

He wasn't spoiling for a fight at all. No, he was laughing and flirting with Sybil Sinclair. Sybil with her blonde curls and her bright blue eyes and a cupid's bow of a mouth that made her look like a porcelain doll. Sybil with her tiny waist and her flawless skin and giddy laugh that actually came out as "Tee-hee-hee."

"My brother is trying to make you jealous," Amanda murmured, coming to stand next to Addie. "Do not let him know that it's working."

"It's not," she insisted, pushing her glasses more firmly onto the bridge of her nose. She straightened to her full height that was still a good three inches shorter than Sybil's willowy five foot four. She brushed back a strand of her hair that had drifted from the practical bun she preferred and tried not to think about how her stick-straight locks would look worn down like Sybil's long curls. "I really couldn't care less if your brother wants to make an utter fool of himself with that…"

"Good to know you aren't affected," Amanda said wryly. "But two can play this game. Come on. Dance with Harlan Stokes."

Just like Jess, Harlan Stokes had a reputation with the ladies. He had never paid the slightest attention to Addie, but he had definitely set his sights on Amanda. She could get him to do anything—even dance with plain Addie Wilcox. Of course, even as he led Addie to the dance floor, Harlan's eyes remained on Amanda, who had accepted another cowboy's invitation to dance. Addie couldn't fault Harlan because her own gaze kept drifting to where Jess was dancing with Sybil. The song was "Sweet Betsy from Pike"—a favorite of Addie's—but she barely heard the tune as Harlan guided her around the floor.

"You think I've got any chance at all with Amanda?" Harlan asked.

Addie glanced up at him. He was only a few inches taller than she was and she knew the other cowhands teased him a lot about his short stature. They even called him Peewee. He looked miserable as he turned her for the sole purpose of keeping his eye on Amanda. Addie knew that her answer called for diplomacy of the highest order.

"Well, you know Amanda is still unsettled in her ways. She's not yet decided on the path she wants to take."

"Not like you, huh? I mean, everybody knows you've been planning on taking over your pa's practice just as soon as you finish your schooling and all."

"Well, not taking over. More like working with him."

Harlan looked surprised. "You've been doing that since you were a kid."

The fact that Harlan's full attention was now focused on her made Addie uncomfortable—so much so that she stumbled and he tightened his hold on her, pulling her closer. "Easy there," he said. "You got your bearings?"

"I'm fine," she said, and knew it came out as a rebuff when he loosened his grip. "Thank you," she added. "I'm not very good at dancing."

He frowned. "You're fine, Addie Wilcox. Just fine."

She was surprised to feel a lump in her throat at his kindness. Blessedly, the waltz ended just then. "Thank you, Harlan. I know that Amanda asked you to take pity on me and…"

"You shouldn't do that, Addie. Put yourself down that way. You're worth two of most of the women at this party."

This had to stop. Addie could feel the heat rise along her neck up into her cheeks. "There's not a whole lot of competition," she said, looking around at the gathering, where men outnumbered the girls and women by a factor of at least three to one.

"You know what I'm saying."

"Why, thank you, Harlan. Does that include Amanda Porterfield?" She was teasing him now.

It was his turn to blush. "Well now, Miss Addie, it would take a lot to measure up to Amanda Porterfield—at least for me."

"You're a good man, Harlan. Thank you for the dance." She punctuated her appreciation with a slight curtsey and laughed when Harlan bowed in return.

"Pleasure was mine, ma'am."

They were both laughing when Addie spotted Jess scowling at her as he carried two cups of punch back to where he had left Sybil waiting.

"Hey, Jess," Harlan called out, "'bout time you got home. The other boys and me have been missing you and your money at the poker game."

Jess kept walking, acknowledging Harlan's greeting only by raising one of the punch cups in a toast. Addie wondered if the cowhands had spiked the drink. She wouldn't put it past them. It was not all that uncommon for the men to add a little whiskey, hoping the spirits might make the girls a little more amenable to their advances. But Jess had never pulled such a trick. Truth was, Jess didn't need to do anything but be his charming self to make a girl like Sybil sit up and take notice.

Stop it, she ordered herself.

Seymour Bunker, the oldest hand on the Porterfield spread who was as good with a fiddle as he was with a lariat, struck up a reel. Harlan took Addie's hand and joined the other dancers. At the same time she saw Jess set down the cups of punch and lead Sybil into the circle. Addie's pulse raced as she realized there was no way she could avoid taking her turn with him in the change of partners required by the dance.

Sure enough, a few minutes later they came together and then circled away and then came together again, sashaying their way down the line of other dancers. She refused to look at him, her mouth drawn into a tight line and her brow furrowed in concentration, as if the steps of the dance were every bit as complex as her study of the thick anatomy text she'd left on the kitchen table back home. Jess tightened his hold on her waist as they made their way down the center of the other dancers. When they reached the end of the line, he let her go without a word.

When the dance finally ended, Harlan's cheeks were flushed. "I'm sorry, Addie. I wasn't thinking. I mean, Jess is a durn fool, if you'll pardon me saying so. Leaving a woman like you the way he did…"

"Please don't concern yourself, Harlan. Thank you for the dances. Oh, there's Amanda, and she's looking this way. Maybe she's free for the next waltz."

Harlan gave Addie a little bow and hurried off. Addie sighed. He wasn't the only one who thought that Jess had left her. Jess's stupid pride had never allowed him to admit the truth—that he had begged her to go with him and she had refused. Well, now he'd come back. She had no idea why, but she'd be willing to bet that it was because the life he'd been so sure was waiting for him in the city had never materialized. It surprised her to realize she got no satisfaction from that thought.

She watched him drink down his punch in one
long gulp while Sybil sipped hers. The one thing that
no amount of irritation at the man could change was
that he was undeniably good-looking. He was tall
and his muscular frame gave evidence of his ability to
work hard. Tonight he was wearing black trousers, a
blue shirt and a leather vest, as if he'd known he was
dressing for a party. And boots, of course—new, from
the look of them. When he'd first arrived he'd been
wearing a black Stetson, but his mother had removed
that as soon as she ran to embrace him. She had
thrown the hat aside and combed his straw-colored
hair away from his forehead with her fingers, all the
while repeating his name over and over as tears of joy
rolled down her weathered cheeks.

A hank of his hair had now fallen over his forehead
and Addie saw Sybil reach up to push it back, but
Jess stepped away from her touch. He said something
to her, smiled and then walked away. Addie's breath
quickened and she closed her eyes, preparing herself
for what she might say when Jess came her way. But
when she opened her eyes again, she saw that he had
not only walked away from Sybil—he had also walked
away from her.

Acknowledgments

First, I want to thank you, my readers, for taking the time to read my books. Your kind emails, letters, and Facebook comments keep me going on the days the writing bogs down or my characters throw a snit and refuse to talk to me.

Second, no words can convey my heartfelt gratitude to Natasha Kern. She is not only a terrific agent, but also a loving friend and wise mentor. I can't say enough good things about her.

I want to thank my wonderful editor, Mary Altman, who shared my same vision for the book. Her suggestions proved invaluable in making my story stronger. Special thanks also goes to the talented and dedicated Sourcebooks team who work so hard behind the scenes.

Finally, a great big thank-you to my family for their loving patience and support. Living with me is like living with an arresting officer. Anything they say or do can be (and often is) used against them in a book!

About the Author

Bestselling author Margaret Brownley has penned more than forty novels and novellas. Her books have won numerous awards, including Readers' Choice and Award of Excellence. She's a former Romance Writers of America RITA finalist and has written for a TV soap. She is currently working on the next book in her A Match Made in Texas series. Not bad for someone who flunked eighth-grade English. Just don't ask her to diagram a sentence. You can find Margaret at www.margaret-brownley.com.